# Where the Yellow Flowers Grow

A Millway Novel

## REBEKAH RUTH

*Sláinte,*
*Rebekah Ruth*

Nickel City Press
Buffalo, NY

Nickel City Press
Buffalo, NY
www.rebekahruthbooks.com
Admin@rebekahruthbooks.com

Publisher's Note: This is a work of fiction. Names, characters, places, and incidents are a product of the author's imagination. Locales and public names are sometimes used for atmospheric purposes. Any resemblance to actual people, living or dead, or to businesses, companies, events, institutions, or locales is completely coincidental.

Because of the dynamic nature of the Internet, any web addresses or links contained in this book may have changed since publication and may no longer be valid. The views expressed in this work are solely those of the author and do not necessarily reflect the views of the publisher, and the publisher hereby disclaims any responsibility for them.

Book Cover Designed by BespokeBookCovers.com
Book Layout ©2013 BookDesignTemplates.com
Where the Yellow Flowers Grow/ Rebekah Ruth.
ISBN 978-0-9909902-8-4

# *Acknowledgements*

Once again I have to thank my fabulous advance readers: Karen Ward, Jenn Roland, Christen Civiletto, Jen Burns, Barb Whalen, LT Kodzo and of course, my mom, Ruthie. Thank you all for reading and giving me your excellent feedback. Thank you to the members of Ink&Keys. The. Best. Writers. Group. Ever. Thanks for critiquing and encouraging me. Christen, Lisa, Laura, Kelly and Marissa—you are such a blessing to me! Love you all.

Thank you to all my readers who have repeatedly asked for the next book in the series. Your excitement and contagious enthusiasm inspired me to get it done! It is for you that I wrote this and I hope you love it as much as you loved *Where the Pink Houses Are.* (I'll even take *almost as much.*) Most of you also left reviews for *Where the Pink Houses* are on Amazon and Goodreads. I can't even tell you how much that means. You rock!

Thank you to my editor, Rebecca Rohan. I'm so glad you know where to put all the commas and the proper use of the semi-colon. (Lord knows I don't!) And thank you to Season Harper-Fox, my writing instructor at Gotham. Your encouragement was priceless and your instruction made this book 100 times easier to write than the first one!

To my Kickstarter Backers...you are AWESOME! Thank you for making this happen!! In particular, I'd like to send a shout out to the following Book Club Level supporters who will be the first to chat with me about Where the Yellow Flowers Grow with their book clubs: Laurie Leenhouts, Karen Ward, Bobby Burns, Sarah Buettenback, Angie Henderson & Donna Visone.

A big thanks goes to my kids: Jo, Jake, Josh and Jonny. I appreciate all your support and your understanding when I'm tied to my Macbook. And lastly, to my number one encourager, Bill. We will celebrate our 25th anniversary this coming year and I couldn't be more thankful for you.

# A word about Accents and Authenticity:

Most of the characters in this book are Irish. I could hear their accents while I wrote the dialogue and I wanted to remind the reader of their Irish lilt without being obnoxious. Therefore, I tweaked certain words throughout the dialogue as cues, but I did not write the dialogue phonetically. For example, when my friends in Ireland say "Matthew" it sounds like "Matchew," or when they say "thirty-three" it sounds more like "tirty-chree." To include all those nuances would have overwhelmed both the reader and me. So, I only tweaked a select few words.

Most of the changes are self-explanatory. However, the word *you* requires some explanation. Sometimes it is actually pronounced just like it is in America, but when you see it spelled *ya* it is really more of a *yih* sound (same vowel sound as in the word *him*). My hope is that these changes will help you hear the melodic Irish accent as you read.

Also of note, the town of Millway is fictional. But my inspiration for the name and location is a town called Millstreet. Not only does Millstreet exist, but it is a wonderful town full of truly hospitable people. When I went to Ireland, I spent a week there at Coolefield House, the home of Mike and Pam Thornton, and the best B&B you'll find anywhere. Their hospitality is second to none. If you happen to visit County Cork, you must spend a few nights in their company.

I gained much of the inspiration for this book during my visit to Millstreet. And while all the characters are a figment of my imagination, I included much of the actual town in these pages, so I hope you feel like you have been transported to this quaint Irish town in County Cork.

*For my friends Pam & Mike Thornton*
*(and Michael and Ava) at Coolefield House*
*Thank you for welcoming me to Ireland with open arms*
*And making my stay exactly what it needed to be.*
*And thank you, Mike, for the wise words:*
*"It's a small world, if you talk."*

# Chapter One ~ January

*Megan*

A freezing wind whipped Megan McKenna's hair into a frenzy as she shivered in the parking lot of her fiancé's flat, trying to get the courage to head toward his door. She'd been in the car for ten hours straight, except for a quick break at a dodgy petrol station so she stomped her feet, coaxing some feeling back into her legs.

Why did Jamie have to move so far away? None of this would have been necessary if he'd just stayed home and worked on his dad's farm, like a normal Irish lad. No, he had to help his Uncle Jack. And of course, Uncle Jack had to live in bloody London—ten hours from Millway. Highly inconvenient!

*Relax, Megan.* She reminded herself to breathe in and out. Kind of a Zen thing. She went to the back of her car and opened the boot. Jamie's mam had baked him some chocolate cupcakes and asked her to pass them along. She'd safely stowed them in the boot because she probably would have consumed them all if they'd been within reach during the long drive. She wasn't always a stress eater, but sometimes ... chocolate simply was the best medicine.

She ran from her car to the stairwell and almost lost the cupcakes twice to the howling wind. She paused just inside the entrance to remind herself why it made sense to be there. She'd known for weeks that something was off. She didn't know what, but something was definitely up with Jamie. They still talked on the phone, but more often than not, she was the one making the calls. She missed the way he used to call her every night.

And now, when they did talk, he said almost nothing. He'd always been quiet, not big on lots of words. But this was more than that. He didn't even sound like her Jamie. The edge in his voice told her something was wrong.

Her friend, Brenna, said he was acting like a guy who was cheating. But she just didn't think that was possible. Jamie wouldn't do that to her. Kind, gentle, loyal Jamie ... he'd never cheat. It had to be something else. So, she was there for answers, under the guise of a birthday surprise.

But the longer she stood there, willing her teeth to stop chattering, the more panic set in. Maybe she shouldn't have come. She should leave. *What if Brenna's right and he's up there with someone right now?* That thought made her angry enough to take the stairs two at a time.

She knocked on the weathered green door and waited. *Breathe. Zen.* But when he opened the door, all her anger melted away. Oh how she'd missed him. Without a word, she handed him the cupcakes and stepped close, wrapping her arms around him and resting her head on his chest. His free arm encircled her and she felt safe for a brief moment.

Too brief. Because as soon as she stepped back and looked him in the eyes, she felt like she was staring at a stranger. His eyes were distant. Hard.

"Surprise," she said, swallowing a stupid lump in her throat.

"Why didn't ya tell me you were coming?" He backed into his apartment. "Ya should've called."

*What a lovely welcome.* She pointed to the box of cupcakes. "I wanted to surprise ya for yer birthday."

"Well, that's nice. But ya should have called."

"Well, it wouldn't have been much of a surprise then, would it?" She tried not to sound ticked off.

He took the box and glanced at the writing on top. "From Mam?"

"Of course." She slung her coat over a chair and scanned the room, searching for clues. Something out of place since her last visit, months before. Some kind of clue to why he was being so weird.

A solitary floor lamp, missing its shade, lit the room with harsh shadows. It was the same bare bones furniture as always. A hand-me-down couch and chair, TV and coffee table—all worn by the years. Nothing stood out. No clues.

He headed to the kitchen and yelled back, "Want some Jameson?"

"Um, no. Thanks." *Whiskey?* "When did you start drinking whiskey?" Jamie had been known to down a few pints but he'd always avoided the hard stuff.

"I dunno. Couple months back."

She touched a family portrait on the wall; it was a couple years old. His parents were smiling. His younger twin brothers, John and David, appeared to be pinching each other and Jamie was standing behind them with a huge grin on his face. He looked so different in the picture. *So much ... softer? No, not the right word. Kinder? Sweeter?* Just so much more like the Jamie she'd fallen in love with.

"Hmm ... Jame, I've missed you," she said, still staring at the picture for a moment. She looked around again. Maybe that chair was new? *Well, there's a real break in the case, Meg. He's got a new chair.* She rolled her eyes and glanced toward the kitchen.

He was leaning against the kitchen doorway, studying her. With a slight curl of the lip, he set his glass down and headed toward her.

"Ya look good Meg." He covered the ground between them in three strides and pulled her close, his hands caressing her back as he looked down at her. "Real good."

Her heart flopped. She opened her mouth—not sure what she was going to say—but he crushed his lips to hers. And despite the strong whiskey flavor, she lost herself for a minute. His stubble burned and she didn't care. This wasn't her cautious, well behaved Jamie ... but man he felt good. She pulled back to catch her breath.

He tucked a strand of her hair behind her ear. "Meg, I've missed you too."

She melted at the words she'd been dying to hear. His fingers slid into her belt loops and he yanked her hips toward his, his hands suddenly sliding down where they'd never been before as he kissed her neck.

"Wait, wait." She pushed his chest back and took another deep breath, trying to clear her head. Wasn't this what she wanted? Proof he wanted her?

"Come on, Meg."

He cupped his warm hand over hers, pulling it from his chest, peppering it with soft kisses trailing up her arm. *Whoa.* Jaime had never been this assertive. It did all sorts of things to her insides.

They had agreed to wait till they were married, even if people said they were old fashioned. So snogging was the most they'd ever done. It had always been an important thing to her ... to wait.

But he wanted her. She could see it in his eyes. His lips were on hers again, this time soft and tender, making her melt, yet again. She couldn't think. She couldn't remember anymore why they'd decided to wait.

"You're so sexy," he whispered in her ear. Tingles raced up her spine and her knees felt like Jell-O. He leaned into her, hand on her back, slowly lowering her to the couch.

She'd given in to the heat and the mindless motion for just a few moments when she saw it—her glaring clue.

Shoes.

Five sets of shoes next to the doormat. One pair of large work boots. One pair of men's runners and three smaller pairs of women's shoes. *Why does he have women's shoes here?*

She tried to push him away.

"Darlin, we don't need to wait. Lets do this." His voice was deeper. His eyes were intense and focused on one thing ... until he followed her gaze.

"Whose shoes are those?" she asked, trying to keep her voice steady.

He sat up and rubbed his stubbled face. "My flatmate's."

"Yer—what? You have a flatmate? A girl?"

He shrugged. "She's a friend of my cousin. We share the flat. But she's not here right now, babes. Just you and me." He leaned back toward her but she shot off the couch.

"You have a woman living here? With you? There's only one bedroom, Jamie. Do you share that too?"

"'Tis no big deal. Don't be so uptight." He shrugged again and stood up.

*Seriously?* Her chest felt weighted, like she'd inhaled a bucket of seawater. She grabbed her coat. She had to get out. Had to breathe.

"Babes, yer not seriously leaving? Calm down. Ya drove all the way up here." He laughed and tried to saunter over to her again. "And things were just getting fun."

"Save it." She held up her hand. "I am not uptight. I'm yer fiancée! Are ya seriously standin' there telling me yer sleeping with another woman but I should calm down?"

"Bloody hell, yer more uppity than I remember. It's casual with me and Annie. Nothin' serious."

*My head's gonna explode.* "Who are you?"

"Who are you?" he snapped. The granite eyes had returned and he lifted his index finger toward the ceiling. "Oh wait—I know—yer the whiny, needy chick I have to talk to on the phone all the time. I'd forgotten, yer much hotter in person. For a minute, I thought ya might be worth spendin' some time with. My mistake." He dropped onto the couch and turned the on the telly.

An icy fury swept through her as she held back tears. She would not let him see her cry. She heard a hushed voice full of venom and vaguely recognized it as her own. "I don't know who the hell ya think you are but I want nothin' to do with you. *Ever.* Don't call me, don't text me and if ya ever have the guts to show yerself in Millway, don't come anywhere near me."

With shaking fingers, she wrenched the engagement ring from her left hand and hurled it at his cheating head. She didn't even stay to see if it hit the mark, although the loud cursing she could hear from the stairwell told her it had.

# Chapter Two ~ March

Millway looks different these days. I've grown up here, so I know what the town should look like. But ever since Jamie (or The Bastard, as I like to call him) cheated on me, it's like there's a grey film over everything. The sun may shine, but it's not as bright. The green hills we affectionately call mountains have lost their vibrant mossy color. And the friendly neighbors on the street don't seem to smile anymore.

Brenna tells me I'm going through the stages of grief: Denial; Anger; Bargaining; Depression and Acceptance. Apparently, she took some kind of psych class before she moved here from America. Makes sense, I guess. I had planned on spending my life with Jamie. No way that will happen now. So that life that I'd planned on is dead. As far as I'm concerned, Jamie's dead—or should be.

I'm obviously in the anger stage.

He hasn't come home to visit his parents, as far as I know, and I hope he never does. His mam treated me like her daughter before, but she's completely turned on me. Wouldn't even give me five minutes to tell her what actually happened. I think The Bastard lied and told her he caught me cheating on him. Me cheating on him? Right. And even better, she obviously told all her friends because everywhere I go, people are whispering. I'm so over the whispering.

Megan closed her journal with a sigh. The park was deserted today, and she liked it that way. It suited her mood. But she knew staying in a prolonged angry state was not healthy. Which is why she had agreed to go see a therapist. And that was why she was writing everything down in a journal.

Doctor Grania Whalen had come highly recommended by several of Megan's friends in Cork City. They hadn't met yet, but she'd given Megan an assignment: to write down how she was feeling, every day. That alone had already been surprisingly therapeutic. She hadn't realized how much writing helped her to process her thoughts. But after a week of writing every day, she knew it was a healthy thing for her. A way to gain some perspective.

She put her journal in her bag and took the footpath toward Main Street. The bell over the door at O'Grady's Grass & Garden sounded like wind chimes and the light cheerful sound soothed her frayed nerves. Maybe she should invest in some wind chimes and just carry them with her, ringing them whenever she caught someone whispering about her. That wouldn't incite more rumors. She gave a half-laugh at the thought.

"Hallooo, Megan!" A melodic voice came from somewhere in the back of the massive, cluttered garden store. Nessa Rose had moved home to run the store for her parents, as they were getting on in age. Megan spied her on a stepladder, hanging a decorative garland above an archway, the ladder swaying slightly.

"Hi, Nessa Rose. Do ya need a hand there?" Megan grabbed ahold of the base of the ladder to offer some stability.

"Oh, thanks, luv. That's much better. I almost fell twice before ya came in. I told Da we need to order a new ladder, but he's so stubborn, ya know?"

Megan nodded. She knew about stubborn parents. Her mother was the Queen of Stubborn. "I think my da has an extra ladder in his workshop. Why don't ya swing by the house later, with yer truck. You can borrow it 'til you can convince yer da. I'd hate to see ya break a leg or something."

"Actually," Nessa Rose said as she descended, "that might work beautifully. The one thing Da hates more than spending money is people thinking he can't afford to. I won't even have to come get yer ladder. I'll just have to tell him I'm *going* to, and he'll be on the phone ordering one within the hour. Brilliant plan, Megan. Truly brilliant. Now, what can I get for ya?"

"Marlene ordered a bunch of flowers. She asked me to pick them up."

"Oh, right. Of course, yer mam's flowers. How silly am I that I didn't think of that?" Nessa Rose tapped her forehead and headed toward the back of the store. "I'll be right back."

Megan smiled, watching her retreat, because Nessa Rose always made her think of a flower. Not because she worked with flowers or because Rose was part of her name, but because she always seemed to look like some sort of flower. Today, she was a daisy. She wore green pants and a white flowing blouse with a yellow collar. Her blonde spiky hair was the center of the daisy, and her willowy walk made Megan think of a daisy swaying in the breeze. The funniest thing was, Megan didn't think Nessa Rose had any clue she dressed like her little botanical friends.

"Here we are. Her pulmonarias are ready to be planted in the ground." She returned carrying a large flat box full of barely blooming, delicate blue flowers. "Actually, probably should have planted them last week, before they bloomed," she mumbled to herself and stared at the plants for a moment.

After an awkward silence, Megan cleared her throat and Nessa Rose came back from wherever her mind had taken her. She handed the box to Megan. "Tell yer mam to make sure they get a good bit of water for the next week or so. They should bloom through April, so she'll get a good six weeks of color from them."

"I'll let her know. Did she already pay?"

"Pay?"

"Yes—my mam, did she already pay for the flowers?"

"Oh, goodness me. Yes, yes. She's all set. Sorry, I'm a little distracted today." Nessa Rose tapped her head again and chuckled. "I know, it's not just today. I'm usually distracted. 'Tis my curse."

"Not a problem. Thanks." Megan smiled and backed out of the doorway, struggling to maneuver the oversized box. As she released the door with her foot, she backed right into someone on the sidewalk and watched in horror as the entire box of plants flipped in the air and landed upside down, scattering potting soil everywhere.

"Brilliant!" she growled as she bent down to salvage the plants, ignoring the man who was above her, apologizing, even though it was obviously her fault.

She righted the box and was scooping the plants back into their plastic containers, one at a time, when the man squatted down and began helping her pack soil into the containers. She noticed his expensive-looking black dress shoes and shiny grey suit pants.

"Didn't you see me coming out of the shop?" she asked with more anger in her voice than she intended, not even bothering to glance up at his face.

"Uh, sorry, no. I had my back to ya. I was waiting fer my ride. Are y'okay?"

"I'm fine." She still didn't look up, too engrossed in getting the plants put back together. Her mother would not be happy. Maybe she wouldn't be able to tell. If Megan grabbed a bag of potting soil and got them all planted before her mam got home, she'd never know.

Except she would, because a number of the plants were damaged from the fall. Her detail-oriented mam would definitely notice. "My flowers are not fine, though. You really should be more careful." She didn't even know why she was scolding the poor guy. Maybe just cuz he was there.

And he was a guy.

"Right. I definitely should be more careful about letting women bump into me like that. Especially if they're carrying dirt."

She realized some of the wet soil had splattered his pretty grey pants. And he couldn't even wipe them off because his hands were now covered in dirt from helping her put the plants back together.

"I'm sorry," she said as she looked up toward the man's face. *Whoa.* He had to be a Hollywood actor or something. His sandy blond hair was tousled on top and short on the sides. He had a gorgeous mouth, which was currently tilted in an amused smile, and his golden eyes made it hard to look away. She didn't even know people could have golden eyes, yet they reminded her of someone. She just couldn't place who it was. "Um, yer pants. I'm really sorry. If you give them to me, I can get them cleaned at Clancy's." She nodded across the street toward the dry cleaners and stood up, shaking excess dirt off her hands.

He stood and did the same. "Well now, I think it's a little early in our relationship for me to be taking off my pants, but I appreciate the request."

"I didn't mean—"

"I'm just teasin'." He winked at her and lifted the box off the ground. "Can I help you get these to yer car?"

Flustered, by both his comments and his gorgeous face, she shook her head. "No, thanks. My car's over at the park. I can handle it." She took the box from him.

"Are ya sure, cuz yer track record—"

"I said I've got it." She winced as her embarrassment came out sounding like anger again.

He lifted up his dirty hands in surrender, laughter still in his eyes. "Okay, 'tis all yers, luv. My ride is here, anyway."

A sleek red car pulled up, a stunning brunette in the driver's seat. Megan wanted to run to her car, but she forced herself to walk away slowly. She could hear the woman telling the man there was no way he was getting in her car when he was covered in dirt. She was saying something about him needing to go take a shower at the hotel.

It struck Megan that she hadn't even thanked him for his help. She certainly wasn't going to go back toward the pretty people convention, especially covered in dirt, but she glanced back. Hollywood guy was wiping his hands on a small towel and—to her surprise—intently watching her walk away.

# Chapter Three ～ April

Grania says I've moved from anger to depression. I told her I already went through the depression when I first broke up with Jamie. She says that the stages of grief don't go in a neat line. They weave in and out of each other. It may take a long time for the depression to subside and I may cycle back through the anger again. Well, that's fan-freaking-tastic. She even suggested medication for the depression. I don't know what to think of that. But I do feel the depression getting a stronger hold on me. Meh.

When it first happened, I stayed in my room for a week, only coming out when my mam insisted I eat or shower. Marlene (yes, I call my mam by her first name. Don't know why. I just do) ... anyway, she doesn't know why I broke up with Jamie. Grania thinks I should tell her. Says it will foster intimacy between us. I told her she hasn't met my mam ... that Marlene's not real big on intimacy. But she made me promise to at least think about it.

So, back to the depression. She's right. It's back. I'm feeling pretty crappy. I set up coffee dates with friends, and then I figure out how to cancel. I go to class in yoga pants and a sweatshirt. Most of the time, I don't even do my makeup. I just don't care. Do I have to care? I'd rather sleep. Sleeping is much better than caring.

*Marlene keeps asking me if my grades are okay. I tell her I'm not ten and she doesn't need to know. She doesn't really appreciate that. I don't care.*

*Have I mentioned I don't care? My da is the only one in the family who gets it. He just hugs me and tells me he loves me. He insists that I'm a gem. But then I wonder why Jamie stopped loving me? What was it about me that made it so easy for him to throw me away? That line of thinking doesn't exactly chase away the depression.*

*Brenna's making me go shopping with her today. Ryan's taking care of the baby for the whole day so we can have a girl's day. We're taking the train into Cork. Apparently, there's some store opening that everyone is going to. I don't care.*

M egan looked in her rearview mirror as she pulled into the train station. *Scary.* Dark purple circles made her green eyes appear wild. Her strawberry-blonde hair hadn't been trimmed in months. Her fringe practically poked her in the eye, and the frayed ends of her hair were currently sticking up out of a haphazard bun. At least she'd put on real clothes. Brenna had threatened to make her change in the middle of the train if she wore yoga pants.

Brenna was waiting on the platform, looking gorgeous, of course. She didn't even need to try. She had naturally dark, thick, curly lashes, so she didn't need mascara. She always looked tan, even though there was hardly any sunshine at this time of year. And she had ruby lips, without a stitch of lipstick or gloss.

Megan wanted to hate her for it. Her own lashes were blonde, so without mascara, everyone thought she was sick. Her lips were so light that they practically blended in with her face. And she was pale. Irish pale. But she couldn't hate Brenna, because Brenna was her best friend. So she loved her in spite of her jealousy-inducing beauty.

"Hey, friend," Brenna said, linking arms with Megan. "Train's due in three minutes. How are you feeling today?"

Megan gave a noncommittal shrug.

The train wasn't too crowded when they boarded and took the first row of seats. It would fill up as they got closer to Cork City. They sat in a comfortable silence for a while. Brenna was a good friend to have when you didn't really want to talk because she didn't force it. She just let Megan talk at her own pace.

"Grania suggested I go on an antidepressant." Megan absently tapped on the small table in front of their seats.

"What do you think of that?" Brenna twisted in her seat to face Megan, pulling her legs up and resting her chin on her knees.

Megan shrugged. And then smiled slightly, knowing that had become her standard answer for everything. "I used to think people who were depressed should just get over it. Like they were just being lazy or selfish. Not trying to get better. I guess I thought they just wanted attention."

"What do you think now?"

"I'm not so sure anymore. My great-Aunt Charlotte always sat in her drawing room with all the curtains closed up tight. If you let any light in, she would complain about her nerves and how you were trying to kill her. I just thought she was a mean ol' bugger. And probably a faker, too. But now I feel bad for her. I don't think anyone ever tried to help her get better." Megan traced a pattern on her jeans with the tip of her finger.

"So do you think the medicine will help you get better?"

"Well, she says she wouldn't normally suggest it for a bereavement case, which is how she's treating the whole break-up thing. But when she did some digging into my history, she found signs of depression reaching back several years. So, if I've been depressed for some time, it makes sense to combine therapy with an antidepressant. She thinks it will help me feel stronger, more able to get past what Jamie did. Cuz I'm not feeling so strong right now—" Megan's voice faltered and she pressed her mouth into a thin line, glancing out the window.

Brenna grabbed Megan's hand and squeezed. "It's okay."

Megan shook her head. "I'm sorry I'm such a mess."

"Please. Are you kidding? Have you forgotten how you had to drag me out of bed when I thought I'd lost Ryan? Don't apologize, friend. There's no need."

Megan wiped tears from her eyes. "Thanks. I'm kind of depressed that I'm depressed." A small laugh escaped her lips. "I know that doesn't make sense. But I feel like I shouldn't be feeling this way. I should be able to pray and trust God to make me better. But I don't even feel like getting out of bed. I am praying, but I'm not sure God can hear me anymore. Like there's something blocking the signal."

Brenna just nodded and waited patiently for Megan to continue. "I guess, I feel like a failure if I take the medication because maybe it means I'm saying God isn't able to help me? But I'm worried if I don't take the medication, it will get worse. I don't want to go through that again."

Brenna cocked her head to the side. "Again?"

"This isn't the first time I've felt like this. When I was seventeen, I went out with this guy, Patrick. I thought he was *the one*." Megan used air quotes for emphasis. "I was sure we were going to get married right out of school and do amazing things with our life together. But a few months before we graduated, he told me God told him to break up with me."

"*God* told him?" Brenna raised a skeptical brow.

Megan shrugged. "Apparently, I was too much of a temptation for him. I gave him *impure* thoughts." More air quotes.

"He actually said that to you? Like it was *your* fault he was thinking with his—"

Megan nodded. "I know. Now I can look back and see he was full of it. But at the time, I believed him. And then I saw him at camp later that summer. Some chick was sitting on his lap, running her fingers through his hair, and they were laughing and having a grand time."

"Ouch."

"Right. I wanted to ram their heads together. But instead, I called my da to come get me, and I practically stayed in my room for a month until I had to go to school. Then even when I started University, I wasn't really better. I might feel good for a few months, but I would always end up back in a dark place. I didn't know it was depression. I just thought of it as good moods and bad moods, ya know? But the bad moods lasted a lot longer than the good ones. And then I guess, over the years, I kind of just leveled out at a medium mood. So, Grania thinks I've been in a mild to moderate depression for several years now."

Brenna stretched her legs under the table. "That's a long time to deal with something like that on your own. Do you feel relieved that you're finally getting some answers?"

"I guess. But I can't help but wonder if maybe that's why Jamie did what he did. Maybe I was just too hard to be with, ya know?"

"Oh sweetie, no. I don't know what Jamie was thinking, but I don't think what he did was your fault."

"But why wasn't I enough for him? What was it about me that wasn't good enough?" Megan sniffled and looked out the window, embarrassed by her continual tears but thankful they were in the front seat so no one else was likely to see her crying.

Brenna rubbed her back. "Friend, he's the one who screwed up. You are not responsible for his cheating. It's not you that's not enough. There's something broken inside of him. That's his baggage, you know?"

Megan nodded and wiped her face on her sleeve. "Maybe. But if I don't get this stuff figured out ... I don't know. I'm just not sure I even know who I am. And even if I want nothing to do with dating, right now, I do eventually want to meet someone. I want to have a relationship like you and Ryan. You guys are perfect together."

Brenna rolled her eyes and smiled. "I've told you before, our relationship is not perfect. Marriage takes a lot of work, and there's no such thing as a perfect relationship."

"Ya know what I mean."

"I know. I wouldn't trade Ryan for anyone else, and I want that for you, too. You deserve to have someone who loves you and treats you right."

"Thanks." Megan smiled tentatively. "Sometimes I feel like I don't deserve that. But Grania says that's the depression talking."

"I agree. Of course you deserve that."

"I don't know. I can't really think straight right now. I kind of think I should try the meds."

"Do it then. What's the worst that could happen?"

"Hmm, good question. I don't think I have much left to lose." Megan glanced down at her stomach. She had a high metabolism and had always been on the thin side, but she could just see a soft pouch forming at her middle. She gave a wry smile as she added, "Other than the few pounds I've gained medicating with chocolate."

# Chapter Four ~ May

### Brenna

Brenna was glad Megan had agreed to come work in the garden. She knew it was a soothing thing for her and to be honest, Brenna hated doing it. *Win-win.* Megan seemed to be doing a lot better, but today she was agitated. Understandable, since she was supposed to be getting married today, and instead she was digging through the dirt in Brenna's flowerbeds.

Megan set down her small spade. "Y'know how sometimes ya see people looking in yer direction and whispering, and you get this paranoid feeling that they're talkin' about ya, but then you realize you're just being silly?" A sudden breeze ruffled the flowers and tossed some potting soil into the air.

"Mm-hm." Brenna didn't look up from her task. Seated on a large blanket, she was changing a diaper. And when you're dealing with a squirming ten-month-old baby boy, you have to be quick and focused, or you will get an unwanted shower. She knew from unfortunate experience.

"Yeah, well, this is not that. People are *still* talking about me. I'm not just paranoid ... hello, are ya with me?" Megan waved her hand before Brenna's face.

"Sorry, yeah. I'm with you. Paranoid. Go ahead." Diaper change accomplished, Brenna looked at her friend. Megan's pin-straight, strawberry-blonde hair was pulled back into a messy ponytail. Her faded jeans, smeared with potting soil, had begun to tear at the knees. And her fingernails, which should have been manicured to perfection on this day, were caked with dirt. No, this was probably not how she had envisioned her wedding attire.

"Well, this morning, I walked into the Tea Shoppe and Old Mary and Mary were sitting at a table along the wall laughing up a storm over something, but as soon as they saw me, they got really quiet, leaned in toward each other and started whispering. They didn't even try to hide it! They were totally talkin' about me." Megan yanked a clump of weeds from the ground with violent force. "I wanted to chuck my scone right at their heads."

"They'd deserve it. Those two are always talking about everyone. I'll pay you if you do it next time!" Brenna grinned, and Megan cracked a smile. "But people know you were supposed to be getting married today, Meg. It would be surprising if they *weren't* talking about it, you know? It'll die down after this, I'm sure."

Megan squinted as the mid-afternoon sun made a rare appearance from behind a cloud. "I doubt it. I've been hearing the whispers fer four months now. 'Can you believe what she did to poor Jamie?' 'I heard she threw the ring right at his face.' 'She had a guy on the side, I heard.' 'She doesn't deserve Jamie anyway … poor lad.' Agghh. If only they knew!"

"Well, they're all obviously getting the story from his mom. And she's gotten it from him. You could try telling people what really happened."

Megan blew out a breath, sending ripples through her strawberry-blonde fringe. "You know I tried to. Right after I broke up with him, I told anyone who would listen that he was a cheating scumbag. Only my close friends believed me. What am I supposed to do, rent a billboard? This is Jamie we're talking about. Even *I* hardly believe me. It just doesn't sound like something he'd do. So now, I'm the liar and the slut and who knows what else." She sighed and rubbed her temples, leaving a smudge of dirt behind.

"Well, I think the billboard idea has merit." Brenna bounced little Ben on her lap, eliciting a fit of giggles. "Oh wait, I know. There's a show in America called *Cheaters*, where they video the guys and catch them on tape, kissing the other woman, then they let the girl confront him. We could start an Irish version." Brenna watched tears slip down Megan's cheeks. "Those aren't laughter tears. I'm sorry for joking, friend. I thought it was okay."

"Of course it's okay." Megan wiped her eyes. "I've moved on. I really have. I'm doing so much better, even if you can't tell today. I've accepted it and I've moved on. But ... sometimes I think about what things were like before. I think about what it would be like if this were all a bad dream and everything was back to normal again. And thinking like that just makes me a little emotional."

"Sweetie, it's okay to cry. Allow yourself a little mourning time today. As a matter of fact, if you wanted to sit in your room and cry all day, there'd be nothing wrong with that. You've had this day looming over you for months now. Just get through it however you need to. Tomorrow will be better," Brenna said.

"However I need to?" Megan pretended to think. "Maybe I'll go bungee jumping. Do people still do that?"

"Okay, amend that. However you need to ... without taking your life into your hands. How 'bout that?"

Megan just nodded and went back to tearing weeds from the garden. Brenna sensed she needed some alone time, so she gave her a quick hug and scooped Ben into her arms.

"He'll need a nap soon. I'm gonna go feed him a bit and put him down. You want some tea after, or are you heading home?" Brenna asked.

"I should probably go. I don't have to work today, but I have some studying to do."

"Hold up." Brenna took a corner of Ben's blanket and ran it under the spigot. "You've got some dirt, just there." She dabbed Megan's temples.

"Nice of you *not* to use yer spit for that." Megan said, and Brenna laughed.

"Well, I *could* use some magic mom-spit if you like."

"No, thanks. I'm good. I'll catch ya later." Megan dusted herself off and ran her hands under the spigot to clean them. She gave a half-hearted wave as she headed to her car.

As Brenna headed toward her back door, she noticed that Megan had been so distracted she'd pulled up half of her flowers along with the weeds. "Text me when you get home," she shouted at Megan's open car window. "Goodness, let's hope she makes it there in one piece!" she said to Ben.

⌒⋎⋉

Megan probably should have gone home. But she hadn't eaten all morning, and she knew there was nothing appealing in the pantry at home. So she turned down Drishane Road and drove the couple miles into Mill-way. Pulling around the back of Rosie's Pub, she took a look at herself in the rearview mirror and sighed. Not a pretty sight. She pulled out the band that held her ponytail and shook her hair, attempting to comb through it with her fingers. Unsuccessful, she piled her hair up into a messy bun. Glancing at her holey, dirty jeans, she decided they completed her "I don't care" look and by definition, that meant she had to stop fussing with herself and just head into the pub.

But her mind whirred so much that she decided to get a journal entry in before lunch.

*So, I've been on meds now for five weeks. I can't believe what a difference it's made. It's like I've been living with only a half-charged battery for so long, I thought that's what a full battery felt like. But no, I actually feel good. I mean, not all the time, of course. It's not magic. I still get ticked off, but it's not constant anymore.*

*Although, today kind of sucks. Today was my wedding date. Crazy how things can change. But even that doesn't feel as horrible as it once did. Jamie is still The Bastard; still a loser, of course. But I feel miles ahead of where I was a month ago.*

*I even feel like Marlene is a little nicer. Maybe she wasn't so bad all along. Maybe it was me? Radical thought.*

*Grania says we're making good progress. She thinks the depression has shown itself as anger in the past so that's what I might want to work on. I've plenty of opportunity to work on it with everyone talking about me, still. You'd think they would have moved on. It's been over four months. But no. Apparently, my imaginary scarlet letter is still showing. Whatever. Maybe I can just let people think what they want to think. Not like I can control it anyway.*

The smell of pot roast gravy and onions—Rosie's perpetual aroma—wafted on the air as Megan opened the door and blinked, adjusting to the dim lighting. She found a seat at the mahogany bar and waved to her bartending friend, Tara, who was wiping up a spill in front of two camera-toting tourists. A low hum of conversation, punctuated by the occasional ding of silverware hitting plates, buzzed around Megan as she watched Tara make her way toward her.

"Hey Meg, are ya eatin'?" Tara asked, tucking a stray ginger lock behind her ear.

"I am. I'll take a burger and chips. And a mineral, I guess."

"Coca-Cola?"

"Diet."

"Sure thing." Tara leaned closer to Megan and whispered, "Just to warn ya, the O'Connors are over at the corner booth. Didn't know if you'd be wantin' to stay or take it to go?"

Megan glanced over and saw The Bastard's parents and brothers. She ran her garden-stained fingers over her haphazard bun. Great. Like she wanted to see *them* when she was a complete mess. Any time she'd seen them in public over the last four months, they'd made exaggerated attempts to ignore her. Well, especially Jamie's mam, Elizabeth. The men just put their heads down and followed Elizabeth's lead.

They weren't looking her way. She could make a quick escape and not have to deal with them at all. She strongly considered it. But then she took a look at the other tables and noticed several pairs of prying eyes peering at her, and she stifled a scream. She had done absolutely nothing wrong here. *Hello ... I'm the one who was cheated on, not the other way around.* It was so unfair that everyone believed Jamie's story over hers. Whatever his story was. She still didn't know exactly what lies he'd told ... just the snippets of rumors she'd heard here and there. But she could imagine she was painted the villain.

Talking about controlling her emotions and actually doing it were apparently two very different things. The anger that lived just under the surface of her healing emotions began to uncoil. She could feel it snaking up through her gut.

"Screw 'em. I'm stayin' put." She stared back, defiantly, at anyone who dared to glance her way. "And skip the mineral. I'll take a pint o' Harp." Grania probably would not approve. Antidepressants and alcohol ... not a good mix. But one pint wouldn't kill her.

Tara's eyebrows lifted in surprise, but she nodded and headed toward the kitchen. Megan fumed. She thought back to the last time she'd seen Jamie, on that frigid January night four months earlier. She'd thought for sure that there had to be another explanation for his strange behavior. Of course, Jamie would never cheat on her. Other guys did stuff like that. Not the Jamie she'd known for so many years.

But he was not the same Jamie. And he *had* been cheating on her. Heat colored her face as she remembered throwing her engagement ring at his head. The gossips had gotten that much right. Not only did she chuck her ring at him but she'd heard him cuss in pain as she ran from his flat, so she knew she'd nailed him. It was the least he deserved.

After that, she'd spent a sleepless night in a dingy motel and spent the whole next day driving home. The first place she'd gone when she'd gotten back to Millway was to Elizabeth O'Connor's place. She'd expected comfort. Expected that Elizabeth would be as horrified at what her son had done as she was, and that she'd hug and console her in a way that Megan's mam never seemed capable of. That was Elizabeth's way. She was like a warm cup of tea—or she *had* been. Megan would never forget the look of disgust on her face when she opened her door that cold night.

"You are no longer welcome in this house." Elizabeth had said as she slammed the door in Megan's face. And that was the last time they'd spoken. Megan called her several times that week, hoping to find out what lies

Jamie had told her. But Elizabeth never answered or returned her calls. Megan knew her good friends believed her side of the story, but Elizabeth's friends were everywhere, and they all looked at Megan as if she were suddenly evil incarnate. Who knew what kinds of rumors were circulating?

Picking up her burger, she watched her hands shake. Just thinking about it all had her blood pressure rising, adrenaline spiking. A few deep breaths calmed her racing heart and she dug in, suddenly aware that she hadn't eaten since lunch the day before. She washed the first bites down with the Harp and felt her shoulders relax after a couple more sips. She thought she was actually managing her anger quite well, thank you very much.

Until the O'Connor family walked past the bar and tested that theory. Jamie's twin brothers, John and David, shot her surprisingly sympathetic looks as their mother began loudly, "Tis a sad day, to be sure. Our Jamie should have moved home by today but he doesn't feel comfortable in his own hometown, anymore. Maybe some people should just go back beyond, to wherever they came from."

The O'Connors had lived in Millway for generations. Megan's family had moved in when she was a baby. So, now, among other things, Elizabeth was calling her an outsider. She felt the hairs on the back of her neck rise so she took a deep breath. *Zen. Breathe in and out Megan.* She turned and faced the bar, stone still, as she heard the front door open and close with their exit. Grania would be proud. Tara rushed over to her with a pained look.

"Oh, Meg, that was so rude! You have every bit as much right to be here as they do. She's being ridiculous. To even think that you would cheat on Jamie."

"Yeah, it's about as crazy as anyone believing that the sweetest guy in Millway would cheat on me, right?"

Tara winced at her words. "Well, ya know I believe ya. Anyone that I hear talkin' about ya gets an earful from me, I promise."

"Thanks, Tara. I know." She drummed her fingers on the bar. She had to deal with this. She'd let Elizabeth off the hook for too long. "I've got to head on." Rising, she threw twenty euros down on the bar and stalked out the door, leaving most of her lunch behind.

The O'Connors were getting into their truck when she snapped, "Hey, Elizabeth!"

Elizabeth slowly turned to face her with a steely gaze. Megan strode toward her.

"Yer so right. Jamie should be here. Why don't you invite him to come home for Sunday dinner, this week. Better yet, you should tell him to bring Annie, the chick he's been *shagging* for six months. She would love yer lamb stew."

The twins shot surprised looks at each other in the back seat. Elizabeth looked stunned as Megan continued, "I don't know exactly what lies yer son has told ya, but I can assure you they are lies. I tried to tell you, but ya wouldn't listen. So when yer ready to hear the truth ... you have my number."

Megan whirled around and stalked to her car without looking back. Her hands were shaking again as she fumbled for the keys. But she felt like she'd just tossed a huge weight off her shoulders. It probably wouldn't make much of a difference, but at least she'd finally been able to defend herself.

# Chapter Five

Brenna put water on for tea, for the third time in an hour. She had never been so distractible before the baby. Now, she needed two more sets of hands and a backup brain. She was pretty sure he was actually sleeping now. He'd been up, crying, the whole night before, so he should definitely sleep well tonight.

She hoped.

She was exhausted and probably could have fallen asleep right at the kitchen table. But she couldn't go to bed yet. Ryan was due home any minute, and she hadn't seen him for a week. She didn't want to be asleep when he arrived, so tea would have to do. If she remembered to put the tea bags in it this time.

She sat down and looked out the window for the tenth time. The long driveway leading to their homey cottage was silent. She guessed it was well after 11:00 p.m., but she'd left her phone on the counter, and she was too tired to move again to check it until it was time to put the water into the teapot. She picked up her book and read to pass the time.

Once the kettle boiled, she shuffled her slippered feet toward the counter and put a couple tea bags in the pot before dousing them with the boiling water. She brought all the tea things to the table and sat back down after snagging her laptop from the desk. She figured a few mindless minutes on Facebook might keep her awake.

She scrolled down and noticed someone had tagged Ryan in a photo. He was sitting at a pub with people she didn't know, all of them smiling and having a grand time. *It's his job, Brenna. He's providing for you and Ben. Chill out.*

Self-talk did nothing to make her feel better. Ryan had been gone so much more than she'd expected. They'd had a bit of whirlwind romance, so she probably hadn't thought through a number of things before saying "I do." Not that she regretted that decision. She would have married him again in a heartbeat, even knowing what she did now. But it had come as a shock, his work schedule.

They met when he was on a long break from work. A big project had just ended and he was in vacation mode. They spent so much time together; she never gave a thought to what would happen when he had to go back to work. But in the year and a half since they'd been married, she'd seen less and less of him.

The economy didn't help. They'd met during the "Celtic Tiger." The boom. Real estate was a great business to be in, and Ryan had done very well for himself over the years. But recently, he'd been more and more concerned about his investments, most of which were in real estate. His construction business was not thriving as it once had, either. They weren't in dire straits, as far as she knew, but the economy was a concern, and he didn't want to keep them afloat with savings.

Which meant he was in Limerick as often as possible, trying to outbid his competitors for the very few jobs that were available now. Often, that meant taking prospective clients to pubs or treating them to dinner. Brenna knew it was his job, not some glamorous double life. She knew that with her head. But when she saw stupid pictures of him hanging out with stupid strangers in a pub, she wanted to punch the computer.

Tires crunched on gravel, and she leapt up from her seat. Even seeing him from the window, she felt a flutter in her stomach. So tall and handsome. Dark hair ruffled by the breeze. Bright blue eyes that lasered in on hers, instantly. The sight of him still moved her. She met him at the back door, and he picked her up, holding her in a strong embrace until she started to giggle. He made it impossible to stay irritated.

"Put me down." She laughed.

He put her down, but he nuzzled at her neck in the process. "I've missed ya, darlin'," he said. "I hate bein' away from ya for so long."

"I hate it, too." She sighed and laid her head on his chest as she pulled him back into a hug. This time with her feet on the ground.

Tipping her chin up, he said, "Yer eyes are tired. Ben's been keepin' ya up, hasn't he?"

"Yeah, teething, I think. The last two nights he's cried so much. He felt kinda warm tonight, too. I hope he's not comin' down with something."

"Poor little lad. I've missed him this week."

"He's missed you, too." She took his hand and pulled him toward the table. "Want some tea?"

"I'd love some."

Brenna poured the tea while Ryan slumped into a chair, and she could see she wasn't the only one who was tired. Despite her weariness, she walked around behind his chair and massaged his shoulders.

"Hmmm, feels so good," he said, barely coherent as he relaxed completely under her touch, dropping his chin to his chest, eyes closed. "When yer done, I'll do yers."

She leaned in close and whispered into his ear, "Promise?"

Suddenly revived, he turned his head toward hers for a quick kiss. Then, in a swift move, he pivoted on his chair, pulling all five-foot-two of her into his lap for a much longer kiss.

A contented sigh escaped her lips. "I've missed you."

"And I you." He pulled her closer, kissed the top of her head and said, "I'm thinkin' I'll give you a five-second head start, and then I'm chasing ya to our room."

Brenna giggled. "Oh really, full of energy now, are you?"

"One ..." Ryan grinned, mischief dancing in his blue eyes.

"No, seriously, we'll wake Ben."

"Two ..."

Brenna squealed and leapt off his lap, dashing toward their first-floor bedroom.

"Three, four, five!" Ryan said in quick succession.

"Cheater!" she said as she hid herself under the covers, laughing. After a minute or so, she peeked over the edge of her blanket, wondering what was taking him so long.

He entered the room holding a lit three-wick candle, set it on the bed-side table and turned off the lights. And just as he crawled under the covers and pulled her close, Ben's high-pitched cry crackled through the monitor on the dresser.

Brenna sighed. "Welcome home, Daddy."

He leaned in and kissed her once more. "Stay in bed. I'll mind him; you sleep."

She told herself she would stay up until he'd gotten the little one back to sleep. She really wanted to. Tired or not, she wanted her husband. But the pull of sleep was too strong.

⌁

"Bren ... Brenna ..." —it couldn't be morning already. She opened her eyes to see Ryan standing over her, holding Ben, with candlelight flickering around them.

"He's really hot." Ryan said, eyes wide with worry.

Brenna's mama instinct snapped into place, and she hopped out of bed, taking Ben from Ryan's arms and putting her lips to his forehead. "Whoa. Definitely a fever."

"I rocked him back to sleep, but it didn't last. Then when I picked him up again, I realized he was too hot. Should we give him something?"

"I've got baby Tylenol in that basket in the kitchen. Grab it for me? I'm gonna go get a cool cloth." She could feel the heat through Ben's pajamas, so she stripped him down to his diaper before grabbing a wet cloth in the bathroom.

"I can't find it." Ryan's frustrated call from the kitchen had her rolling her eyes.

"It's there! You have to move stuff around. It's there."

Why was it guys could never find things when they were right in front of them? Ben whimpered as Brenna wiped the cool cloth over his chest.

"It was behind the basket," Ryan said, returning to the bedroom. "How much?"

Brenna held out her hand. "I've got it. Can you find the thermometer? It should be around the same place."

If she weren't worried about her baby, she would have laughed at the look on his face. He knew he was hopeless. He never found stuff on the first try. Usually. But concern for Ben must have sharpened his skills, because he was back in thirty seconds with thermometer in hand.

Swiping it across Ben's forehead, she waited for the beep. Nothing. She tried again. Still nothing. "Geez, why can't I ever make this stupid thing work?"

"Maybe something happened when you reprogrammed it for Fahrenheit. It's an Irish thermometer, and ya confused it with yer Americanizing."

"You're hilarious." Brenna deadpanned. She tried it on her own forehead and got a reading of 97.5 so she knew it was working. She tried again on Ben and this time when the beep went off, it read 103.8.

"Geez, that's really high, isn't it?" Ryan peered over her shoulder.

Brenna nodded, feeling sick to her stomach. It was after midnight. Why did babies always get sick after doctor's hours? She hated calling the answering service. She didn't want to be that overprotective, first-time mom who panicked over every little fever or chill. But almost 104 was high. "We can wait and see if the meds bring his fever down, or we can call Doctor Rob. What do you think?"

Ryan shook his head. "Rob's in America, on holiday. He won't have his cell on. New doc just started; he's probably the one on-call."

Putting her lips back to Ben's forehead, she felt the heat still radiating. She held the washcloth up toward Ryan, and he took it to re-wet it. Brenna glanced at the alarm clock. 12:15 a.m. Not likely that Anna was still up. But there was a chance. She was the closest thing Brenna had to a mom, and she would know what to do.

"Brenna?" Anna answered on the first ring. "What's wrong?"

"Sorry to call so late."

"I was still up. What's wrong?"

"Ben has a fever. It's 103.8. I don't know what to do. Should I call the doctor?"

"You gave him Tylenol?"

"Five minutes ago."

"Okay, too soon to know if that's helping. Have you tried a cool cloth?"

"Yeah, wiping his forehead as we speak." Ben was in and out of sleep, even as she ran the cool cloth over his face. The fact that he didn't fully wake up was enough to tell her he wasn't himself.

"Well, you can call the doctor, they're used to late-night calls. Or you can give it another half hour. See if the fever goes down so he's more comfortable."

"What would you do?"

"I'd wait. If it's not down significantly in thirty minutes, ring the doctor. But babies can get pretty high temperatures. Was he acting sick?"

"He's been really grumpy. Not sleeping well."

"Is he worse when you lie him down?"

"Yeah, actually. He seems okay during the day, but the last two nights he's cried most of the night."

"Hmmm, well, that sounds like it could be an ear infection. If so, he'll be fine till morning. Can't get him antibiotics before then, anyway. But if it'll ease yer mind, give the doc a call. And then call me in the morning and let me know how he's doing."

"Okay, I will. Thanks."

"Ah, sure. 'Tis what grandmas are for, ya know. Don't worry yerself. He'll be fine. Bye, luv."

Brenna hung up, feeling a little less worried.

"What did she think?" Ryan asked.

"She thinks it sounds like an ear infection. She said to call the doc if it will make me feel better."

Anna wasn't related to Ben by blood, but she was his grandmother nonetheless, and Brenna trusted her advice. Five minutes later, the doctor confirmed what Anna had said: it was likely an ear infection. "Keep him on Tylenol or Motrin if you've any handy. I'll see him first thing. I've an

8:30 open, and I'll make a note for Peggy. Just call the office in the morning, and she'll give you that appointment."

"Thank you, Doctor—I'm sorry, what did you say your last name was?" Brenna asked.

"O'Brien. But Doctor David works fine."

"Okay, thank you, Doctor David. Sorry to wake you."

"Not a problem. I'm on call. That's why I'm here."

# Chapter Six

"Have you seen the new doctor?" Brenna asked Megan as they warmed their hands on freshly poured cups of tea. Megan was stalling. She should be home, studying for Monday's exam. But she was the queen of procrastination, so when Brenna had invited her for a late morning tea, she'd gladly closed her books and headed over.

"No. Someone at the pharmacy mentioned Doctor Rob was bringing on someone new. Didn't know he already had. You've been to see him?"

"Just this morning. Remember how I said Ben was crying yesterday? Turns out he wasn't teething. It was an ear infection. I felt bad I had to call last night after midnight. But the doc had us come in first thing and got Ben on some antibiotics. He's finally sleeping now."

"Poor lad," Megan said. "Oh, speaking of the doc's office, did ya hear Shannon's moving back? One of Doctor Rob's nurses goes on maternity leave in June. Shannon's going to fill in."

"That's awesome. So she's a full-fledged nurse now?" Brenna said. "I don't think I've seen her in at least a year. Actually, I was big as a house, so it's definitely been over a year."

"Aye, she's been working in Dublin for a while. Tara and I had lunch with her this week when she was in Cork for a meeting."

Brenna set a cutting board and some peeled potatoes in front of Megan.

"Here, earn your tea. I need them quartered."

"Yes, ma'am." Megan saluted.

"So, Tara will be glad to have her best friend back in town."

"Aye, she's excited. We should plan a chick flick night."

"Definitely. So, back to the doctor ..." Brenna's eyes danced with humor.

"What, is he that good looking?"

"Well," Brenna glanced toward the living room and lowered her voice, "don't tell Ryan I said so but, as we'd say back in the States, he's a hottie."

Megan's eyebrows lifted. "Hmm, guess I'll have to get a look at him. But I don't really see why Doctor Rob needed to bring on someone else. I've never had trouble gettin' in to see him, have you?"

"No, but I think Rob's dad is getting ready to retire. Besides, Doctor David is more specialized in pediatrics. I mean, he's still a GP, and he's taking patients of all ages, but he said something about focusing more on children's medicine, eventually." The scent of basil wafted on the air as Brenna stirred some bubbly concoction on her stove.

"Ah, makes sense then. Still, I don't care how hot he is, I'm done with men for a while." Megan tried to give her best "I mean business" look.

"You may want to wait till you see him up close to make that an official policy. Not kidding, Meg. He really is gorgeous. Great smile. Golden hair. I bet every single woman in town will come down with a cold this week, just to get a chance to meet the charming Doctor David O'Brien." Brenna laughed.

Megan gulped her tea too quickly in an effort to interrupt. She ended up in a coughing fit when the tea went down the wrong way.

"Are you okay?" Brenna asked.

Megan nodded, eyes watering. "David ... did you say ..." She coughed again. "Did you say David O'Brien?" It couldn't be the same David O'Brien, she thought to herself. The David O'Brien she remembered from secondary school had been tall and skinny. Scrawny, even. With bad acne, coke-bottle-thick glasses and a horrid overbite that had kids calling him "Beaver Boy." She'd never called him that, but most kids did.

Brenna was patting her back, "Yes, David O'Brien. Why? Do ya know him?"

"Geez, I hope not. The David O'Brien I knew would probably still hate me for ignorin' him during most of his fourth year!" *Among other things.*

"Fourth year ... that's tenth grade?"

Megan nodded.

"Can't be the same one. No one could ignore this guy. I'm tellin' ya, Meg, I kept trying not to blush around him, and I'm happily married with my very own hottie in residence! It was embarrassing."

"I'm sure you're right. 'Tis a common enough name. I still feel bad for how I treated that poor lad." Megan took the cutting board full of potatoes to the sink and began rinsing them off. "Anyway, doesn't matter how gorgeous the doctor is. I don't need a man to come in and screw with my life again. I finally feel like I'm over the whole Jamie thing. The wedding date has passed now, and I'm done thinking about it."

"Maybe the good doctor could help you get over him completely," Brenna said with a sideways grin.

Megan rolled her eyes. "I do not need a rebound guy. I just need to be on my own for a bit. Get my balance back. I didn't realize how much I'd been waiting just to get past the wedding date. But it's a new day. I'm starting fresh, and I need to figure out what I want, for me, without a guy getting in the way."

Ryan walked into the kitchen. Now there was a good man. The most eligible bachelor in town for years, and Brenna had managed to snag him within months of moving to Ireland. Some of the girls in town were still ticked that he'd been snatched up by an "outsider."

But Megan was happy for them. They fit together, against the odds. Ryan was a good seven years older than Brenna, who had been a widow and only twenty years old when she'd arrived in Millway. She deserved Ryan. She'd been through so much in those first twenty years that to Megan's thinking, she'd earned the right to pick any guy that made her happy. And Ryan did.

"Hey," Ryan greeted Megan with a kiss on the cheek. "How's my favorite singer been?" She and Ryan often sang together for the church college group, Veritas.

"Fair, and yerself? How's Limerick?"

"'Tis getting old. All this back and forth," he said with a sigh as Brenna nodded in agreement. "I'm working on trying to move my operations here, but it's not looking feasible, at the moment."

"Well, I'm sure you'll figure something out," Megan said, patting his arm.

Ryan snagged a scone and poured himself a cup of tea, offering Megan and Brenna a refresh before putting the teapot down. "So, we met the new doctor today," he said with a grin and a nod toward Megan.

"Ah geez, not you, too!" She rolled her eyes and laughed at the silly matchmaking grins Brenna and Ryan shared. "Well, I'll take that as my cue to leave. I'm off to grab a quick bite to eat at Rosie's, and then I've some studying to do."

"You could have lunch with us, you know." Brenna said.

"I know, thanks. But you've not seen each other for a week, and I'm sure you could use some," Megan shaped air quotes with her fingers, "family time. I'll see ya later." She gave each a quick goodbye kiss on the cheek.

Megan was halfway through her bowl of lamb stew at Rosie's Pub when he walked in, and she almost choked. The gorgeous Hollywood guy that she'd dumped dirt on took a seat in a far booth with a pretty blonde in a gunmetal grey suit.

Heat filled her face as she remembered his frequent appearances in her dreams. She'd kept an eye out for him for a few days, curious to know who he was. But she hadn't seen him once in the two months since she'd bumped into him, so she figured he'd just been passing through. Which is why she hadn't worried too much about seeing him in her dreams. He was just some Hollywood stranger. It was like dreaming about Brad Pitt. No strings attached. But now her stomach was flittering erratically, seeing him again, in the flesh. Thank God he could have no idea he'd been in her thoughts.

"He's gorgeous, isn't he?" the server, Brigit, said in a whisper.

Megan nodded and blushed again at having been caught staring.

Brigit fanned her face. "I may have to come down with flu, just so I can go visit him, ya know?"

"Um ..." Megan wondered what she was missing. "Visit him?"

Eyes wide, Brigit plopped into the seat opposite Megan. "Aye, visit him. He's the new doctor. Ya didn't know?"

Megan shook her head, puzzle pieces fitting together with uncomfortable speed. "No, I had heard there was a new doctor, but I hadn't seen him yet."

"Well, now ya have. Good luck not staring. I'm gonna go see if Katie will switch tables with me. She's already got a boyfriend." Brigit laughed and headed toward the kitchen.

Megan's stomach rebelled against the half cup of lamb stew she'd already consumed, and she swallowed hard, taking a few deep breaths. Hollywood guy was the new doctor, David O'Brien. But the real question ... was Doctor David O'Brien once Beaver Boy? The same David O'Brien she'd known in school? She watched him intently for a few moments, until Brigit walked past her and winked. Megan put her head in her hands, embarrassed at feeling like a stalker. But how was she supposed to figure out if this was the same David without watching him a bit?

She gave a few more casual glances. His sandy blond hair and golden eyes were what gave him that Hollywood look. And that sizzling smile ... geez, even from across the room and not directed at her, it was potent. He couldn't possibly be Beaver Boy. And yet, he was familiar to her. She had to admit there was something about him that she recognized—and not just from the dirt incident. Even when she'd seen him in her dreams, there was something familiar. *It's something about his eyes.* She put her head back in her hands. This was not good.

She hadn't told Brenna everything. Beaver Boy had been "fierce in love" with her —his own words. He had tutored her when she was twelve, and they'd gotten to know each other a little. And then, a couple years later, he'd written her a love letter and delivered it with a bouquet of delicate yellow buttercups. How he'd known they were her favorite flower, she had no clue. But she was fourteen and completely shocked and embarrassed by his attention. She'd smiled at him when he gave her the flowers and letter, but as she turned back to her friends, she rolled her eyes, lest they think she liked him back.

Then, after seeing the look of horror on her friends' faces, she did something that still haunted her. She dropped the flowers and letter in the trash bin, knowing he would see her do it, and laughed with her friends as they all headed to class. No one saw her sneak back and pull the letter and flowers out of the bin, minutes later, when the crowd had dispersed. Reading that stupid letter had made her feel even worse about how she'd behaved. It was the sweetest thing she'd ever read, even if it was from a lad the kids called Beaver Boy.

He'd been a couple years ahead of her in school, and while she wouldn't have said they were close friends or anything, she'd thought he was a sweet guy ever since he'd tutored her, and she had always made it a point to be nice to him—until that day. Then, after what she did, she didn't even have the courage to look at him. He'd moved away at the end of that school year. And ever since then, whenever she saw yellow flowers, guilt pinched her and made her feel queasy.

Now, ten years later, was it possible that Beaver Boy had turned into Doctor Dazzle? She shook her head. It couldn't be. She pushed her bowl away, appetite gone, and waited for Brigit to come back with her bill. All the while, she tried not to look in his direction again. Reaching into her purse for her wallet, she noticed a package of Vitamin C drops she'd picked up at the pharmacy. She popped two of them in her mouth. She didn't plan on being sick any time soon.

⚓

Megan tried to think of anything but the doctor as she drove home in a bit of a daze. Home was a cream-colored plaster cottage with blue shutters and flower boxes. A riot of blue flowers splashed across the window line. Her mam kept the boxes filled with azaleas, peonies, and plumerias. Megan would have chosen a variety of wild flowers in sunny, warm shades. But her mam loved all things blue and green. From her earrings to her scarves to her shoes, everything fell on the blue-green end of the color spectrum.

"Meg, that you?" Marlene called from the laundry room as Megan set her things down on the kitchen table.

"'Tis."

"Good. I need yer help a moment? In here?" Marlene's auburn hair was swept up into a snug bun. She wore cream slacks with a thin teal belt and a matching blouse, and turquoise earrings swung from her ears. She was holding a teal picture frame against the wall with one hand, a nail between her red lips and a hammer in her other hand. "Hold this right here, would ya?" she said around the nail.

Megan held it steady while her mam used the nail to make a mark for where she should place it in the wall.

"Are the boys at hurling practice?" Megan asked.

"Till half-five. Thanks, hold this one now?" Marlene placed another teal frame against the wall, and Megan held it in place as they repeated the process.

"Looks nice in here." Megan said.

"Thank you. I like the shelves better there. More streamlined, don't ya think?"

"Mm-hm." Her mam was constantly rearranging furniture or redecorating rooms. Megan had stopped giving her true opinion years ago. It was more efficient. If she disagreed with her mam, it would mean a half-hour discussion until she was so worn down that she'd just agree out of desperation, anyway.

"Were you out studying?" Marlene asked.

"No, I was at Brenna's. Heading to my room to study now."

"Hmmm." A loaded sound escaped Marlene's lips.

"What?" Megan knew she should just ignore it.

"It's just, if you don't pass your exam, you'll have to take the course again, and it'll throw off your whole plan. I know it's been a tough year, but you really need to make it a priority. Just one more weekend of focus."

"Yes. I know, Mam. That's why I'm heading up to study." *I'm twenty-four, Mam, not fourteen.*

"Good. You'll be a wonderful teacher. I know you'll love it like I do, and like yer grandmother before me. 'Tis a proud tradition." Marlene smiled and patted Megan's cheek.

"I know, Mam." *You're driving me crazy, Mam.*

Megan unclenched her fists and took a deep breath as she took the stairs to her bedroom. The pounding hammer sound echoed off the walls matching the pulse in her head. She was good and truly stuck. She'd known for years that she didn't want to teach. But instead of taking a stand, she'd gone along with it like a leaf swept along by the river current.

Opening the door, she took a good look around her bedroom. It was in desperate need of a makeover. It probably looked exactly as it had ten years ago, with the exception of a few quilt changes over the years and a bit more hair and makeup products on her dresser. She knew why she didn't update it. Because she wanted to move out, and if she spent the time and money to fix up her room, it would be as good as signing a five-year lease. So, she slept with frilly curtains and pink flowered wallpaper surrounding her and daydreamed of getting her own flat.

Flopping across her bed, she reached down and pulled a wooden box from underneath. It was a little larger than a shoebox with beautiful scrollwork along the top edges and her initials carved into the center of the lid. *MCM.* Megan Ciara McKenna. Her dad had made it for her fifth birthday. She only kept the most important keepsakes inside, since it was so small. No room for art projects or books. But it held small tokens of her childhood experiences.

Thinking about her teen years had made her a bit sentimental. So, ever the procrastinator, she thought maybe she would open it and go through her memories, one by one. But even if she didn't want to admit it, her mam was right. She needed to study, and although it had been years, she knew from experience that opening the box meant at least an hour of reminiscing. So, with a sigh, she ran her hand along the scrolled edges and then placed it back beneath her bed and sat at her desk with her class notes.

Stupid class notes. Why was she even doing this? It wasn't that she was bad at it or even that she hated it. But she didn't *enjoy* it. Why should she sign up to do something every day for the rest of her life, that she didn't even *like* doing? She had thought that she might be able to find something else to do after she'd gotten her Bachelor in Education. She had worked in a preschool, the town offices, the library, and now at the pharmacy. If she could find something she enjoyed and still use her degree, she might be able to talk her way out of being a teacher.

But nothing had seemed to fit that description and before she knew it, she was back at UCC getting her post-grad in primary education. She had hoped that maybe the post-grad program would give her something more to like in the field. But instead, as each month passed, she felt more and more panicked. Like she had to get out but instead she was being swept away.

*This summer*, she thought, as she grabbed her textbook from the desk, *this summer I will figure out how to change course.* Just one more exam and then three months of freedom. Maybe more, if only she could figure out how to escape the current.

# Chapter Seven

Well, I think I've hit every one of the stages of grief, at this point. The latest one is the best. Acceptance. I still don't know why Jamie did what he did but I've come to the place where I'm okay with not knowing because I'll probably never get an explanation. I actually feel good letting go and not worrying about it any more. Even if there were something I was doing that upset him, a healthy guy would have talked to me about it, not shacked up with some other woman.

So, I've truly moved on. Grania seems very encouraged by my progress. I asked her if she thought the medication had done its job and now I could go off of it, since I'm feeling so much better. She agreed that I'm doing a lot better but said it's way too soon to stop taking the meds. She said a minimum of six months is recommended and then we will re-evaluate. Makes sense, I guess. I hate being dependent on meds. But, she's the expert. I'll give her the benefit of the doubt.

I haven't been writing as much. Grania says it's okay. We've worked through a lot and she says she's proud of me and I only need to write when I feel like I need to work through something now. Hopefully that means I won't be writing much at all. Here's to smooth sailing from here on out. (Wishful thinking?)

⌒⊀

"Hey, Meg?" Tom Burke, Megan's boss, yelled across the back room of the pharmacy.

"Over here!" she replied from her crouched position, counting boxes on the lowest shelf. It was Friday afternoon, and she was frustrated. Inventory was taking longer than she'd planned and wasn't her favorite thing to do, anyway. She'd been hoping to stop by Brenna's for tea, but time was getting away from her.

"I need you to run this up to Rowan Family Practice. They have a little guy there who needs it right away." She looked up to see him standing over her, little white bag in hand.

She swallowed hard. "No problem, do ya want to finish up this part of inventory?"

Tom nodded and playfully bumped her out of the way, taking her clipboard in the process. She didn't want to let on that anything was amiss, but this was exactly the situation she'd been avoiding all week long. Working for one of only two pharmacies in town, she figured she'd eventually have to come face to face with Doctor David O'Brien. She was just hoping it would be later rather than sooner.

It was a short walk to the doctor's office. Red and pink flowers were blooming in all the window boxes on Main Street, and Rosie's Pub had a new paint job, the fumes making her feel slightly dizzy as she walked by. She'd considered renting one of the flats above the pub, just to have her own space. Ryan owned the whole building, pub on the first floor and apartments above and he'd told Megan he'd give her a "friends and family" rate. But her parents said she was crazy to spend the money when she lived for free at home. She supposed they were right. At least until she finished school or decided what was next.

She checked her hair in the reflection from the window, then crossed the road. As she approached the tan plaster building that housed the Rowan Family Practice, she rehearsed in her mind what she would say to David.

"Hi David, it's nice to see ya. Been so long!" No, too casual. As if they'd been close friends.

"Hi David, it's Megan McKenna. Remember that time I was a horrible witch to ya? Really sorry about that." Too abrupt.

"Hi David, weren't we in school together?" That was neutral enough to work. She shrugged, blew out a breath and opened the door. Peggy, the receptionist, flashed a warm smile.

"Why Megan, haven't seen ya around much lately. Been hiding, have ya?"

Megan laughed, knowing Peggy had no clue she actually *had* been hiding.

"I have a delivery for Doctor Rob?" She held up the white bag.

"Ah, sure. Thanks. Not for Doctor Rob though, he's not back yet. New doc." Peggy winked and waved at her face as if a hot flash were coming on. Then she whispered, "Have ya seen him?"

Why did everyone keep asking her that? Megan smiled, nodded, and set the bag on the counter just as the phone rang.

"Rowan Family Practice, can you hold please?" Peggy put her hand to the receiver and said to Megan, "Be a dear and take that to Exam Room Two?" She didn't even wait for a reply, just went right back to her phone call as Megan stood there, not wanting to comply.

She sighed, grabbed the bag, and headed through the waiting room door to the hallway beyond. She knocked on the exam room door and Doctor David opened it. He excused himself from his patient and quickly slipped out into the hallway. Up close, he took her breath away. In her flustered state after dropping the plants, she hadn't really taken in how good-looking he was. Every thought she'd had of what she was going to say fled her mind and she just stood there holding the bag out, like an idiot.

David smiled, and her heart started thudding. With just a look and a smile, she could feel a blush creeping up her cheeks. Wow.

"Is that a delivery fer me?" he asked, politely.

"Oh, yes. From Tom, at the pharmacy." She extended the bag toward him.

He took it with his left hand and held out his right. "I'm David."

Shock kept her silent for a moment. Did he not remember her? Oh, that would be rather convenient. Or was it truly not him?

"Megan." She shook his hand and smiled, feeling like a giddy schoolgirl who's just been spoken to by the captain of the rugby team.

"Well, thank you, Megan. Have a great day." He smiled again and went back to his waiting patient.

Megan released a breath she didn't know she'd been holding. She left the doctor's office in a confused daze. That was the last thing she'd expected. Polite, gorgeous—stunning, even. Amazing smile.

And completely clueless as to who she was?

He didn't even seem to recognize her from the plant incident. Yet, upon such close inspection, she was sure it had to be the same David O'Brien. The hair color was right. But even more so, the amber colored eyes. They were unique. A golden color surrounded by a ring of soft brown.

She had seen young David without his glasses only a couple times that summer that he tutored her in math, but she now remembered noticing how beautiful his golden eyes were and thinking what a shame it was that they were distorted by Coke-bottle glasses. Those same eyes had just held her captive for a brief moment in the hallway outside Exam Room Two. That was why they had drawn her attention on the plant-dropping day. She had thought it was because they were so unique. But really, it was because she'd seen *those exact eyes* before.

She crossed the street near Rosie's Pub, the fumes again assaulting her nose. Thoughts swirled like fall leaves caught up in the wind. Maybe she hadn't made such a horrible impact on him when he was a teen. Maybe she'd overestimated how much he'd liked her. Although, if her memory was right, it was pretty clear from the letter he'd written. But it was a long time ago and maybe he'd actually forgotten about the letter and yellow flowers. Maybe that would buy her some time to work up to an apology.

Still, for him to not remember her at all? They'd been in the same school for years and he had tutored her three times a week for a whole summer. And *she* still looked much the same. It made no sense at all. Strangely, instead of relief at his lack of recognition, she felt disappointed. And the fact that she was disappointed that he didn't know her made her downright irritable. She didn't like feeling like a silly schoolgirl with a crush.

She decided that a chocolate pastry would make her feel much better, so she ducked into Rosie's. Their new pastry case, stocked by Ryan's cousin, Bettie, was calling to her. What Bettie could do with a little flour and sugar was incredible. She ran a local bed and breakfast but had recently branched out, making pastries for a few Millway shops.

Tara was behind the bar as usual. "Hello there, what brings you in here in the middle of the workday?" she asked.

"One word." Megan smiled and nodded toward Bettie's pastries. "Chocolate."

"Ah, you're not the first today, and you won't be the last, either." Tara pulled a small waxy sheet from a box behind the pastry display and picked up a chocolate treat, gently nestling it in a bag. "That all then?"

Megan told her it was, paid three euros, and said goodbye to her friend. As she set a brisk pace back toward the pharmacy, the wind picked up and played with her hair. She tried to hold it down but eventually gave up and just let it fly. It matched her emotions right now. Scattered. Untamed. She couldn't believe he didn't know her, which led her to believe he was toying with her. To what end? Why would he pretend not to know her?

She needed to run all of this past Brenna. They took turns being wise for each other. Why was it so much easier to give someone advice about her situation than it was to figure out what to do about your own? It was like cleaning, she decided. Always easier to clean a friend's place than your own. Maybe she'd still be able to stop by Brenna's after work, if inventory didn't take the rest of the night.

～ଟ✕

## David

David laughed to himself as he shuffled through paperwork on his desk. He was seeing Megan's face in his mind, her reaction to his handshake. He hadn't planned to pretend not to know her. It had just happened. But he thought it was pretty brilliant. He figured they'd both rather forget the yellow flower incident. She, because she was so mortified by his attention, and he because he was so crushed, at the time, by how she'd re-acted.

It wasn't so much that she hadn't returned his feelings. He wasn't an id-iot, and he'd had a mirror. He'd known he was a long shot. But she'd al-ways been kind to him before that, so the tossing of the flowers and letter into the trash—in front of everyone—that had shocked and hurt his sixteen-year-old self. She never even looked him in the eyes again after that, ap-parently so repulsed by his attentions.

Then, just a few months later, his father had been transferred, and they'd moved to America. End of story. He hadn't thought about her too much after that. The move was good for him. His mother decided it was easier to homeschool him than try to integrate him into an American high school for his final two years. David was relieved and took advantage of the time. He convinced his parents to let him get braces; he worked out daily and began to change his Beaver Boy image. By the time he started university, Beaver Boy was history.

And by the time they returned to Ireland, a few years later, no one in Millway would have recognized him. But his dad had been transferred to Dublin, anyway, not back to Millway. David had gone to University Col-lege Dublin for med school and really hadn't thought of Megan much at all. Until the day of his interview with Doctor Rob. The day she dropped dirt-filled plants all over the sidewalk at his feet while he waited for his sister to pick him up.

He hadn't recognized her at first. He was more amused by her snippy attitude than anything else. But when she'd looked up at him, anger sim-mering in those green eyes, he realized exactly who he was talking to. And he knew she had no idea. It had been kind of fun to watch her without her having a clue. And if he was honest, the thought of working in Millway became even more appealing at that moment.

Landing in Millway had been a fluke, really. He hadn't requested to come here. He'd spent the last two years of med school, as required, at St. Vincent's University Hospital, and then he'd been an intern at Beaumont in Dublin. But he'd grown tired of the city. He wanted to see what general practice had to offer in a smaller town. Any smaller town. It didn't matter much to him.

Then the position in Millway just came up at the right time. A doctor at Beaumont hospital was friends with Doctor Rob and knew he was looking for some temporary help that could turn into a permanent position.

David hadn't even thought about people remembering him as Beaver Boy. He was used to what he looked like now. That scrawny, geeky kid from his past was just a memory. But he had to admit, it had been fun to get the shocked looks all week long. Most people had no clue who he was until they heard his name, and the responses were always the same, "Wait, David O'Brien? Did you grow up here?" He could tell they wanted to ask if he was Beaver Boy, so he would preempt them.

"Aye, 'tis me, Beaver Boy, in the flesh." And the shock was always apparent. He really didn't mind too much. He had a few pictures of himself from those days, and they were right, he *had* looked sort of like a beaver. Kids are stupid and cruel, and he'd gotten over it long ago.

Plus, he wasn't very social back then, so he didn't have many friends, but it was by choice. He liked being alone, spending hours working on intricate Lego designs or reading some epic fantasy series. He was basically a loner. It wasn't until college that he learned how to be social. So, he saw the uncomfortable looks on people's faces when they realized who he was. But because he didn't seem to hold those days against anyone, it seemed people were quickly forgetting about Beaver Boy. Now he was just Doctor David.

The ladies, in particular, seemed very pleased to forget about Beaver Boy. He was aware of his effect on women. Most tended to blush around him. He wasn't sure exactly why. Was it just a natural response to him, or were they thinking things that embarrassed them? He didn't know. But he enjoyed it. He enjoyed that he never lacked for a date if he wanted one. But he also never got serious with anyone. At least, he hadn't for many years. He was having fun just keeping his relationships casual. He could go out with a lass on Friday, have a nice dinner, watch a movie, drop her off at home, and not think about her again.

But since arriving back in Millway, one woman had entered his thoughts repeatedly. And he kind of resented it. He wasn't consciously giving Megan special real estate in his brain, but she was setting up shop there, nonetheless. All it took was seeing her a few times across the street or in the pub. He had seen her looking at him last weekend at Rosie's. He'd thought about saying hi but she was gone before he had a chance. A part of him worried that talking to her might bring out his inner geeky teenager. Seeing her again when he opened the exam room door had caught him off guard.

But at least he hadn't made a fool of himself. He hadn't reverted back to Beaver Boy. He'd been Doctor David and if he wasn't mistaken, he'd totally surprised her. Maybe even thrown her off balance a little. Was it mean to pretend not to remember her? No, it had felt natural. He wasn't the same guy, anyway. So a fresh start might just be the best thing. And maybe now that he'd talked with her, she'd stop occupying his mind.

Even as he thought that, he saw her through the window, strawberry-blonde hair whipping in the wind as she walked away from Rosie's pub. No, she wasn't moving out of his head any time soon. Damn.

# Chapter Eight

Brenna loved Sundays for many reasons. First, because Ryan was almost always home on Sundays—top reason. But she also enjoyed seeing friends at Mass and hearing Father Tim's thought-provoking homilies, and she loved everyone fawning over her adorable boy. He was a joyful little guy with a huge smile willingly offered up to anyone who even looked at him.

And then, there was Sunday dinner. It was a tradition that went back long before Brenna had arrived in Ireland. The Maloney Bed and Breakfast was started and operated for years by Auntie Pat. She was the great-aunt of Brenna's first husband, Ben. Brenna and Ben had only been married four months when he was killed in a car accident along with his father, Joe. It had been a horrific time for Brenna and her mother-in-law, Anna. A trip to Ireland, financed by Auntie Pat the following year, had originally been just a vacation but had turned into a new life for the both of them.

And since she'd arrived, she'd been having Sunday dinner at the bed and breakfast almost every week. Long ago, Auntie Pat had decided that Sunday morning checkout was by 10:00 a.m. sharp and the B&B then closed for the day. No exceptions. Auntie Pat's daughter, Bettie, had taken over the running of the B&B as Auntie Pat got older and her mental health declined. And Bettie was a phenomenal cook. So a Sunday dinner from her kitchen was rarely ever turned down.

Although, Brenna *had* actually stayed away for a few weeks after Megan and Jamie broke up. Bettie was very close to Jamie's mom, Elizabeth, and had made it clear that if sides were chosen, she'd be on Jamie's. And nothing Brenna said would change her mind. No matter how good Bettie's cooking was, Brenna had been tempted to stay away longer than a few weeks. But Ryan, the ultimate peacemaker, convinced them to call a truce. They would just avoid the subject. Family was family and could love each other even if they didn't agree on everything.

Brenna inhaled deeply as she entered the back door of the B&B, straight into the cheery yellow kitchen. "Are we having rosemary potatoes today?" she asked Bettie, who was pulling scones out of the oven.

"That we are, pet. With some fresh salmon from the Blackwater. Tom brought it by this morning. Can't get fresher than that!" she said with a wink. Brenna hadn't even liked fish before she moved to Millway. But Bettie had been horrified at the thought of her never having fresh salmon and had set out immediately to cure her of her aversion. It had worked. There was probably nothing Bettie could make that Brenna wouldn't eat. She had a gift.

Ryan followed her in with a sleeping baby on his shoulder. Bettie set her spoon on the counter and headed straight for them. "How am I lucky enough to have the two handsomest men in all of Ireland, here in my kitchen?" Ryan bent to kiss her cheek and she placed a soft kiss on little Ben's forehead. "He fell asleep between here and the church? Wish I could nod off so fast. Takes me nigh an hour to fall asleep most nights."

"Well," said Ryan, "Tis a gift usually bestowed on men, I'm told. The small one here is just taking after me."

Ryan took Ben to a tiny room off the kitchen that Bettie had outfitted with a Pack'n Play, a rocking chair, and a few other baby essentials. She was almost as bad as Anna in her doting over Ben.

"Where's Anna?" Brenna asked.

"Ah, she'll be along soon. She's helping Father Tim with something, I guess." Anna lived at the B&B with Bettie and Auntie Pat. She helped Bettie every morning with changing sheets and towels and tidying the place. And then she worked for four hours at Sacred Heart, the only church in town, as Father Tim's administrative assistant.

"Hmm, she says he'd be lost without her." Not for the first time, Brenna thought it a shame that priests couldn't marry. Because Anna and Father Tim would make a great couple.

"True, not sure how he got along before she took the job." Bettie said as she shooed Brenna toward the living room. "Off ya go, yer little one's asleep, so you should be relaxing."

Ryan joined her moments later, and they took advantage of a few private moments before they heard Anna's voice through the kitchen door. She breezed through and came to collect hugs and kisses from Brenna and Ryan, both.

"I heard my little peanut is asleep. How am I supposed to smother him with kisses if you let him fall asleep every time ya drive over here?" Anna asked with a smile. "Will ya take some tea?"

"That sounds perfect. I could use a little caffeine." Brenna yawned, as if on cue.

"Aw, Ben's been keeping you up at night again, has he? Some tea should be just right then." Anna said as she walked back toward the kitchen.

Ryan grinned at Brenna, poked her side and whispered, "Ben's been keeping you up, is it? I'm sorry."

Brenna giggled. "Shhh, stop, that tickles." She playfully swatted his hand away, still laughing. He knew very well that Ben had been sleeping fine for the past week. And he was not sorry in the least.

～✕

Dinner was served promptly at one o'clock. Auntie Pat wasn't feeling well and wouldn't be joining them. Brenna worried about her. She had begun the early stages of Alzheimer's around the time Brenna had moved to Millway. Now, a couple years in, she was struggling. Some days, she seemed to be losing herself to the disease. Other days, she was her feisty 82-year-old self, perfectly lucid, telling them all what to do and how to do it.

"How's Patsy doing?" Brenna asked as she passed a serving dish clock-wise, around the table.

"She doesn't know who I am, today." Bettie said.

"I'm sorry, Bettie. That must be so hard to deal with."

"'Tis okay. I'm getting used to it. Not every day is bad. So, I look for-ward to the good days and get through the bad ones. She's got a cold today, too. I've made her some soup for when she wakes."

"I'll take it up when you're ready," Brenna said.

Bettie nodded, a sudden smile breaking across her face. "Oh, did ya hear about the new TidyTowns project?"

Anna chimed in, "'Tis wonderful news."

Brenna wondered what could have them both so excited. TidyTowns was a nationwide initiative that had been around for many years. Towns competed with other towns of similar size with the purpose of making their town a beautiful and welcoming place to live and work. And of course, placing in the competition was always a goal, as well. Winners were an-nounced each September. They planted flowers, organized groups to re-fresh paint in public areas, spruced up streets and footpaths, organized anti-litter campaigns, and kept an eye out for anything that would improve community life. Both Anna and Bettie were active committee members.

"So," Bettie folded her hands on the table. "You know Mountdonovan, right?"

Brenna nodded. "Yeah, the old estate behind town, with the big tree, right? Where the yellow flowers grow." Megan loved to go there to be alone, but Brenna certainly wouldn't be bringing up Megan's name with Bettie around.

"Aye. And it has been empty all this time. Fallen into ruins, really. And, ya may not know that it's been owned all these years by a Donovan descendant living somewhere in America, herself too old to do anything with it. Well, apparently she's passed on—God rest her soul—and she's left the whole of the estate to the town to be used as some sort of tourist attrac-tion and educational campus. Specifically requested the TidyTowns Committee to see to it, she did."

"Wow, what are they going to do with it?" Brenna asked.

Anna answered, "It's still in the planning stages. 'Twill be a TidyTowns project this summer, but obviously, won't count for this year, as there's only a couple weeks left until this year's judging starts. But I'm sure it will give us a leg up on the competition for next year. It's a lovely project with great possibilities. There's some grant money available for educational projects so that will help fund the renovations and whatever needs doing. I think they are talking about restoring the manor house for a visitor's center. Using some of the outbuildings for educational purposes, maybe a folk village, and even a small organic farm on-site."

"That sounds like a huge project." Brenna said.

"'Tis, and I imagine it will take a while to get it all planned out and organized to the point where we can make it look beautiful. But rest assured, when it's time, TidyTowns will be ready for the job." Bettie smacked the table in emphasis.

"I'm sure you will all make it look lovely. And I'm sure you won't be wanting my help." Brenna smiled.

"Well now, we know gardening is not your strength." Anna said with a wink. "But you're artistic and creative, so I'm sure we'll find a way to put ya to work. As ya know, we do much more than gardening."

"I know, you've mentioned it a time or two." *Sarcasm.* Anna had been trying to get Brenna to join the TidyTowns Committee for the past year, saying they needed some younger blood. She put her off every time. Not on principle or anything. She thought it was a great thing that benefited the community. She just wasn't ready to commit to anything when she was still trying to figure out how to handle a baby and a house and laundry ... never ending laundry. Maybe one day she'd have time for committees. But this was not that day.

After dinner, Brenna carried Auntie Pat's soup upstairs. She set the tray on a small table in the hallway and knocked.

"Hello, Patsy ... it's Brenna. I've brought you some delicious potato soup." She knocked once more and opened the door.

Auntie Pat was sitting in a rocking chair staring out her window, white hair sticking up like stretched out cotton balls. Her tiny, backlit frame looked even smaller than normal.

Brenna forced herself not to look concerned. "I have your dinner for you, Patsy. Are you hungry?" She set the soup on a table and sat herself on a stool in front of the rocking chair. She took Auntie Pat's cool knobby hands in her own and watched as the older woman slowly turned to face her.

False recognition sparked in Auntie Pat's eyes. "Pam, what are you doin' here? Shouldn't ya be home with yer flock of small ones? If you've one you've twenty, crawlin' around that house of yers."

Pam was Auntie Pat's sister and Ryan's grandmother. She had died of cancer years ago. Her five children were all grandparents themselves, living in the Limerick area, one of them being Brenna's father-in-law. No point in trying to correct her, though. It was best to just play along.

"I've just come to bring you some soup, luv. I'll leave it here on your table for you." Brenna brought the small TV tray to the front of Auntie Pat's chair and set her soup and tea down within easy reach.

"Thanks, Pammy. 'Tis good of ya to come."

"Do you want to visit?"

"No, I'm tired. Is Jack home?" Her long-deceased husband.

"Not right now, Patsy." Brenna squeezed her hand, and held back tears at the bony feel of it.

"Alright then, will ya make sure wee Bettie gets some dinner? Jack should be home soon."

"Sure, I'll take care of her."

Brenna left the room with a lump in her throat. Every time Auntie Pat had a good day, Brenna let herself believe that she was getting better. That she would make a recovery. But she knew that wasn't possible. Alzheimer's was slowly but steadily winning this battle. And it was painful to watch and not be able to change it. Sometimes she avoided coming to visit so she could avoid the pain, but she never stayed away long. Auntie Pat, Bettie, Anna ... they may not be blood, but without question, they were her family, and she would do whatever she could to support them.

Conversation had moved to the kitchen while she'd been upstairs. Anna was holding Ben, letting him bounce on her lap, over and over. Brenna knew that would last only so long. He wasn't quite crawling yet, but he could scoot himself all over the place and staying in one spot was definitely not something he did for long, these days.

Bettie looked toward Brenna as she sat next to Ryan and grabbed a cup for tea.

"So, how is she?"

Brenna shrugged. "She didn't know me, either. I was Pam today."

"Ah, yes. I've been Pam a lot lately, too." She sighed and sat herself down as well.

Ryan stood up and slid behind Bettie's chair, rubbing her shoulders for a bit. She smiled and patted his hand. "You always know how to make me feel better, luv." Ryan's ability to make his loved ones feel special and cared for was one of his most endearing qualities.

Since Ryan's dad was one of Pam's five kids that Auntie Pat had mentioned, Anna and Bettie were his second cousins. It seemed to Brenna that all of Ireland was made up of cousins, just once or twice removed. Her parents had each been an only child, so Brenna had no cousins of her own. At least not until she moved to Millway, where everyone seemed to adopt her into the great big family that was Ireland.

# Chapter Nine

Millway was a small town nestled in the hills of County Cork with maybe 1,500 residents. They were small, but they were also a proud town. Proud of their heritage, proud of their people, and proud of their accomplishments. As such, they took the TidyTowns competition very seriously. And since TidyTowns judging was to commence soon, the whole committee was aflutter with things that must be seen to. Megan hadn't been involved in an official capacity, but she often volunteered for project days, which is how she found herself in the Town Park on Saturday morning, picking up litter and pulling weeds from flower beds.

She enjoyed gardening—the feel of cool soil between her fingers relaxed her, which is why she refused to wear gardening gloves. They took all the enjoyment away. Her mother—who was not just a card-carrying TidyTowns committee member, but the chairman—continually nagged her about it. "You'll get farmer hands if ya keep sticking your hands in the dirt. Look at yer nails, Meg. You need to take better care." On and on she would go, and Megan would just tune her out. She knew her mam meant well, but it was easier to ignore her than try to explain.

But on this particular morning, her mam was at a teacher's conference, and Megan was completely enjoying herself. Work was going quickly. It seemed to her that they had far more volunteers than normal.

She wiped her brow with her forearm and looked toward the next flowerbed. Why would five people need to be working on a plot no bigger than her car? And that's when she saw himself—David O'Brien. He was saying something—Hollywood smile flashing—while bent down, tossing weeds into a bin. And the silly girls around him were hanging on every word. Ridiculous. Could they be more obvious?

She looked around the park and noticed that the extra volunteers appeared to be women, of all ages. Apparently, none were immune to his charms. She wanted to feel smug and say that *she* was immune. But she knew it wasn't true. If she were over there at that other flowerbed, she'd probably have the stupid puppy-dog look on her face, too. Which was why she would simply avoid him. Better that than act like an idiot.

She stood back and looked at her work. Quite satisfactory. She moved in the opposite direction of the Doctor Fan Club, past the playground and into her favorite spot in the park.

Old, bent trees fully shaded the spot, but sunlight broke through the leaves in thin golden shafts. A small wooden bridge arched over a barely-there stream, and a tiny waterfall made tinkly sounds, which made her think of a mountain hike through untouched land. Of course, this wasn't untouched land. It was fifty feet from a bright red and blue playground. But it was just secluded enough that she could trick herself into feeling like she was alone.

She took off her hat—wide-brimmed to keep the sun from her face, wouldn't Mam be proud—and sat down on the solid wooden bench near the waterfall. She closed her eyes and let the light breeze play with her hair.

⌐⌐⌐

David almost hated to disturb her. She looked angelic. Eyes closed, face upturned, tiniest of smiles on her face, and strawberry-blonde hair moving with the breeze. But he wanted to talk to her, and if he didn't act quickly, his many "assistants" would discover him and the moment would be lost.

"May I?" He spoke softly, so he wouldn't startle her and pointed to the bench just opposite hers.

Megan opened her eyes, confusion clouding her expression. "Oh ... of course." She looked uncomfortable, like she was about to bolt.

"How are you, today—Megan, right?" *Laying it on too thick, David?*

"Yes. I'm well, Doctor O'Brien. And yerself?" She glanced down at her dirty hands and pulled a wipe out of her bag to clean them off.

"Call me David ... please." He smiled, hoping to put her at ease. She didn't react to him like most women did. She seemed more nervous than interested, and he wished he knew what she was thinking. "I'm much better now that I'm sitting. All that squatting and bending has my legs aching. I must be getting old."

She laughed. "I think we're close in age, so I may have to take offense at that."

"My apologies."

"I'm surprised ya made it this far without your following," she said with a nod back toward the park.

"Well," he leaned in closer to whisper, "truth be told, I had to lose them by going to the jacks." He laughed and nodded toward the bathrooms.

Her laugh was musical, and dimples appeared on her cheeks. "Ah, that was brilliant ... although, I know some of them. You're lucky they didn't just follow you in." She absently twisted a strand of hair. "And, I'm surprised they weren't waiting for you when ya came out."

"They may still be. I used the back exit and took the long way 'round."

She laughed again and looked more at ease. "Well, on behalf of Millway, I apologize for the behavior of some of our younger—and not so much younger—residents. You really shouldn't have to be sneaking out back doors and running for cover." Her eyes were bright now, engaged.

"No apologies needed. They're harmless. So, you work at the pharmacy, then. Full time?"

"Part-time. Tom Burke is a family friend. He's let me have part-time hours since I went back to school. I'm off school for the summer, though. Gives me more time to pull weeds in the town park." Her lips curled into a half-smile.

"And what are ya studying?"

"Post grad ... teaching." She waved her hand as if to dismiss the topic. "So, how are you finding Millway? Has it changed much since ya left?"

So, she did remember him.

"Ah, not really. Not much, anyway. We were in school together. I didn't think you remembered me."

A rosy color crept up her cheeks, and she lowered her gaze. "Well, you have changed—a bit."

He nodded and laughed. "America was good for me—"

"There you are! We need your help, Doctor; we can't lift the bag of potting soil," said a middle-aged woman with a loud voice and louder clothes. The pretty young lady standing just behind her, with bright red cheeks, had to be her daughter. Mammy was looking for a son-in-law. He saw amusement in Megan's eyes even as he tried to stifle his irritation at the interruption.

"I'll be right there," he said as he stood and turned back to Megan. "It seems I'm found. Mustn't keep the ladies waiting. 'Twas nice to catch up with you, Megan. I hope we get a chance to chat again."

⌒⌒⌒

*So much for avoiding him.* Megan had the urge to stick her face in the stream. She was sure it was bright red. And her heart was beating double-time. The man caused a powerful reaction in her, and it was work to keep it from showing.

But, in all, that had gone quite well. He hadn't brought up the yellow flower incident, but he remembered her, so he surely remembered what she'd done. And yet, he was still nice to her. Friendly, even. Maybe it had been way worse in her mind than reality. Maybe she'd been feeling guilty all these years for no reason. Or maybe he was just the nice guy she had always thought he was, and he was giving her a break.

She dusted off her hat, placed it back on her head, and headed for the closest flowerbed, feeling invigorated. She might not even cringe anymore when she saw wild buttercups growing in the fields.

# Chapter Ten

"I think I may explode." Brenna pushed away from the food-laden table and leaned back in her chair, hoping to give her stomach more room. She never ate as much in one sitting as she did at Bettie's place on Sundays.

"Well, as long as you've saved room for dessert," Bettie said as she eyed Brenna and all the others seated around the large table. Ryan, Anna, and Auntie Pat all looked ready to dig in to a sweet delight from Bettie's kitchen.

"I think maybe you don't understand my whole 'explode' comment."

Auntie Pat chimed in, "Oh, come now, ya always make room for dessert. She's made a chocolate cream pie. You'll find room." She was bossing people around which meant she was herself, today. And she looked better. She must have been eating this week.

"Well, why didn't you say that in the first place? I'm sure I'll find some room." Brenna slid the plate away from her as if that would clear some room in her stomach. She placed the last of her cut-up carrots on Ben's high chair tray and smiled as his eyes lit up. "In a while."

"Of course ya will." Auntie Pat stacked her plate on top of Brenna's and gathered the dirty silverware on top of the plates. "So, that Megan outdid herself today, didn't she? I expect that's what angels will sound like in heaven."

Brenna could see alarm in Anna's eyes at the mention of Megan singing at morning Mass. Auntie Pat hadn't caught on to the unspoken agreement not to bring up Megan at dinner.

"I'll get that, Patsy." Brenna stood up and began clearing the dishes, and Ryan did the same on the other side of the table.

Bettie chimed in, as she headed toward the kitchen, "Well, 'tis true she's a lovely voice, but some say she shouldn't be singing in church at all. Not sure I'd disagree." Anger pressed on Brenna's chest. She set the plates on the table and felt Ryan grab her hand.

Anna jumped up from her seat. "I'll get those dishes, luv. You two go relax in the living room. Shoo. I'll get Ben cleaned up, as well."

Brenna let Ryan pull her to the next room and onto the couch.

"Why does she start things like that? She says something just as she's walking in the kitchen. I'm not afraid to follow her in there and finish the conversation, you know." Brenna fumed. They hadn't had a big blowup about the Megan-Jamie situation in months, but every once in a while, it was as if Bettie couldn't resist just laying one more dig out there.

"Oh, I know." Ryan said as he took her face in his hands and gave her a quick kiss.

"That's not going to make me forget what Bettie just said."

"I know it won't. I just think you're really cute when you're all mad and flustered. Couldn't help myself." Ryan said with a mischievous grin.

Raised voices could be heard coming from the kitchen. Brenna could pick out Anna and Auntie Pat's voices and a low, more whispered voice that must be Bettie.

"Sounds like Anna and Patsy are finishing the conversation for ya." Ryan massaged the back of her neck. "Bettie can't help it. She's grown up with Elizabeth O'Connor. Of course she'd be sympathetic to her."

"Well, then she's basically calling me a liar. I told her what really happened."

"No, she's not calling you a liar. She's calling Megan a liar. She and Elizabeth believe Jamie. And I can understand that, can't you? If anyone other than Megan had told you Jamie was a cheater, would ya have believed it?"

Brenna sighed and furrowed her brow. "Stop making sense. It's annoying me."

"I can't help it if I'm brilliant. I'm also really good at distraction. What do ya say we go home, put Ben down for a nap, and I can take your mind off all this nonsense?" His blue eyes danced with humor, and Brenna could feel her anger evaporating. Man, he was good.

"Okay, on one condition. Use that winning smile of yours and snag us two pieces of pie to take home while I gather Ben's things and load up the car."

"Deal." He kissed her again and winked as he sauntered toward the kitchen.

～

*Standing up in front of the church is hard some days. Most days, I stand up there and force myself not to care if people have the wrong impression of me. I just pray and ask God for strength. Besides, I talked to Father Tim back in January when it all went down. Told him everything that had happened with Jamie, and I'm confident he believed me. But I can't help watching when people whisper as I get up to sing.*

*I've thought about quitting. I only make a small stipend for singing at the Sunday Mass and the Veritas College group. But I love to sing, and I won't admit defeat. So, I keep getting up there week after week—pretending none of it bothers me.*

*But if Patricia Kennedy would just curl up in a hole and die, I'd be hard-pressed to shed a tear. The woman is evil. I'm quite sure she sits in the front at Mass just so she can stare at me with that disgusted look etched on her too-perfect features. I know I'm not supposed to hate people, but she makes that really hard to accomplish.*

*Char is a piece of work in her own right but even she had the grace to look embarrassed at her mother's behavior today; even coming to my rescue, in her own way. Never thought I'd say it but I feel sorry for Char. Can't imagine having that woman for a mother.*

Megan was the first one home from Mass. Her dad had stopped at the store to deal with some work issue. He didn't usually work on Sundays, but managing a grocery store that was open every day meant he was on-call. Her mam and brothers had stopped to buy groceries for the week. And that gave her a few precious moments of quiet to write down her thoughts, which she desperately needed today.

She had been walking to her car in the church parking lot when she noticed Patricia Kennedy was parked right next to her, standing between the two cars so that she blocked Megan's door completely. Turning her back to Megan, she spoke loudly into her cell.

"Oh, yes. Mm-hm. I know. It makes me uncomfortable too. Well, Mary, have you told Father Tim how ya feel? Because I've expressed my concerns to him several times now. Maybe if more of us made it clear how we feel having a woman like ... that ... in a leadership position within the church, he would consider doing something about it."

Megan imagined tackling the woman like a rugby player. She said, "Excuse me." But Patricia obviously pretended not to hear her. She just went on with her conversation, as if she didn't know she was there. People were beginning to stare. *Do. Not. Cry.* Megan willfully held back tears. Her only options were to yell at the woman to move, shove her out of the way, or go around and crawl through from the passenger side.

Just as she decided that shoving Patricia would be the most satisfying solution, Char opened her driver's side door, stood up and yelled, "MOTHER, would you get in the car?"

Patricia had no choice but to respond to her daughter, so she ended her conversation, turned toward Megan, and with her mouth curled into a sly smile, slid into the passenger seat.

Megan slammed her door, so angry she thought it might not be safe to drive. But she could feel people staring at her just sitting in her car, so she peeled away from the church and drove straight home. Deep breathing the whole way, she prayed that God would calm her down before she hurt someone.

And now, sitting at her kitchen table, hot tears streamed down her face, dripping onto her journal. And she let them flow. Her body shook with sobs as she pulled her knees up to her chest and rested her forehead on them. *God, this is so unfair. Why do I have to go through this? I didn't do anything wrong. Why do I feel like I'm being punished?*

She cried herself out and was still sitting in a curled up ball when her dad came through the door.

"Meggie, what is it?" He was instantly on his knees at her side. She sniffled and leaned over as he put his arms around her. "Shhh, it's okay, luv. It's okay." She let him pull her up and he held her, stroking her hair. She could remember standing on a chair, ten years old, being held in his arms in just the same way after she'd been in a huge fight with her mam. He was her rock.

"Da, why are people so mean?"

"Usually because they're unhappy," he answered and placed a kiss on top of her head. "What's happened? Something to do with Jamie?"

"Not exactly. It's just all the people thinking that I'm the one who cheated. I don't know what he told Elizabeth, but it's something like that. I just want to drive up there and choke him until he admits to his mother and every other gossip in this town that he's the lying, cheating bastard, not me."

"Let's go. I'll drive." He gently moved away from her toward the door and Megan realized he was serious.

"Really?"

"Really. Don't think I haven't imagined doing the same to the boy, myself. You asked me to stay out of it, and so I have. But if ya want to go up there, I'll drive and pay for the petrol, meself." She caught the dangerous glint in his eyes.

Megan sighed. "No, I don't really want to see him. I'm doing better." She laughed at his raised eyebrows. "I really am, Da. You caught me at a weak moment, but I'm really doing fine, in general. It's just dealing with always feeling like people are talking about me, it's making me a little crazy, today."

"Megan McKenna. You need to remember who ya are. You are a lovely young woman who has always treated everyone with kindness and dignity." Yellow flowers in a trash bin flashed through her mind, and she cringed. "Okay, I know you. Yer thinking of something you've done wrong. I'm not saying yer perfect. But yer heart is right. You put others first. You love God and people, and that is more than can be said fer some of the women who are giving ya grief. You have to decide that you know who y'are and where y'come from and that is enough. They can't make you feel like less if ya don't let them."

She reached out for another hug and relaxed in his embrace.

"Thanks, Da. Yer really smart, ya know that?"

"Aye, but don't tell yer mother. She'll start expectin' more from me." He tapped her nose like he had when she was younger. "You are an amazing young lass, and I couldn't be prouder."

She squeezed him and gave him a kiss, then headed to her room to fix her face before heading out to have lunch with Tara at the Tea Shoppe. As she washed her face, she thought about the truth of her dad's words. *They can't make you feel like less if ya don't let them.* She had given Patricia and Elizabeth, and anyone else with judgmental glances, way too much power over her. *She* knew that she wasn't what they thought she was. And that would have to be enough.

～✕

The Tea Shoppe smelled like a bakery, no matter what time of day you walked in. It had opened on the outskirts of town, but when a Main Street vacancy opened up last year, Maura, the owner, had cashed in all her retirement funds to get the prime location. And it had paid off. What had started out as a small tea and pastry shop had now turned into a cozy restaurant that served homemade soup, sandwiches, and fresh salads. Even in the current economic climate, she did a brisk business.

Megan breathed in the sugar-cookie smell and tried to figure out what she wanted for lunch. They were seated in a snug corner booth, Megan's favorite spot because it was partially blocked off from the rest of the dining room by a half-wall and a cluster of plants, making it cozy and secluded. Tara studied the menu as if she would be taking an exam on it any minute.

"What are ya havin'?" Megan asked.

"Veg soup," she said without looking up from the menu.

"You alright?"

Tara glanced up and looked like she was going to be sick. She blew out a breath. "I need to talk to ya about something, and I don't know how."

"What is it? You can tell me anything." Tara looked back at her menu until Megan snatched it from her hands. "It's not going to tell ya how to say whatever it is yer not telling me. Just say it. Whatever it is, it's okay."

"Okay, well ya know how I was kind of dating John O'Connor back when you started dating Jamie, but then I broke up with him?"

"I remember."

"Well, John's been calling me. A lot. And he's not giving up and I just didn't know if you would be mad if I ... ya know ... went out with him again."

Megan breathed a sigh of relief. "Geez, woman. I thought you were gonna tell me you were dyin' or something."

"Oh, no. Sorry to scare ya. No, I just feel guilty talking to John when his family has treated you so badly."

"Yeah, well, John's never said anything to me about it. And it's not like he's the one who's a cheater, right?"

"No! He would never cheat on—" Tara stopped with a horrified look on her face.

Megan waved her concern away. "Tara, I have no issue with John. He shouldn't be punished for what his brother did. And neither should you. Go for it. You're really sweet to talk with me about it but ya didn't have to."

Tara's shoulders relaxed and she smiled. "Thanks. You've just been through so much. I didn't want to add to it."

"It's fine—really. Should we go order, then?"

They went to the counter to place their orders and waited for their food, chatting. The bell over the front door sounded as Megan grabbed her tray of food and headed for their booth. She resented the fact that her heart started pounding as soon as she saw David walk in with a pretty brunette. He noticed her and gave a casual wave before turning back to the woman beside him.

Megan spent the rest of her time with Tara trying *not* to look toward David's table. She knew he couldn't really see her through the plants but she had a perfect view of the chestnut haired woman with her pearly white teeth and flirty smile. At least three other women stopped by the table to chat. Geez, it was like he literally had his very own fan club. Every time she saw him she was more convinced that he had to be a player. That image didn't fit with the guy she'd talked to in the park. But come on, he practically oozed women. It was ridiculous.

Ken and Brunette Barbie only had tea and scones and were gone before Megan was done eating. As she said goodbye to Tara and walked to her car, she found herself wondering if the dark-haired beauty was just a date or his girlfriend. Someone had picked him up in a flashy red car back when she spilled the dirt on him. So maybe he wasn't a player and that brunette was his steady girlfriend. The thought furrowed her brow. Then she reminded herself that she didn't care, in the least.

# Chapter Eleven

David hated Mondays. The phones rang incessantly, and most Monday morning patients had been dealing with whatever their complaint was all weekend long, and by the time they arrived, they were out of sorts. Some weeks he looked at it like a game. He tried to see how many moods he could turn around. Other weeks, he just didn't have the energy.

Today was an "other week." His back and legs ached, and his head was pounding for no apparent reason. He hadn't had a moment to breathe since he'd walked in four hours earlier. So, when the billing manager, Patricia Kennedy, asked if he had a minute, he wanted to snap and tell her no. But he took a deep breath and invited her into his small office. There was only room for his desk and chair, a small bookshelf and a second chair in front of his desk. It was a first-year doctor's office, to be sure. At least he had a window.

Patricia took a seat. She was a pretty woman. Old enough to be his mother but she didn't look it. Yet there was something about her that bothered him. Her beauty didn't reach her eyes. They were cold, even when she smiled.

David motioned to his sandwich. "Do ya mind if I eat? I've only a few minutes."

"Of course not. Please." Patricia waved a hand and looked toward the papers in her lap. "I wanted to check a few of these billing codes with you. Being new, you may not have all the codes memorized just yet." She proceeded to flip from statement to statement, highlighting his errors. He was usually very detail-oriented. But Doctor Rob had just returned from vacation, and Doc Rowan had one foot in retirement, so the bulk of the patients had fallen to him in his first couple weeks, and he hadn't really had a chance to get acclimated.

"Thank you for bringing these to my attention. I'll work on it. Is that all?"

Patricia eyed his meager sandwich and squared her shoulders. "Actually, I imagine you're in need of a good home-cooked meal. I wanted to invite you to dinner. My son, Matthew, is in town from Dublin and my daughter, Char, will be there. I'm sure both would like to meet you. Have ya plans tonight?"

"No ... I was just—"

"Perfect. I've a nice lamb stew in the slow cooker at home." She scribbled her address onto a sheet of paper and passed it to him. "We'll see you at half-six, then."

She was out of his office before he could object. Well, a free meal was a free meal, he supposed. He finished his sandwich and looked at his schedule. His next appointment was in five minutes. Just enough time to grab a much-needed cup of coffee.

⌇

Brenna tapped her foot to the music in the waiting room. It was a Scottish band; she couldn't remember the name, but they were popular and she liked their sound.

"Benjamin?" The nurse said from the doorway, with a big smile on her wrinkled face. "He's getting so big, isn't he?"

"Hi, Ailish. I think he's sneaking food from the fridge while I sleep." Brenna hoisted Ben onto her hip and grabbed his diaper bag. After all the typical weights and measures, they were ushered into Exam Room One to wait for the doctor. She didn't really see why a follow-up appointment was necessary. Ben's fever had been gone after a day on the antibiotics, and he'd been sleeping well ever since. She was confident the ear infection was gone. But she tended to follow the rules, so here they sat.

After a quick knock on the door, Doctor David entered, glancing at Ben's chart and flipping pages. He looked tired, and she suddenly had an image of him being chased through town by a flock of women. She gulped down a laugh. Megan had told her about his gardening friends. The poor guy. He probably wondered what he'd gotten himself into, coming to Millway. Eligible bachelors were not left alone for long. And one that looked like he did and a doctor besides? He was toast.

"Hello, Mrs. Kelly. Nice to see you again." He reached out to shake her hand. "So, ear infection two weeks ago. How's he been since?"

She turned Ben to face outward as the doctor wheeled his stool closer. "Good. The medicine seems to have worked. He's back to his jolly self."

"Excellent. Well, let's have a look, shall we?" He examined both of Ben's ears and declared them clear of infection. He was quick and efficient.

A sudden thought struck Brenna. "Doctor O'Brien?"

"Doctor David, please," he said.

"Yes, but the O'Brien is what I'm wondering about. You're from Millway, originally? I'm wondering if there's any relation to my husband, as it seems that all of you are related to each other somehow."

He looked back at Ben's chart. "Mrs. Kelly? I don't understand the connection."

"Oh, sorry. My first husband, Ben O'Brien. He passed away. But his mom and dad are from Millway. Joe O'Brien?"

His eyes softened, and he tilted his head in thought. "Hmm, sounds familiar, actually. I'll have to ask my parents, but I think he was my dad's cousin."

Brenna laughed. It was true. They were all cousins. "Small world, huh?"

"Actually, my mam says, 'It's a small world, if you talk,' and she's usually right. Sorry for your loss, though. Do ya mind me asking what happened to your first husband? You seem awfully young to be a widow."

"I don't mind. I am. I was a newlywed, just nineteen years old when he died. It was a freak car accident during a storm. He and Joe were both in the car." She still had pain in her chest when she told the story. "Neither survived."

Sadness and compassion warmed his eyes. "I'm so sorry, Mrs. Kelly."

"Thank you. And it's Brenna. I didn't mean to get all serious on you. I'm doing very well and this little guy," she kissed Ben on his chubby cheek and he giggled and pulled on her nose, "keeps me grounded. And, since we are related, I think you should come have dinner with me and my husband, Ryan."

"I would like that." His genuine smile was powerful, and she had to force herself not to stare. She could see why the local girls were all aflutter. But to her thinking, there was only one local girl that was worth his time, and that was Megan. Now all she had to do was help the both of them see that.

"Good. I'll check with Ryan and get back to you. Should I call you here, at the office?"

"Um, no. You can text me, if ya like." He wrote his cell number on his business card and handed it to her. "It's been nice talking with you, Brenna. I'll look forward to dinner with you and your husband."

# Chapter Twelve

"He's coming for dinner?" Megan asked, bouncing Ben on her lap as she watched Brenna struggle to attach the baby gate to the playroom doorframe.

"Yep, Friday night. You're welcome to come."

"Tomorrow? No way. I've got—stuff to do."

"Right. Stuff."

"Oh! Actually, I'm not lying. Well, I mean, I *was* lying, but I just remembered I have to pack. We're going to my aunt's place up in the Burren for the weekend."

"Well, it's okay, I didn't really want you to come anyway. It will look too much like a set-up, and I'm too crafty to be so obvious." Brenna grinned. She finally got the gate into place, scooped Ben into her arms, and placed him into his toy-filled playroom. "I'd like to kiss whoever invented baby gates!"

"I bet. I'm exhausted just watching you chase him around. He doesn't stop, does he?"

"Not until he crashes at nap time. He may have started crawling late, but he's making up for lost time."

"And how are things with Ryan? He seems stressed lately."

"He is; I am. I mean *we're* fine. But it's stressful, the job stuff. If he commutes, that's almost three hours of driving a day. If he doesn't, we don't see him all week. Wasn't so bad before; he could work from home and only go to Limerick once or twice a week. But lately, he's been gone a lot."

"I wish I could do something to help."

"You do. You give me projects to keep my mind off of the stress." Brenna's mischievous grin was back.

"My love life—or lack of one—is not a project, darlin'. So you can just take up knitting or something."

"Might as well take up baking and gardening." Brenna rolled her eyes.

"Well, let's not go crazy." Megan smiled and glanced toward Ben, who was having a delightful, unintelligible conversation with a toy hammer.

"Seriously, though, I don't have a hobby. Not that I have time for one right now, but I don't have any real skills, you know?" Brenna drummed her fingers on the table with a slight pout on her face.

"Sure ya do. You're a good reader. I've never met anyone who reads as fast as you do."

"Hmm, true. I'm sure that talent will come in handy ... never." Brenna said as she got up grab the kettle from the stove.

"Well, there must be something you like doing. Something that makes you feel more alive when ya do it?"

"Actually ... I like to paint. And draw. I haven't really done it in a few years. But I used to paint when I lived with my gram. And I was taking some good art classes in college, before the accident."

"Perfect—you should start painting again, then. Or at least start doing some sketches or something. Just to ease back into it."

"Yeah, maybe. I've done a few sketches since I got here but not much of anything good. Now that I have a lovely little jailhouse set up for Ben, I might be able to give it a more focused try." Brenna smiled and poured the hot water into the teapot.

Megan went to the cupboard for the cups and saucers and, glancing out the window, saw Ryan parking his truck. "Yer man's home. You sure ya don't mind me stealing him to play guitar for me tonight at Veritas?"

Brenna grabbed a third cup and set it on the table. "You don't steal him often, and I love to hear you guys sing. So it's all good. Especially because it gives me a night out. Anna's thrilled to get her hands on Ben."

Ryan came in through the back door, and Brenna greeted him with a long hug. Sometimes, it was painful for Megan to watch them together. It reminded her of Jamie. Of what she'd had and lost. But not today. Today, when she watched them, a blond with a stethoscope popped into her mind. She sighed. At least it was an improvement—proof she was healing. And the growl in her stomach was proof she was hungry.

"Hi, Ry," she said, getting up and giving him a kiss on the cheek.

"Meg. How are ya?"

"Hungry. Where's Bettie's shortbread? In the press?" she asked, as she searched through Brenna's cupboard.

"Oh, no ya don't," Ryan said, walking to Megan and spinning her from the cupboard. "Bettie told me, specifically, that the shortbread was mine and mine alone. So don't even think about it."

"Ahem," Brenna said. "You two always fight over the shortbread, which is just so silly. Obviously, Bettie made it for *me*. Which is why ..." Megan and Ryan turned in time to see her pop a piece of shortbread into her mouth, chew and swallow, "I just ate the last piece."

"Oh, you'll pay for that," Ryan said, and Brenna squealed and ran from the room. He turned to Megan. "Duty calls. I'm going to go teach her a lesson and then we can run through the songs for tonight."

As Ryan chased his wife into the living room, Megan's thoughts again wandered to David O'Brien. That was happening much too often, lately, and she didn't really appreciate it. After all, she was done with men. Maybe.

# Chapter Thirteen

Ryan had worked from home, so Brenna had plenty of time to make a tasty lamb stew without Ben underfoot. She might not be much of a baker, but her cooking skills weren't too shabby. The house smelled of fried onions and lamb, which were now tucked into the Dutch oven with potatoes, carrots, and a hearty broth. Ryan and David were in the living room watching Munster rugby and, by the sound of their shouts, Munster was winning. Which was good. Because dinner would be much more enjoyable if Munster won.

Brenna grabbed three beers and brought them to the living room. Ryan pulled her onto his lap and then shouted at the TV, oblivious to the nearness of her ear.

"Ouch, you big lump." She smacked him in the chest playfully, spilling some beer onto her shirt.

"Ah, Doc," Ryan said, "do ya see how she beats me? 'Tis a shame. You'd best be careful what ya say and do, or she may come after you, too."

David made an exaggerated move away from Brenna and laughed. "I'll be on my best behavior."

"Whatever." Brenna smiled, rolled her eyes, and dabbed at her shirt with a burp cloth. "Now David, since the commercial is on, I wanted to ask, did you check with your parents about Joe? Because I asked Anna, his wife, and she said he had three cousins she knew of, in town. Paddy, John, and Trevor."

"Aye, Trevor would be my father, and he also confirmed it. We are related. Shall I call ya cousin?"

"Absolutely! It's about time I had a cousin around here. Everyone else has twenty!"

"Brilliant." David held up his beer for a toast, bottles clinked all around. "Slainté, cousin!"

Brenna lost them moments later when Munster returned to the screen, so she went to check on her stew. She pulled the piping dish from the oven and set the table. Listening to the men shouting again, she smiled. It was nice, Ryan having someone to watch the game with. He knew practically everyone in Millway, but with his job taking him away so often, he rarely actually did anything with another guy, other than his once-a-week coffee with Father Tim.

She loved Father Tim. He and Ryan had been friends for years, but he was fifty years old. She liked the idea of Ryan having a younger friend. She hummed along with the radio as she pulled a pan from the cupboard, or the press, as they called it in Ireland. Bettie had made some bread for her earlier in the day, so she popped it into the oven just to warm it a bit.

"How much longer?" She yelled toward the living room.

"Five minutes!" came the reply.

Ben was happily playing with his toys. The playroom was a lifesaver. "Hey, little boy," she said as she reached over the gate for him. His smile was like a bright light filling the room. He was the happiest baby she'd ever seen. She knew she was lucky and figured her next baby would probably be a tyrant, just to even the scales. By the time she had him strapped into his high chair, Munster had won. Ryan and David joined them, and stew was quickly ladled into bowls. Brenna pulled the bread from the oven and sat down to eat.

"Cousin," David grinned as he said it. "This is the best thing I've eaten all week."

Brenna blushed, "Oh, stop."

"No, seriously. Most nights in my flat I eat something from a can. But I've had lamb stew three times this week and yours is, by far, the best. I'm not just sayin' so cuz we're family." He grinned again.

"Well, thank you then. I'm glad you like it."

"Our Brenna is a terrific cook." Ryan said around a mouthful of stew. "You'll have to come back for her pot roast. It's cousin Bettie's recipe, and it melts in yer mouth."

"Do you get a lot of dinner invites?" Brenna asked.

"Hmm, I guess. I don't always accept. By the time work is done, I'm usually ready to be alone."

"I used to feel that way when I worked at Rosie's. I could only talk to people for so long." Brenna said.

"Exactly. It's like I use up my words for the day, and then I've none left. But I suppose it depends on the company. Some people are just easy to be around. Others, not so much." David reached for a piece of bread and slathered some butter on it. "For example, this past Monday, our billing manager marched into my office and basically told me I was coming for dinner. So, I did. And it felt like work. Awkward pauses. Forced conversation. Bland lamb stew." Brenna smiled at that. "Just not what I want to do at the end of the day. Not to mention, I think she was trying to set me up with her daughter. I mean, I have nothing against meeting pretty women," he said with a grin, "but agendas annoy me."

Brenna was suddenly very glad she'd not pushed Megan to come to dinner. Ryan caught her eye, and she quickly shifted her attention to Ben, cutting up some potatoes and carrots for him to pick up off his plate.

"Your billing manager, that would be Patricia?" Ryan asked.

"Aye, you know her?"

"We do, but we're not exactly friendly." Ryan winked at Brenna. Patricia was one of her least favorite people.

"Well, I've only worked with her a few weeks, but she doesn't strike me as someone many people are friendly with. More like people seem to either obey or tolerate her."

Ryan laughed. "Brenna calls her Ice Queen."

David raised his eyebrows, "Hmm, she can be quite chilly."

"So you met Char?" Ryan asked while ladling more stew into everyone's bowls.

"I did. She's a pretty girl. I'm guessing she's high maintenance, though."

"She's better than she used to be. But you still might want to steer clear of that one." Ryan said.

"Oh, no question. I told Patricia the next day that I wasn't interested in a relationship with anyone right now. I doubt she'll give up. But truth is, even if I were looking, I wouldn't be looking in Char's direction. Too much of a possibility she'll turn out like her mother." David shivered on the word 'mother.'

"I knew I liked you." Brenna pointed at him with her fork. "We are going to get along quite well, I think. More bread?"

# Chapter Fourteen ~ June

Grania's moving. Her husband was transferred to Dublin, so she's leaving in two weeks. That means I have one more session with her. She's been a lifesaver. I'm not thrilled she's leaving. But I'm glad it's now instead of two months ago.

She referred me to a colleague. But I don't want to start all over again with someone and honestly, I think I'm good. I feel better than I have in a long time. I have more energy and I just feel ... more in control of myself and my emotions.

There were still a few issues that we were going to work through. Ones that weren't directly related to all the stuff with Jamie. Things like my relationship with my mam and the fact that I have no clue why I'm going to school to be a teacher. She had a field day with that revelation. But those are things I was dealing with before and I think I can handle them on my own.

Since I don't want to see a new therapist, she suggested that she could fill our family doctor in on my case, so that he can monitor the medication over time, like when I need refills or if we need to adjust the dosage. I've always seen Doc Rowan, but I think he's retiring. I certainly don't want David to be my doctor, so I asked her to make sure she speaks to Doctor Rob, only.

*Knowing I won't be seeing her anymore makes me a little nervous. But I'm so thankful I had her help for at least a little while. And she told me if I really needed her, she would only be a text away. Very kind of her.*

———

Megan pulled her car around the back of Brenna's house. The sky was grey, and a light drizzle misted her windshield. She could see weeds popping up around the geraniums and azaleas in the flowerbeds. It was obvious she hadn't been here in a week, but she wasn't dressed for gardening today. She would have to make a point to stop by and tend the flowers this weekend. The back door was unlocked, as usual.

"Hey, stranger," Brenna said while toting Ben toward his playroom.

Megan noticed a bite to Brenna's words and realized she might be in trouble. She shut Brenna's back door and leaned in to kiss Ben on his forehead. "Hello, my little man." She tousled his chestnut hair before Brenna set him down to play.

"You've barely answered my texts for days. What's goin' on?" Brenna said, an unmistakable irritation in her tone.

"Ugh. I'm sorry. I need to get a new phone! Mine keeps dying. Holds a charge for like an hour. I only got one text from you this week, so obviously it's been losing texts." Megan dropped into a chair, slamming her phone onto the table. "Really sorry, Bren. I haven't been ignoring ya. I got your text that dinner with the doctor went well on Friday. But then I was gone for the weekend, and Tom needed extra help at the pharmacy this week, so I've just been running. All lame excuses, I know. I'm a horrible friend."

"It's alright. I'm just glad you aren't dead in a ditch somewhere." Brenna said with a slight pout. "But get your phone fixed, will you? And you *are* a horrible friend, so I don't think I'm going to share any of Bettie's shortbread with you today."

Brenna's pout had turned into a mischievous grin, and Megan knew that she was forgiven. She accepted the shortbread ban as punishment and patted the table, urging Brenna to sit. Megan's phone vibrated on the table. With a glance, she said, "Ah, there are yer last three texts coming through."

Brenna rolled her eyes. "I sent those yesterday."

"Yes, and now you have proof that my phone is a reject."

"I'm tempted to drive to Killarney myself and get you an iPhone. But Anna's coming for dinner so your reject phone gets a pass for the day." Brenna poured Megan some tea, topped off her own cup and offered the shortbread, after all, with a tilted smile. "So, I haven't talked to you, really, since David came for dinner. Wanna hear about it?"

Megan hated that her stomach did a little dance at just the mention of his name. "No, I don't. I'm sure it was a lovely meal, but I don't need the details."

"Okay. I won't tell you about how Patricia's trying to get her claws into him." Brenna's nose wrinkled like she'd caught a bad smell.

"Ew, she's old enough to be his mother!"

"No, not for herself, for Char."

"Oh." Why should she care? She was NOT going to get involved with anyone right now. Besides, he was a major flirt.

And not her type.

And probably totally full of himself.

But Char? Char was beautiful and she had, to everyone's surprise, gotten a bit nicer over the last year. In the past, you could count on her to be a witch and scare off just about any sensible guy that came around. But now? "Okay, you win. Spill it."

Brenna grinned as she grabbed a laundry basket from the hallway. "Patricia cornered him into dinner at her house last week. Of course, Char was there. Probably freshly waxed and tanned."

"So, is he interested in her?" Not that she cared.

"Nope, totally blew her off. Said he could tell she was high maintenance and even told Patricia the next day that he wasn't interested."

Something like relief flooded her and she exhaled, not even realizing she'd been holding her breath. "Well, I'm glad he's smart enough to steer clear of that family." She had dated Char's brother, Matthew, for a total of about three weeks during university. He was a tool. And Patricia was much, much worse.

"He's very smart." Brenna folded cute little baby jeans and onesies into neat piles on the table.

"He always was. Top of his class every year. He even helped me with arithmetic right before I started second year. I was twelve years old and totally embarrassed that I needed help." She hadn't thought much about that summer until recently. She had struggled all year with math, and her teacher had suggested to her mam that she find a tutor over the summer months to get her up to speed before the next year, when things would get more rigorous.

Her mam had scoffed at the idea of a hiring a tutor when she, herself, was a teacher. She could certainly help her daughter with her arithmetic. So, she had started working with Megan even before the school year ended, but it didn't go well. They got along even worse than normal, and her dad had swooped in and saved the day, suggesting David as a solution.

David had been bagging groceries for him at the SuperValu, and her dad knew he was bright and a hard worker who was always looking for more hours. He couldn't give him more at the store, but he could hire him to help his daughter with math a few times a week.

"Aw, he tutored you? That's so sweet. Megan got schooled by the Doctor," Brenna said while wiggling her eyebrows.

Megan rolled her eyes. "Yer ridiculous. We were kids. And he certainly didn't look like he does now." He was sweet, though. After an awkward few sessions, as they both got over the normal boy-talking-to-girl embarrassment, she had actually looked forward to him coming over. He was easy to talk to. And he did help her figure out math. Helped her understand it in a way that made sense to her right-brained way of thinking. But once school started again, they didn't really hang out anymore. She had a good group of friends, and he hardly ever seemed to be around.

"Why don't you even want to give him a chance, Meg?"

"Hmm?" Brenna's words brought Megan back from her childhood memories. "Oh, sorry. I was somewhere else."

"Why won't you give him a chance?" Brenna repeated over her shoulder as she grabbed Ben from his playroom and strapped him into his highchair for a snack.

Megan sighed. "I'm sure he's a nice guy. Actually, I was surprised how nice he was when we talked in the park, although I think he's a little full of himself. But even if he showed the slightest interest in me, which he doesn't, I'm just not ready to even think about dating. I feel like I need some time to figure out who I am, now. Does that make sense?"

"Ahh, total sense. It's like you had already envisioned out your whole future—get married to Jamie, have kids, live happily ever after—and all that was suddenly yanked away from you. Now you feel a little lost."

"Exactly. Wow. You nailed it, Bren." Megan took over the folding as Brenna cut up a banana, putting small pieces on Ben's tray. "I don't think I could have explained it like that, but it's exactly how I feel."

"I felt that way after Ben died. Rocked. Like I couldn't figure out which way was forward."

"Right."

"Don't worry, friend. You'll find your feet again. Sorry about trying to push David on you. I just want to see you treated right. But I didn't know how you were feeling."

"I know. I'm not very good at being totally honest about how I feel. I'm good at listening to other people and helping them. Not so good at the whole vulnerable thing."

"I do know that about you." Brenna said, squeezing Megan's hand. "I know this whole thing has been a grieving process. But I think you're on the other side of things."

"I do, too. I don't feel broken anymore. Just a little unsure. I know I joked I was done with men but I'm not saying I'll never date again." Megan placed the stacks of baby clothes back into the laundry basket. "But when I do decide to date someone, I don't think I'll be rushing into anything. I had trust issues *before* Jamie. Now?" Megan laughed. "I can't even imagine what kind of hoops I'll make some poor guy jump through."

Brenna laughed. "Okay, I'll try to back off on the David stuff."

"Thank you—."

"If," she held up her index finger, "you promise to be friendly to him and not totally close that door."

Megan sighed. "I don't think there's a door ..." Brenna skewered her with a look. "Okay, okay. I won't close the door." She rolled her eyes and cringed when the image of David jumping through hula-hoops drifted through her brain.

# Chapter Fifteen

Megan picked dead flowers from the boxes on Main Street as she walked from Burke's Pharmacy to Rosie's Pub. It was likely the job of someone on the TidyTowns committee, but she couldn't walk past and not do it. She should probably be hurrying along and not even glancing at the flowers. She had a backlog of inventory to stock and would likely end up staying a little late. But she just didn't feel like rushing.

It was a gorgeous day, sunny and breezy without a hint of a rain cloud. Days like this weren't common and always made Megan want to sit in the garden and soak up the sun. But since she couldn't do that, walking slowly down Main Street would suffice.

Rosie's was crowded. A Blarney Castle tour bus must have come through town, as Megan saw cameras around many necks. She had to jostle a bit to reach the bar where she would pick up her to-go order. Tara nodded from the other end of the bar, where she was building a Guinness. As she waited, Megan noticed David having lunch with yet another pretty woman. Geez, where did he find them all? She sighed. It didn't matter. Despite Brenna's hopeful wishes, there was no door.

"Sorry for the wait. Here ya go." Tara said, a bit breathless.

"Thanks. I'm all set," said Megan as she placed ten euros into Tara's hand.

Back out in the sunshine her mood lifted again as she smiled up at the sun, swinging her bag as she walked.

"Megan, wait up." She turned and her stomach did a little dance as she saw David jogging up the street toward her.

"Oh, hi there."

He reached her in seconds. Slightly winded. Gorgeous as ever. "Hey, are ya headed to Burke's?"

"I am, back to work."

"Great, mind if I walk with you? I'm heading just past there, to the bank."

Megan looked around, wondering where the pretty blonde had gone. "Weren't you just eating with someone?"

"Oh, she's off to her next client. She's a drug rep."

"Ah, well sure." As they started back toward the pharmacy, Megan smoothed down her hair and wondered if her makeup was still on. Then she cursed herself for even thinking about it. "How's the new job?"

"Good. It's a nice pace compared to the hospitals in Dublin. Residency was brutal. I was looking for a small-town practice and this just came up. Couldn't believe I got an offer back in my hometown." He smiled, and she tried not to look at his lips.

"That worked out well. So, where are yer parents, then?" Megan noticed a dead flower she hadn't seen on her way but before she could get to it, David had plucked it off and tossed it away without even seeming aware of it.

"They're both in Dublin, for now. They got divorced a couple years ago."

"Oh, I'm sorry."

He shrugged. "Thanks. It was for the best. My mam is a lot happier now. She's staying in Dublin until my sister's done with dental school. She'll probably move to wherever Molly does after school. They're pretty close."

"A doctor and a dentist. There must be at least one more sibling going for lawyer."

"Nope. We're it. My poor parents will have to make do with a doctor and a dentist."

"I'm sure they'll deal with the disappointment," she said and he laughed. She had to admit, she liked making him smile. "So, are you thinking you'll settle here, or is the position still temporary?"

He looked at her sideways. "You're well informed. 'Tis a temporary position which may turn into something more, if both Rob and I are agreeable to it. He knows I have plans to do some missions work, so we'll see if that fits into what he needs or not."

"Missions? Where are you going?"

"Well, nowhere any time soon. But I'm hoping to get back to West Africa eventually."

"You've gone before?" Megan said.

"Aye, a couple times. Once you go, it's hard not to go back." He looked wistful, almost sad.

"I really admire that. It takes guts to head to Africa and do something that makes a difference. Most of us just think about doing something. It's great to meet someone who actually does it." She paused outside Burke's.

"Well, I'm part of C.A.M.P. Ireland. Have ya heard of it?"

"No, is it a camping place?"

David laughed. "No, sorry. Camp stands for Christian Alliance of Medical Professionals. It's a group that raises money for certain causes in Africa. We support a children's home in Sierra Leone, and we've provided food and water for some of the villages. When we do take medical crews to Africa, we choose from the people in the organization. You should come check it out." David's eyes lit up.

"Me? No, I don't have any medical skills—"

"—First of all, that doesn't matter. All you need is a good attitude and a heart for people. But you do have skills. With the small amount you probably know from Burke's about medications, you'd practically be a pharmacist in Africa. And we always set up a pharmacy on the trips. So, if you check it out and like what ya see, maybe you'll end up on next year's trip?" He leaned casually on the plaster storefront and the slight breeze played with his golden hair. "So think about it."

Megan's mind was whirling. It was crazy to think about going to Africa. But maybe getting involved in something charitable was exactly what she needed. She was sick of thinking about her own life. Maybe helping someone else would be a nice change of perspective. She smiled. "I guess it couldn't hurt to check it out."

"Great. I can email you the info I have. We have a meeting in Killarney next Wednesday night. If ya want, you can come and meet everyone and talk to Donal, our group leader. He can answer way more questions than I can."

"Okay, well, maybe." Megan pointed toward the door. "I'm here. I should go in. But hold on and I'll write down my email address." She wrote her email down and considered writing down her phone number. *No, he probably gets ten numbers a day. Just email.* Handing it to David, she said goodbye and headed in to work, feeling somewhat excited for the first time in a long while.

❧

David closed his office door, a signal to the nurses that he wasn't to be disturbed unless there was an emergency. His next patient wasn't due for fifteen minutes, and he wanted just a few moments of quiet. He hadn't planned to invite Megan to join C.A.M.P. She seemed to have some strange power to make him do things he wasn't planning to do.

He wasn't sure what he thought of her yet, but he knew that the more he was around her, the more he wanted to be. That was different. Most of the women he went out with kind of bored him by the end of the first date. He had a feeling that wouldn't be the case with Megan. A sharp knock interrupted his thoughts. The door opened slightly and Patricia put her head in.

"Sorry Doctor, have you a minute?"

David sighed. "Come in."

She sat down and handed him a file folder. "I wanted to show you the new forms we're using for patient visits." David scanned the form as she continued. "It's pretty similar to the old one but will work better with the billing software."

"Looks pretty self-explanatory."

"'Tis. Shouldn't be a difficult transition." She smoothed her skirt and looked out the window. "So, I hate to meddle, David, but I just felt it was my Christian duty to warn ya ..." She looked uncomfortable for the first time since he'd known her. In his experience, though, any time someone said they felt it was their Christian duty to tell you something, the next thing out of their mouth was decidedly un-Christian.

"What is it, Patricia?"

"Well, I noticed you were walking with Megan McKenna. She is a very beautiful girl, no question. And she seems all sweet and innocent. But I'd be remiss if I didn't warn you. And if I didn't care for you," she reached across the desk and patted his hand, "I wouldn't say anything. But I saw you looking at her in Rosie's and thought maybe you seemed ... interested?" She looked down again.

David's stomach twisted, and he wasn't sure if it was anger at her for intruding or worry over what she was about to say.

"You see, she was engaged to my best friend's son, Jamie. They seemed like a perfect match. The whole town thought so. But he had to work out of town for a long time, and it seems she couldn't deal with the separation. He caught her with his cousin. On his birthday, of all days. It was horrible. She made excuses, said she'd planned to tell him. Poor lad was crushed. It was a huge scandal. So, I figured you might hear about it from the gossips around town but it was better if you heard the real story from a reliable source."

David felt like he'd been kicked in the stomach. "Well, thank you for your concern, Patricia. I appreciate it. I do need to get ready for my patient." He motioned toward the door and she took the hint, closing the door as she left.

His mind whirred through painful past images. Images of a lass with smiling bright blue eyes and long lashes. *Katie*. He hadn't thought about her for quite a long time. But now she filled his thoughts. He could hear her laugh as he remembered the good times, when they'd first started dating. And then he could see her with bed-head and a sheet wrapped around her, begging him to wait and saying it wasn't what it looked like.

He knew what it felt like to be cheated on. It was one of the worst things he'd ever experienced. He was surprised, though. Megan didn't seem like the cheating type.

But then, neither had Katie.

# Chapter Sixteen

David enjoyed an early morning run—once he was running. What he didn't enjoy was the evil alarm clock going off at 7:00 a.m. on his day off. But by the time his feet hit the pavement, he felt energized. On this particular Saturday morning, the sun was hidden behind clouds, as usual. But it wasn't raining yet and looked like it might hold off for a while.

David veered off the road and took the path that led to the Mountdonovan Estate. With an easy climb over the stile he was on the property and it was as beautiful as he remembered. Being an Irishman, he was used to the many-hued green hills, but something about this view always inspired him. He slowed to a walk and took in the sight of the valley spread below and the patchwork hills beyond.

The main house looked much worse than it had when he was a kid. Back then, the roof had still been mostly intact, and it had looked like a lonely stone giant with blacked out eyes and mossy hair. Now it just looked like a ruin. But with imagination, you could see what it had once been. A grand house; the host of elegant dances and hunting parties alike. Massive Greek columns still framed the oversized, faded, red door.

David remembered the time his little sister, Molly, had dared him to try to get through that door to the murky house beyond. He'd been terrified of what may have been lurking in the shadows, but since his sister was a blabbermouth who would surely tell if he chickened out, he'd scoffed at her and told her any sissy could walk through the front door. A real man would climb the vines that encircled the far right column, all the way to the top. She was in awe as she watched him shimmy to the topside of the twenty-foot column. Of course, she had no idea he'd been climbing it—and every other vertical structure around—for years. So, the ease with which he handled the task silenced her for any more dares, and he avoided ever having to enter the mouth of the giant.

Memories continued to drift through his mind. By far, his favorite place to climb had been the huge tree in the front lawn. It made him think of "The Party Tree" from *The Hobbit*. And it was full of branches and heavily leaved, so no one ever saw him up there. He wandered toward the tree and sat down in its shade, his back against the ancient trunk.

This was where he'd first seen Megan. He'd forgotten that. He was probably around eleven, so she would have been about nine. He had climbed the tree with a book in hand, probably some *Hobbit*-like fantasy, and had been reading for only a short while when he heard singing somewhere below. It had taken him a few moments to find the source of the pretty voice floating on the air. It was a lass with strawberry-blonde braids swinging past her shoulders as she twirled and sang a lilting tune he'd never heard before.

He didn't usually pay attention to girls. Likely, because they didn't pay much attention to him. But something about her had him mesmerized for several minutes. She was twirling in the tall grasses, just outside the shadow of the house, and every once in a while, she would bend down and then straighten up again. He was puzzled until he finally realized she was picking wild yellow flowers, a growing bouquet in her hand. But just then, he'd lost hold of his book and as it hit the ground with a thud, she'd startled and run off down the pathway, toward town.

From then on, he'd seen her everywhere. In the store, at the park, occasionally back at Mountdonovan. But he never had the courage to talk to her. Until her dad had asked him for a favor, one day. By then he was about fourteen and worked for a couple hours a day, bagging groceries at the local store. Megan's dad was the manager and one of David's favorite people. He was kind to everyone and paid attention when people spoke. He always asked David how his day at school had been and truly seemed interested in the answer. And when he asked if David would consider a summer job helping his daughter with math, he happily agreed.

It ended up being the favorite summer of his childhood. He remembered being a little scared of Mrs. McKenna. She was strict and kind of scary. But Mr. McKenna let him tinker with the tools in the workshop behind their house after each tutoring session. And after a few awkward work sessions together, Megan seemed to enjoy his company, as well. Of course, he developed a full-blown crush on her and pined for her for a long time without ever having the courage to tell her.

Until that fateful day, in fourth year, when he decided it was time to reveal his feelings. He'd written five letters that had landed in his rubbish bin before he finally had one that said what he wanted. Now, he couldn't even remember what it had said. But at the time it had meant everything so it had to be perfect.

He'd stopped by the Mountdonovan place to pick the yellow flowers she seemed to love. A bouquet would accompany his letter announcing some sort of undying love and probably a declaration that he and Megan were soul mates. His cheeks colored a bit, even now, thinking of what must have been in that letter. Thankfully, she'd never read it. At the time, it had almost killed him when she chucked it and his flowers into the trash bin. But looking back, he was very thankful no one had seen his sixteen-year-old thoughts on love and life.

Now, he wasn't sure what to make of the woman who had been that strawberry-blonde, flower-loving lass, all those years ago. She was still pretty. Beautiful, really. Until the flower incident, she had always been kind to him, like her father had been. And the woman he'd spent just a little time with since returning to Millway seemed to still be that kind-hearted girl. But from the rumors he was hearing, the real Megan was probably more in line with the heartless teenager who'd humiliated him and then never bothered to speak to him again.

That would explain why she still intrigued him, he thought with a frown. He seemed to have a weakness for wolves in sheep's clothing. But since he didn't seem to be able to ignore her or stay away from her, he decided he'd have to spend enough time with her to figure out if she was a sheep or a wolf.

⌒⌒⌒

Brenna woke to her favorite sound coming over the baby monitor. Ben was in his crib babbling nonsense with the occasional real word thrown in. She donned her robe and went to his room.

"Hey buddy, how are you doin' today?" His delighted squeal and giggle when she spoke to him made her melt.

Five years ago, if you'd told her she'd be living in Ireland at twenty-three, married to an Irishman with a giggling baby boy taking up her days, she would never have believed it. Eighteen-year-old Brenna would have told you she'd go to college to be an art teacher; marry Ben O'Brien; get a job; buy a house. And maybe start having kids by her mid to late twenties. But nothing in her life had really ever gone as planned. And now, not much surprised her.

But last night, Ryan's confession that his business was in trouble had done just that. She had seen a change in him over the last few months. He was stressed, although he hid it pretty well. Still, little things clued her in. The way he'd stare off into space when he didn't know she was watching. The way he'd started tensing up when she talked about buying something for the house. The fact that his temper was a little quicker to show. She'd known something was off.

But it was worse than she realized. When she told him she was thinking of getting some art supplies and taking an art class or two, he acted weird and when she pressed him, he admitted things were not going so well at Kelly Construction. He was looking for a buyer and if he didn't find one soon, would probably have to sell at a small loss before it turned into a big loss. She wasn't happy that he hadn't bothered to let her know sooner, but he was so stressed, she kept her thoughts to herself.

She hadn't slept much. Her mind wouldn't turn off. But mamas don't get to sleep in just because they've been up half the night, and Ryan was out for an early Saturday morning business meeting. So, she got Ben dressed and shuffled to the kitchen for some coffee. Tea was fine for most of the day. But after a night without sleep, coffee was essential. Ryan had set the timer to brew her a fresh pot. She breathed in the hazelnut-laced aroma and felt slightly more awake.

With Ben settled into his high chair, and a steaming cup of coffee in hand, she sat at the table and opened her laptop. Maybe she could find a job and help ease some of Ryan's stress. Looking over at her little guy, she felt a pang of sadness. What if she had to leave him every day to go to work? She couldn't imagine doing it. But at least she could see what options were out there. Feeding Ben with one hand, scrolling through job listings with the other, she didn't even hear Megan pull up. The knock at her kitchen door startled her and the spoonful of banana goo landed on her shirtsleeve as she called for Megan to come in.

"Hey there," Megan said with a bright morning smile. "I brought chocolate pastries, because I'm an awesome friend."

"You are an awesome friend. I've got coffee, but would you rather have tea?" Brenna went to the sink and wet a towel to scrub her sleeve with.

"Sure. I'll make it." Megan put the water on to boil. "Hey there little Ben-ben." She kissed Ben's nose and his big blue eyes crinkled when he smiled up at her. "Well, if he isn't enough to set a girl's biological clock ticking."

Brenna laughed. "I think you've still got a bit of time, old maid."

"Yeah, well, that's not what I came to tell you." Megan went back to the counter to pull out the teapot and all that went with a cup of tea. "Guess where I'm thinking about going?"

"Um. Dublin?" Brenna sat back down to finish feeding Ben.

"Funny. No, farther."

"I don't know, where?"

"Come on, you can at least guess."

"Okay ... New York."

"Nope. Africa!"

The beaming smile on Megan's face told Brenna her friend wasn't kidding. She looked like she'd just won the lottery.

"What—why are you going to Africa?"

"Well, I'm not going any time soon. But I'm looking into joining a medical missions group that takes trips once a year. It's too late for me to get in on this year's trip; I think they actually already went. But just the idea of doing something to help people who need basic things like food, shelter, water—I'm so excited to start *doing* something." Megan poured their tea and slid into the seat across from Brenna.

"Wow. Sounds cool. Tell me more." Brenna wiped Ben's hands and face and put his favorite stuffed lion on the tray, mimicking a lion's roar as she did, sending him into a fit of giggles.

"I guess they do fundraising projects throughout the year. They support a children's home and other efforts to help people rebuild their lives after the horrible civil war in Sierra Leone. Did ya see *Blood Diamond*?"

"Yeah, I think so. Leo DiCaprio?"

"That's the one. It's based on what happened in Sierra Leone. I've looked through the organization's website to see what they do, but there's a meeting in Killarney on Wednesday so I can ask more questions then." She didn't seem able to stop grinning. "I wondered if ya might want to go with me?"

Brenna choked on her tea. "To Africa?"

"No." Megan laughed. "To the meeting."

"Oh. Yeah, I probably couldn't get a babysitter for Africa, but a meeting in Killarney is doable." She smiled. "How did you hear about it?"

Megan's face reddened. "Oh, Doctor David mentioned it yesterday, said I should check it out cuz they always need people with pharmacy experience."

"And Tom Burke isn't really David's type." Brenna said with a glint in her eyes.

"Ha-ha. Funny. But really, I can't explain it, Bren. It just feels like God is opening a door for me to walk through. I don't know what's on the other side of it, but I have to go through. Does that make sense?"

"Yep. It's how I felt when Anna asked me if I wanted to stay in Ireland. I wasn't sure exactly what I was saying yes to, but I was sure I was supposed to say yes."

"Exactly. Remember last Sunday, when Father Tim talked about puttin' yer yes on the table? Saying, 'Okay God, the answer is yes, now what is the question?'"

"I remember." Brenna wondered if she was supposed to be saying yes to finding a job. Her stomach soured.

"Well, I went home on Sunday and literally wrote in my journal, 'Okay, Lord. My yes is on the table. Show me what my next step is.' And then within the week, someone invites me to join a group that helps people in Africa and I may go there myself? How surreal is that?"

"It's pretty incredible. So, you just want some company for the meeting?"

Megan shrugged. "David offered to drive, but I don't want it to be just the two of us in the car."

Brenna rolled her eyes. "Why not? Do you know how many women around here would pay to have an hour in the car with him?"

"Well, I'm not all those women that he's always having lunch with, or whatever. And I don't really want to be alone with him."

"Why?"

Megan sighed. "Because. I don't like how he looks at me and smiles like I'm going to fall at his feet and beg for a date, or something."

"Wow ... he's got you wound up, hasn't he?"

"Shut it." Megan scowled even as her cheeks pinked up. "I would just feel more comfortable if you're with me. If you can't come, I'll ask Tara."

"No. Chill, I can come. I'm sure Anna will watch Ben." Brenna was amused at Megan's obvious confusion over the doctor. She had never seen her so flustered.

"Thanks. Now, enough about me. What's up with you? Ya looked spooked when I walked in. So what's happenin'?"

"Dang, I can't hide anything from you, can I?"

"Since when have you ever been able to hide anything from me?"

She was right. Megan was almost always one step ahead of her. Even when she found out she was pregnant, Megan had already guessed it.

"Since never. Okay, obviously this is between us. I don't know how much Ryan wants me to share. But if I don't talk with someone about it, I'll go crazy." Ben started screeching and hitting the sides of his chair. "Shhh, can you say, 'Down please?'" She took him from the chair and set him down to crawl around in his playroom. "So, Ryan told me last night that business is really down. He thinks he's going to sell while he can still make a little something off the business. He's worried if things keep going as they are and he waits it out, he'll lose money on the sale."

"Oh no! That stinks. What will he do if he sells his business?"

"I don't know. He was hoping to find something local to do. He has his Auctioneer's license but selling real estate won't do much good when the market is so bad. He has some properties he can take over the management of, locally. But that would put Fergus, his manager, out of a job and he doesn't really want to do that. I don't know." She breathed out a sigh.

Megan patted her hand from across the table. "Hey, it's gonna be okay. Ryan will figure it out. He's a smart one."

"I know. I'm sure he will. It's just that I'm wondering if I should be looking for a job? I could probably pick up some shifts again at Rosie's. I don't know what he needs me to do. I barely slept last night. Can't stop my mind from whirring."

"Well have you asked him if he wants ya to look for a job?"

"No. I don't want to show him that I'm worried. Thought maybe I'd talk it out with you first.

"I'm here for ya, luv."

"Thanks." Brenna squeezed Megan's hand and reached for the chocolate pastry bag. "And chocolate pastries are always helpful, too."

# Chapter Seventeen

Megan loved Killarney. It was bigger than Millway and often had a festival atmosphere, from the colorful shops to the street vendors to the curious old gentleman playing the drum-violin-harmonica combo rigged to cause yellow, wooden, cutout elves to dance to the beat of the drum. Lively. That was the best word for Killarney.

The meeting for C.A.M.P., the Christian Alliance of Medical Professionals, was held in the basement of a stone-faced Anglican church. The temperature dropped as they descended the winding staircase, and the mixed smell of dampness, mothballs and coffee made Megan sneeze. Twenty or so chairs were arranged in a semi-circle; a few were already filled. A handful of people mingled around the large coffee urn at the corner of the room, and Megan was so glad Brenna was with her.

The car ride had been easy. David was surprised she'd brought a friend, but since they were "cousins" or something, Brenna and David did most of the talking while Megan, who had finagled the back seat of David's sporty car, half-listened while her mind wandered to what Africa might be like. The only pictures in her mind were safari-type settings she'd seen in movies or the dusty, parched desert lands shown in commercials begging for help for needy children.

Now, in the meeting room, she noticed strings had been stretched along each wall and large pictures of African children were fastened to them with clothespins. Most of them were smiling, and their warm, chocolate eyes held her gaze.

She startled at the feel of a hand on her back and turned to see David standing much too close as he said, softly, "That one, there, is Alahaji." He pointed at a boy of about six with a crooked grin and laughing eyes. "When I first met him, he had sores all over his body. The villagers had shunned him and his mother, because they considered the sores a sign that he was cursed."

"Seriously?" Megan noticed a few slight scars on the young boy's cheeks.

He nodded. "There are a lot of tribal traditions and superstitions, especially when ya get out of the city."

"He looks so happy." She glanced toward Brenna, who was at the coffee table, and walked over to see Alahaji up close. David followed her.

"He was. We were able to treat him for the sores, and his skin healed up quite well. He was accepted back into his village since the 'gods' had healed him, and he was doing great, last time I was there."

She looked at David and noticed his usual suave, charmer persona was absent. Kind of like a shield was down. When he looked at Alahaji, he almost looked like a man looking at his son.

"How many times have you been there?"

"Twice. I couldn't go last time. But I went the two years before that."

Brenna joined them, carrying three coffees, and David explained the boy in the picture. Moments later, a small man with a big voice called out for everyone to take their seats. Brenna sat to Megan's left, David sat to her right and leaned in to whisper, pointing out a few of the people he knew from past trips. She noticed that most of the group looked to be college-aged. Probably med or nursing students.

"Thank you all for coming. My name is Donal Magee." He was even shorter than Megan had first thought, probably no taller than Brenna's five-foot-two. His wiry grey hair stood up at odd angles and his rimmed glasses sat slightly askew. He had a bookish look, but the confidence of someone very accustomed to standing in front of a crowd. "As most of you know, I am the director for C.A.M.P., here in Ireland. Lovely to see all of your smiling faces again. Those of you who've just returned from Africa, I'm glad to see you've all had proper showers. I'm sure you smell better than the last time we saw each other, too." A smattering of light laughter followed as Donal grinned. "Now, for the benefit of those who've just joined us, let's go around and each share our name, profession, and how we came to be here tonight."

David leaned in again, whispering, "Donal just took a group to Sierra Leone a few weeks ago. I was originally planning to go, but when the Millway job came up, I had to back out."

"Ah, that's a shame." Megan whispered back. "Has he been doing this for a long time?"

"Aye, he started out as an engineer and then a professor at University College Dublin. Took a group of students down to Freetown years ago and was actually there when rebels started to take over the city. They barely got out. You'll have to ask him to tell you his story sometime."

A chill snaked down Megan's spine, partly from the thought of being there when rebels attacked and partly from David's face so close to hers.

"Are ya cold?" he asked quietly.

"No, thanks. I'm fine," she whispered back as Brenna started to introduce herself.

"Um, I'm Brenna. I'm not going on a trip or anything. Just came as moral support." She shrugged and turned toward Megan, obviously glad she was done with her turn.

"Hi, I'm Megan McKenna. I'm a grad student in education, and I work in a pharmacy. David mentioned you might need someone with pharmacy experience when ya go back next year? I just wanted to check out what you all do."

Donal nodded. "Excellent. Nice job, David, finding us a pharmacist—"

"Oh, I'm not an actual pharmacist." Megan interrupted, cheeks coloring, as soft chuckles could be heard around the room.

"Well, as our veterans can attest, the smallest amount of experience here makes you somewhat of an expert in the mission field. But no worries, my dear. You don't have to make any promises right now. You can just check out the events we do throughout the year. There's plenty of time to decide if you'd like to actually go with us or not."

Donal motioned for David to introduce himself, and the rest of the group followed suit. Then, Donal handed out a flyer with the calendar for the remainder of the year. They had a few more meetings scheduled and then a large benefit to raise funds for a children's home in Freetown, Sierra Leone.

"You'll notice," Donal said, "that the location for this year's benefit is listed as To Be Announced. We had booked the Killarney Room at McGoverns, but they have a new owner and it's possible we won't be able to use their facility, due to renovations. So, if any of you know of a place that can hold a few hundred guests, please let me know. Most of the planning is done but once we have the venue decided, we'll be needing plenty of help. Moira?" He nodded toward a stocky, ginger-haired woman beside him, who took the cue and stood.

"Hello all, I'm Moira—for the few of ya that haven't been here before. I've a sign-up sheet for the benefit." She held a clipboard aloft and continued in a brisk voice, "As Donal has said, we've done most of the planning, but it will take a large team of volunteers to pull off an event of this size, especially if we end up having to change the venue. We've a lot to get done in a relatively small timeframe, so if yer interested in helping, put yer email down and I'll be in touch, soon. And do remember, each event you help with, gives you a percentage toward yer trip, should ya decide to join us next year."

Moira passed the clipboard to a gangly young man with unruly brown hair and a wide toothy smile. He eagerly filled in his name and passed it to his left.

"Right, thank you Moira." Donal nodded toward her as she took her seat again. "Now I know how much you all love my ice-breakers—" An exaggerated groan rippled around the circle. "Come now, you know it helps us get to know one another, so as long as we have at least one new person here, I like to do one quick little game. And as there's only about twenty of us here tonight, this shouldn't be too hard. Let's all stand."

He proceeded to explain that they would each say their name and something they like that starts with the same letter. "For example, I would start with Donal loves donuts. And then Moira?"

In a flat voice, Moira said, "Donal loves donuts and Moira loves movies." She had done this before.

The young man with the toothy grin said, "Donal loves donuts, Moira loves movies and Niall loves ... nuts." He looked expectantly to his left. Megan quickly calculated that she'd have to recite the names of at least ten people when her turn came. She didn't dare look at Brenna; she could already feel the searing glare. Brenna hated things like this. Anything that made her stand up and speak in front of people usually had her hiding behind a plant or something. But there was no way she could hide, so Megan knew payback would be coming her way.

Before long, they had made their way around the circle, and Megan was surprised at how effective the game had been. She could easily name each person in the room by the time they were done.

Donal addressed the group a final time. "Folks, thank you very much for yer time tonight. We are especially glad to meet the three or four newcomers. If you should have any questions, please email or call me. My contact info is on the bottom of the calendar I passed out."

Papers rustled as the group began to disperse. David said he needed to ask Donal about something but he'd be right back. Megan tucked the calendar into her bag and gave Brenna a sheepish smile. "Thanks for coming?"

Brenna narrowed her eyes. "You're lucky we didn't play one of those games where you pass an orange from neck to neck or end up sitting on strangers' laps. Cuz Megan Loves Monkeys might not have made it home in one piece."

"Calm down, Brenna Loves Bananas. You did fine." Megan poked her friend in the side, breaking her fake frown and forcing a dimpled smile.

Outside, with a mischievous glint in her eye, Brenna slipped into the back seat of David's car before Megan could object, saying something about sleeping on the way home.

Payback.

David opened Megan's door with a slight bow accompanied by a "M'lady." Full charmer mode re-engaged. She pretended she thought he was silly, even rolling her eyes for effect, as she slid into the smooth leather seat. But she had to admit, he was incredibly charming.

Within minutes of leaving Killarney, soft snoring noises came from the back seat. David chuckled and said in a hushed voice, "She wasn't kidding."

"Poor thing." Megan glanced back at her sleeping friend and smiled. "She told me she didn't sleep well last night. Some friend I am, dragging her out till after ten."

"You're a horrible friend." He laughed. "But seriously, why did ya ask her to come along?"

*Wow. Nothing like putting me on the spot.* "I don't know. I guess I just felt nervous about meeting a bunch of new people, and she makes me feel more relaxed." Liar. You just didn't want to be in the car alone with him because he makes your heart beat faster and your palms get sweaty. She wiped her palms on her jeans.

He nodded and sat in thoughtful silence for a few minutes. "So, are you seeing anyone?"

*Again with the direct questions. Geez.* "Um. No. I'm busy with school and stuff. You?"

He shook his head. "No, no one serious. Focusing on my job right now. Takes most of my energy. "

"I can imagine." She thought about the fact that practically every time she saw him in town, he was with a different woman. "You seem to have a lot of pretty lady-friends, though."

He looked at her sideways, his mouth with the slightest upturn at the corner. "Do I?"

She nodded. "From what I've seen at Rosie's and The Tea Shoppe, yes."

"Well now, I can't help it if I get asked to lunch a lot."

"Must be a burden for you." She looked up, and he was grinning at her. She laughed and wondered how he did it. Even when she wanted to frown and roll her eyes, she felt powerless against that smile.

"Aye, 'tis a burden. But, we all have a cross to bear."

Now she did manage a roll of the eyes but she couldn't wipe the smile from her face. For the rest of the drive, she peppered him with questions about his past mission trips, and in turn answered his questions about school and her family. Although she may have imagined it, it seemed like he was probing for information about her past relationships, but she carefully dodged all questions that would have led to Jamie. That wound had nicely healed over and she didn't plan to pick at the scar.

The trip home felt much quicker than the trip there, and Megan was surprised to realize she was disappointed when they arrived at Brenna's, where she had parked her car. And while she admittedly had had a good time, she couldn't decide if David was actually arrogant or if that was just a clever act. She suspected it was the latter, which made him all the more intriguing.

# Chapter Eighteen

Megan loved the Mountdonovan property. She'd gone there a lot when she was young, even though kids said there were ghosts living in the old place. She may have seen and heard things that spooked her, occasionally. But she'd always ended up venturing back.

A small alcove, behind one of the smaller buildings, had a tree that had grown close enough to form a roof overhead, making it a perfect secluded spot to think or read. It was her spot. The place she went when she just needed space to think. It had been her private thinking place for as long as she could remember. She eyed that spot as she walked toward the large, stone main house. It always called to her.

But she wasn't here alone, today. Today, there was work to do. She could see the TidyTowns organizers, her mother being one of them, gathered in front of the house talking to Ryan Kelly.

To her left, the valley was obscured by fog and the farmer's patchwork hills beyond were barely visible. Even with the fog, the scene always transported her to another time, when ladies would sit beneath the shade of the huge tree on the front lawn, easels set up, painting landscapes. She and Brenna enjoyed Jane Austen movie marathons; *Pride and Prejudice*; *Emma*; *Mansfield Park*—all favorites. And this place reminded her of those stories. It was inherently romantic.

Which is why she wasn't sure how she felt when she saw David, surrounded by giggling ladies, on the far side of the group of volunteers. She didn't blame them for hanging on him. He looked—well, Brenna was right—he was hot. Jeans slung low on his hips, white T-shirt, blond hair ruffled by the wind. He made a fine picture.

She had been thinking about him since Wednesday's meeting. The look on his face when he talked about the little boy, Alahaji, had struck a chord with her. She still wasn't sure what she thought about him, other than the obvious ... that he was gorgeous. She supposed she didn't know him well enough, yet, to decide what kind of guy he was. But she had spent longer than normal getting ready this morning, knowing he would probably be here. She would never have admitted that to Brenna, though. And thankfully, Brenna was home, so she wouldn't have the chance to call her out.

As she neared the group, she saw David's attention shift from the women around him. His eyes locked on hers, and he smiled. He certainly did weird things to her stomach. She felt something like butterflies dancing in her belly as she smiled back. Mortified at the thought of anyone knowing how she felt, she gave a quick wave and purposely headed toward Anna instead of him. But not before she saw the women gathered around him turn to see who had stolen his attention. Some looked surprised, others looked disgusted and Megan, used to those looks by now, just looked away.

"Good morning, Anna. How are ya, today?"

"Oh, hello, luv. I'm fine, and yerself?"

"I'm looking forward to using up some energy on these weeds. I'll bet the gardens haven't been touched since before I was born."

"I'd be surprised if they've been touched since I was born. I remember everything growing wild, back when I was a wee one," Anna said.

Megan noticed Anna looking behind her with a smile. She followed her gaze and saw David walking toward them. Stupid butterflies started dancing again.

"He's a pretty one, isn't he?" Anna whispered, and Megan could feel her cheeks heat.

"Hi there," David said, smiling as always.

"Hi, yerself. Have ya met Anna O'Brien?" Megan nodded toward Anna, who held out her hand to shake David's.

"I have not had the pleasure, but I hear that we are cousins by marriage, Anna."

"So Brenna has told me. Nice to meet you, cousin. I remember yer dad from when we were kids—"

"Anna!" Bettie was calling to Anna from a crouched position in one of the front gardens.

"Oh, excuse me. Looks like I'm being paged. I'll talk with you later, Megan. And pleased to meet you, David."

David nodded and turned toward Megan. "So, after a couple days to think about it, how did ya like the C.A.M.P. group?"

"I'm intrigued. I've been looking for something to do that's more about helping others. I'd say it's a good fit." She shrugged. "I have a hard time wrapping my mind around the idea of going to Africa. But I guess that's a long way off, and I shouldn't worry about it. Still, it's hard to picture what it's like there."

"Aye, tis almost impossible to do till you've been there. And then you'll never forget it." Again, that vulnerable look passed over his sun-lit eyes and she wanted to know more.

"Have you ever thought about going there for a long-term mission?"

He tilted his head as he considered. "I've thought about it. Usually when I'm there, I think about it a lot. But it's a very hard place. Honestly, I'm not sure I could handle it."

Before she could reply, a sharp whistle came from behind her, quieting the crowd, and she turned as she heard her mother's voice addressing the group.

"Hello, all. The TidyTowns committee wishes to thank you all for volunteering your time. Our goal is to get some cleanup done today and next week. And hopefully after that, we can fix up some of the outbuildings in preparation for the renovation crew, who will start work as soon as possible. Our own Ryan Kelly has secured the bid to use his crew for the renovation and he's generously agreed to do the work at cost—" A rowdy applause interrupted her. Megan, knowing Ryan's business was struggling, wondered what Brenna thought of him doing the work pro bono. Her mother smiled in approval of the applause and raised her hand to quiet the group.

"Yes," she continued, "'tis a very generous offer and it allows us to include the folk village many of us were so excited about. The committee will be taking applications for the position of Mountdonovan Program Director over the next several weeks. So, if you know of anyone who would be interested, please direct them to our website for an application."

Megan felt spark of excitement ripple through her. Program director? She didn't even know what it would entail, but just the thought of working on this property instead of in a classroom gave her a thrill. But then she thought about the fact that Patricia and Bettie were both on the committee so she'd probably have no shot, not to mention that she would have to admit to her mother that she didn't want to teach. That wasn't gonna happen any time soon. Megan realized her mother's mouth was moving, and she'd been paying no attention at all. That wasn't really new. Thankful her mother couldn't hear her thoughts, she tuned back in.

"Now, for today, we need half of you to work removing debris from around the old kitchen building in back. Please don't climb on any part of the building, but all the loose timbers on the ground need to be stacked, and any rubbish can be put in the large construction bin. The rest of you, I hope you've brought your gardening gloves because we have a lot of weeds to pull. We'll start with the weeds along the side of the house and the buttercups—those little yellow flowers you see everywhere—those can go too. I know they're pretty. We'll leave them in the field but here along the house ..."

Megan didn't hear what she said next. Her heart was pounding so loud it was all she could hear. She had forgotten about the buttercups near the house. The exact flowers David had given her that she'd tossed in the trash. Maybe he wouldn't notice.

She chanced a quick sideways glance and found him looking at her, his expression unreadable. She swallowed hard and decided to deal with it head on.

"Can I talk with you for a minute?" she asked in a whisper as she tilted her head toward the big tree just behind them.

He nodded and headed toward the leafy cover. She followed, jamming her hands into her pockets so she wouldn't feel them shaking. Once they were under the tree, David turned around and leaned against the trunk.

He spoke before she had the chance. "Listen, we were kids. It's not a big deal, Megan. I'm sure I embarrassed you." His words were kind, but there was an edge to his voice that she hadn't heard before.

"David, I have wanted to apologize to you ever since that day. I was such a jerk and I'm so sorry."

He raised an eyebrow. "Truly?" He didn't sound convinced.

"Truly. It was a cruel and heartless thing to do."

"It's okay." He shrugged. "I imagine attention from Beaver Boy was the last thing a fourteen-year-old girl wanted."

"Well, I think that kind of attention from *anyone* would have embarrassed me back then. But I felt rotten for how I treated you, and I should have apologized that day. Instead, I felt so ashamed of how I acted, I avoided you for the next few months and then, suddenly, you were gone. I was sure you must have hated me by then."

"Hmm." He looked like he was measuring her words.

"Hmm, what?"

"I always thought you avoided me after that because you were disgusted by me or something."

"No." She shook her head. "I was disgusted by *myself*. Seriously. I haven't been able to look at those flowers since, without feeling like I was gonna be sick, cuz they're a reminder of how rotten I was to you. I was just a coward. I cared too much what other people thought. I think I'm finally cured of that, though," she said with a wry laugh.

He stared off into the distance for what felt like forever. Now her palms were sweating, so she took them out of her pockets and casually wiped them on her jeans.

"So, do you forgive me or not?" she asked, desperately wanting the conversation to be over.

He raised an eyebrow, and his lips curled into a crooked smile. "Ah Megan, if I held grudges against everyone who did something cruel to me when I was a kid," he lowered his voice and leaned in, "I'd have very few people left in this town to talk to."

She winced. It must have been rough being Beaver Boy, and she hadn't made it any easier. "So, is that a yes?"

He smiled. "Of course I forgive you." She let out a breath, relieved and then startled when he stepped even closer and took her hand. "But I think you at least owe me a date."

Her heart thudded in her chest again as he pulled her hand to his lips and kissed it, without taking his eyes off hers. Butterflies had stopped dancing and were now in a full on riot. "I ... um ..." She tried to remember why she had insisted to Brenna that she wasn't ready to go out with anyone. But with those golden eyes staring at her, not one coherent thought surfaced.

"Come now, after that heartfelt apology, there's no way ya can turn me down a second time."

She laughed. "Well, when ya put it like that, I guess you're right. Looks like I owe you a date."

"Damn straight." He grinned. "How's Friday night?"

Friday night. Why did that sound familiar? Ah, Ben. "Can't. Brenna's doing a birthday party for Ben. Turning one."

"Right. I forgot about that."

"I'm free Saturday."

He laughed and shook his head. "I've a meeting in Cork, Saturday. And then my week is jammed. Next Friday?"

He had released her hand but she could swear it was tingling. "That works for me."

"I'll pick ya up at six? We can have dinner at the new hotel restaurant, Blackwater. The food is pretty good."

"Okay." She was glad to feel her heartbeat returning to normal.

"We should probably get back?" He motioned toward the volunteers scattered about the property, pulling weeds or hauling garbage.

Megan had forgotten all about the cleanup work. "Oh, right. Yes, we should. I think my mother gave me a scolding look when we walked away. I'll hear about it later."

"Ah, yes, Mrs. McKenna. She never seemed to be a fan of mine, back in the day."

"Really? Well, don't take it personally, I wouldn't say she's always a fan of mine, either." Megan laughed.

David casually placed a hand on the small of her back, starting them walking back toward the main house. He tilted his head as he looked at her. "Hmm, well, I know your da thinks the world of ya."

She smiled and tried to ignore the fact that his touch had the butterflies rioting again. "My da is awesome."

"He was a great boss. How's he doin' these days?"

"Great. You should stop by and see him. He thought the world of you, too, ya know."

"I'll do that. But, before we get to work, I do have one very important question to ask ya." He tried to look serious, but there was laughter in his eyes. "Are ya sure you didn't just apologize because you think I'm so gorgeous now?"

She laughed. "Well, you're *okay* looking, but what really turns me on is your humility." He laughed loud enough that heads turned, and she was acutely aware of the hostile looks from a few of the ladies who had obviously wondered where their Prince Charming had been hiding. "Well, it seems I've kept ya from your adoring public for long enough."

He nodded, "Aye, 'tis important to spread the wealth. Can't have one woman monopolizing all my time."

"Heaven forbid." She smiled, enjoying the banter. She laid a hand on his arm. "But, seriously, thank you for being so forgiving. It means a lot to me."

He surprised her yet again when he leaned down and kissed her cheek, right in front of anyone who might have been looking. Heartbeat. Red face. Butterflies. He whispered, "It means a lot to me, too." Then, he bent down, picked a bright yellow buttercup, and winked as he handed it to her and started to walk away.

Her heart skipped at the meaningful gesture.

"Hey, David," she called out just loud enough that only he would hear. He turned back toward her. "Just to clarify, the apology had nothing to do with the fact that I think you're gorgeous." She winked at him, tucked the flower behind her ear, and walked away toward the gardens beside the house.

～✕

David couldn't help casually looking for Megan the rest of the morning. They didn't talk again, but he was acutely aware of her presence. When he was clearing timbers from around the old kitchen building, she was pulling weeds behind the house. When he was pulling vines off the sides of the stables, she was just over the hill moving some rocks and debris from one of the gardens. He almost thought he could have pinpointed her location without looking, he was so drawn to her.

He had already been attracted to her before, but that whole conversation had been charged with electricity. He wondered if she could feel it. It had been an effort, under that tree, not to pull her to him and kiss her like he wanted to. Even now, two hours later, he wanted to go grab her and kiss her. Especially when he caught her looking back at him and smiling.

He grabbed his bottle of water and poured the whole thing over his head. A makeshift cold shower.

"Hey, how's it goin'?" Ryan said, walking toward him.

"Tis goin' very well. Yerself?"

"Better now. I've been meeting with five women for the last hour, going over plans and blueprints. I don't think they agreed on a single thing." He shook his head and pulled a hammer from his tool belt. "I'm lookin' around for something to hit."

David laughed and shrugged. "Ya can't handle it the way you'd handle a group of lads. You have to know what ya want, goin' in. Then use the looks God gave you to smile and charm them into thinking they've just come up with an idea that was yers all along."

Ryan laughed but still looked stressed. "Sounds like you've perfected the skill."

"Comes natural. I could join you at yer next meeting. Show ya how it's done?" David said, amused by himself.

"Thanks, but I'm done with meetings for now," Ryan replied with a wry grin. "I've a second hammer in my bag, though. Wanna help me pound some nails out of those timbers over there?"

"Aye, be glad to."

They worked in an easy silence until they needed a water break.

"So," Ryan said, "I noticed you and Megan talking under the tree, earlier."

"Aye, she's close with Brenna?"

"Very. She's a great lass, and she's been through a lot."

David thought back to Patricia's warning. "I've heard some things."

Ryan glanced at him and took another swig of water. "I bet ya have. But unless you've heard those things from Megan or Brenna, they're probably not true."

David sat down on a fallen tree. "That so? Well, I guess I'm willin' to take yer word for that. They do say you shouldn't believe everything ya hear."

Ryan joined him on the tree. "Especially in this case. Most of the town has the story completely wrong. I don't feel right discussing Megan's business. But I thought you should know, she's a special girl. And she's been hurt pretty bad, so be careful with her." David raised an eyebrow and Ryan added, "Ya look at her differently than the others. I think you already know she's special. I just wanted to let ya know yer right."

"Well, thanks. I'm glad to hear the rumors aren't true." David stood up and looked toward Megan. "And don't worry, I'll be careful with her."

# Chapter Nineteen

Megan waved to Anna as she drove past the B&B and pulled down the long driveway to the O'Connors' rambling yellow farmhouse. She'd been at work when Elizabeth called her and asked if they could talk. That was four hours ago and still her stomach was bubbling with nerves and her hands felt like ice. She had just agreed, without asking questions, because she couldn't really talk at work. Also, she had probably been in shock.

So she had no idea if she was walking into an ambush or a white flag. She wouldn't have thought the second option was possible, but Elizabeth's voice on the phone was not like the woman who had been freezing her out and spreading lies about her for months. It was the old Elizabeth. The one who had made her chicken soup when she was sick. The one who had been like a second mother to her.

Elizabeth was on the wraparound porch, waiting for her. She was a tall woman with long black hair and grey wisps at the temple. Red and weary eyes followed Megan as she parked and walked toward the house. A trickle of fear gave Megan a chill. Elizabeth had clearly been crying. Was something wrong with Jamie? She wasn't even sure how she'd feel about that.

"I'm glad ya came," she said while grasping both of Megan's freezing cold hands. "First, I have to tell you how sorry I am for how I've treated ya these past months. I ... I'm ashamed."

The unexpected apology stunned Megan into silence for a moment. Then, when she tried to ask what had changed, the words stuck in her throat and came out as a solitary sob. She pulled her hands from Elizabeth to cover her face.

Elizabeth spoke again, "I hope you will forgive me, dear. I know I was monstrous, but I know now that Jamie was lying and that I've had the whole thing upside-down and backwards."

The pressure in Megan's chest overruled her desire to compose herself, and she couldn't hold back the flood of tears. Hands still covering her face, she shook with the force of the odd pain of finally hearing the apology she'd wanted for so long. She stiffened as she felt Elizabeth's warm arms encircle her.

"Shhh, 'tis okay, luv." Elizabeth whispered as she smoothed Megan's hair, still holding her close. "I'm so ... very sorry."

At the hitch in Elizabeth's voice, Megan looked up to see tears streaming down her face as well. She sighed and pulled away. "I don't know what to say."

"You don't have to say anything. I'm surprised you even agreed to come after how I've behaved. But I'm really glad ya did. Come, let's have some tea." Elizabeth led her into the house to the long country table where they'd shared so many meals together.

The spacious farm kitchen looked just the same as always had. Warmed by the huge yellow Aga stove along the wall, the room smelled faintly of pancakes. Their cat, Jax, wound his way around Megan's legs, as if to say he'd missed her. She took a seat and wiped her face and nose with a tissue Elizabeth offered, then took a steadying breath. "Sorry I lost it there."

"No, I think you're exempt from ever having to apologize to me about anything, leastwise for crying after I've treated you like a ... harlot or something. I've gone through two boxes of those tissues, cryin' about the matter myself. The boys have been slinking around here the whole week, afraid to show their faces, lest they should have to deal with female emotions on the loose."

Megan smiled. "My brothers usually hide, once a month, at our house."

"Aye, that happens here, too. I don't want to make you cry any more. Are y'okay to talk for a bit?"

Megan nodded.

"Well, tis no excuse, but like ya said that day at Rosie's, Jamie lied to me about everything."

Megan nodded. "I figured he must have."

"I want ya to know, I didn't believe it when he first called me. I told him he must have misunderstood. That you would never cheat on him. But then he told me he'd walked in on you and there was no way to misunderstand." Elizabeth looked down at the table and smoothed the linen tablecloth. "He said that he had planned a romantic night out for the two of you, to celebrate his birthday. That he'd reserved a hotel room for you to have a place to stay and that he was to get you at half-five but he was stuck on the farm with a birthing mare."

Megan's pulse raced. "All of that is a complete lie, so far."

"I didn't know that, at the time. But I believe you." Elizabeth poured tea into delicate cups and sat down across from Megan. "We can just go right to you telling me what actually happened, if ya like?"

Megan shook her head. "No. I'm probably the only person in town who *doesn't* know what lies he told about me. I want to know." She could hear the edge in her voice but she didn't even try to control it.

Elizabeth winced, took a deep breath, and resumed her story. "Alright. So, he said he couldn't call you while he was dealing with the mare but his cousin, Declan, was leaving the house for work. He asked him to text you and let ya know he'd get ya closer to half-seven. But things went quicker than he expected so he cleaned up and got to your hotel room early where you were ... in a compromising position ... with Declan."

"He said I was sleeping with his freaking cousin?" Megan's face felt like it was on fire, and she put her teacup down for fear she'd crush it. Elizabeth looked at her, probably unsure if she should continue. With a deep breath and a wave of her hand, Megan said, "Go ahead, finish the story. But I take no responsibility for any names I may call yer son. Go on."

Elizabeth looked extremely uncomfortable. "So, he said he took off, furious, and that you followed him to his apartment. That you explained yerself, saying that you'd fallen for Declan on yer past visits and that you didn't want to hurt Jamie, but that you had planned to tell him after his birthday was over."

"You believed all this?"

Elizabeth eyed her over her teacup. "He was very convincing. He said the two of you fought and he was angry and he shoved you and ya fell back. And when he tried to help you up you pushed him away, took off yer ring and threw it in his face, giving him a good-sized gash above his right eye."

"Wow." Megan took several slow breaths before she could speak. "Okay, well the only piece of that whole idiotic story that is actually true is me chucking the ring."

"Aye, well, he has a scar to show for that part."

"Good. He deserves it. I didn't walk in on him, but the story is basically reversed. He's been living with Declan's friend, Annie, for who knows how long. There's only one bed, and he pretty much admitted he's not sleeping on the couch."

Elizabeth nodded. "I know—"

"It was so crazy. He was acting weird on the phone for a while, but I just figured it was the distance or something. I know I said I was going up to surprise him for his birthday, but really I wanted to check on him. See what was going on."

Elizabeth picked at the fringe on the woven table runner. "I thought he was acting strange on the phone, too. But I thought I was just imagining things. And then, when he fed me that whole story, I figured he had been acting weird because he suspected something was wrong with the two of you. I'm sorry. I put the whole thing on you. But I didn't know then what I know now."

"So, how did ya figure it out?" Megan asked.

"I drove up there last weekend. He wasn't home, but this Annie answered the door. So, I played along as if I knew who she was. We had tea. I asked her how long they'd been together. She said six months. Which was before his birthday, so I knew."

"Did she know I'd been there?"

Elizabeth shook her head. "She didn't even know he was engaged. She had been out of town visiting family, said she felt guilty she missed his birthday. She had no clue about anything that happened while she was gone. He told her he'd gotten the cut at work."

"So he lies to everyone now. Did ya see him? He was different, right? Like he was a totally different person." Tears filled Megan's eyes, again, as she was transported back to his apartment on that cold night.

Elizabeth's lip trembled as she nodded. "There's more to the story, Megan. I found out some things while I was there that will answer a lot of questions for you." Megan could see tears forming in Elizabeth's eyes and a jolt of fear shot through her, once more. "What I'm going to tell you may be hard to believe, and I don't want you to think I'm making excuses for what he did. But you have a right to know what's happened."

Megan's stomach swirled. "Yer kind of scaring me."

Elizabeth nodded. "Do ya remember when Jamie was sick back in November?"

"With the flu? When his Aunt Denni made him go to the hospital?"

"Aye, well, that wasn't the full story. He didn't have a bad flu, like we were told. He had an accident on the farm and his head was injured."

"What happened?" Megan remembered telling him she was coming to see him in the hospital, and Denni getting on the phone and telling her that he was really contagious and they weren't allowing visitors, anyway. But that they thought he'd be feeling better within the week. He was released later that week, but he told her he was swamped with work and he'd see her at Christmas. Of course, he hadn't ended up coming home for Christmas, which is why she went to see him in January.

"Well, Jamie actually doesn't remember the accident or much of the weeks just afterward. But here's what I've pieced together after talking with Denni and Jack. He may have been hit with something in the barn or fallen and hit his head. Either way, he didn't have a visible head injury, but Jack found him unconscious in the barn."

Megan felt like she was going to be sick. "Why didn't they call and tell us right away?"

"That's a whole other part to the story. I'll get to that in a second. They called an ambulance and by the time they joined him at the hospital, he was awake and, according to Denni, he begged them not to tell us. Said he didn't want us to worry and that the doctors said he was going to be fine, anyway."

"You don't believe her?"

"I'm not sure. My husband has not been on great terms with his brother for years. He never thought Jack should have moved to England, and they don't speak much. He didn't take too kindly to Jamie even going up there to help his uncle. So, from some of the things I heard when I was there, I think Jack was worried that James might sue him, if he knew Jamie had been hurt on the job. I know they're not in a good place, financially, and it seems to me that they figured, no harm—no foul. If Jamie was fine anyway, why cause a fuss, right?"

"Okay, so they hushed it all to cover themselves. But he was fine, right? He was out of the hospital in a week."

"Aye, he was released, but he wasn't fine. Have ya ever heard of TBI, Traumatic Brain Injury?"

Megan shook her head.

"When I was growing up, my friend Mary's dad, Teddy, was kicked in the head by a horse, when we were around ten. And Megan, it changed him. A head injury like that can completely alter someone's personality."

"What ... alter how?"

Elizabeth took a deep breath. "It varies, case by case. In Teddy's case, it was drastic."

Megan was seriously in danger of being sick all over Elizabeth's pretty tablecloth. "Explain."

"Teddy was a sweet, gentle kind of guy. Everyone called him Teddy Bear. But, after the accident, he was different. He could get mean. And even violent. 'Twas horrible and Mary's mam eventually left him, to protect herself and her kids. It wasn't until Mary was grown that doctors realized he'd had TBI, stemming from that kick to the head."

Megan knew where this was going, and she realized her hands were icy and shaking. "So you're saying Jamie has TBI?"

"Yes. He wasn't diagnosed at the time because it sounds like the doctors didn't get the full story from Jack, and Jamie never went back for his follow-up visits. And since it's mild TBI, it often goes undiagnosed. Denni and Jack had never even heard of TBI, so they didn't know. Like me, they assumed his change in behavior had to do with issues he was having with you. Although, Denni did say that the hospital had called her a few times trying to reach Jamie. She says she told him, and he said he'd call them back. But he obviously didn't."

Megan was having trouble processing. "So how do ya know it's TBI?"

"Because, when I saw him, I knew something was very wrong. He was forgetting things he should know. I noticed he had sticky notes on his door that reminded him to take his keys and wallet. And one over the stove that said to turn off the stove. It was bizarre. Sometimes he seemed normal, but other times, particularly if he was stressed, he was more like a stranger."

"That's what I thought, that he seemed like a different person." Megan shivered.

"Aye, and the way his temper flared up so quickly immediately reminded me of Mary's dad. So, I started asking questions, trying to find out if he'd been hit in the head recently. And that's when Denni told me that he might have been. They weren't exactly sure. From there, it all clicked into place. I made him go to the doctor first thing Monday morning, and they said he very likely had mild or moderate TBI. There was some discrepancy in his record as to how long he'd been unconscious. At the time, the doctors were under the impression he'd only lost consciousness for a few minutes. But it may have been longer. So, last week they had Jamie come back for several tests and gave the official diagnosis on Wednesday morning." Elizabeth let out a shaky breath.

"Well, is it something they can treat?" And what would that mean for her? Could things go back to the way they were? Would she even want them to?

But Elizabeth shook her head. "I don't know. There are things they can do to help him recover, in some ways. But it's all very vague. They say that every case of TBI is different, and every person responds to it differently. Some people have very few symptoms. Jamie's were subtle enough that it went undiagnosed, and that's not helpful for recovery. Early intervention is important, and we've lost that time." She stared off for a moment. "But there are people who say that much of what's lost can be improved with consistent therapy. Right now, they're just trying to sort through his symptoms."

"What other symptoms does he have?"

"I don't think he's been sleeping well, at all. And he told the doctor that he has headaches every day. I definitely think he's depressed. I don't know if ya could tell over the phone, but he's been drinking a lot. It's one of the things Denni noticed and thought it was because he was upset over what happened with the two of you."

"He offered me whiskey. I thought that was weird because he never seemed to like it before. He hardly even drank beer."

She nodded. "People with TBI, especially if it's undiagnosed, know that something's wrong but they don't know how to fix it. So, to cope, they often turn to a bottle or to drugs."

"He must have felt so alone." Megan held back fresh tears. "I wish I had known. I would have done something. I would have driven up there and taken him to the doctor, myself."

"Aye, me too. But he's been hiding it and staying away from us, because he was ashamed of how he was acting. He didn't know why he was acting like he was and forgetting things and feeling irritable all the time. And it's almost like he's at war with himself. One part is desperately trying to hold on to the old Jamie and the other is depressed and very angry. Meg, I don't think he will ever be the same again—" Elizabeth choked on her words as tears fell.

And amidst all the confusing emotions whirling through Megan's head, an overwhelming empathy rose to the surface and she grabbed Elizabeth's hands. "Are you okay?" What must it be like to find out that your son may never be the same?

Elizabeth wiped at her eyes and nose with a tissue and shook her head again. "No, I'm not okay. I'm a wreck. But I feel a little better now that I've told you. I know it's a lot to take in. But I thought you'd want to know."

Hot tears stung Megan's eyes and she let them fall. "I don't even know what to think, right now. I need to process all of this."

"Of course you do. I've had a week to process it and I'm still confused and emotional."

Megan wiped her face with the back of her sleeve. "So, what happens now? How's Jamie taking all of this?"

"Hard to say. I can't read him anymore. He's confused but I think he's also relieved. It must have been horrible to know something was wrong but not know what or why. He recognizes now that he needs to see the doctor, and he's taking that seriously. Denni makes sure he gets there."

"Don't ya want him to come home?" Megan had never wanted to see him again. Now, a part of her wished he were here so she could give him a hug and tell him it would all be okay. Even if it wouldn't.

"I do. But for now, he can get better care in London than he can here. We convinced him to move in with Jack and Denni. She's keeping an eye on him, and then next week I'm going to go up there and stay for a while."

"Do you trust her, after all this?"

Elizabeth sighed. "I trust her to do what's right, now. I don't think they would have kept it quiet if they'd known about the TBI. I think they were selfish, but I don't think they were malicious."

"Denni always struck me as a sweetheart. I can't believe they didn't tell us."

Elizabeth nodded. "There's a part of me that is so angry ... I could probably break every dish in the press. But I have to deal with the anger later. Right now, all I care about it making sure he gets the help he needs."

Megan had such conflicting emotions racing through her. She had spent so much time hating Jamie for what he had done, but now she didn't know how to feel. She stood abruptly, chair legs scraping the ground and Jax, who had curled up beneath her chair, went racing from the room with a squeal.

"I'm sorry, I need to go. I have to think."

Elizabeth stood and came around to Megan's side. "Again, I'm sorry, luv. I know you need some time to sort through all of this. I hope you'll forgive me for how I've been, but I will understand if ya don't. I just want you to know that I'll do my best at damage control. Once the story gets out, I imagine there will be many other apologies coming your way."

Megan shook her head. "Listen, I was definitely hurt that you didn't even give me a chance to talk about things, but I don't really blame you for believing him. Nothing about Jamie would ever have made ya think he'd lie like that. I'm just glad you know the truth, now."

Elizabeth sniffed and pulled her into a hug. "I am, too. Don't worry. I'll tell everyone."

Megan relaxed and allowed the hug. "Thanks. But focus on helping Jamie. Don't worry about me. I'm pretty tough."

"Megan, you are a much stronger woman than I. Once ya process all of this, let me know if you want to talk, okay?"

Megan nodded, grabbed her purse, and forced herself not to run to her car. Her heart raced as a panic rose. She just had to go somewhere, but she didn't know where. She left the farmhouse and drove down the road until she found herself at Mountdonovan. She parked beside the stile and ran all the way to her alcove, where she collapsed onto the ground and burst into tears.

# Chapter Twenty

Ryan was staring at his breakfast without eating. Brenna had fallen asleep last night before he got home, so she had told him about Jamie at the breakfast table.

"Crazy, huh?" she asked.

He looked up at her. "I can't even imagine what his parents are feeling. Or Megan, for that matter. What did she say?"

"She was pretty out of it when she called. She told me about her talk with Elizabeth, but I don't think she even knows how to feel. I mean, he cheated on her, but is that really his fault or is it like an insanity defense? Does she go back to him and try to help him with his recovery? Does she walk away?" Brenna shook her head and moved toward Ryan, lowering herself into his lap as he wrapped his arms around her.

"It's seriously messed up," he said.

"I know. Especially since she was finally starting to move on. Hasn't she been through enough? I mean, really?" She clenched her fists. "Makes me so angry but I don't know who to be angry at, anymore. It was easy to be angry at Jamie, before. But now? Now, it's just a mess."

He pulled her closer and kissed her brow. "I've gotta go to work, soon. She comin' over today?"

"Yeah, I convinced her to call in sick. She'll be here a little later." Brenna moved off his lap and picked up the juice cup that Ben had just tossed over his playroom gate.

"Okay, tell her she's in my prayers today," Ryan said as he grabbed his bag.

"Will do. Are you meeting with that buyer today?"

Ryan nodded. "Aye, but he's looking at three different companies. Not sure where he stands, right now."

"Well, I'll be praying for *you*, then. Keep me posted."

Ryan scooped Ben out of his playroom. "Hey, little man. Take good care of yer mammy, today, okay?" He smothered him with kisses and Ben dissolved into a fit of laughter. "Whoo, I think he's stinky. That's my cue to leave." He held him out toward Brenna.

She took her stinky boy and smacked her man on the butt, saying, in a perfect Irish brogue, "Get out of here, then. Yer of no use to me."

She went about her morning routine, mindlessly. Ben was changed and happily playing with the new block set that Anna had bought him. Brenna had laughed at her bringing him gifts so close to his birthday, knowing full well she would say they didn't count as birthday gifts. He was actually turning one on Thursday, but they weren't having his party till Friday night. Anna would probably bring him gifts on both days. Brenna was making her bed when she heard a car in the driveway.

Megan walked into the kitchen looking like she hadn't slept all night long. Her messy bun was barely on top of her head, and day-old mascara flakes dotted her cheeks.

"How ya doing today?" Brenna asked, opening her arms for a big hug.

"Probably about as good as I look." Megan sighed. "He called."

"Jamie?"

"Aye. Last night."

"Holy crap. Sit down. You want tea?"

"Coffee." Megan, who hardly ever drank coffee, sank into a chair with a heavy sigh.

"Coffee? Oh man. You didn't sleep at all, did you?"

Megan shook her head as Brenna grabbed two coffee mugs from the cupboard. She pulled out some of Bettie's shortbread and set in on a plate in front of Megan, next to her coffee. She took a quick look into the playroom to check on Ben and then sat down across from her friend.

"So, he called you. What did he say?"

Megan rubbed her face with both hands and dropped her head into them, sighing. "I'm trying to think of where to start."

"Take your time. You don't have to talk if you don't want to. You can even go take a nap if you want. I just changed the sheets."

Megan shook her head. "No, I want to tell ya. I just don't know how coherent it will be."

"I'll decipher. Start with the phone call. He calls, you answer, then what?"

"Okay, so I was lying in bed, and my stupid phone isn't even showing me phone numbers, now, so I didn't know who it was. When I heard his voice, I just wanted to cry. But it was hard to understand him. I think he was really drunk. He asked how I was doing. Told me he knew his mam had told me. Then he said he was really sorry for what he did."

"Wow."

"I know. I don't even know what to think, anymore. I'm so freaking confused." She pushed the shortbread away and laid her head on the table.

"Meg, I'm so sorry you're going through all this. What did you say to him?"

"I told him I forgave him." Megan's voice echoed off the table when she didn't even raise her head to answer. "What am I supposed to do? It's so confusing." She lifted her head and rested it on her palm, as if it weighed too much to stay up unassisted. "I don't even know if he can be considered in his right mind. So how can I blame him for what he did? None of it makes any sense."

"Well, an apology is good, right?"

She nodded. "I bawled like a baby when I got off the phone. I didn't realize just how badly I'd wanted to hear those words from him. Needed to hear them. But he was also really drunk. He may not even remember our conversation."

"True. But I'm glad he apologized, even if he doesn't remember it." Brenna sipped her coffee. "So, if the personality changes are from the injury, does that mean he can get better, with treatment? Be like he used to be?"

Megan shook her head. "I don't know. Of course I wore out Google looking for information. I read until my eyes started burning, but it doesn't seem like there are any concrete answers. Most of what I read seemed to indicate that personality changes that last this long could be permanent. But again, nothing's set in stone. Everyone responds to head trauma differently."

"It just seems unreal. Did he seem like himself, or like the guy you saw in January?"

"Hard to tell through the whiskey. He sounded more like the old Jamie; he wasn't nasty. But he still didn't seem like himself. Still kind of felt like I was talking to a stranger."

Brenna tried to imagine how she would feel if Ryan were in Jamie's shoes. It was just too messed up to comprehend. "So, what are you gonna do?"

Megan dropped her head to the table, again and in a muffled voice, said, "I have no idea."

"Sorry, luv." Brenna moved to the chair next to Megan and rubbed her back in soft slow circles.

Megan sat up and looked at Brenna, tears glistening. "He said he misses me. Do ya know how much I wanted to hear that, fer so long?"

"Yeah, I know."

"Well, here's the thing. When he said it, I didn't even say it back. There was a time when a call like that would have sent me driving back to London. But I don't know who he is anymore, so I don't even know how to miss him. I miss the old Jamie, but not the guy who was living with another woman while he was engaged to me." Megan's balled fist struck her chest.

She took a ragged breath and continued, "So what does all this mean for me? I'm supposed to just accept his apology and ... what? Try to make things work with the new Jamie, trusting that there's enough of the old Jamie in there to hold us together? I mean, I may have done that if I'd known right away. But it's been almost six months! Six. Damn. Months. It's so unfair. And now, just when I'm finally starting to feel normal again, BAM, all of this comes out. I just don't understand what God wants from me."

Brenna warmed her hands on her coffee mug. "I don't know either, friend. It's crazy."

"I'm so angry." Tears rolled down her cheeks. "But I don't even know who to be mad at anymore. I've spent all this time being furious with Jamie and then with his mam, and now I can't be mad at either one."

The side of Brenna's mouth curled upward. "Well, you could safely still hate Patricia." Megan gave a tired laugh as Brenna continued, "But seriously, I just said the same thing to Ryan. I can't figure out who to be mad at for you. Do you think you're mad at God?"

She stared off for a moment. "Probably. He could have prevented all of this. Why did Jamie have to get hit in the head? Take away five seconds of his life, and I'm a married woman right now, just back from her honeymoon and talking to you about curtains or stupid bedding sets." Megan's laugh was bitter. And Brenna didn't blame her.

"Well, I'm not a theologian or anything. You know that. But I do think it's okay for you to be mad at God. He's big enough to handle it. I'm sure He wants you to be honest with him. That's one of the few things I remember our pastor telling me after Ben was killed. Because I thought the same thing. Why didn't God stop it? One minute faster on the highway and that girl would have missed him altogether. But I never got an answer. I just slowly figured out how to trust God, in spite of the crazy things that happen. I have to believe that He is good, even when things look bad."

Megan nodded. "I know. I'm sure I'll get there. I just need some time to sort through how I feel."

"What do you feel most right now? Anger?"

"Confusion."

"Okay, so let's talk through it. I think you're confused because you don't know how you're supposed to feel about Jamie, now, right?"

"Exactly. This is the man I was getting ready to spend the rest of my life with. Till death do us part, sickness and health, all that. I walked away because he cheated, but if he wasn't really himself, does it still count? Is it still okay that I left him? You're right. I have absolutely no clue how I'm supposed to feel about him."

"So, don't worry about how you're *supposed* to feel, then. Just think about how you actually feel. What do you feel when you think about him?"

Silence filled the air between them for a few moments.

"Empathy. That's all. I feel bad for him."

"Okay—"

"And guilt, too. I feel guilty because I don't think I can love him again. I can't picture going back to him and then I feel like the most horrible person on earth because I can just turn my back on him." Megan's anguished green eyes pierced Brenna's heart.

"Aw, friend. I'm so sorry. It's definitely complicated. Did Grania recommend a new therapist when she left? Maybe you should talk with someone?" Brenna heard Ben's sippy cup hit the floor again. She got up to return it to him, and added, "It also might help to write down how you're feeling. That always helps me see things more clearly."

Megan nodded. "Grania had me start a journal when I started therapy. I've been writing in it a lot. But at the moment, I don't want to hear more of my own thoughts. I'd really just like someone to tell me what to do."

"Well, I don't know what you should do. But I can tell you what my gut says. Take it for what it's worth, okay?"

Megan nodded and looked at her expectantly.

"I think you might be able to be his friend, and be supportive as he walks through this, but the man you fell in love with, the one you were going to marry, doesn't really exist anymore. From everything you've told me about him, especially the way he was when you were there, he's not Jamie. Now, if you were already married, then you would have a lot more to think about. But you're not married. I know it sounds harsh, but you don't owe him anything. Even if his actions are related to the injury, he still chose to cheat on you, Meg. He wasn't forced. The man he is *now* made that choice. Who's to say he wouldn't do it again?"

Megan's brows rose in surprise. "Whoa, I didn't even consider that."

"I know it's not pleasant to think about. But it's true, isn't it?"

"'Tis. When did you get so wise?"

"Ha, I don't think I'd go that far. It's just my opinion."

"Well, it helps. Thanks," Megan said with a weak smile as she laid her head back down on the table.

"Let's go." Brenna reached for Megan's elbow. "You're going to take a nap. Come on." She led her to the bedroom and tucked her in like a mama would her child. "Get some sleep. You'll feel better if you do."

Megan mumbled something as she turned toward the wall and covered her head with the blankets.

# Chapter Twenty-One

After sleeping away half the of the previous day at Brenna's, Megan was sure she'd wake up early Wednesday morning, even though she wasn't scheduled to work. But the sun had been up for quite a while before she opened her eyes. A quick glance at her alarm clock told her she'd slept for twelve hours, but her head still wasn't clear. Thoughts whirled constantly and handling other people's medications would definitely have been a problem, so having the day off was a blessing.

After a quick bowl of porridge, she took off toward town. She parked by the stile at Mountdonovan, grabbed her large bag from the trunk, and took the pathway to her spot. She was excited for all the proposed changes to Mountdonovan, but last weekend it hit her that she was going to lose her private little alcove. She hated the thought.

She pulled an oversized quilt from her bag and sat on it with her back against the cool stone wall. It was warm out; the first day the sun had shone in several days. She watched the sunlight filter through the canopy of trees, little dust motes floating in and out of the shafts of light.

With so much on her mind, she'd been feeling the urge to pray and ask God for help to sort through the mess. But every time she closed her eyes to pray, her thoughts scattered, and she found herself thinking about random things rather than communicating with God. So, instead of her regular journal, she'd brought along a new one that she intended to use as a prayer journal. A way to focus her thoughts into prayer rather than allowing them to drift.

She ran her fingers along the embossed edge of the butterfly design on the cover. Vibrant blue and orange wings with metallic gold veins shimmered in the sunlight. Squinting, as the light hit her eyes, she shifted to the other corner of her alcove. The sunlight still warmed her legs as she pulled her favorite pen from her bag.

*Lord,*

*I need some help with all of the thoughts crowding my head. I know I haven't been very focused when I've tried to pray lately. But I need to talk with you. To tell you what's on my mind, even though you already know. I haven't been ignoring you. Not really. I think I've just been really mad. Mad at Jamie. Mad at Elizabeth.*

*And honestly, mad at you. I've always trusted you. And I think I still do, but I don't understand why you let bad things happen to people who love you and serve you. Jamie was one of the sweetest guys I've ever met. He loved you and loved people. He went out of his way to help friends and strangers and even enemies. I never even saw him get angry at anyone. He settled me. Kept me grounded. When I wanted to fly off the handle, he calmed me down. And all that is gone. I don't even know him anymore. Why? Why is this okay with you?*

*It feels like he's dead, but he's not. How do I handle that? Sometimes, I think it would be easier if he had actually died. And then, I feel horribly guilty for thinking such a thing. God, he was a really good guy. He didn't deserve this.*

*Of course, you know he called again, yesterday. But this time he sounded angry, not weepy. He was cussing all over the place and he was blaming me and I ended up just hanging up on him. I know you don't expect me to take abuse like that. I guess that's a pretty good indicator of what I should do. The guy who called me crying on Monday might have been sorry. But the one who called yesterday was just like the one I saw in January. Cold, sneering. No one I want to spend my life with.*

She shook her hand to loosen a cramp and closed her eyes to think. When she opened them, she could see a breeze tickling the long grasses, still dotted with some buttercups.

*And then, there's David. I know how he makes me feel ... like a stupid schoolgirl with a crush. But those feelings aren't something to build a relationship on. I don't even think I want a relationship. Ugh. I'm so confused! And I'm not even sure what he's really all about. Seems to me he's pretty happy to go out with a new girl every few days, and not take any of them seriously. He's gorgeous, but he knows it. I would have thought he was just a conceited, shallow guy. But the way he looks at the pictures from Africa, there's a lot more there than he lets on, I think. And that makes me want to know more.*

*But, I'm a little fragile right now, God. If he toys with me, messes with me ... I'm not sure I could take it. I keep thinking the safest thing to do is just to keep things professional and completely platonic. And when I'm not around him, I'm confident that's what I'm going to do. But then I get within twenty feet of him and I can't think straight—*

Megan heard voices close by and getting closer. She stood and hastily swiped at her jeans; a few stray leaves floated down. She would have just stayed hidden and waited for whomever it was to pass, but she could tell they weren't just walking along the path. They were behind the building already, close to where she stood. So, she began folding up her blanket and was just stuffing it into her bag when she heard a familiar voice.

"Hey, Meg. Sorry, we didn't know you were back here in your spot." Ryan said, hands stuffed in the pockets of his jeans. Next to him stood the man she'd just been writing about, and her face heated with the irrational thought that he knew what she'd been writing. He wore khaki pants and a crisp, white, button-down shirt. His eyes sparkled as he shot her his usual, killer smile. It struck her to realize that he almost made Ryan look plain, and that was hard to do. She forced herself to look at Ryan only. It helped regulate her heartbeat.

"Hey Ry. 'Tis no problem. I was just leaving. What are you guys up to?"

"Ryan's showing me some of the plans for the renovation." David motioned toward the main house.

Ryan chimed in, "I'm picking his brain on some of the techniques used in American construction. David's actually got a good bit of construction experience."

"Really? When does a med student have time to pick up a hammer and nails?"

"High school and undergrad. My father's an architect and worked in construction. I spent five summers on a construction crew helping him. It's kind of in the blood."

She remembered all the time that David had spent in her dad's woodworking shop after their tutoring sessions. She picked up her bag and started to walk with them, back toward her car.

"That's cool. You two should have plenty to talk about then," she said. David lifted the bag from her shoulder and continued walking. Chivalry. He was definitely a charmer. She made a move to take her bag back. "I can carry that, ya know."

"I'm sure you can. So can I." He winked at her and kept walking.

Ryan caught her playfully rolling her eyes, and his mischievous smile had her wondering what he was thinking.

"So," he nudged her with his elbow, "Brenna's made a wonderful potato soup for tonight. David's coming over for dinner. Care to join us?"

*Nice try, Ry.* "Aw, thanks. I'd love to, but I already promised Aidan I'd come to his match tonight." A small thrill coursed through her when she saw disappointment cross David's face. "I'll be there for Ben's party tomorrow, though."

"Well, we'll miss you tonight. Brenna said you're coming to help her get stuff ready tomorrow afternoon?"

"Aye, have her text me if she needs me to grab anything from the market before I come."

"Will do." Ryan stopped suddenly on the path and looked around. "Dang. I think I left my bag back by the main house. Be right back."

"We'll meet you by the stile," David said and turned back toward Megan as they walked. "Ryan said that was your spot?"

"Yeah, the little covered alcove. Kind of where I come to clear my head or just get away. Been doing it since I was little," she said.

David laughed.

Megan cocked an eyebrow. "Why is that funny?"

"Because I came here all the time, when I was younger."

"You're teasing me."

"No, I'm not. You probably never saw me because we were on opposite sides of the house. My spot was up in the big tree."

"Really? That's hysterical. But I can't believe I never even saw you."

"I was stealthy." He grinned and raised his hands in a martial arts position. "Ninja training."

"Wow. A doctor, a construction guy, *and* a ninja. Impressive."

"Aye, I've lots of hidden talents." He wiggled his eyebrows. "I can juggle, too."

She laughed. "Ah, a juggler. That explains why the ladies get all fluttery around you."

He set her bag down, and she leaned against her car. "Fluttery, huh? But you don't get fluttery."

"Me? No, I'm not the fluttery type." *Liar.* "Now, if ya could do balloon animals—well then, that might be a different story."

"Hmmm, I'll have to work on it," he said quietly and stepped closer to her, his hand reaching toward her hair as he leaned in. *What is he doing? He wouldn't kiss me, would he?* She couldn't think with his gorgeous mouth so close. And then he pulled his hand away with a couple of leaves that had apparently stowed away in her ponytail. Lovely.

"Thanks." She ran her fingers over her hair to make sure all the leaves were gone and she could feel the pink climbing her cheeks. Thank God he had no idea what she'd been thinking. Just then, Ryan jogged up, giving her a moment to recover from the fact that she had totally thought David was about to kiss her. He wasn't, of course. That would have been crazy. They hadn't even gone on their date yet. *Their date.* The thought of a whole evening alone with him suddenly had her feeling dizzy. "Well, I'd better go. Aidan's match starts soon. See ya."

She slipped into her car, and they waved, walking off toward the other entrance to the property. She watched them walk away and sat there for a few more minutes, letting her heartbeat return to its normal pace. Why did she always need recovery time after being around the man? It was very inconvenient.

⌒⟋✦

*What the heck?* David leaned back on Ryan and Brenna's couch and rubbed his hands over his eyes. He had almost kissed her! He was used to being very in control of himself around women. *He* set the pace. *He* decided who he was interested in and who he wasn't. Usually. But Megan had him constantly off balance and she didn't even seem to know it. Of course, that was because he was a good actor. Even if he was rattled, it was rare that anyone knew it. It was part of what made him a good doctor. Nothing appeared to shake him. But somehow, Megan did shake him.

Was it because she was his first crush? Maybe it all went back to that. Maybe her rejection, all those years ago, had impacted him more than he'd admitted even to himself. That was the best explanation he could come up with. He didn't like feeling off balance. And yet, he was drawn to her. Moth to flame.

Today, she'd been playful and funny, but she'd seemed sad, too. He found himself wanting to know why. What was going on in her world that had her spending her day curled up in the shadow of a ruined building? Brenna would know. Maybe he would try to glean a little information from her.

He could see Brenna from where he sat. She was in the kitchen, stirring her soup; Ryan had gone upstairs, at her request, to give the baby a quick bath since he'd gotten ahold of some sticky substance and was covered in red blanket lint. This left David sitting by himself in the living room with too much time to think about Megan, whose face was looking up at him from a picture frame on the side table. The telly was on, but he couldn't focus on his favorite sports show. Not with her green eyes staring up at him.

He wandered into the kitchen. "Might I be of any use?"

"Um, sure. You could cut the bread for me. It's over there." Brenna pointed to the end of the counter. "Cutting board and bread knife are in the drawer right below. Thanks."

"My pleasure." The smell of crisp bacon had his stomach grumbling.

Brenna yelled up the stairs, "Babe, dinner will be ready in about fifteen. You guys be done by then?"

Ryan's voice floated down. "Aye. He's one sticky boy. We'll be done, though."

She turned her attention to the bacon, setting it onto a paper-towel covered plate. "I can't believe he's turning one tomorrow. People say it goes fast. They're so right."

"He seems like a really good baby."

"He is. I'm definitely spoiled." She grabbed a spoon from the drawer to test the soup. "Hmm ... more pepper, I think." She grabbed a second spoon and offered a sample. "What do you think?"

It tasted perfect to him and he told her so, and then laughed when she added more pepper, anyway.

"So, what kind of birthday party do ya throw for a one-year-old?"

"Well, I'm not one for big, fancy, *Pinterest* parties. I'm impressed with people who can pull those things off, but I'm not one of them. I'm more about the company than the party favors. So, I think we'll just have some pizza and cake, visit with friends and family, take pictures of him covered in chocolate frosting and that should do it. You're coming, right?"

"I am. 'Tis my first one-year-old birthday party invite. Wouldn't miss it."

"Hmmm, I think it's my first one-year-old birthday party, too." She laughed. "So, Ryan says you've got some good ideas for Mountdonovan."

He shrugged. "I hope so. I worked with my father on a similar project in South Carolina. 'Twas an old estate that had been commandeered by the Confederate Army, eventually burned down and had been left as a shell for years. At some point, a descendant of the original owners claimed it but couldn't afford to restore it. Eventually, the state acquired the property and wanted to turn it into a museum and educational complex. It turned out really well. Mountdonovan has even more potential. 'Tis a fine property."

"It's beautiful. I'm excited they're going to fix it up. Have you joined the TidyTowns committee?"

*Perfect segue. Thank you.* "No, I've just helped out on volunteer days. I've seen Megan there a couple times. Is she a member?"

Brenna smiled. "No, her mom is the chairman so Megan just helps out, sometimes. She's got a great eye for landscaping, and she's very good with plants and flowers. My entire flower garden would be dead if it weren't for her."

"First time I ever saw her, she was picking flowers at the Mountdonovan place," David said, absently, as he finished slicing the bread.

Brenna raised her eyebrows as she handed him a breadbasket. "Really? When was that?"

"Ah, we were young. She was probably nine or ten?" He adjusted his hold on the bread to avoid slicing his fingertips as he neared the end of the loaf. "And Ryan and I just ran into her there, this afternoon."

"She likes it there. Calls it her 'thinking spot.' She's gonna have to find another place to think, I guess." She pulled bowls from the cupboard and set them on placemats.

He nodded. "I used to go there when I was a lad, climb the big tree, and think or read. There's just something about the place that makes ya relax."

"That's what she says, too. That it's peaceful."

"'Tis." He set the basket on the table. "She seemed a little sad today, though."

He was showing too much interest, he knew. But it seemed that even when she wasn't around, she had him doing things he didn't intend. Brenna studied him as she stirred the soup again.

"She's going through a lot," she said, then hesitated, like she was weighing how much she could tell him.

His dad had always said, "First one to speak, loses." So, he kept his mouth shut, hoping she'd offer a little more information. He scraped the crumbs from the cutting board and took it to the sink to wash it.

She motioned for him to sit. "You've probably heard that she was supposed to get married last month?"

He nodded. "I heard. One of the O'Connors? I don't know them but I remember some younger boys with that name in school."

"Yep. Jamie. He was one of the first people I met when I moved here. Actually, I thought Megan hated me that night when we met."

"When you met Jamie or Megan?"

"Both. We were at a street festival, and Tara had asked Jamie to teach me how to dance. I saw Megan watching us and could tell that she was not happy. They weren't dating yet, but I think Jamie was the only one in town who was unaware of her feelings for him. I guess my presence was enough to push her to tell him how she felt, and she made it clear that she wanted me to stay away from him."

"Sounds like an odd beginning to a friendship."

She smiled. "She definitely didn't see me as a friend at that point. But she apologized later and then she stood by me through a really rough time. She's the best girlfriend I've ever had."

"And now you've been there for her."

Brenna nodded as she pulled the rinsed cutting board back out of the sink and began chopping up the bacon. "She's had a crappy year. What have you heard?"

He hesitated. "You don't really want to know, do you?"

She studied him, again. "You don't have to tell me. But I am curious about what people are saying. Most people know that she's my best friend, so they don't repeat the gossip in front of me."

David sighed. "Well, the most vocal one has been Patricia, so I'm sure you can imagine."

Brenna's eyes narrowed. "You know she's one of my least favorite people. Ever. Right?"

"I do. And that's why I'm not sure I should tell ya while you're holding a knife."

She grinned and pointed the knife in his direction. "You're a smart man. But I promise to do no harm."

He blew out an exaggerated breath. "Well, among other things, she said that Megan was cheating on Jamie, with at least one guy, possibly two. And that he was so devastated, he called off the wedding and wouldn't even come home to see his parents."

Brenna set the knife down on the counter and turned to face him. "Do you know which part of that is crap?"

"I'm guessing all of it?"

"Like I said, smart man. The truth is *he* was cheating on *her,* and *she* broke it off. But he lied so convincingly to his mom that most of the town believed his version over Megan's."

"Doesn't sound fair."

"No, but if you knew Jamie, you might understand it better. Everyone loves Jamie. He's one of the nicest guys you'd ever meet, or he used to be. So, I understand why it was hard for people to wrap their minds around it." She slid the bacon pieces into a small glass bowl and set them on the table. "But Megan is just as sweet as Jamie, so it's pretty rotten that they wouldn't give her the same benefit of the doubt that they gave him. I would have thought that the fact that he won't come back here would have been a big red flag to everyone that he's lying, though."

"Sometimes people choose not to believe the truth, even when it's right in front of them." David's thoughts went back five years to a tiny flat in Dublin. When he'd walked in on Katie with her ex, he'd hardly believed it, and he'd seen it with his own eyes. When she'd tried to calm him down, he wanted to believe that there was some explanation. But there wasn't anything that could explain away what she did. Still, he knew they had mutual friends who'd believed her version of the events over his.

"I know. Even some of our family members have made nasty comments about Megan. It's been crazy."

"So, why is she so sad, now? It's been a while, right? Is she still in love with him?" David tried to keep his tone detached, clinical, as if he were discussing a medical case. In reality, the thought of Megan still being in love with her ex had him clenching his fists and breathing deeply to slow his heart rate.

Brenna held up one finger. "Hold on." She turned off the burner and poured the soup into a serving bowl, then covered it with a lid. She excused herself and yelled up the stairs again, "Almost done?"

"Aye, just gettin' him dressed. Two minutes," Ryan yelled back.

She turned back toward David and sighed. "I don't know how much I should tell you, because it's her business, but I'll just say that things got way more complicated this week. She's just trying to figure some things out."

Maybe Megan would tell him what was happening when they went out next week. "Did she tell you I asked her out?"

A smile lit Brenna's face. "She did. Next Friday?"

He nodded. "Do you think she'll cancel because of whatever she's going through?"

"Not if I have anything to say about it. She needs to go out and do something fun." Brenna rinsed and dried her hands. "I don't think she'll cancel."

"Well, I'll have to think of something fun to take her mind off her troubles. Let me know if ya have any ideas."

Ryan came in with Ben. "Sorry that took so long. Kid's got a lot of rolls, and he's after having red lint in every one of them."

Brenna walked toward Ryan and leaned in to kiss Ben on the head, inhaling as she pulled away. "Mmmm, clean baby smell. I love it. Thanks, babe. Can you put him in his chair?"

Dinner banter was entertaining. David didn't hang out with too many married couples, but he found that he was more relaxed in the Kellys' kitchen than he was in his own. There was something about the way Brenna and Ryan were with each other that just seemed true and real. It was refreshing. He got the feeling that they would have the exact same lively conversation, even if he weren't there. It wasn't an act.

It was a sharp contrast to what he'd seen in his own home, growing up. His parents would talk and laugh when company came. But when no one was around, they were more like business partners, which is probably why their marriage dissolved as soon as his little sister went to college. Partnership no longer effective. Split the assets and move on. He couldn't imagine Brenna and Ryan ever getting to that point. It ignited the smallest flicker of hope that maybe he wouldn't repeat his parents' mistakes. Maybe, if he ever got married, it could look more like the Kellys than the O'Briens.

# Chapter Twenty-Two

Megan spent Friday afternoon helping Brenna clean her house. Not that it was particularly messy, but she understood the desire to have the bathrooms sparkling and the cereal vacuumed out of the rug before a large group of people descended upon your home.

When the sinks were shining and the floors were free of debris, Megan sat down for a break while Brenna put Ben down for a late nap. The teapot was already on the table and piping hot. She poured a cup and pulled the markers and poster board closer. She was supposed to make a birthday sign. But as she sketched out the basic bubble letters, her mind wandered. Just under two years ago, it would have been hard to believe that this special day would arrive.

She could see herself sitting on Brenna's bed at the B&B, Brenna surrounded by tissues with tear tracks through her mascara. She was a wreck and rightly so. She had fallen for Ryan, who had rejected her for no obvious reason, driving her right into the arms of Luke Dillon, town heartbreaker. But Ryan realized his mistake in a few short days and came back to town, sweeping Brenna off her feet, admitting that he loved her. It was like a storybook romance. Until that day when, sitting there on her bed, she told Megan she was pregnant—with Luke's baby.

Megan had already suspected and was horrified to be right. And then, Brenna told her the plan. She would break up with Ryan and move back to

America, and he would never have to know. It was a stupid plan, and obviously God had other plans that Brenna couldn't see. Because He took that messed-up situation and made something beautiful out of it.

Luke signed away his rights to the baby, and Ryan took Ben as his own. And God used what looked like the worst possible thing to create an amazing new life for Brenna. And Ryan. And Ben. It was close to a miracle. And thinking about it made Megan wonder if God would take her mess and make something beautiful, too.

She couldn't see how. Couldn't picture a scenario that would make things better. But then, she couldn't think of one that day sitting on Brenna's bed, either. And she didn't have to. Brenna decided that instead of running, she would trust God to work things out, and He did. Could Megan do the same, now? Just trust that no matter what, He would work things out?

Brenna's phone vibrated on the table, snapping Megan back to the present. She glanced at the caller I.D. and dropped her teacup onto the saucer. *Luke Dillon?* No freaking way. Her spine tingled. What were the odds that he would call just as she'd been thinking about all that had happened between him, Brenna, and Ryan? Adrenaline surged. No way he was going to do anything to ruin this day. Without another thought, she snatched the phone and answered.

"Luke? It's Megan. What are you doin' calling Brenna? Are ya crazy?"

A pause. "Well, hello to you, too, Megan. Been a while. Yep, I'm doing better. Thanks for asking."

She let out a breath, looked toward the stairs and took the phone outside. "Sorry. I wasn't trying to be rude. I didn't want Brenna to see her phone and get upset. I didn't think you two had talked since ... well, since you signed the papers when you were in jail."

"We haven't. I thought maybe enough time had gone by that I could call."

Megan shook her head, even though he couldn't see her. "Bad idea, Luke. Ryan will freak! Why do ya need to talk to her, anyway?"

Another pause. Longer this time. "Cuz I ... I know he turned one yesterday. I didn't call right on the day. I didn't want to interrupt anything. But ..."

"Jesus, Mary, and Joseph, are ya out of yer mind? Ben is Ryan's son now. Practically speaking, he always has been. You signed the papers, Luke. You can't be coming back trying to be a daddy."

"I'm not. I know I don't deserve that. But sittin' in a jail cell for months gives a guy lots of time to think. I don't have a right to be a father to him, but does that mean I can never see him? Never have any part in his life?" She could hear real emotion in his voice, and it stunned her.

She sat down on a large garden rock to keep from falling over. "Luke, I don't even know what to say. I think it does mean that. Donating the sperm doesn't make you a father. You know that. You don't have any place in their life. It would be incredibly selfish of you to try and make one." She couldn't believe she was having this conversation. "It's not all about you, Luke. It's about that little boy, and he has a da. A great one. If you ever cared about Brenna, you will leave her and her family alone."

Silence again. "Well, don't tiptoe around it, Megan. No need to use kid gloves." That was the cocky, sarcastic Luke she remembered.

"Are ya back in town?" The thought horrified her.

"No, I'm still in Dublin."

"Good. Listen, I gotta go. I don't mean to be harsh, Luke. But ya have to use your head, here. Please don't call her again, okay?"

"It was nice talkin' to ya, Meg. Just like old times. See you around." Click.

Megan's hands shook, and a chill snaked down her back. Now what? Did she delete the call and keep it quiet? Did she tell Brenna? Certainly not before the party. In about ten minutes, Ryan would be home and twenty minutes after that, the house would be full of family and friends. No way she was gonna bring it up now. But she would have to tell her. It wasn't the kind of thing she could keep from her. She deleted the call and headed back inside, hoping she could keep her mouth shut for the whole night. *Lord help me.*

David didn't know exactly what to bring to a baby's birthday party. Thankfully, he had plenty of help picking out a present. He'd gone to Nora's Boutique on Main Street and no less than four elderly ladies took turns suggesting different gift options, two of them adding a pinch on the bum.

In the end, he went with Nora's suggestion of a stuffed monkey. Hard to go wrong with a stuffed animal. She had wrapped it and done a bag up with festive ribbons. He also wanted to bring a gift for the hostess, but that was easier. One of the few things he'd brought with him from Dublin was a nice wine collection. He chose a mild red that he thought Brenna would like and didn't bother with ribbons or bows.

As he pulled up the long drive, he noticed cars parked at odd angles along the lawn. There didn't appear to be a system, so he found an empty spot on the grass and walked the pathway through the fragrant flower garden. Before he even reached the door, he could hear the clamor of many voices packed into a small space. He blew out a breath and knocked. He didn't love crowds, but he could act like he did.

A stunning, dark-haired woman answered the door with a gorgeous smile. "Well, hello there. You must be the handsome new doctor I've heard so much about." The petite woman wove her arm through his and relieved him of his gifts in one fluid move. Resting her free hand on his arm, she ushered him toward the living room. "I'm Darcy, Ryan's sister, by the way."

He smiled, "Pleased to meet you, Darcy. I'm David."

Her laugh was loud but had a lilting quality. "Oh, I know. I've already had a lengthy conversation about you, and I've only been here twenty minutes."

"All good things, I trust?"

"Of course, all good things." She patted his arm and led him toward a slightly balding, dark-haired man who was standing in the corner, absorbed in his smartphone.

"Goodness, gracious, Pete. Could ya put that thing down for just a few minutes?" He looked up with a grin. "David, this is my husband, Pete.

Pete, David is the new doctor in Millway. Apparently, the ladies are fawning all over him."

She was a trip. He'd thought Ryan was outgoing. But he was a wallflower compared to Darcy. Pete held out his hand, and David shook it. Strong and calloused. With that and his short, muscular build, David pegged him as a construction guy.

The next few minutes consisted of Darcy escorting him around the living room, introducing him to various friends and family. He met Ryan's parents, Mary Catherine and Ryan, Senior, an Auntie Pat, a Bettie, Ryan's friend Danny from Limerick, and Anna was there, of course. He met Darcy's kids. A shy seven-year-old named Trevor, and a cherub-faced, five-year-old with a riot of chestnut curls. She introduced herself as Erin Elizabeth Kenny and shook his hand with a grip that rivaled her father's. But everything else about the lass was Darcy. He didn't envy Pete. In about ten years, this one would probably have him tearing whatever was left of his hair out.

Little Erin grabbed his free hand as they continued the rounds. He casually scanned the rooms but saw no sign of Megan. Before long, Brenna came up, playfully smacking Darcy in the arm. "Good grief, woman. You're going to scare him back to Dublin. Let the poor man breathe a bit before you introduce him to anyone else."

Darcy laughed. "Ah, yes. I forget how taxing a party can be for you shy types." She tapped Brenna's nose at the word 'shy' and turned toward David with a bright grin. "I haven't scared ya in the least, have I, Doctor?"

He matched her grin. "What man would complain about being escorted around a party by a gorgeous woman and her stunning daughter?"

"Hmmm, you're right, Brenna. He's as smooth as he is gorgeous." Using every bit of her four-inch heeled boots, she reached up, kissed his cheek and flounced off toward the kitchen.

He noticed Brenna's cheeks color at Darcy's comment, so he looked elsewhere for a moment, then said, "Full house, eh?"

"It is. Darcy's personality takes up a whole room though, so it seems like there are more people than there are."

They both laughed. "I like her," he said.

"Everyone likes her." Brenna said with a glance toward the kitchen. "She doesn't accept anything less."

"She and Pete live in Limerick?"

"Yeah, for now. But Ryan's parents have been talking about moving back here. If they do, Darcy and Pete probably will, too."

"That's a good thing?"

Brenna nodded. "I'd love to have Darcy around more. She's great. Plus, she absorbs all the spotlight so I can just flitter around in the background and do whatever needs doing. Speaking of, I need to go to the garage for more pop—or, ya know, minerals." She patted his arm and headed for the door, saying over her shoulder, "Ryan's in the kitchen."

Part of David had wanted to ask where Megan was, but he resisted. He needed to slow it down. He'd grown irritated, as he'd found himself thinking about her all day at work. The last time he'd thought about a woman constantly had been when he'd met Katie. And thinking of *her* did not take him to a happy place. He thought a good goal would be to not think of Megan at all until they went out next Friday.

He knew it wouldn't happen.

Ryan was taking a second pizza out of the oven as David wandered in. The pleasing aroma of bread, sauce, and cheese washed over him. He hadn't had homemade pizza in a long time. "Now that's my idea of party food," he said, rubbing his stomach.

Ryan glanced over. "Hey, I guess you've met the family by now?"

"Aye, I think I've met the entire guest list."

Ryan nodded. "Just about. Megan and Tara went to go pick up their friend Shannon from the train station. You've met Tara, haven't you?"

"She's the bartender at Rosie's?"

"She is. And Shannon, who's coming on the train, is going to be working in your office, come Monday."

"Ah, the new nurse. I've heard about her coming but wasn't here yet when she interviewed."

"Well, you'll meet her in about—" Ryan glanced at the digital clock on the stove, "I'm thinking about five minutes."

Just then, Megan and Tara walked through the kitchen door with a tall, familiar-looking woman, whose black hair fell in curls down to her elbows. Brenna came in from the opposite direction carrying two six-packs, and a round of hugs and kisses began as a mini-reunion took place. David stood there feeling awkward. He didn't want to leave to go back into the living room, but he felt like he was intruding. Brenna suddenly realized introductions were needed.

"Sorry, David. I should have introduced you right away. This is Shannon Maguire. She'll be starting in your office on Monday."

"Aye, I've heard. Pleasure to meet you, Shannon." He shook her hand and tried not to look at Megan, who was standing just outside his peripheral vision. "Have we met?"

Shannon's cheeks flushed. "Um, yes. Last year in Dublin. Christmas party at Doctor Murphy's?"

"Oh, right. Nice to see you again." *Crap.* Now he remembered. He'd gone on a date with her and never called her again. And now she was going to be working in the same office. Brilliant. He would have to apologize later.

The ladies took off in herd-like formation, toward the living room. Megan hadn't even said hello. He wondered, for the one-hundredth time, what had happened this week to upset her. Whatever. He didn't need to know since he wasn't going to think about her until Friday, anyway.

⌖

Brenna introduced Shannon to the few people she didn't already know. Within minutes, Tara and Shannon were in the corner, heads together, discussing some juicy gossip, she guessed. She glanced around wondering where Megan had gotten to. She was about to try texting her when she saw her going up the stairs on Bettie and Anna's heels. That was weird.

She wondered if she should go rescue Megan, but at that moment, her mother-in-law came up from the side and put an arm around her. "Lovely party, dear. The pizza was delicious."

"Thanks, Mam." Mary Catherine had insisted Brenna call her Mam from the day she and Ryan had gotten engaged. "It's one of the traditions that I remember with my parents. Pizza and pop at every one of my birth-day parties." Brenna's parents had died in a plane crash when she was just ten. So, holding on to the few traditions she could remember was extreme-ly important to her.

"Well, I'm glad for it. I love it. I keep meaning to get the dough recipe from ya."

Brenna laughed, "I'll write it down for you. It's the only dough I can ac-tually make, so it should be a snap for you."

With over twenty people in the house, there was no table large enough for all. So, pizza had been a find-a-seat-where-you-can kind of meal. And Brenna's stomach rumbled as she realized she had not eaten a thing since lunch.

"Honey, I heard that. Did ya get some pizza?" Mary Catherine asked.

"No, but I'm fine. I'll eat once we finish the cake." She had trouble eat-ing when she hosted a party. She was always a little nervous about every-thing going smoothly. So, she usually ended up stuffing herself once everyone went home. Ryan knew her pattern, and she was confident he'd stashed some food for her in the fridge. "Want to help me round everyone up to sing happy birthday?"

"Of course," she said.

"Great. I think the kitchen will work best. We can squeeze. If you round up this crew, I'll grab some who went upstairs?"

Mary Catherine nodded and set about her task while Brenna headed upstairs. She could hear voices coming from the guest room, so she knocked softly and opened the door. Megan and Bettie were in the middle of the room, hugging each other. Each with tear tracks on her face, and Anna stood on the other side of them, beaming. Relief flooded Brenna as she realized what must have happened. Elizabeth must have told Bettie that Megan was telling the truth all along. Megan glanced toward Brenna with an odd sheepish look.

"Can I join in?" Brenna said as she rushed over for a group hug. Anna joined them, laughter bubbling up from the group.

Bettie turned toward Brenna. "I owe you an apology as well, luv. I'm sorry. I didn't know, but I should have listened to you. Instead, I made it uncomfortable for the whole family."

Brenna kissed Bettie on the cheek. "All is forgiven. I can't tell you what a relief this is. Sunday can go back to being my favorite day of the week."

By the time they got back downstairs, Ryan had Ben in his chair and the cake set on the table, one large candle in the center. Bettie had made the cake, of course, because her cakes were better than anything Brenna could buy and certainly better than what Brenna could make.

Within moments of the birthday song, her chubby little guy had chocolate smeared on his nose and both cheeks, and a good bit of it laced in his dark curls. And as soon as he realized there was nothing left on his tray and he wasn't getting more, he began to cry while tapping his fingers together, sign language for "more."

Brenna laughed a little as she tried to wipe his moving hands enough that she could pull him from the chair.

"Well, it is past his bed time," she said.

Anna swooped in with a warm cloth and cleaned him up quickly, while Brenna removed the tray and stashed it in the sink. She'd deal with the mess later. As soon as he was released and in Anna's arms, Ben reached toward Brenna. Tears still clung to his long lashes as he said, "Mamama-mama" and buried his face in her neck when she held him. His soft little hand rested on her cheek and she melted.

There was no feeling in the world like the one she got when her little boy reached for her and only her. He was good about going to most anyone. But at the end of the day, only she was Mama. It was her daily miracle.

She had intended to have one of the grandmas give him a bath and put him to bed, so she could visit with friends and family. But she realized that was not going to fly tonight, and she was secretly happy he wouldn't go to anyone else at the moment. Because there was truly no other way she wanted to end his first birthday than rocking him to sleep herself.

Ryan would take care of the guests, and she would just be Mama tonight.

Megan hadn't tried to ignore David; she had just been extremely distracted. The fact that Luke had called had her avoiding eye contact with Brenna and Ryan all night long, so she wouldn't blurt it out. And since David had mostly been with Ryan or Brenna the whole evening, she'd avoided him without trying.

And now, as her hands moved through the hot, soapy water in the sink, she could feel him studying her from across the room. He was talking with Ryan, but she had glanced over a couple times and each time, he quickly looked away and back at Ryan.

She wouldn't exactly be able to explain her behavior, but she wasn't even sure he'd noticed. Still, as she worked on the last of the dishes, she wondered if he would bail on their date. She wasn't exactly giving him encouraging signals.

The hollow feeling in her stomach at the thought of him canceling had her realizing how much she'd been looking forward to going out with him. Even with all the craziness her week had brought, she still wanted to hang out with him. When it came down to it, whether anything came of it or not, lately she always felt better after she was around him. She had fun, and he made her laugh. There hadn't been much laughter in her life over the last six months.

Maybe it was because he was new in town and hadn't been around for all the drama, so he was untainted by it. She wiped down the counter, grabbed a towel to start drying the dishes, and had an "aha moment." David was like a breath of fresh air because when she was around him, she completely forgot about Jamie and all the tangled emotions that went with him.

"Can I dry?" He was suddenly standing close and as always, her heart answered with a rhythmic thud.

She started to say that she was done washing and didn't need help, but just then Anna dropped another stack of dirties into the suds. "This is the last of it," she said with a smile. "Now, I'm off to collect the empties." She breezed back out of the kitchen and Megan turned back toward David.

She handed him the towel. "That would be great, thanks."

His smile was tentative. It wasn't his, *Look at me, I'm Doctor Dazzle* smile. It was almost shy. And oddly, it relaxed her.

She added a little more hot water and plunged her hands back under the suds. "So, ya had Brenna's potato soup last night. Amazing, right?"

"It was delicious. I think I'll have to finagle another dinner invite very soon." Same shy smile and as he looked back down toward his task, she noticed his thick blond and copper lashes.

They washed and dried in silence for a minute. She wasn't sure she'd ever seen him so quiet. It dawned on her that he might actually be hurt that she hadn't spoken to him all night.

"Hey, I'm sorry I didn't say hi, earlier. It wasn't intentional. I was really distracted by some stuff."

His shoulders visibly relaxed, he looked at her sideways and said, softly, "Good. You had me a little worried. Wondered if I had upset you, somehow."

She shook her head. "No! You didn't do anything. I'm sorry I worried you." The revelation that he cared surprised her. Because he was so cool and confident all the time, she had assumed he wouldn't be upset by whether or not she spoke to him.

He smiled again, still on the shy side but definitely wider than before. She had the strongest urge to dry her hands on his towel and wrap her arms around him. *Geez, Megan. Control yourself!* She suddenly wondered if he could feel what she did. Like there was a current running between them. She was afraid to look at him, sure that he'd read her thoughts or sense her racing pulse. So, instead, she turned around and searched the room for any dishes Anna may have overlooked. But Anna was too efficient.

She headed toward the door that led from the kitchen onto a side porch, saying over her shoulder, "I'll be right back. Just gonna check outside for stray dishes."

The minute she was outside, she blew out a breath and fanned her face. Was this what hot flashes felt like? Her mother had been complaining for months about them. Maybe she should have been a little more sympathetic.

Her cell phone vibrated in her pocket, and she dug it out, but not before the call went to voicemail. She looked at the caller I.D., and the stress of the week dropped back on her like a cold, wet blanket. It was Jamie. Sure, *now* her phone decided to tell her who was calling. She stuffed the phone in her pocket and headed back inside to visit with David a little while longer. Because now she knew that was the quickest way to take her mind off all of the madness.

# Chapter Twenty-Three

Megan hadn't bothered to knock on Brenna's door. She had just gotten her hands right into the dirt, as therapy. She'd been weeding Brenna's flower garden pretty regularly, but she still managed to find some undesirables to toss. She hadn't slept well because she didn't want to talk to Brenna about Luke, but she knew she had to. She had waited around till everyone else had left the party, the night before, but Brenna had never emerged from Ben's room. So she had to think about it all night long, and she was over it. Which is why she was in Brenna's garden before Brenna had probably even opened her eyes.

Megan worked at a leisurely pace. The garden was large, taking up much of the front lawn, and as she worked the final corner under the kitchen window she could hear signs of life inside. The faucet running—for tea, she hoped. The happy, squealy sounds of a bubbly one-year-old boy. And then, the surprising sound of raised voices.

She had never heard Ryan and Brenna argue. And now she felt trapped. If she made her presence known, she'd interrupt them and most likely, Ryan would head out, leaving their argument unresolved. She didn't want that. But, if she stayed where she was, she was a complete eavesdropper. She didn't want that, either.

She glanced toward her car. If she stayed low, she might be able to make it and pull out before they noticed her. But it wasn't likely. One of the kitchen windows faced out on the driveway. And if they hadn't noticed her car yet, they would soon. She crawled to the outer edge of the garden and continued weeding, pretending she hadn't heard anything.

Within ten minutes, she heard the kitchen door slam and saw Ryan walking toward his truck. When he saw her car, he looked toward the garden and waved quickly without saying a word. He took off, gravel spraying as he barreled out of the drive.

The only time she'd ever seen Ryan that upset was when Luke was around. But there was no way he could have found out about the call. She had erased it. Unless ... unless Luke had called again. What an eejit! She went from concerned to instantly angry. She had told him not to call again. What was he thinking?

Dusting off her jeans, she marched toward the porch and into the kitchen. Ben was crawling around his playroom, babbling to himself. Brenna was seated at the table, head on her arms. She glanced up sharply and then laid her head back down when she saw Megan.

"Hey, are you okay?" Megan washed her hands at the kitchen sink.

"No. I'm so ticked right now."

"I can't believe he called back," Megan said.

Brenna looked up, puzzled. "Ryan called? When?"

Megan's stomach flipped. *Crap.* It wasn't about Luke. "Oh, wait. No, I'm confused." Megan sat at the table. "What happened?"

Thankfully, Brenna was upset enough that she could be pulled off track. "I'm just tired of it. He's in Limerick all the time. More than he's home. He was supposed to be gone Monday through Friday this week. But he gets up today and tells me he has to go early. It's Saturday! I had planned a picnic for today with Anna. And then we were supposed to have Father Tim over for dinner tonight. And this isn't the first time, either. I'm so over it."

"Must be really frustrating. Why did he have to leave so suddenly?"

Brenna sighed. "Apparently, there's another buyer who may be interested in his company, but he's only in Limerick for the day."

"Well, a buyer is a good thing, right?"

Brenna leveled an irritated glance her way. "It seems like there's always another buyer and none of them pan out. I'm not sure he'll ever sell his business, and in the meantime, I feel like a single mom, half the time."

"Did ya tell him you feel like a single mom?"

"Yeah."

Megan winced. "I'm guessing he didn't like that too much?" Ryan was the most involved dad she knew. He couldn't do much when he was away, but when it came to Ben, he did everything Brenna asked and more.

"No, he didn't. He said something about not knowing any single moms who didn't have to worry about how to pay their bills, blah, blah, blah. That's not what I meant, and he knows it. I wasn't talking about actually being a single mom. I just meant that when I have Ben, by myself, all day and night for a week at a time, it's tiring. So, when I'm expecting him to be here and then he suddenly has to take off to Limerick again, it ticks me off."

"Sure. That's understandable. I bet he doesn't like it either."

Brenna narrowed her eyes. "Don't take his side, Megan."

Megan waved her hands and shook her head. "Nope, not taking sides at all. I don't think you guys are on different sides, anyway. I think there's a lot of built up frustration, probably for both of you. And it just gets to a boiling point, sometimes. But Bren, you're a fair person. You have to see that he doesn't like leaving, anymore than you like to see him go, right?"

"I don't know." Brenna picked at her sweatshirt where a frayed edge had started to come apart. "He seems to be plenty happy enough in all the stupid Facebook pictures. It's not like he's going and sitting in a little office, Meg. He's going to lunch, golfing, taking clients to dinner. I wouldn't feel too sorry for him."

"Brenna Kelly, that man lights up when he's around you and Ben, and you know that's where he most wants to be. I love you, but I think you're being unfair to him. It's not like he's out there having an affair. He's doing all that stuff so he can be here with you for the long run. Whenever I get upset with my mam or someone, you always tell me to try and look at things from their perspective, right?"

Brenna rolled her eyes and got up to check on Ben, who had pulled himself into a standing position at the gate and was beaming with his accomplishment. She knelt down in front of him. "Good job, big boy! You are sooo big!" He beamed more and she kissed his chubby cheek and then returned to her seat. "I know he's doing it for us. I *know* that. But I don't have to like the process, you know? I don't have to jump up and down with excitement when he keeps leaving."

"I seriously doubt he's expecting that. I'm sure he could be more understanding of how you're feeling. But that goes both ways, darlin'."

Brenna nodded, went to the cupboard, and came back with some of Bettie's shortbread in a tightly sealed container. She sighed as she set it on the table. "I wasn't very nice. I guess I'd better call him. Enjoy." She motioned toward the shortbread. "But don't eat it all. I'll be back."

Brenna's absence gave Megan a few minutes to grapple with how she was supposed to bring up Luke now. Brenna was already in a bad mood. And now she was going to find out Luke called? Megan's stomach started roiling again at the thought. She nibbled on some shortbread, hoping it would soothe her stomach.

Several minutes later, Brenna came back with a smile on her face. "All better. Thanks for kicking my butt a little."

"That's what friends are for. I'd expect the same from you."

"Okay," Brenna said with a triumphant look as she settled back into her chair, "then how did things go with David, last night? Didn't even look like you talked to him once. Just because things are confusing with Jamie, doesn't mean you need to ignore David."

"Touché. But I didn't ignore him. After you went upstairs, we had a very nice talk. He helped me with the dishes." At just the thought of standing next to the sink with him, her face heated.

"Oh, good. Well, I'm glad, because I had a lecture all prepared for you. Guess I'll save it for the next time." Brenna grinned.

She considered keeping Brenna in the dark, because admitting how David made her feel somehow made it more real. But she realized she might need to butter her up a bit before admitting she took the call from Luke and then erased the evidence. So it was time to let her in.

"I gotta be honest, Bren. The guy gets to me."

Brenna crooked an eyebrow. "In a bad way or a good way?"

"Oh, in a very good way."

Brenna's eyes lit up and she grabbed Megan's arm. "Really? Geez, I was starting to think there was something wrong with you. Who could ignore attention from a guy like that?"

"Trust me, I haven't been ignoring it. I've just been acting like he didn't affect me. But, wow, I've never felt anything like what I feel around him. It's kinda scary."

"Oh my gosh, you're a better actress than I thought."

Megan bit her lip. "I've been trying to convince myself that he didn't get to me. I don't want to be interested in anyone right now. I want to stand on my own. Be independent. Figure out what I want to do for a living. A guy will complicate all those things. But I can't stop thinking about him."

"He asks about you all the time."

"He does?" Megan felt a flutter in her stomach.

"Yep. Tries to act all casual, like he doesn't really care. But I can tell he likes you."

"Well, that's just the thing. I think he likes lots of girls. Every time I see him he's with a different woman. He's a total flirt, and I sooo didn't want to be one of the silly girls crushing on him. But I can't help myself." She rested her chin on her palm. "I'm sunk."

Brenna laughed and clapped her hands. "Yay, I've been hoping that you'd be sunk. He's a great guy, Meg. I think he shows Ryan and me a different side of himself. Like he's really relaxed here, and we get to see the real David. The way he is out in public, it's like that's a character he plays. Playboy, smooth, cocky. But the real guy is kinda quiet, really funny, and deeper than he seems at first glance."

Megan blew out a breath, causing her fringe to stir. "I hope you're right. I'm not sure what I think of that cocky, playboy guy. But the few times we've talked, I feel like I've seen the real David, too. And that's the one that I want to get to know more. You really think he likes me?"

"I think so. Hasn't he given you any indication? I mean, he asked you out; that has to say something."

"Yes, but I already told you, he goes out with lots of women. So, that doesn't say much. But ..." Megan's mind flashed to the day at Mountdonovan when she'd been sure he was about to kiss her.

"But what?"

"I think he almost kissed me."

"What? When?" Brenna's eyes grew wide as Megan filled her in.

Brenna playfully smacked Megan's arm. "Why am I just hearing about this now? That goes against best friend code, ya know."

"There's a code?"

"Of course there's a code. All first kisses and near misses must be discussed within twenty-four hours. It's in the handbook. I'll get you a copy."

"Well, sorry for going against code." Megan laughed. "I'll do better next time. But it might have just been my imagination."

Brenna shook her head. "Nope. Women have a sixth sense about these things. If you thought he wanted to kiss you, he did. No question. I bet he'll kiss you on your date. It's Friday, right?"

"'Tis. I don't know if I want him to kiss me, though. I mean—I *want* him to, whenever I'm around him. But when I'm thinking clearly, I just want to slow things down a little."

Brenna eyed her over her teacup. "Okay, so slow things down. He can't kiss you if you don't let him. Just keep your distance a bit."

"You don't understand. I can't think clearly around him." Megan worried her lip. "Last night, we were standing there by the sink and I had to leave the house to cool down cuz I couldn't handle being so close to him. I don't know if he could feel it but it was like there were sparks flying between us." She ran her fingers through her hair. "It freaked me out. With Jamie, it was a slow and steady kind of feeling, like a hot simmer. I knew I liked him, and I told him so, and I found out he felt the same. But it wasn't like this. Did you ever feel that with Ryan? That electricity?"

"Hmmm," Brenna looked uncomfortable as she nodded her head slightly. "I did feel an overwhelming urge just to be with him. And it was a little different from how I'd felt with Ben. But I'm nodding cuz I remember the first time I ever felt those really powerful sparks ... and that was with Luke." She cringed.

Ugh. Megan's stomach dropped. *Perfect segue there, Meg. Tell her about the call.* "So you felt that way with both Luke and Ryan?" *Stop stalling. Tell her.*

"Yeah, but with Luke, it was just all about the physical. He wasn't the total package. With Ryan, it was more like an ache, deep down. Like I hated being away from him and when I was around him, even when we weren't dating yet, I wanted to be close to him."

"Hmmm, this feels like the two of those combined."

"Dang, girl. That could be dangerous!"

"I know. And, speaking of dangerous, there's something I need to tell you."

Brenna cocked her head to the side, "What?"

Megan blew out another breath and closed her eyes.

"Hello?" Brenna said. "You can't just say you have something dangerous to tell me and then clam up. What's up?"

Ben was yelling again from the gate and this time, Megan got up. She eyed Brenna as she walked toward him, sure Brenna knew she was stalling. "Hello, buddy, aren't you just the cutest thing ever?" He was dressed in little blue jeans and a green, plaid onesie, with "Nana's Boy" embroidered on the front. He put both hands up toward her and immediately a look of fear crossed his face as he realized he was no longer holding on to the gate. He plopped to the floor and started to cry, so Megan reached in and pulled him out. "Shhh, it's okay, sweetie, Auntie Megan's got ya."

She kissed his head, handed him a stuffed monkey, and brought him back to the table with her, sitting down and pushing the dishes away so he couldn't grab them.

Brenna was studying her. "Okay, so now you're using my son as a shield. What in the world do you need to tell me?"

Megan laughed softly, realizing Brenna was right. "Okay, here goes. Yesterday, before the party, your phone rang. It was Luke." Brenna's eyes popped wide with shock. "I answered it because I didn't want him to upset you right before the party. And then after we talked, I deleted the call, so ya wouldn't see that he'd called until I could tell you about it."

"What did he want?"

Megan grimaced. "He knew Ben had just turned one. He was asking about him."

Brenna's hands flew to cover her mouth as she inhaled and exhaled sharply. "Oh, God. If he tries to see him, Ryan might kill him!"

Ben, probably seeing a look of terror in his mother's eyes, started to cry again. Megan whispered into his silky hair, "Shhh, it's okay. Shhh."

Brenna took him and held him close, as if someone were trying to take him from her. She took a deep breath. "Tell me everything. I want to know exactly what he said."

Megan relayed the conversation, in detail, and finished with an apology. "I didn't mean to keep it from you overnight. I totally planned to tell ya last night—"

"It's okay. I would have done the same thing." Brenna waved her off and shook her head. "I didn't even realize his number was still in my phone. He's gonna call back."

Megan nodded. "Probably. He didn't say he wouldn't, even when I asked him not to."

"What am I gonna do? You, Ryan, Anna and Father Tim are the only ones who know that Ben's actually from Luke. No one else. Oh, except Shannon. She knows. Which means Tara probably knows, too. Ugh. Do you think everyone actually knows?" Ben began standing and jumping on Brenna's lap, occasionally leaning toward her ear and touching her ear lobe, curious and giggling.

"No, I don't think so. I mean ... maybe a few people that saw you and Luke dancing together that night could suspect, but no one could know for sure. And it really doesn't matter. Everyone knows that Ryan is truly Ben's da."

"What is he thinking? Why now?" Brenna put Ben in his chair and cut up a banana for him. "I spent the first three months of Ben's life terrified that Luke would show up and make trouble. You remember, I had nightmares about it. But, I haven't even thought about it for months. Why is he calling now?"

Megan shook her head. "I don't know. Honestly, he sounded sad. Like he regretted some of the things he did."

"Great, that's what I need. Luke to shape up and think he's ready to be a dad." Brenna grabbed a fistful of her hair. "I have to tell Ryan. But I don't want to."

"I don't blame you. He sees red when anyone mentions Luke."

"I know. That time when Luke got drunk and broke my ribs, I really thought Ryan was gonna kill him."

"Well, he did beat the crap out of him."

"Thank God that's all he did. He doesn't think straight when it comes to Luke." Brenna wiped banana goo from her fingers. "He's gone until Friday, so that means I have one week to figure out how to tell him. Hopefully, Luke won't call back right away. Ryan will take it better if he knows I didn't actually talk to him."

"Well, if he calls, you could just ignore the call," Megan said.

Brenna shook her head. "Luke is very persistent. He gets what he wants. *Obviously.* That's why we're even having this conversation. If I ignore him, it will just push him to come back to Millway. That can't happen."

"No, that would be bad."

"Very bad."

# Chapter Twenty-Four

David knew his mother would be horrified at how little he'd attended Mass when he lived in Dublin. He knew he should go. That a good Catholic made time to go to Mass, regularly. But truth be told, he wasn't sure he wanted to be a good Catholic. He believed in God, but he wasn't sure what he thought about the church. She would be even more horrified to know that he'd attended a Protestant church several times—and had enjoyed it.

But, since returning to Millway, he'd started going to Mass every Sunday, for a couple reasons. One, there were no other options. Sacred Heart was the only church in town. Two, there was his work. Doctor Rob had explained that it helped people to trust him as a doctor when they saw him sitting in the pew, week after week. It made him relatable, and he suggested David do the same. So he had come—week in, week out.

Sacred Heart was a stone building, a chocolate color with an offsetting tan stone trim around the arched doorway and the large stained-glass windows. Inside, it was brighter than one would have expected. The cream-colored walls depicted Biblical scenes in various-sized tile mosaics. Even more than Mountdonovan, this place brought David back to his childhood. He could remember being very young, staring at the apocalyptic frescoes on the ceiling, terrified by the black, leathery-winged creatures being tossed into a burning lake. Now, as an adult, the paintings didn't faze him.

He was more interested in the strawberry-blonde that usually stood at the front of the church.

He'd told himself, that first week he had come, that he was just following Doctor Rob's orders. But after hearing Megan sing, he knew he'd come every week just for that treat.

It surprised him how nervous she always looked when she stood up there. You would think if she were nervous about singing, it would show in her voice. But the opposite happened. As soon as she started to sing, the nervous look disappeared and she seemed to lose herself in the music.

Today, she looked a little less nervous. She had been smiling and chatting with a middle-aged, dark-haired woman just before Mass began. And now, as she waited for her cue to begin the singing, he saw her scanning the first few rows. She smiled at a few people and then her expression cooled. He could see she was looking right at Patricia, who was looking anywhere but at Megan. *Interesting.*

Father Tim raised both hands to indicate he was about to speak, and then he asked for everyone's attention. "Today, we are going to do things a little differently. Megan, dear, if you could take a seat, we're not going to start with a song. We have a guest speaker who would like to say a few words." With a puzzled look, Megan quickly took a seat in the front corner as the woman with the long black hair walked toward the microphone.

"Thank you, Father Tim. I appreciate yer willingness to give me a few moments." She looked out at the congregation. She held a sheet of paper and it shook as she took a deep breath and cleared her throat. "Ahem ... hello. Most of ya know me, but for any that don't, my name's Elizabeth O'Connor. I asked Father Tim if I could speak this morning because I want to apologize for something I've done. I know this is a bit unorthodox, but I hurt a dear friend, and I did it in such a way that the only way I can come close to fixing it, is to do it publicly, like this."

She blew out a quick breath and continued. "Many of you know my son, Jamie, has been living near London for the past year and a half, working with his uncle. He called me in January and told me something that I had trouble believing, but as he wasn't the type to lie, I was soon convinced. He told me his fiancée had cheated on him and broke off the engagement when he confronted her. I was hurt for him, and I reacted badly. When his fiancée tried to tell me her side of the story, I accused her of lying and refused to listen to her."

At the mention of Jamie's name, David realized this was about Megan, and he had an almost overpowering desire to go sit next to her and help her through whatever was about to be said. He could see her profile from where he sat, and he was pretty sure he could see tears streaming down her face. But she was holding her head high and looking directly at Elizabeth. The silence that had descended when Elizabeth stood up now turned into a soft rustling noise as people began whispering to each other.

Elizabeth cleared her throat again. "But I found out, recently, that the lies had actually come from my son. Megan, his fiancée, had been telling the truth." Audible gasps could be heard as she turned toward Megan. "I've confessed my sin. I've already told Megan how sorry I am, and she has accepted my apology. But, I needed to do this publicly because I spread those lies about her, and even if I thought they were true, I should never have done that. The only way I could think of to fix the damage I did with my gossiping mouth was to come stand here, in front of all of you, and tell the truth. I know that Megan has been treated badly by people who thought they were being loyal to me."

She scanned the crowd, and David was sure she was making eye contact with some of those "loyal" friends. He saw movement near Megan and realized Brenna had snuck up to the front row to sit next to her. He exhaled as the tension in his shoulders eased. He hadn't wanted to create problems for Megan, so it had taken every ounce of control he had not to do what Brenna had just done. But it was better this way. People would expect Brenna to be there with her.

"While I appreciate my loyal friends, I want to publicly encourage you to apologize to Megan for anything you may have done to hurt her." As she said this, she looked directly at Patricia, who once again looked away. Brenna's arm was now circling Megan's back, and he could see Megan shaking, fully crying now. And he was surprised to realize that it was physically painful for him to watch.

After a brief explanation of Jamie's TBI diagnosis and a plea for patience with the changes anyone might notice in her son, Elizabeth walked straight to Megan, bent down and hugged her, and then took her seat.

There was an awkward silence. Applause didn't seem appropriate, but neither did silence, so another wave of rustling whispers ensued. Father Tim quickly stood back up and raised his hands again, asking for silence.

"Thank you, Elizabeth. That was a very brave thing you just did, and I know Megan appreciates it." He nodded toward Megan and winked. She had wiped at her face and appeared calm. "Usually, it is not in perfection that we best understand what God has done for us, but in our brokenness and the grace that He shows us in regards to our mistakes. That's where we see Him in action. Forgiveness is a powerful force. And the way God can heal relationships is an amazing witness to His life-changing power."

Father Tim continued on to his homily, but David didn't hear it. His mind was actively sorting through what he'd just heard. Piecing together what he'd already known with what he'd guessed and had now heard from Elizabeth, Megan had been through an incredibly difficult time in the past six months.

Her fiancé cheated on her. She broke off the engagement. She came home, probably expecting support, and instead had most of the town turned against her. She'd probably endured biting insults and dirty looks. Suddenly, her nervous stance at the front of the church each week made perfect sense.

And now, six months after the shock of finding out her fiancé cheated, she finds out that he has an injury that may have been partly responsible for his behavior. David had worked with TBI patients before. The severity of their symptoms ranged greatly. Some seemed to be hardly affected and only those close to them would have any clue. Others were severely impacted, losing motor and cognitive function. For his mother to have had no idea, all this time, he would have to be closer to the milder end of the spectrum. And if it was mild, maybe he would even recover, with proper therapy.

And if he did, would Megan take him back? The weight of what she'd been grappling with over the past week settled on his chest. The thought of her going back to Jamie had him clenching his fists. And that was when he knew. He didn't just like Megan, he was well on his way to falling for her. And that scared the crap out of him.

⌒⌖

It had been a very long time since Megan had been invited to Sunday dinner at the Maloney B&B, but she would have accepted an invite from anyone to avoid having to go home and face her mother. She understood Elizabeth's desire to make things right. But Megan hadn't told her mother the whole truth about what had happened with Jamie. Her dad knew, but not her mam. She had just said that Jamie had been acting like a jerk and she didn't want to do the long-distance thing anymore. And when Elizabeth had given Marlene the cold shoulder, Megan had explained that she was angry at her for breaking up with Jamie and asked her mam not to get involved.

But now, in front of the entire church, Elizabeth had unknowingly called her bluff. She had felt her mother staring at her throughout the entire service. So, she immediately ducked into the church offices as Mass ended. She only came out when Brenna texted her with an "all clear." She would face Marlene later. For now, she was looking forward to whatever Bettie had whipped up for dinner. She was hoping for pot roast. No one made pot roast gravy like Bettie.

She pulled around the back of the B&B to the family entrance and knocked on the kitchen door. Bettie opened the door and put her arms out for a hug. This was the Bettie she had known before. Always first with a hug and a scone to go with it.

"My, my, you must be exhausted after that. Come, dear, I'll get ya some tea." Bettie said with a motion toward the wooden kitchen table in front of a large lead-paned window.

Bettie put a gentle hand on her arm and led her to a chair. From the window, she could see the O'Connor farm, and a familiar pang of sadness had her staring into space. The emotional morning had taken a lot out of her. But as Bettie set a tray before her, loaded with shortbread and scones, she decided the day was looking up. She inhaled, deeply, and caught the scent of Bettie's famous pot roast gravy. Definitely looking up.

Bettie set the tea things on the table. "Brenna had to run home for something. She'll be here soon."

Megan nodded. "She texted me."

"Anna and Mam went to the store, they'll be here soon, too."

"Okay. I'm fine to just sit and drink some tea." Megan smiled.

"So, you didn't know Elizabeth was going to do that, did you?"

"No. No clue. She didn't have to. I told her I was fine."

"Well, you and I both know she had to find some way to make things right. She would never have been able to sleep if she didn't do something. I hope that will put an end to all that you've had to deal with around town. Brenna told me how people have been. I know I was angry for what I thought you'd done, but I can't see myself doing like some have done to ya." Bettie shook her head and tsk'd as she stirred something on the stove.

Megan shrugged. "I've learned from it. I'm not very quick to judge anyone these days. Especially based on gossip. I figure if I can find a lesson to learn from this mess, then nothing is wasted."

Bettie nodded thoughtfully. Tapping her spoon on the edge of the pot, she set it on the spoon rest and turned toward Megan. "I know that my sister-in-law has probably been the worst to you."

Megan could feel anger snaking back, building tension in her shoulders. "Patricia has never been particularly friendly to me. She doesn't shop at my dad's store because they got into an argument years ago when Da fired Matthew. She's barely spoken to me since. But she went out of her way to make me miserable this year. I'll never like her, but I'm sure I'm supposed to try to forgive her. It's not an appealing thought."

"Aye, she can be pretty mean. I'm sorry, luv. I think yer on the right track, though. Forgiving her will help you feel better, ya know."

"I know. I've heard it before. Something like, *Forgiveness sets a prisoner free, who'd have known the prisoner was me?*"

"Exactly, holdin' on to anger just makes ya sick."

"Well, I always thought I was pretty good about forgiving people. But I've learned that it's a lot harder when they don't admit what they've done."

Bettie sat down opposite Megan and reached for her hand. "I've known Patricia my whole life, and I've never seen her apologize to anyone about anything. If ya wait for that, you'll probably still be waiting in yer grave. Better to let it go, and then she'll have no power over you." Giving Megan's hand a squeeze, Bettie stood up again and headed back to her spoon and her pot.

She continued, "Trust me. I know this from experience. When she and my brother, Danny—God rest his soul—first married, I found her very ... hard to deal with. I was hurt by her superior attitude, and I just kept getting hurt. Eventually, Danny sat me down and told me not to let her get to me. He said she put on a good front, but she wasn't as confident as she acted. He told me about her childhood, and honestly, after what she went through as a wee one, it's amazing she's not worse."

Megan tried to imagine Patricia being "worse," and shuddered at the thought. She was curious about what had happened in Patricia's life that had given Bettie enough sympathy to ignore her rotten behavior all these years.

"Was she abused?"

Bettie looked at her for a moment before answering. "Aye. That's a mild term for it. You'll understand, I don't feel right giving specifics. But trust me when I tell ya, she had a very rough start."

"Well, I supposed that might make it easier for me to forgive her. But she's still not my favorite topic." Megan spooned some sugar into her tea and stirred in the milk. "So, how are things around here? Business good?"

Bettie sighed. "Too good, really. It's too much. I'm finding it hard to keep up with the B&B, the pastry business, and taking care of Mam. Don't tell anyone," she dropped her voice to a whisper, even though no one else was in the house, "I've contacted an auctioneer. I'm wondering how much I could sell the B&B for." Megan tried to keep the shock from her face. "I know, Mam would be horrified if she knew. But the thing is, she's rarely even in this century, so I'm not sure she would even notice. I just can't do it all. Even with Anna's help, it's overwhelming."

"I can help you, Bettie. At least for the summer. I'm only part-time at Burke's."

"Ah, yer a sweetheart. I'll keep that in mind, I will. But I need some pretty drastic help if I'm going to make things work. If I don't keep up with the B&B we'll lose customers, and eventually it won't be worth as much if I sell. I'm turning down pastry orders every day because I just don't have the time. And then, some days, Mam needs me all day. While other days, she hardly needs me at all."

"You could close down the pastry business."

Bettie nodded. "Aye, that seems the most logical. But the thing is, that's what I enjoy most. I've always dreamt of opening my own bakery. I never planned to run the B&B. I just came to help Mam out. It's not something I love to do. But making my pastries and sellin' them, that is the closest I'll get to my own bakery, and I'd hate to give it up. I truly love it."

"Hmmm ... well, I think Brenna was toying with the idea of getting a part-time job. Maybe she could help you." At the wry smile on Bettie's face, Megan added, "Not with the baking, of course. But maybe with the B&B?"

"Aye, 'tis a thought. I didn't know she was thinkin' of goin' back to work. Is she bored? She can't need the money. Ryan's a good businessman. He must have plenty saved."

Megan shrugged. "I don't know, exactly. Maybe I shouldn't have said anything."

"Tut-tut. No worries. I'll not say anything unless she brings it up, alright then? And by the same token, please don't mention the auctioneer to anyone?"

"I won't. And thanks."

As if on cue, Brenna came through the kitchen door with a sleeping Ben on her shoulder and his diaper bag slung on her other shoulder. "Bettie, is his playpen set up?" she whispered.

"Aye, luv. All ready. I know he can't make it here on a Sunday without fallin' asleep." Bettie opened the door to the pantry-turned-baby-nap-room and Brenna got Ben settled.

Soon, Anna arrived with Auntie Pat, who was quite lucid for a change. Before long, they were all seated, enjoying a lively conversation. Bettie's pot roast was even better than Megan had remembered. She asked for a rare second helping and ended the meal feeling like she could barely move. She stalled as long as she could, but eventually, she had to go home and face the music. So, she said her goodbyes and drove home.

# Chapter Twenty-Five

Pulling into her driveway, Megan noticed all the usual cars plus one. It was a shiny silver sports car, and she knew who it belonged to. What in the world was David doing at her house? She checked her face in the rearview mirror, added a little lip-gloss, considered putting her hair into a quick ponytail just to get it out of her face, but decided against it.

The side door of the cottage led directly into the tidy, efficient kitchen. Marlene McKenna had a place for everything, and everything was in its place. So, as trained, Megan immediately hung her keys on the rack by the door and ventured in to see what was going on. No one was in the kitchen, but she could hear men shouting in the living room. Either hurling or rugby was surely on the telly. She wondered if she could just slip upstairs and not be noticed. It had been a long day, and weariness was setting back in. But she took too long to decide because just as she was about to make a break for it, her twenty-year-old brother, Aidan, came sauntering into the kitchen.

"Meg, when did you get home?"

"Just now. What's happenin'?"

"Munster kicked butt, that's what."

"Where's Mam?" Not that she wanted to see her. More like she was trying to figure out how to avoid her.

Aidan cocked his head toward the stairs and whispered, "Went to bed early. What did you do? She was spittin' mad by the time she got home from church today."

Megan raised a brow. "How do you know it was me?"

Aidan looked at her with an amused grin. "Process of elimination, my dear sister. Michael and I were here all morning, and she was fine when she left. Da headed straight to his workshop when he got home, but she didn't follow him, so it wasn't him. You're the only one left who could make her that mad. So, I'll ask again, what did ya do?"

At that moment, her da and David walked into the kitchen carrying stew bowls and empty beer bottles. Her da, setting down his armload, clapped Aidan on the back. "Best to leave all that between the women, son. Take my advice: don't get involved."

Aidan nodded and took his dad's unsaid cue to leave the room.

"Hey Megan." David's tentative smile was back.

"Hello," she replied, hearing the weariness in her own voice, but having no energy left to pretend.

Her dad walked toward her with outstretched arms, "I'm thinkin' you're in need of a hug, Meggie."

She relaxed in his safe arms and barely held back tears, only because David was standing three feet away. She pulled away and busied herself with the dishes.

"So," her da said, "I see you two have been reacquainted. David tells me he's part of that Africa advocacy group ya mentioned."

Megan nodded. "He's the one who told me about it. I didn't tell you that?"

"No. Slipped yer mind, I'm sure. Just glad I ran into him at the store this afternoon. He was going to watch the game alone. Imagine."

David replied, "Well, sir, I told you, it's not uncommon. I'm a single chap. I'm alone a lot, and I don't mind."

"Aye, but 'tis practically a sin to watch Munster alone." He chuckled. "And no more of this 'sir' business. Pat or Paddy is just fine. Yer a grown man now, and no longer one of my employees. I think we can dispense with the formalities. Don't you, *Doctor*?"

David laughed. "Okay, you win, *Paddy*. Just call me David."

Megan listened to their banter as she filled the dishwasher and rinsed the empty bottles. She thought about making tea, but it required too much effort.

"Meggie, I've got to go finish a project in my shop for one of yer mother's TidyTowns ideas. I've told David about yer lovely gardens out back. I bet he'd like a tour, wouldn't ya David?" Her dad grinned and patted his ample belly. He was pleased with himself. He always patted his belly when he was happy about something.

She looked sideways at David, who smiled. "I'd love a tour, if it's no trouble."

She tried to hide her sigh. It wasn't that she didn't like being around him. It was that she didn't have the energy to pretend she wasn't that interested, so she worried she'd embarrass herself if she were left alone with him too long. But, it was obvious her dad knew there was something going on and was determined to give them alone time.

"Sure, let me just go change out of my church clothes. Give me five minutes." She wiped her hands on the dishtowel and kissed her da's cheek on her way to the stairs.

～

Megan inhaled deeply; the scents of chamomile mixed with lavender had a soothing effect. She always felt better surrounded by plants, and her wise father knew that. David walked quietly beside her as she described the different plants and flowers she'd chosen for the rambling garden. She wasn't as nervous around him as she usually was. Probably because she was in her element.

He was unusually quiet, and she didn't know what to make of it. Once they entered the wooded portion of the garden, she felt his hand slip into hers as he pulled her up short.

"Megan, I know I don't really have a place in your life ... yet," he was facing her and he looked almost nervous. Just the touch of his hand had her heart pounding. "But from the moment you sat down in church this morning, I've had the strongest urge to ... well let me just ask you. Would you mind if I gave you a hug?"

She hadn't been sure what he was about to say, but she didn't expect that at all. A hug?

He didn't wait for her answer. He just pulled her close, encircling her with his strong arms. She laid her head on his chest. At first, she thought her heart had sped up even more, but she realized, with a shock, that it was his heartbeat she was hearing. And it was pounding. It made her feel more relaxed, and she wrapped her arms around his trim waist and held tight.

He kissed the top of her head and whispered, "I'm so sorry for all that you've been through this year."

At his kind words, emotion snapped through her like a whip, and tears spilled out in a slow, steady stream. She nodded her thanks and tilted her face so that it nestled at his neck. She inhaled. He smelled of musky spices and fresh-cut wood. She knew her tears were slipping down and wetting his T-shirt. But she couldn't stop them. His hand rubbed her back, and she closed her eyes. It had been a long time since she'd felt the comfort of anyone's arms other than her da's. It warmed her, and although she kept thinking he might get tired and let her go, he didn't. He just held her.

After a long while, he pulled back, only slightly, and tipped her face up. With his thumb, he wiped the tears from below her eyes. "Are you okay?"

She had trouble not looking at his mouth, so close to hers. She nodded. "I am now. Thank you."

He smiled, sweet and tender, and brushed his lips over her misty lashes. She closed her eyes and took in every sensation as if time had slowed. She could feel his breath on her cheek and then his lips, soft and gentle, kissing her tear tracks. He moved to her other cheek, barely touching it with his lips. Her legs felt weak, so she held tighter to his waist. She felt his hand on the back of her neck and in her hair. She opened her eyes. His gold-flecked amber eyes locked with hers, and she knew two things. He was about to kiss her, and she'd never wanted anyone to kiss her so badly.

David watched her as he kissed her cheeks. Her eyes were closed, face tilted up, and the smallest of smiles on her rose-colored lips. He wasn't sure he'd ever seen anyone more beautiful. Even with a tear-stained face, she was breathtaking. He couldn't hold himself back any longer. But he warned himself to stay gentle. He was sure she needed tender and careful right now. But if he didn't kiss her for real, he might explode.

Then, she opened her eyes and in them he saw hunger. She wanted him to kiss her, and the realization thrilled him, sending a surge through his body. He brought his mouth to hers with more passion than he planned, but she responded with the same intensity. Time stretched. Her hands roamed over his back as she drove the kiss deeper, pushing him close to the edge of control. He needed to rein it in.

"Megan—" he said between breaths. "Meg, hold on."

She stilled, and he could feel her body stiffen under his arms. She whispered, "I'm sorry."

Sorry? He pulled her away to look at her face. "Why are you sorry?"

"Because I know you were just trying to be nice, and I didn't mean to turn it into ..."

He put two fingers over her lips. "Shhh. You have nothing to be sorry for. I wasn't just trying to be nice. I care about you ... a lot. Like I said, I've been wanting to hold you all day, and I wasn't expecting anything else. But, Megan, that was amazing. Say anything but sorry. Besides, I think I kissed you first, ya know?"

She relaxed, still in his arms, and smiled. "Well, I certainly kissed ya back."

"Aye, that ya did."

"I don't normally kiss guys I'm not even going out with. I said sorry cuz I didn't want you to get the wrong picture." A breeze rippled through her hair.

"And what might that wrong picture be?"

"That I lured you back here, into the woods. That I'm just like all the other girls in town, throwing myself at the gorgeous new doctor."

He had to laugh. "You are nothing like the other girls in town, Megan. But you're forgetting one important thing. I don't want to kiss those other girls. But you? I've wanted to kiss you for a very long time."

She giggled and tilted her head. "Aw, ya have?"

"I have. And I have to say, it was worth the wait."

She blushed and looked down. "It was really sweet of you to hold me like that. I didn't realize how much I needed it. Although, not exactly how I pictured our first kiss starting. With me crying all over you, like a silly girl."

David grinned. "So, you pictured our first kiss?" He had first pictured it when he was fifteen years old. Reality was much more satisfying.

Her face flushed even more. "Well, since I'm embarrassing myself anyway, yes. The other night at Ben's party, that day at Mountdonovan when you picked the leaves out of my hair, when you told me about Alahaji, pretty much any time I've seen ya in the last two weeks."

"Hmmm," He tucked a stray hair behind her ear. "You have good instincts. You should act on them more often."

She nodded. "I should." She put both arms around his neck, fingers curling into his hair and pulled his face toward hers, kissing him again. Gently, though. Full of feeling but soft and smooth. And her deliberate, slow touch had his pulse racing once again.

She pulled away and laid her head back on his chest. He held her as both of their heart rates returned to normal. And he knew, as he felt her breath tickling his neck, that somehow, his heart was becoming hers. Putting his heart in the hands of a woman again slightly terrified him. But he also realized he had very little say in the matter. His heart had probably been hers all along.

"David?" She interrupted his thoughts, her head still on his chest. "My life is really complicated right now."

"I know." Did they really have to think about it? "Let's talk about it another day. For today, let's just follow our instincts, okay?"

"Deal." She nodded. "But David?"

"Hmm?"

"Right now my instincts are telling me that if I get any more comfortable, I'm going to fall asleep." She stepped out of his embrace.

He looked at her eyes. Poor girl did look exhausted, but he couldn't resist. "Now Megan, are you asking me to take ya to bed? Because I know I said we'd follow our instincts, but I think that it's a little early—" She smacked his chest, playful but hard. He laughed and rubbed his chest. "I'll have to remember you've grown up with brothers to tease you. You've a strong arm, there."

"I do, and I know how to use it. So, be careful which instincts you follow." She grinned and he kissed her once more.

"I guess I should let ya get yerself to bed, then. I don't think I can wait till Friday to see you again, though."

They began walking, and she looked at him sideways. "How about lunch at Rosie's? You pick the day."

"Perfect. I'll have to look at the schedule tomorrow, but I'll make it happen."

She smiled and smoothed her hair down and grinned mischievously. "Only, do I have to wear a suit, like all your other lunch dates?"

"Those are business lunches."

"Mm-hmm."

"What, did those girls make ya jealous, Megan?"

She narrowed her eyes. "Of course not. Just noticed you take a lot of pretty women to lunch."

"Aye, well, it seems the pharmaceutical companies are hiring more beautiful women than they used to. But I will look forward to lunch with you, much more than I do with them. Alright?"

"Okay, text me. Only day I can't do is Wednesday."

"I would text you, but I don't have your number," he said as he leaned against his car.

She laughed. "Yeah, I guess we really should have each other's numbers at this point. I'll give you mine, but I warn you, my phone is a reject. If ya don't hear back from me, try again."

They switched phones and each entered their number into the other's phone. David chuckled, "I didn't know they still made slider phones. How do ya even use this?" He laughed again at the way she crinkled her nose and tried to look offended as she swiped the phone out of his hand.

"I know I need a new one. Brenna has threatened me with bodily harm if I don't do it soon. Maybe Wednesday night, when I go to Killarney for the C.A.M.P. meeting, I can go early and get new phone."

"How 'bout I drive and we grab a bite to eat before the meeting, as well?"

"Even better. So, text me when you're free for lunch."

"I will. And can I kiss you goodbye, out here, where anyone might see?"

Megan looked toward her house. He could tell she was fighting between wanting another kiss and maybe not being ready to be seen as a couple. The kiss won.

# Chapter Twenty-Six

Brenna had the tea ready when Megan walked in. It was still early, so a chilly breeze swept in before Megan closed the kitchen door. The first thing Brenna noticed was an ear-to-ear grin on Megan's face. She was practically glowing.

"What in the world happened between yesterday and today?"

Megan went to the cupboard and pawed through it. "Hold on, I'll tell ya in a minute." She was probably looking for shortbread. Not finding any, she pulled out some scones in a plastic bag.

"Were you just humming?" Brenna hadn't seen her friend this happy in at least a year.

"Was I?" Megan shrugged. "I didn't realize."

They sat and poured tea as Megan began. "Okay, I'm still within the twenty-four hour period mandated by the best friend code—"

"He kissed you!"

Megan smiled even wider, and her eyes went dreamy. "He definitely kissed me."

Brenna laughed. "Look at you, you're a goner. What happened to, 'I'm gonna slow things down?'"

Megan winced. "I know, I know. But I also told you I can't think straight when I'm around him."

"Okay, spill it. I need details." Brenna tapped the table in excited impatience.

"Wait," Megan looked around, "where's Benny boy?"

"Anna had the day off and asked if she could have him."

"Sweet. What are ya gonna do with a whole day to yourself?"

"Probably figure out where to bury your body if you don't tell me what happened, right now."

Megan laughed and recounted the events of the previous day with enough detail that Brenna felt like she was watching a scene in a movie.

"Megan, that's so freakin' romantic. He just wanted to hold you? Did you melt when he said that?"

"Of course. He really meant it, Bren. He told me on the phone last night that he had to restrain himself in his pew because he just wanted to come sit with me and wrap his arms around me. He said he was so relieved when you did just that. He knew it wouldn't have been appropriate for him to do it. How precious though, that he wanted to."

"Aww ... I guess you should thank Elizabeth for her speech. It drove him to your house, literally."

"Kind of ironic, huh? But I do have fallout to deal with. I still haven't talked with my mam. She never came down last night and was gone before I got up today. Actually, I'm shocked she didn't wake me up. Usually, she would, if she had something she was mad about."

"Well, maybe it will be good for you guys to talk, ya know? You can't shut her out forever."

"I'm not shutting her out. Not really. It's just easier not to talk to her about things. I know she loves me, but sometimes I feel like she doesn't really like me much. Like I'm a disappointment to her."

"Meg, what would she be disappointed in? You're a great daughter; you're going to be a teacher just like her. I'm sure she's very proud of you."

Megan shook her head, fixed her eyes on the table in front of her and said in a hushed tone, "I don't want to be a teacher."

"You don't?"

"No, and I haven't for a long time. But I didn't know how to get out of it, and I know my mam is going to be so upset with me. I think that's why

I've avoided talking to her about anything in so long. I was afraid she'd figure it out and be furious."

"Well, that explains why you get so grumpy whenever I ask you about school. How come you didn't tell me?"

Megan twisted a strand of hair that had come loose from her ponytail. "I didn't tell anyone. I kept thinking I'd start to like it. That something would change and I would be more interested in it."

Brenna was surprised. Not that Megan didn't like teaching. She'd never seemed overly enthusiastic about it. But that she had gone so far into the career path without standing up and saying how she felt. Megan wasn't shy. She wasn't the type to do things she didn't want to do. "What are you gonna do?"

"I don't know. It's not that I don't like kids, or even teaching. But I hate feeling like I'm confined to the classroom. It feels like a sentence more than a career. I've been wracking my brain for a solution. Nothing comes. Well, I've had a few ideas, but I don't know. Right now, I'm just trying to trust that God will open up another door for me and that I'll recognize it when He does."

"I still don't understand why you waited so long to say anything. It's not like you."

"I know. It's because I know how much my mam wanted me to be a teacher. My grandma was a teacher, too. She's been talking about it my whole life! It's a family thing. I just wanted her to be proud of me."

"I'm sure she'll be proud of you, no matter what you do." Brenna patted her hand. "I have a benefit you don't have. I know what a mom feels for her child. Give her more credit. She may just surprise you."

Megan sighed. "You're probably—" Brenna's cell phone rang and her heart dropped to her stomach when she saw Luke's name on the caller I.D.

"Oh no. What do I do?" Panic laced through her.

"I'll answer it again, if ya want."

Brenna blew out a breath. "No, I need to do it. But stay here."

She swiped the screen to answer and kept her tone cool. "Hello, Luke."

"Hi, Brenna. Don't hang up, okay?"

She paused. "Why are you calling again?"

"Megan told you, huh?"

"Of course she told me." Brenna almost laughed as Megan scrunched her face and mouthed, "Duh."

"Listen, I don't want to bother you. I don't want to make your life harder, but I thought ya should know I'm probably moving back to Millway, soon."

Brenna felt all the color drain from her face. "Why? If you don't want to make my life harder, you won't move back here." Megan's eyes popped wide with alarm, and she grabbed Brenna's free hand.

"My parents moved back a few months ago and they've been asking me to come home. So, what, I should never move back to my home because it would make you uncomfortable? That's not right. I'm sorry for what I did, Brenna. I already told ya that when you came to see me in jail. You said ya forgave me."

*Deep breath.* "I did forgive you, Luke. I really did. But I'm not the one you need to worry about. I don't know if Ryan knows how to let it go. He heard your parents were back, and he was in a bad mood for days. Can't you understand how he might feel?"

Luke chuckled. "What, is he worried I'm gonna try to win ya back?"

Anger coursed through her. He thought this was a joke? Megan looked pained, not being able to hear Luke's side of the conversation. "That would be impossible, Luke."

"Ouch." He paused. "No worries, I'm not interested."

"Yeah, well, Megan said you asked about Ben. Let me make myself very clear. If you try to see him or interfere with our life at all, I will take legal action. I've done it before, and I'll do it again. You know I will." She pulled her hand from Megan's and ran it through her hair. "Don't force me to do that."

"Listen, this was a courtesy call. I didn't want you to be shocked if ya saw me walking down the street. I'm not asking you for anything, so just calm yourself."

"Luke, I'm begging you not to come back. Even if you don't do anything, just your presence in town will cause me all sorts of problems. Please, reconsider."

"I don't know. I haven't made a final decision. Do you want me to let ya know what I decide?"

She exhaled and tried to hold her tears back. "Yes. But don't call me for any other reason, okay? I have to go. Bye, Luke."

She dropped her phone to the table and put her head down on her arms. She could feel Megan's hand rubbing her arm.

"You got the gist of that?" she asked, lifting her head.

Megan nodded. "You okay?"

"Nope."

"So did he say he would reconsider?"

"No, just that he hadn't made a final decision. He'll call me if he's going to move back."

"Why does he need to come back? There are plenty of other places he can live. Geez."

"His parents moved back. You knew that, right?"

Megan nodded.

"So they want him to come home. Of course, they have no clue about Ben. What if he tells them? Are they going to claim to be his grandparents? Want to come to birthday parties? Can you imagine?"

Megan got up and put the water on to warm up their tea. "Are you gonna tell Ryan?"

Brenna dropped her head to the table again with a thud. "I'm so screwed. I have to. But if I tell him, he'll be furious and impossible to live with. And that's just with the threat of Luke moving back. If he actually does, I'll be freaking out every time Ryan goes into town, worried he'll run into Luke and Luke will make some smart-ass remark, like he does, and then? Then, Ryan will kill him. I'll be a prison widow, and Ben will grow up without a dad and—"

"Shhh, slow down, hon." Megan was standing over her, rubbing her back. "Ryan won't actually kill him. It'll be okay."

"Meg, you don't understand." Brenna sat up and rubbed her temples. "Luke can turn Ryan into the Incredible Hulk."

"Maybe enough time has gone by that he'll surprise you. Maybe it won't be as bad as ya think."

Brenna shook her head. "Pretty sure it will be. Last time we argued about it, he apologized and said he would have a better attitude about it. But I don't know if he can keep that promise. And if I don't tell him Luke called, and he finds out, he'll read into it and think I still have feelings for Luke."

"No." Megan looked stunned. "He knows there's no comparison between him and Luke."

"You would think so. But I'm telling you, as much as he tries to be, Ryan's not rational when it comes to Luke. I'm just plain screwed."

⤚⤙

Megan walked into Rosie's and scanned the room for David. He wasn't there yet. Sam, the manager, caught her eye with a nod.

"Are ya gonna sit at the bar or will ya be needin' a table today, Megan?" he asked.

"A table for two. Thanks, Sam."

"Pleasure. I've a nice little booth over here for ya." He ushered her to a small booth along the side wall.

Megan sat and expected Sam to walk away. Instead, he stood there, wringing the towel in his hands.

"Did you need something, Sam?"

"I don't like getting involved in stuff, but me wife knows you're in here a lot, and she told me to tell ya she thinks yer very brave and she's sorry for all y've been through."

Shock rippled through her. "Really? Well, tell Margaret I said thank you."

Sam grinned, obviously relieved that his message-boy duties were done. "I'll do that. Brenna meeting ya?"

Megan shook her head. "No, another friend."

"Can I get ya started with a drink? Brigit will be a few minutes."

"Aye, tea would be great."

Just then, David came through the door. She wondered if her stomach would ever stop reacting to the sight of him. Sam took his cue to leave as David slid into the booth across from her.

"Hey," he said with a smile.

"Hey, yerself." She knew she was grinning but couldn't help it. "How's work?"

"It's Monday. My least favorite day. But you are a bright spot in it. I'm glad you could make it on short notice." He had texted her just as she was leaving Brenna's.

"It worked out well. I have to work in an hour, so this is perfect."

Brigit brought a pot of tea with two cups and took their order. Megan could see the question in Brigit's eyes. *Did you snag him?* She pretended she didn't know what the meaningful look was about and glanced out the window as Brigit headed for the kitchen.

Megan glanced at David's strong hands, resting on top of the table, and immediately sat on her own. She was having trouble not putting her hands in his, but she wasn't ready to do anything publicly yet. And she knew she had to talk about it.

David was studying her. "You got quiet all of a sudden. Are y'okay?"

She nodded. "I said yesterday that my life was complicated."

He blew out a breath. "So, it's already time for the talk. No more following instincts?"

"I liked following instincts." She smiled. "And I plan to do more of it. But ..."

"Do ya regret what happened yesterday?"

"No! Not at all. I just thought we should talk about where we go from here."

David's lip curled in a sly smile. "Wherever you want to go."

"Seriously ... like I said, it's complicated. I want to get to know ya more. I want to hang out with you. But I need to take it slowly, especially in public." She glanced at Brigit as she walked by.

"Alright. What does that mean? How slow?" His eyes were intense, and her heartbeat was the opposite of slow.

She leaned in and whispered, "For example, right now, I'm sitting on my hands because what I really want to do is hold yours." He grinned. "But I need a little while before I'm ready to kind of ... go public. "

His eyes danced with mischief. "I'm fine with private, ya know."

"I'm sure," her stomach was twisting again. "But you know what I'm saying, right?"

"I think so. You want to see where this goes, but ya don't want to be seen as a couple, yet?"

She let out a relieved sigh. "Yes. This is the first day, in over six months, that not one person has given me a dirty look or cold stare. I'd just like even a few days' break before talk starts up again. And you know it will. Taking you off the market might just land me right back in the Public Enemy Number One spot."

He laughed. "I doubt it will be all that bad. But if people do talk, there's one big difference this time."

"What?"

His amber eyes held hers for a moment. "You won't be alone."

Unexpected tears filled her eyes. "True. Thanks." She quickly wiped the tears away and chuckled. "Where've ya been the last six months?"

Brigit arrived with their lunch, and Megan noticed how her eyes lit up when she spoke to David. Even with Brigit's suspicion that there was something between them, she obviously couldn't help but flirt with him. Megan choked down a ridiculous wisp of jealousy. If things with David did move forward, and she expected they would, she would have to learn to how to handle the looks other women gave him. She couldn't let herself get jealous every time someone batted her eyelashes at him, or she'd be jealous twenty-four/seven.

She made it through the entire lunch without touching him and was amazed at just how difficult it had been. He walked her to Burke's on his way back to the office and kept a respectable distance between them, honoring her wishes, even though she could tell it was as difficult for him as it was for her.

"So, Wednesday, I'm off work at four. Can I pick you up at half-four? We can take care of your phone first and then find a bite to eat before the meeting?"

"Perfect. I work nine to two on Wednesday. I'm looking forward to the meeting."

"Aye, me too. See ya Wednesday." He stood there looking at her for a moment. If they weren't trying to keep things quiet, he would be giving her a kiss goodbye, and they both knew it. So instead, she returned his smile and said thank you, knowing he knew exactly what she meant.

She started to watch him walk away but forced herself to turn and enter the pharmacy. She had a short, three-hour shift, and then she would have to go home, and there would be no avoiding her mother.

Entering the kitchen, Megan hung her keys up and took a deep breath. "Mam?"

No answer.

"Mam, where are ya?" Her car was there. She had to be home. But still no answer. She checked the downstairs rooms and looked out the back window, then headed upstairs and knocked on her parent's bedroom door. Still not getting an answer, she opened the door and realized her mam was probably out on her balcony behind the closed French doors.

She knocked lightly on the glass so she wouldn't startle her, then opened the door, letting a warm breeze wash over her face. Her mam was seated at a small table, heavy-laden with various books. She looked at Megan with eyes that were more sad than angry.

"Can we talk?" Megan asked.

Marlene nodded and motioned toward the second chair. "You can put the books on the floor."

"Are ya working on ideas for next school year already?" Megan moved a stack of books and sat.

"No, I've agreed to teach a summer course on Irish Literature."

"Ah." Megan twisted several strands of hair at her temple. "Well, Mam, I wanted to say I'm sorry."

Her mother nodded. Unusually quiet. Megan had steeled herself for an argument. She had been prepared to apologize and try to calm her mam down. She wasn't expecting a silent, sad reception. All her rehearsed defensive arguments were worthless.

"You're not mad?" Megan said.

"I was." Her mam eyed her and a glimpse of her usual fiery tempera-ment flared and then quickly subsided. "But I don't know what to feel now."

"I didn't know Elizabeth was going to do that. I would have told you the truth if I'd known. I'm sorry you had to find it out that way."

Her mam ran her finger along the binding of a Maurice Walsh book. "It was a horrible feeling ... to be there in church and suddenly people are looking over at me to gauge my reaction, and I have to act like I knew what was going on; meanwhile I'm angry at you for not telling me and angry at the people who've obviously been mistreating you. I just don't understand why you kept such a big thing from me." Hurt radiated from her eyes.

"It wasn't planned out or anything. It's no secret you and I don't see eye to eye on a lot of things."

Marlene arched an eyebrow and pursed her lips. "Tis true we look at the world differently. I don't see why that would keep you from telling me your fiancé cheated on you. I would have been able to help you. Or at the least understand why you've been so emotional."

Megan sighed and tried to find a way to explain herself. A memory of her childhood dog flitted through her mind. "Remember when I was ten and Rex got hit by that car?" Marlene nodded with a furrowed brow. "Well, I was so sad, and I just wanted to be sad for a while. But you kept pushing me to put it behind me and then you said we should get a new puppy. I know you were just trying to help, but I didn't want a new pup-py. I just wanted to grieve for Rex for a while. So I told you I didn't want a new puppy, but you got one anyway."

"I thought it would help you get over Rex, if you had a new little one to take care of and play with."

"I know, Mam. And that might have worked for you. But I told you over and over that I didn't want a new dog."

"I thought you didn't know what ya wanted." Marlene looked down and her hands, neatly folded on the table.

"You thought your way was the only way." Megan said quietly, trying not to incite anger. "You do that all the time. You don't listen to me, you just bulldoze and do what you want to do."

"I do not do it all the time." Marlene's voice grew louder. She paused and took a calming breath. "But regardless, what's your point?"

"Well, again, it's not something I planned out. But when I came back from London and Elizabeth slammed her door in my face and I felt so lost and desperately sad, I couldn't face telling you. I thought you would go talk to Jamie or Elizabeth. I thought you would take over, try and fix things. And I didn't want things fixed. I didn't ever want to see Jamie again. I didn't want a new puppy. I just wanted to grieve and move on in my own time and my own way."

Marlene was silently staring out at Megan's wild gardens. "I would have wanted to protect you."

"I know, Mam. I know you always mean well."

Tears filled her mother's eyes. "You know that I love you, right?"

"Of course. I know that. But sometimes I think you don't really like me very much."

Shock registered on her mom's face. "Megan, of course I like you. Why would you say such a thing?"

Megan struggled for the words. "I think you like me more when I do what ya want. When I act like you. But I'm not like you and that should be okay with you. I want you to love me for who I am, even if that means you don't agree with me, and I don't want ya to try to fit me into your mold. I've tried, Mam. I've tried to do what you want and be who you want me to be, but it's not real. It's not true and I can't do it." Now tears filled Megan's eyes and she looked down, avoiding Marlene's gaze.

"You're right."

Megan looked up in surprise.

Her mam continued, "You were always such a free spirit. Even when you were very little, you wanted to pick out your clothes and mix red and purple and other ghastly combinations. I thought it was my job to teach you those colors didn't match and show you what to wear." Megan remembered the exact outfit her mam was talking about. It was a purple dress with small yellow flowers on it, and she'd had red tights and red shoes, and they were her favorites, so why not wear them together?

"I remember. I didn't get why it was such a big deal to you. Or why ya got so angry with me."

"I didn't understand you. I think it's why you and your father are so close. Somehow, he innately understood you, and it made me feel like a failure. Megan, I'm sorry I've tried to make you more like me. I guess I thought if I could just make you see things my way, maybe we would have a relationship like you and your da. Instead, I pushed you further away to the point that you didn't feel safe telling me the most important, painful thing that's ever happened to you."

Megan fiddled with a ring on her thumb. "I should have told you."

"You should have. But I can understand, now, why you didn't. I've spent the last day trying to figure out why you hate me so much—"

"Mam, I don't hate you!"

"Well, you said you didn't think I liked you very much. I could say the same."

Megan wanted to deny it, but she was right. Neither of them acted like they liked the other. "Maybe we can start over. If we can figure out a way to appreciate what makes us unique, instead of trying to change each other? That would go a long way toward making things better."

Marlene nodded and looked out over the gardens again. "I wish I could plant wild and crazy gardens like you do. I think they're beautiful."

"You do? I always thought ya hated my gardens."

Marlene laughed. "I'm jealous of them. I can't visualize things like you can. I play by the rules and plant in straight lines. I don't know how to do it any other way."

"I wish I could keep my stuff neat and organized, like you do. I don't like having to search for my keys, my purse, my *sanity*. You never waste time searching for anything. You always know exactly where everything is."

Marlene smiled and patted Megan's hand. "This is nice."

Megan could feel her heart pounding. This was her open door. She had to tell her mam about school but she didn't want to ruin what was a very good moment. Yet, if she didn't tell her, she'd just be lying to her still.

"It is nice. But I have to tell you something else that I haven't told ya because I'm afraid you'll get really mad."

A look of dread passed over her mother's face. "Is it worse than Jamie cheating on you?"

Megan shrugged. 'Not to me, but it might be to you."

Marlene blew out a breath. "Okay, lay it on me."

"I don't want to be a teacher."

"What?" The trees rustled with the wind, and Megan pictured them whispering to each other about what a disappointment she was.

"I don't want to be a teacher. I haven't wanted to for a long time, but I kept hoping I'd change my mind and start liking it." Megan watched her mam process her words, impressed with the obvious effort she was making to not look angry.

Marlene's head shook, slightly tossing her ginger hair. "I won't lie—I'm shocked."

"I should have said something a long time ago. I just didn't want to let ya down."

"This is just more of the same issue, Meg." Marlene rubbed at her temples. "It all goes back to me trying to make you fit into a package I can understand. The fact that you would spend all this time and effort doing something just because I wanted it shows me just how much I've messed things up."

"No, it's not your fault, Mam."

"Well, no sense in arguing over who's to blame. I think your idea of starting over is a very good one."

Megan smiled. "Me too."

Marlene absently stacked the books into three piles. "If you don't want to teach, what do you want to do?"

"I don't really know. I've spent so much time and energy trying to like teaching, I haven't taken any time to figure out what I actually like. I think I want to do something that allows me to work with kids, but not in a classroom setting. And, obviously, my favorite thing to do is gardening. I also really enjoyed running the events for the library. Unfortunately, that was a volunteer position, and I can't live on a volunteer's nonexistent salary."

Marlene cocked her head to the side and raised her brows. "Hmm, interesting."

"What's interesting?"

"Well, the TidyTowns committee met last night to discuss what we're looking for in the Program Director position for Mountdonovan. It didn't cross my mind at the time, because I didn't know you were looking for something. But I actually think you'd be really good for the position."

"You do? What's involved?" Megan remembered the feeling of excitement she had the first time the job was mentioned.

"You would be in charge of planning and organizing the educational program, which would bring in schoolchildren for field trips. And you would need to oversee the management of the facility, in regards to special events and other programs held on the property. It's somewhat unclear, as we aren't exactly sure how the facility will be used. But that's one reason we're looking to fill the position soon, so that the director can help with the planning as the renovations take place. There's some more info on the website. You should fill out an application—" Marlene stopped herself mid-sentence, her face reddening. "Of course, that is, if you think it would be something of interest. I'm not trying to tell you what to do."

Megan laughed. "It's okay, Mam. It does sound interesting, and I will definitely look into it."

"Good. Let me know if I can help."

Relief flooded Megan. She wouldn't have thought it was possible to have this calm, reasonable talk with her mam. For years, she had pictured this conversation, and it always ended with screaming and tears and a slamming door. So it took her a moment to register the fact that her mam had just stood and held her arms open for a hug.

After the hug, Megan went to her room. She needed to process all that had gone on since the morning before, and more and more she was realizing she processed her thoughts best by writing them down.

Between Elizabeth telling the whole town that she wasn't to blame, to her incredible time with David, to this completely shocking conversation with her mam, the past two days probably qualified for the best two days in a row, ever.

She pulled out her prayer journal and flipped to her first entry. It was a half-finished one from last Wednesday, when Ryan and David had found her in her alcove. She started a new entry.

*Lord,*

*Wow, what a crazy couple days. First, what Elizabeth did. That was really amazing. I feel like I've been set free from a curse. And then, David. It's a little scary how fast I'm falling for him. I need help there, Lord. I don't want to go too fast. Help me to be more rational around him. But thank you for him. The way he just held me, it almost felt like a gift from you... like you knew I needed that and you sent him to me.*

*And the biggest one of all—Mam. I don't think we've ever had such an honest talk. It will be hard to start over, cuz I think we've both hurt each other over the years. But I think, now that we both are working on it at the same time, we might actually be able to have a good relationship. I'm so thankful, Lord. I know you are working in my life. You've taken the horrible things that have happened and planted them, like seeds, in my life. And now I can see the first shoots of what you're doing.*

*Thank you Lord. Help me learn more each day how to trust you and how to be more like you.*

*And, Lord... if this director job is something I'd be good at, help me make it happen.*

# Chapter Twenty-Seven

*D*avid watched Megan leave her house and approach his car. She wore a pale yellow dress made of some kind of flowy fabric. She made him think of a faerie. Apt comparison—she'd certainly bewitched him. He knew how he felt. And he was pretty sure she felt the same. But, in his mind, Jamie was still a wild card.

Opening the door, she slid into the passenger seat, and he inhaled the vanilla scent of her.

"Hey, beautiful." He wanted to lean in and kiss her but instead, he grabbed her hand. No one outside the car would see that. She squeezed his hand and smiled wide, dimples fully engaged. He hated to pull his hand away, but he needed it to shift gears.

"How was yer day, today?" she said.

"Good. Busy, but good. Doctor Rob is pleased with the patient load I've been carrying, and we're going to talk about the possibilities for the future at the end of the week. His dad is only seeing a few patients now, so I think it's pretty likely he'll make the temporary position a permanent one."

"That's great!" She grabbed his hand again.

"Aye. I like the office and the staff, for the most part." Patricia had been in a foul mood all week, and he'd steered clear of her. But in general, they were all fine to work with.

As they neared the last stop sign in town, he needed his hand again. She giggled as he reconsidered and reached across his body to shift with the opposite hand, knee on the steering wheel. He'd never wanted an automatic transmission before today. But he was starting to see what some of the benefits might be.

"So, Shannon started working this week, right?"

Warning bells. *Does she know we went out before? Should I tell her?*

"Aye, she started Monday. She's very good, especially for someone just out of school." And she'd done a good job of not making things awkward. She didn't bring up their date or the fact that he'd never called her afterward.

"She's a natural. I don't think I could be a nurse. I don't have the temperament. But she's been like that as long as I've known her. She was always the one bringing birds with broken wings home, to try to patch them up. Drove her mam mental." She smiled.

As they talked, she absently ran her fingernail up and down his forearm and he wondered if she had any clue what she was doing to him. By the time they were fifteen minutes outside of town, he felt like an out-of-control teenage boy who could only think of one thing. He blew out a breath and took his hand back.

"I need a few minutes without you touching me, okay?"

Her surprised look had him laughing until it turned to a frown.

"I'm sorry. I didn't mean to annoy you," she said, the words clipped.

"Annoy me? Are ya kidding? It's all I can do to not pull off on one of these country lanes and do unspeakable things to you. You're driving me crazy."

"Oh!" she said in wonder. "Really?"

He laughed again. "Yes, really." Did she truly not know the effect she had on him? He needed to change the subject, and he knew exactly which topic would equal a cold shower for him. "I wanted to ask you about something."

"Sure, what's up?"

He hesitated. Unsure if she would be willing to talk.

"Is something wrong?"

"No, I just don't want to upset you." He turned the radio down all the way. "Are y'okay to talk a little bit about Jamie?"

"Oh, um, sure. What do ya want to know?"

"Is he coming back here?"

"I don't know. I know Elizabeth wants him to move back home, but he's got certain doctors he's working with in London, and they want him to stay there for a while, I think."

So, he probably would come back at some point, which meant David would have to deal with an ex, again. That hadn't gone too well for him with Katie. In the end, she'd chosen her ex, blatantly. He had to keep reminding himself that Megan wasn't Katie.

"When's the last time you saw him?"

She traced the logo on the glove box with her long, slender fingers. "The day I broke up with him, back in January."

"So, have ya talked to him since you found out about the TBI?"

Now she was hesitating. "Yes, briefly, on the phone."

That meant she'd talked to him very recently. David knew he had no right to be angry, but he felt it simmering beneath the surface, anyway.

"Did *you* call *him*?"

She looked over at him, sharply. "No, he called me. But if I had called him, would that be a problem for you?" The irritation in her voice was unmistakable as she turned and stared out the window. "You know *he* cheated on *me*, right? I'm not going back to him."

David shrugged. "Sometimes people change their minds. I'm not trying to be a jerk—"

"Well, how's that workin' for ya?" she snapped.

How was he managing to say everything wrong? He tried to take her hand again, but she snatched it away from him.

"Megan, I'm sorry. I *am* being a jerk. I didn't mean to."

She narrowed her eyes. "I don't appreciate the third degree when the conversations that I had with Jamie were one, perfectly understandable, and two, before anything happened between us." She crossed her arms, obviously quite pissed. "Not to mention, you have a lot of nerve acting jealous when I'm the one who will actually have to deal with real competition, fifty times a day."

He was botching this whole conversation. He saw a small dirt road and pulled off in a cloud of dust. She had turned her entire body to face the window.

"Megan, look at me, please?" She turned and looked at him through misty eyes. Damn. He'd made her cry. And he could tell that made her even more mad. "First, I'm sorry. This is my baggage I'm dealing with, not yours. And second, you have no competition. No one makes me feel like you do. There's no one else that I think about when I should be working. No one else I think about when I should be sleeping. And it's because I like you so much that I'm acting a little crazy. I'm not used to ... caring so much. I'm really sorry. Forgive me?"

She sighed. "Do you have any idea how many women look at you when you're in a restaurant or walking down the street? I can't help it if that feels like competition."

"Listen, I can't control what those women do, but I can tell you that I don't even notice them anymore. I'm too busy looking at your adorable dimples."

Her dimples sprang to life again, probably against her will, which made her laugh. She sighed and took his hand. "I'm sorry I overreacted."

"No, that was all on me. I was out of line. Forgive me?"

"Yes, I forgive ya."

He leaned in, and they touched forehead to forehead. "Thanks." He cupped her cheek. "Since we're not in Millway, I think it's safe for me to kiss ya. What do you think?"

She grinned. "I think you should follow that instinct."

~∕〜

Following that instinct had them arriving in Killarney ten minutes after the Phonesaver cell store closed.

"Crap. Brenna's gonna kill me." Megan had promised her friend she'd get her phone either fixed or better yet, upgraded. Brenna didn't appreciate ignored texts and Megan's phone was still constantly dropping texts. Or just plain not working.

"Well, we can drive back this weekend. I'm free on Saturday. We could go to Muckross House, too."

She grabbed his forearm. "I love it there! Have you walked through the gardens behind the Manor House?" The beautiful estate, in the first National Park of Ireland, was one of her favorite places to visit, even if it was overrun with tourists. Queen Victoria had even stayed there once. And the thousands of acres that surrounded the estate were gorgeous. It was the kind of place Megan enjoyed getting lost in. It would be even more enjoyable getting lost in the woods with David. She smiled at the thought.

"A long time ago, but yes. I remember them. I love the trees that look like they don't belong—"

"Yes! They look like they're from Japan, don't they? Those really tall ones with the reddish-tan trunks?"

"Aye, those are the ones." He was scoring brownie points right now, no question.

They were driving in circles, looking for a place to park that was near a restaurant and the church where the meeting would be. They settled on a little Chinese restaurant that was not much more than a hole in the wall, but Megan had been before and knew the food was excellent. After a quick dinner, they walked to the church. David reached for her hand, and she hesitated.

"Sorry, it's just that anyone could be driving by. Slow, remember?"

He nodded. "So, how about at the meeting? No one else is from Millway. Are we allowed PDA there? Can I sit next to you, or would it be better if I were across the room?"

She smacked his arm and then had to rub her hand. Rock hard biceps, geez! "Stop teasing. I thought you understood why I wanted to be cautious."

He laughed. "I do. And I am teasing you. It's fun." He nudged her with his elbow, eliciting another smile. He was good at that. "But I know why ya want to take things slowly. It's the smarter way to handle things, even if it doesn't feel so smart whenever I'm near you."

"I just need a little more time. Everyone is being so sweet to me. I don't want to look like the heartless chick who starts dating another guy right after she finds out her ex-fiancé has a life-altering injury. Ya know? Especially not the most eligible bachelor to hit town in years. Girls are going to hate me."

"I'm sorry. I won't pressure you anymore. You set the pace." A sad smile crossed his face.

"Even just a couple more days. Tell ya what, let's just get to Friday. That will be our first official date, and I'll be ready to handle any backlash by then. I promise."

"Deal. Till Friday." He held out his hand for a handshake and she took it, noticing he held the shake for longer than necessary and shot her a wink when he finally did let go. He was used to getting his way. She could tell this was new for him, being held at arms length.

The old church still smelled like coffee and mothballs. Different pictures were hung on the strings this time. She looked for Alahaji but didn't see him in any of the shots. David went to get them coffee while she looked at a scrapbook Donal had put out on the information table. Glancing across the room, she laughed to herself when she noticed that David still hadn't made it to the coffee table. Someone stopped him about every three feet. She picked up a map of Sierra Leone and a flyer about the Müller Haven House for Children, located in Sierra Leone's capitol, Freetown.

"Megan?"

She turned at the familiar voice. "Shannon! What are you doing here?"

"Remember when I went on the mission trip to Uganda? That was with C.A.M.P. Hoping to get back to Africa, maybe next year. Have you been here before?"

"I've been just the one time. You weren't here at the last meeting."

"No, I was still in Dublin and I never really got involved with the chapter there. I hear there's a big benefit to get ready for, so I told Donal I'd do my best to start coming to the meetings, now that I'm back in town."

"Ah, how did you connect with C.A.M.P.?

"Donal took a student group to Uganda my freshman year, and I was chosen by my professor to go. It was amazing. I learned so much, and I've been dying to get back to Africa ever since." Megan remembered looking at Shannon's pictures from that trip. Shannon glanced across the room, and her eyes grew wide. She grabbed Megan's arm. "Doctor David is a member?"

"He's the one who told me about it." Megan watched as a telltale flush crept up Shannon's face.

"Cool," she said absently as she continued to stare in his direction.

"How's the new job?" *Hello?*

"Hmm? Oh, good. I love it. I already knew the whole staff. It's great. A little awkward with Doctor David, but I'm sure that will fade." She still hadn't taken her eyes from David, who was about twenty feet away, holding two coffees, surrounded by four women who appeared to be peppering him with questions. He looked cornered and shot Megan a "help me" look, and then something like alarm passed over his face as he noticed Shannon standing next to her.

"Why awkward?" Megan asked.

Shannon finally turned her attention to Megan as if she'd just realized they were having a conversation. "Oh, because we went out when I lived in Dublin. It's a little weird, now that he's my boss. Good Lord, he's gorgeous, isn't he?"

Megan just nodded, and Shannon hardly seemed to notice. They had just talked about Shannon in the car, and he hadn't mentioned dating her. Why? Was he trying to keep it a secret? Did he still like her? Was he keeping her on the back burner in case things didn't work out between them? Shannon was a very pretty girl with porcelain skin, big dark eyes, and lots of wavy black hair. If he was interested in her, he certainly wouldn't want the two of them talking. Megan glanced back toward David. No wonder he looked alarmed.

"So, ya think he's still interested?" Megan asked, careful to sound nonchalant.

"I have no idea. It's hard to tell. It's been over a year, and I don't think he knew I was the one who was hired, so he looked pretty shocked at Ben's party. But he was really friendly this week, so I'm hopeful. If I can just keep from acting like a babbling fool around him. He makes me nervous, and I act like a silly schoolgirl, and I forget how to think! It's embarrassing. Oh, here he comes." Shannon squeezed her arm, again. "Act natural."

David appeared to be studying Megan's face as he approached. She smiled wide and acted "natural."

Shannon, oblivious, greeted him enthusiastically. "Hi there! I had no idea you were a C.A.M.P. member."

He smiled, somewhat stiff. "No, I didn't know you were either. Small world." He continued to look at Megan. She knew he was trying to read her. She smiled, acted casual, and suggested they take their seats, as Donal was approaching the front of the room. She noticed Shannon waited until they had both taken seats so she could take the seat next to David.

David's body language shouted that he wasn't interested. But was that just for Megan's benefit? Shannon seemed completely clueless to the undercurrents, which was odd, because she was a sharp girl. Megan decided she would just ask him about it on the way home and focused her attention on Donal as he addressed the group.

"Folks, thank you for coming. You will be thrilled to know that I will be skipping the icebreaker this evening, since we just met a couple weeks ago." A round of applause and whistles had Donal holding his hands over his heart in mock pain. "Come now, the games aren't that bad. They build camaraderie. However, you shall be spared today, as we only have the church for an hour tonight, and we have several things to cover for the Müller Haven House Benefit. We've just gotten word that we will indeed need to find a new venue. Highly inconvenient at this late stage, but that's the way it goes. So please let us know if you think of anything."

*Mountdonovan.* The thought flew through Megan's brain like an arrow. What if they did the benefit as a grand opening of the Mountdonovan Estate? Even if she didn't get the director job, she could help organize the event. And what better way to open the estate than to do a benefit for a children's home? Ryan's team had already begun the renovations. How quickly could they finish? Her brain was buzzing, and she'd barely heard any of what Donal was saying. *Focus, Megan.*

" ... and Moira emailed you all with details about the different committees we'll be needing for the event. So, she will be splitting you up into those committees so each area gets a start on an action plan. Now, I need the doctors to come meet with me upstairs, as we have some medical things to review from the team that returned last month."

David gave a quick wave as he followed Donal and three others up the stairs. Moira introduced the heads of the committees who in turn called out names of those who'd been assigned to their group. Those who didn't have a group were free to choose.

Megan had expressed an interest in helping with the decor and the floral centerpieces, so she met with that group and Shannon, who was unassigned, joined her. Introductions made and tasks delegated, the remainder of the time was spent chatting and getting to know one another. Megan's mind was elsewhere, though. She was preoccupied with the idea of proposing the benefit to the TidyTowns committee, and she was anxious to talk with David on the way home about his and Shannon's supposed relationship.

As the meeting wound to an end, Shannon made a call. Megan looked for David but didn't see him, so she figured she could just find him upstairs on the way out. With Shannon still on her phone, Megan mouthed a good-bye, but Shannon waved her hands, indicating she wanted Megan to wait. David joined them just as Shannon finished her call.

She turned toward Megan. "Would you be able to give me a ride home, Meg? That was my aunt. She's my ride, but she met her friends here for dinner and won't be done for another hour. I didn't realize the meeting was a short one tonight."

"Well, I didn't drive. David gave me a ride." Megan turned to David. It was his choice.

Shannon's flustered face turned pink. "Oh, would you mind giving me a ride? I live a couple miles past Megan's place."

Irritation flashed over David's face so quickly that Megan doubted Shannon's rose-colored glasses allowed her to see it. He glanced at Megan and then answered, "Sure, not a problem."

So much for asking him about Shannon on the way home. Megan almost laughed as they neared the car and Shannon asked if she'd mind if she sat in front. "I get carsick in the back," she said.

"No problem." Megan replied and smiled as she caught David rolling his eyes. The entire ride home, Shannon chattered like a magpie, and Megan grew amused as she noticed David's jaw twitching. She'd never heard Shannon talk so much. She wasn't kidding that he made her nervous.

When he dropped Megan off in her driveway, he looked miserable and mouthed that he would call her. She went to her room to get ready for bed and waited. But no call came. She wondered if maybe her phone was just acting up, so she tested it by calling the pharmacy, knowing it would just go to after-hours voicemail. She held her breath until the connection went through and she heard the voicemail kick in. Disappointed, she tossed her cell onto her bedside table. Phone was working just fine. So, he'd simply decided not to call. Which made her doubt her read on the situation.

Maybe what she took as irritation at having to bring Shannon home, was merely discomfort at having two of his prospects in his car at one time. Maybe all that talk about her not having any competition was a load of crap, and he was getting reacquainted with her competition right now. She could practically feel green vapors of jealousy oozing from her pores. She turned out the lights and stared at her ceiling, willing herself to sleep but having no success. She rolled over, grabbed her phone again, and checked the ringer. It was on. No missed calls. She wondered if she should call him. And then she pictured his car windows full of steam and punched her pillow several times.

No way. He would have to call her, if he dared.

She texted Brenna, instead: *Had a very weird night. Text if ur still up and I'll call u.*

She waited a minute and tried again: *Hey ... still up?*

She wasn't answering. Must have gone to bed early. Megan's thoughts were swirling and she begged God to just turn off her brain so she could sleep. But it just continued to swirl.

Apparently, He wasn't answering her either.

⚓

The woman did not shut up. When he had seen her at Ben's party, David had remembered they'd gone out but couldn't remember why it had only been once. She was pretty and smart, so why hadn't he called her again? The ride home from Killarney was a good clue. After twenty minutes, he'd completely tuned her out and tried to think of a way he could drop her off first, before Megan, but there was no logical way to do it. They lived on the same road, it was a dead end, and he'd have to pass Megan's house to get to Shannon's.

He decided he would just call Megan after. She might not even know he'd gone out with Shannon, but it was time to tell her, now that Shannon had made it so freakin' obvious that she was interested. The last thing he wanted was for Megan to get the wrong idea. He'd been watching her all night. She didn't seem angry; she seemed amused. He wished he could laugh at the situation, but not being able to explain had him on edge.

Megan smiled when she got out of the car. That was a good sign, right? If she were mad, she wouldn't be smiling. He tried to let her know he'd call her and then pulled away. The two miles to Shannon's house felt like ten as she prattled on about some course she had taken in the spring.

He pulled into the long drive and expected her to get out, but she didn't. She kept talking. He tried to be polite. He had to work with this woman and didn't want to cause problems at the office, but after five more minutes of her talking, and not taking a single hint, he decided he would just get out and go open her door. But just as he reached for his door handle, she got quiet. Maybe she'd finally run out of words.

"Well, see you at work tomorrow." He barely smiled, not wanting to encourage any more conversation.

Shannon took a deep breath. "Can I ask ya something?"

*No. Freaking. Way.* "Go ahead."

"Well, that time we went out, I had a great time. And I felt like we connected. And then you never called and ya didn't text me back, when I texted you. So, I always wondered what happened."

*Seriously? I have to talk about this now?* David could feel time ticking in his brain. He *had* to call Megan. But he also had to work with Shannon. He couldn't just blow her off. But neither could he just tell her the truth: that she talked so much it made his ears bleed.

He hesitated, trying to think of what to say.

"David, I know we work in the same office now, so I don't want to make things uncomfortable. That's why I didn't say anything earlier this week. But running into you at the meeting like that, finding out you may be going to Sierra Leone next year and I might, too ... it all just makes me wonder if there's some bigger plan at work here."

He could just tell her he was falling in love with Megan. But he'd promised to wait till Friday before they made their new relationship public. And he knew, in a small town like Millway, if he told Shannon tonight, it would be all over town by lunchtime tomorrow.

"Listen, Shannon. You're a really nice girl, and I had a nice time when we went out. But at the time, I wasn't looking for any kind of relationship."

"And now?" Her big, brown eyes were full of hope.

"And now ..." He should just tell her the truth. He wasn't interested. They weren't a good match. He was falling in love with Megan. " ... now we work together." *Coward.*

She looked down and nodded. "I understand." She opened her door. "Thanks for the ride. Sorry I talked so much. I don't usually, but I ramble when I'm nervous."

"It's okay." He gave her a genuine smile. "Don't be nervous around me. I'm harmless."

"Thanks. See ya tomorrow."

"Bye." She closed the door and he closed his eyes, soaking in the silence.

He waited until she was inside and then turned the car around so he could navigate the long driveway going forward. Reversing down that thing in the dark would surely land him in a ditch. He parked at the very end of the drive and called Megan. No answer and no voicemail. Damn.

He texted her: *Hey, r u still up?*

Nothing. He drove the two miles much quicker than he should have. But when he slowed down outside Megan's home, all the lights were off. He was tempted to try the pebbles at the window trick; it worked in the movies. But he didn't want to make a big deal out of the Shannon thing, especially if Megan didn't already know. She was probably peacefully sleeping. He would have to be patient and wait until tomorrow.

# Chapter Twenty-Eight

Megan's eyes fluttered open as sunrays poured through the wavy windowpane by her bed, splitting into a shower of tiny prisms. She'd always loved that one windowpane. It was original to the house, so probably a couple hundred years old. And with time, the glass had shifted and sagged until its wiggly pattern made it impossible to see out of. As a kid, she had imagined rainbow faeries were sent to wake her up each morning. But on this particular morning, she cursed the rainbow faeries and wondered why she felt like she had a hangover.

Then she remembered all her tossing and turning. The last time she'd looked at the clock, it read 4:23 a.m. Now, it read 7:02 a.m. and she was too tired to even do the math in her head, to figure out how little sleep that meant she'd gotten. She groaned and rolled over, covering her head and squeezing her eyes shut, hoping she could drift off.

But she knew it was pointless. She could never fall back asleep once she was awake. Never. She'd even tried to teach herself how to do it at university. All her friends could nap at any time of day, but she never could get her body to obey.

Her phone sprang to life, vibrating and beeping on the nightstand. Three, four, five messages registered on the screen. The last was from Brenna: *I'm assuming you sent that text last nite. But I didn't get it till just*

*now. Which means you still have your reject phone. Grrr. So, if you get this*
*some time this month, call me.*

The other four texts were all from David:

*Hey, r u still up?*

*I'm outside. If ur up, text me.*

*Woke up thinkin of u.*

*Little worried ur not replying or answering ur phone. Call me?*

She had three missed calls, too. One from Brenna and two from David.
Well, it was nice to feel loved. But if she didn't get her phone fixed ASAP,
she might lose a best friend. She sent off quick texts to both Brenna and
David, apologizing for her stupid phone and promising them she'd try to
reach them later.

At least David hadn't blown her off the night before. It was her phone's
fault. That had her relieved, and even feeling a little guilty for all the nasty
thoughts she'd had.

Usually, she showered and dressed before she ventured downstairs.
But this morning, she needed coffee more than anything else. So she
wrapped up in her robe and slippers and shuffled toward the stairs. She'd
smelled the sausage as soon as she opened her door and then the scent of
coffee drifted past her and she smiled, following the scent down the stairs.

"Hey Mam," she said as she grabbed her favorite coffee mug. It was
decorated with a riot of colorful flowers and the words "Time Began in a
Garden" in a flowing script on the side. Yes, corny. But she was a gardener,
so she liked it anyway.

"Morning. How was yer meeting?" Her mam was fully dressed and ac-
cessorized.

"Good." Megan blew her off by habit and then felt a pang of guilt. She
had promised she'd be honest and try to build a better relationship. She
decided to try something she hadn't done in years—let her mam in and ask
her advice. "Actually, it was a really weird meeting."

Marlene turned off the burner and faced her. "Weird how?"

"Well, I'm trying to figure out a new relationship, and it just kind of
feels like a roller coaster sometimes."

"David, right?"

Megan nodded. "It's that obvious?"

"No. I was clueless," she admitted with a wave of her hand. "Your da told me he thought something was brewing."

"Oh, it's brewing." Megan knew she was blushing.

Her mam sat down across from her with a deep breath and a smile. "You can tell me as little or as much as ya want. Yer call. I'm just going to sit and listen."

Impressive. Megan had been bracing for an immediate, strong opinion. Patient diplomacy was more than she'd hoped for.

"Okay. Well, I'll try to sum up. I got the feeling he was interested in me, but then I had the feeling he was interested in a lot of women, so I tried to steer clear of him. But that was hard. He kept showing up and talking to me or even just smiling at me." *Geez.* Her stomach fluttered at just the thought. "He's got a killer smile."

"I've noticed."

"Ya have?"

"I'm old, not blind," her mam said with a wry smile.

"Good point. But you're not old. You're just ... mature."

She nodded. "I'll take that. So, have you gone out with him?"

"Not exactly. We had lunch this week. And we went to the meeting last night. But he's made it—um—clear that he's attracted to me." Blushing again. Megan was all for getting closer with her mam. But she would not be giving details about her Sunday walk in the garden.

Marlene smiled. Normally, in a conversation like this, she would be in full interrogation mode by this point. Who? What? Where? When? Why? Instead, she just patiently waited. Megan could definitely get used to this.

"Here's the thing: there's no question we are attracted to each other, but I don't know if I trust him. I can't build a relationship on attraction alone. And I don't want to set myself up to be hurt. I can't take any more drama."

Marlene nodded. "Sounds to me like you just need to take things slowly and get to know him. There will come a point when you will know that you can either trust him or not. In the meantime, spend time finding out who he really is."

"I know. I need to keep things slow. But it's really tricky when I'm around him. I don't think straight."

Her mam laughed. "I remember the feeling."

"With da?" Megan wrinkled her nose at the thought.

Marlene nodded and smiled. "Mm-hm."

"I don't want to know, Mam. Sorry."

Laughter again. She was enjoying this, wasn't she? "I don't expect you do. I'm just telling you I understand what you're talking about. But you can slow it down. You have to be wise about where you spend your time getting to know each other. Go out in public. Walk in the park, go to Rosie's, keep things in public, and it will help you deal with the temptation to speed things up."

"That is a very good idea. Thanks."

"May I ask why you're not sure you can trust him?"

"Well, last night we were driving to the meeting, and he got all weird about Jamie. Like jealous, and we kind of fought about it, but he apologized and it was fine."

"Well, I don't like the sound of that. If he's jealous and you're not even really together yet, that may be a red flag."

"I know. But it wasn't like that. It wasn't like he was nasty or anything. He did say something about his baggage, and I didn't ask him to clarify. But the argument isn't even what I'm concerned about. After that we talked about Shannon starting at his office this week. I think I asked him about it, and he said she was doing a good job. That was all. Normal conversation. But then, Shannon turns up at the meeting, and then she tells me she and David went out last year in Dublin, and she's obviously very into him. I mean, so into him that it was like I wasn't even there."

"And how did he act toward her?"

"No interest. Polite. But what bothers me is that he didn't mention they went out. You would think he would, unless he had a reason not to. So, now I'm wondering what's actually going on? Was last night an act for my benefit, just so I wouldn't think he liked her? I'm wondering if he's kind of keeping her in mind as a backup in case I don't work out. I don't know. It really didn't seem like he liked her. But I'm just confused."

"Well, I would have thought he would have called to explain himself."

"Oh, right. My phone is messed up. So, he did try to text me and call me last night. Should I stop in to see him at work? Call him?"

"I think you do need to talk to him. I would call."

Megan was so pleasantly surprised at having a rational, calm, and helpful conversation with her mam that she popped up from the table and gave her a tight hug. "Thanks, Mam. I'm really glad I talked to ya about it."

And although Marlene turned away quickly, Megan thought she may have seen a tear in her eye. Grabbing a pancake and piece of sausage from the counter, she headed back up to her room to call David.

⌐⊷⊷

David had sent Megan two more texts this morning and tried to call her. Either she actually was mad, or her phone was messed up again. He considered driving out to see her before work, but he was starting to feel like a stalker. So, instead, he made himself some breakfast and forced himself to review some medical journals.

His phone rang, and he answered it before the first ring ended. "Hey, Megan. Is everything okay?"

"Aye, sorry about the texts. My phone seemed like it was working fine last night, but it wasn't showing me texts or taking incoming calls. If you're still up for going to Muckross House on Saturday, I really need to get a new phone on the way."

"Definitely. Are ya free tonight? I'd like to see you ... talk with you." He needed to tell her about Shannon, even if she didn't know they'd gone out. It had kept him up all night.

She hesitated. "I want to talk with you, too. But I'm working when you probably have lunch, today. And then I'm singing at Veritas, and I'm supposed to go to Brenna's afterward for a Jane Austen movie night. Don't laugh." He laughed anyway. "Hey!"

"No, not laughing at you. Just at the fact that ya told me not to laugh. I actually like Jane Austen flicks. Now it's your turn not to laugh."

"Seriously, you like chick flicks?"

"Well, not *all* chick flicks. I like the period pieces, if they're well written. But ya don't have to pass that around. It might get my man-card re-
voked."

Now she was laughing, and he could picture her dimples. "So you can't
make it work today?"

"It's kind of hard today, and since we're going out tomorrow night, we
can just talk then, right?"

He didn't want to wait till then. But he also didn't want to make a big
deal out of nothing. "Aye, we can talk tomorrow. I've made reservations for
6:00 p.m., at the Blackwater. I'll pick you up at a quarter till?"

"Sounds good. Have a nice day."

"You too. Bye."

At face value, the conversation was fine. But something about it wasn't
right. She was acting weird. Maybe Shannon had said something after all.
He'd just have to be patient until tomorrow night. Then he would explain,
and she would be fine, and they could move on.

⌒➤⤙

Brenna parked her car at the B&B when she dropped Ben off with Bettie. It wasn't raining, so she decided to walk into town for her lunch with
Anna. She enjoyed the ten-minute walk. It reminded her of when she'd
first moved to Millway. She'd lived at the B&B and worked at Rosie's, so
she could probably still make the walk in her sleep.

Anna's office at Sacred Heart was behind the sanctuary. It was a large
room, painted in soft browns, with a couple doors leading out of it into various storerooms and offices. She was the administrative assistant, so her
desk was centered in the room, directly in line with Father Tim's door.
Anyone who wanted to see him would have to go through her, literally.
When Brenna walked in, Father Tim was sitting on the corner of Anna's
desk, and they were laughing heartily about something.

He was a few years younger than Anna, with salt-and-pepper hair, cut
short and gelled into place. He'd been a bit overweight when they'd first
met him, but in the last year he'd lost a good thirty-five pounds, and it suited him well. Some said he'd had a scare with his heart. Others said he was

sick, and that's why he'd dropped so much weight. But Anna assured her neither was true. He'd simply joined a new gym last year, and regular workouts had him feeling better than he had in years.

"Ah, Brenna, how are ya doin', young lady?" He stood and greeted her with a hug and a kiss on the cheek.

"I'm well, Father Tim. Sorry, again, that we had to cancel dinner last weekend. We're still on for this Saturday?"

"Aye, wouldn't miss it." He patted his stomach, a leftover habit from when there'd been much more to pat.

Anna gave her a hug and kiss, as well, and then grabbed her sweater. "I'll be back in an hour," she said to Father Tim, "want me to bring you anything?"

He smiled and pulled out his wallet. "Sure, chicken salad would be great. Thanks, luv."

She waved off his money. "My turn. You bought Monday."

Brenna watched them with interest. Neither of them would ever admit it, but there was something there between them. It was quiet and far below the surface, but she knew Anna well enough to see what Anna might not even see, herself. There was no point in bringing it up, though. Father Tim was a Catholic priest and could not marry. And he was a wonderful priest. But the no-marriage thing was a shame.

Anna looped her arm through Brenna's as they walked down the narrow sidewalk toward Rosie's. "How are ya doin'?

"Fine. I miss Ryan when he's gone so much. But I understand why he has to leave."

Anna nodded. "I imagine it's hard on the both of you."

"Yep. But we make up for it when he gets home," Brenna said with a grin, and Anna rolled her eyes.

"Now, don't be givin' me too much information, girl."

Brenna laughed. "Sorry. Just missing him a lot today. It helps me to think about what happens when he gets home. I'll keep it to myself."

"I appreciate that." Anna opened the door and held it as Brenna walked into Rosie's.

As they sat at a booth and ordered lunch, Brenna wondered how it would feel if she had to come back to work. She had enjoyed it when she was a server. But it was a tiring job for her. Not physically. Just having to talk to so many people and always being "on" wore her out.

She didn't miss that aspect of the job. But watching Brigit and Tara talking and joking about something, she missed the camaraderie of the workplace. She spent her days with Ben, and she loved it, but if she had to leave him with Anna or Bettie a few nights a week, so she could bring some money into the household, it wouldn't be all bad.

"You're quiet today." Anna said, once their meals had been delivered.

Brenna shrugged. "Lot on my mind, I guess. Ryan's had some good meetings this week. The prospect that he went to meet on Saturday is looking good."

"So, if he sells his construction business, what will he do for income?"

"He's looking to structure the deal so that he has a small stake in it still for at least a while, and he would manage any jobs from here to Killarney."

"Ah, that's good. Will that be enough for ya to live on, though?"

"I don't know. He's got a lot of money in the bank and in investments. He hardly spent anything before we got married. But as far as the income to live off of, I'm thinking about what I can do to help. Any thoughts?"

"Yes, actually. Would you be interested in helping out at the B&B?" Anna stirred cream and sugar into her coffee.

"Sure. But I'd do that for free. I don't want to take money from Bettie and Patsy."

"Well, Bettie's the one who suggested it. She's overwhelmed since she took on the pastry business. If she doesn't pay you, she'll end up paying someone else. May as well be you, right?"

The thought had occurred to Brenna before, but she didn't think it was a viable option. "What would she need me to do?"

"You'll have to talk with her. It's nothing glamorous, but I think she could use help with both the workload at the B&B and delivering pastries. She turns down pastry orders every week because she doesn't have time. If she had help, she could easily make enough to cover what she'd pay you and more besides. Not to mention, she can keep an eye on Benny-boy while she's baking, leaving you free to make deliveries or whatever needs doing."

"Hmmm. I would love to help her. I'll talk to her this week." She picked at her salad, not very hungry. "So, anything new with you?"

Anna laughed. "No, I'm pretty routine. Get up, change beds for Bettie, go to work, come home, help Bettie with tea time snack, have tea with Auntie Pat, dinner, bed."

"Aw, Anna. That makes me sad. Do you regret the move here?"

Anna raised her brows, "No! You know me, it's my way. I like routine. I'd be just the same, back in the States. No, I don't regret the move, even for a second. Joe and I had actually talked about retiring here." Anna always had a wistful look when she talked about her late husband.

"That would have been nice." Brenna knew she missed him. Even with Ryan in her life, she still missed her first husband, Ben, at times. Something would remind her of him, and she'd find herself wondering how life would have turned out if he and his dad hadn't been on the highway that night. She knew the same thing happened to Anna. Those memories would come out of nowhere, and you just had to deal with them when they came. Allow yourself to still grieve, when you needed to.

Anna flagged Brigit down for a refill on her coffee and asked her to put in the order for Father Tim's salad, to-go. "So, how's Megan, after Elizabeth's speech at Mass?"

"She's really good, I think. Except she has a dumb phone that doesn't work half the time." Brenna rolled her eyes. She was actually getting very tired of Megan's phone issues. "It was the right thing for Elizabeth to do, and I think it's made a huge difference for Megan in just how she feels out in public. It was so bad before. People can be so judgmental and cruel."

Anna nodded. "It broke my heart, how people treated her. I've hardly spoken to Patricia in months because she was always trashing Megan, and I couldn't take it. I even quit book club."

"You did? I didn't know that. I know you're close to Elizabeth, so the fact that you trusted my take on the whole thing meant a lot to me." Brenna speared a piece of chicken onto her fork.

"Well, none of it made sense. But I can read people well, and I thought Megan was telling the truth. Poor lass has been through so much. It's nice to see her smiling again."

Brenna nodded. "It is."

"I think a certain doctor may have something to do with that smile, too." Anna grinned over her coffee cup.

"What makes you say that?" Brenna had promised not to say anything about Megan and David until they made it public. She was very tempted to give Anna just a little bit of information. But she kept her tone neutral.

"Nothing specific, and I see you're not going to be of any help in giving me specifics. But it's just something about the way they act around each other. It's very cute."

Brenna nodded, giving away nothing. "Well, I think they would make an adorable couple."

"And they'd make gorgeous children!" Anna laughed.

No question, there. "They'd look like a Hollywood couple, wouldn't they?"

"Aye, have ya seen what happens when he walks down the street? Practically stops traffic."

"Oh my gosh, I know!"

Brigit brought their bill and Father Tim's salad. Brenna heard a text come in. It was from Megan:

*Hey, we're still on for Jane night, right?*

Brenna replied: *Absolutely! I've got a bottle of wine that David brought to Ben's party. Can't wait. I'm thinkin' Mansfield Park. Sound good?*

They paid their bill, left Rosie's, and headed back toward Sacred Heart. Brenna glanced at her phone twice along the way. No reply. "Grrrr. Megan's phone is driving me crazy!"

"Why doesn't she get it fixed?"

"She was supposed to get a new one last night, but she didn't get to the store in time. I swear, if she doesn't get it taken care of this weekend, I might ban her from my house until it's done!"

"Well, we can't all be as tech-savvy as you, my dear. Maybe you should just go with her to Killarney or Cork and help her."

"Apparently, I'm going to have to." Brenna noticed David just coming over the rise at the top of Main Street. "Hey, let's count how many women turn their heads as he walks by."

Anna laughed. "You're terrible."

"Two. Three.. Four."

"That was a guy."

"Still counts." Brenna was laughing and couldn't keep up her count. There had only been about ten people between them and David, and she guessed most of them had turned to look at him.

"Hey, cousin," he said as he approached. "You two look happy."

Anna answered, "We've just been talking about girlie things."

"Ah, well, I'm definitely not part of that conversation, then."

"No, definitely not." Brenna said with a smile. "Heading back to work?"

"I am."

"Well, have a nice day, Cuz."

"Aye, you too. Enjoy your Jane Austen movie night," he said as he continued on toward his office. Brenna wondered if Anna noticed the slip-up. Why would he know about the movie night? It's not likely she would have mentioned it to him, which means if Anna were paying attention, she'd know he and Megan had talked about it. One more day, and all the silly secrecy would be done, and the Hollywood couple would be the talk of the town.

# Chapter Twenty-Nine

It had been difficult to concentrate on work all day because Megan was so excited for her date. Brenna had talked her down a bit last night. She didn't think David was hiding anything intentionally, so Megan decided to trust Brenna's gut and just let it go.

She changed her outfit three times and then settled on the first dress she'd picked out. Turning back and forth in front of the mirror, she took an honest assessment:

Not much to work with on top—thank God for bras that offered a little assistance. A quick glance over her shoulder confirmed that she still had not acquired even a fraction of J Lo's bum. Nope. Still quite flat and not much in the way of hips, either. She sighed. Sometimes, she thought she looked like a boy.

But she did have a tiny waist, which gave the illusion of having more curves than she actually had. She had pretty good legs. She would admit to that. And she usually chose dresses and skirts that let her show off them off, with the hopes that they would draw attention away from her small chest and flat bum.

*Now on to the face.* She crinkled her nose as she made her appraisal. Not too shabby. Without makeup, she looked rather plain. But with a little effort and hair spray, she cleaned up pretty well.

She heard a car door. David was right on time. Her phone beeped with a text message as she grabbed it, and her sweater, and headed down the stairs. The text was from David. He was texting her from the car? Wow. You'd think he'd come to the door, at least. She clicked the text icon: *Hey, sorry, but would u mind meeting me at Blackwater? Late patient. Won't be done till about six. Don't want to miss our rez.*

Who was in her driveway, then? The rest of her family had gone to Limerick for a game. She shot a quick text back to let David know that was fine, that she'd need to stop for petrol, but she'd meet him soon. Then she went to the door.

And almost fainted.

Through the window she could see Jamie's tall, lanky frame, taking halting steps up the path. Instantly, her heart felt like it was beating double-time. She hadn't seen him since that day in January. What was he doing here? And why now?

Another text came in from David: *Thx. Really looking forward to seeing u.*

And then the doorbell rang. Could she just hide? No, her car was parked right in front. He knew she was here. She could *not* do this right now.

She sent off another text: *Gonna be late. sorry. unexpected company.*

The doorbell rang again as her phone made a funny noise. Looking down, she saw the lit screen go blank. It was completely dead, even though she had just charged it!

"Damn, damn, damn."

She blew out a breath and opened the door, with a tentative, "Hello."

"Hi, Meg, I'm sorry to just drop in like this. I just got home, and I wanted to see you first." He rubbed the back of his neck. "I need to do this properly. Can I come in?"

She didn't move. Wasn't even sure what to think.

"Please?" He sounded and looked just like the old Jamie. She couldn't tell him no. She moved out of the way, the room swaying a bit with the surreal feeling of having him in her kitchen after so much time.

"So, are ya just home for a visit?" she asked as they sat at the kitchen table.

"Aye, just for the weekend. But I'll be moving back pretty soon." He looked down at his fidgeting hands. "Megan, I needed to see you in person. You're the reason I came home this weekend. I know my mam told you about the TBI. And I just wanted to see you, face to face, to tell ya how sorry I am for what I did." He looked at her through his long, dark lashes and then looked down again.

The lump in her throat was almost painful. He'd already told her he was sorry, on the phone. But having him sitting in front of her, saying it to her face—and sober—it was much more powerful. She was finding it hard to stay detached.

"You really hurt me, Jamie." Tears were brimming in her eyes. And she was shocked to see the same in his.

"I'm sorry." He was looking directly into her eyes, now. "There's no excuse. I know the TBI affects me, but I can't blame what I did on that. Not fully. I was upset and confused, but I didn't reach out for help. I didn't want you to know about the stupid things I was doing, cuz I was ashamed. So, I just convinced myself that you were cramping my style and I lied to you ... myself ... my parents. Everyone. It was like I was two people. I could see what I was doing was wrong, but I just kept doing it. I'm so sorry I hurt you, luv. You didn't deserve it. I hate myself for what I did to you."

"Um ... wow." She rose and grabbed a tissue from the counter, dabbing her eyes as she leaned against the sink to give herself a little space. She also plugged in her phone to see if it would come back on, but no such luck. "I'm glad you're sorry. After all this time, I have to be honest. I don't really even know how to feel around you."

"I know. I don't blame ya. I'm not expecting anything from you. I just want ya to know that I'm sorry."

"Thanks." Her voice broke, and she whispered, "I forgave you, already."

"I know, ya said that when I called. But I needed to look into your eyes and make sure it was true."

He looked so sad and defeated. Her heart went out to him; her mind had no say. She reached for his hands and pulled so he would stand. "It's true. I do forgive you. Come here." She held her arms out and let him hug her. Standing there, in such a familiar place, she realized not only had she forgiven him, she still loved this man, deeply.

But not in the way a woman loves a man. Things had changed. She had changed. Whether it was what he'd done or the things she'd been through since then, she wasn't sure, but she just didn't feel the same way about him. And that revelation had her realizing how much she cared about David. He was the one she wanted to spend her time with. If she'd had any doubt that she was over Jamie, it was erased. She did want to see him get better, though.

"I'm sorry for all you're going through, Jame," she said, softly. And she felt him tremble. And then silent sobs began wracking his body, and she thought she might fall apart. What woman can stand to see a man cry? "Hey, hey, it's okay. Shhh. It's gonna be okay." She rubbed his back.

Jamie didn't stop crying. Instead, he released her and went to his knees, still shaking. "I screwed up my whole life, Meg. I don't understand how I got here. How this happened. It doesn't make any sense."

She knelt down in front of him and pulled him into another hug. They stayed like that for several moments. "I don't understand it, either. I've asked God to make sense of it so many times. I've never gotten an answer. But, this last week I've been praying for you. And seeing you now, I feel like God has answered some of my prayers. You seem like the old Jamie, to me. How do ya feel?"

Noting the tears on his cheeks, Megan pulled away to grab the box of tissues and then sat back down on the floor, offering the box to him.

"Thanks." He grabbed several tissues and wiped his eyes and nose. "Sorry I lost it. I don't really know how to answer yer question. Sometimes, I feel like I'm exactly the same. But then I forget simple words or something happens and I get frustrated, or mad and I handle it differently than I used to. I'm not patient, like I was. I blow up ... go from zero to sixty without warning. I hurt people I love." He looked at her as his voice faltered. "I'm glad to know that there's a reason though. You can't imagine what it's been like, not having any clue why I felt so different, why I kept doing stupid things."

"It must have been scary." She took his hand and squeezed.

"It still is. I don't think I'll ever get back to the guy I was. That scares the fecking shit out of me." A bitter laugh escaped his lips. "Right there, that was something I wouldn't have said before."

She smiled, as she had just thought the exact same thing. "I think you need to give yourself a lot of grace and time. I know you said you can't blame what you did on the injury. But I'd say it's got to be about ninety percent of it. I mean, I know you made certain choices. But you wouldn't have made those before the injury, ya know?"

Holy crap. Was she really sitting on her kitchen floor defending Jamie ... to Jamie? *Twilight Zone.* She caught sight of the clock and winced. 6:22 p.m. She had no way to know if her last text went through to David and no way to contact him since she only had his number stored in her stupid phone which was still just a black screen. The thought of him sitting alone at the restaurant wondering where the heck she was tied her stomach in knots. But she couldn't exactly tell Jamie she had to get to her date when he was sitting on her kitchen floor, weeping.

"Aye, unfortunately, grace is one of the things I can't seem to find anymore. Along with patience, peace, sleep, forgiveness—"

"I really do forgive you, Jamie."

He rubbed her hand. "I know ya do. I'm talking about not being able to forgive myself. I knew what I was doing, when you came to visit. I mean, being an ass. I didn't deserve you anymore, and I wanted you to hate me, cuz I hated myself."

*Wait. What?* "So, that was an act?"

"No, I wouldn't say that. But it was me *not* trying to be the old Jamie. I was miserable, and I was doing stupid things. I think on some level, it was me, trying to show you what ya would have to deal with if you stayed with me." In a strange and twisted way, she thought that sounded like him loving her the only way he could at that time.

"And this, this is you trying to be the old Jamie?"

"No. This is who I am. I'm just not always like this. There are other parts to my personality that I never had before ... things I never dealt with, before the accident."

Megan took a deep breath and nodded. "You were drunk when ya called me, last week."

"Aye." He nodded. "That's not uncommon, lately. I get overwhelmed and the only thing that seems to help is a drink. Docs are giving me some other coping techniques, though. I haven't had a drink this week."

"That's good." She squeezed his hand again.

"'Tis. But I've a long way to go. I'd appreciate it if you'd keep sayin' those prayers. I'm not sure I know how to pray, anymore. Not sure I even want to." He stood and put the tissue box back on the counter, then turned back, offering a hand to pull Megan up.

She had to move him along but didn't want him to feel like she was pushing him away. She kept hold of his hand and began walking toward the front door.

Outside, they stood in front of his car for several minutes, talking about his treatment and what the doctors had told him about TBI, until Jamie said he needed to go.

"Well," Megan took his hands in hers, "I don't think there's any script for how to handle all this, or what happened with us. But I want you to know, you were my friend for a long time before we were anything else. And you're still my friend. I'm here if ya need me, okay?"

Jamie looked at her with a mix of pain and relief. He took her face in his hands, leaned in, forehead to forehead. "You were the best thing that ever happened to me. I never got to say goodbye." And then he kissed her, as tears rolled down his face. "Thank you for not hating me."

She let him pull her into one final embrace. It felt like goodbye. And although she was sure she would see him again, she knew they both understood it would only be as friends.

As Jamie drove away, she ran back inside, grabbed her phone, sweater and keys. Her phone was still dead. Damn phone. The wall clock said 6:48 p.m. What must David be thinking? She would have called him from the home phone if she knew his number. She realized she didn't know any numbers. Brenna would have David's number, but she didn't even know *her* number. She made a mental note to get an old-fashioned paper address book.

She sat in her car for a minute, just breathing slowly. She felt numb about what had just happened with Jamie. And she didn't have time to think it through. David was either waiting for her at The Blackwater or he'd given up on her. She intended to find him, either way. She wanted to tell him she didn't care if he'd dated Shannon before. And she didn't care if the whole town flirted with him. She was ready to go public. She wanted to know him more, to be with him, and she didn't care what people had to say about it.

～

David checked his phone as he left his office. It was 6:05 p.m. Great. Their first official date, and he'd blown off picking her up and was still late. He shot off a quick text to let Megan know he was two minutes away.

The Blackwater was fairly crowded. It was a dinner crowd more than a bar crowd. But David did notice Shannon sitting at the bar by herself, with a whiskey in her hand and another one on the bar in front of her. Thankfully, her back was to him. As the hostess approached, he scanned the room for Megan, but she wasn't there yet. Well, at least she wouldn't be upset at him for being late.

The Blackwater Inn and Grill, Ryan had explained on a recent tour through Millway, had been a dilapidated hotel, and the only one in town until about a year ago, when a wealthy businessman who'd been born in Millway gave it a complete makeover.

Golden-brown textured walls highlighted the abundant, rich, walnut trim. And you could tell they had put money into the bar. It was also made of the dark wood, but the bronze accents and polished granite top gave the whole restaurant an air of elegance. The stone fireplace and wooden tables, in contrast, gave it a comfortable, homey feel.

David was seated in a cozy booth near the fireplace and he'd only ordered water, so he could wait to see if Megan wanted some wine. But he was growing concerned. She hadn't replied to his texts asking if she was okay, and now she was almost twenty minutes late, and she only lived five minutes away. He warred between concern for her safety and irritation that he was essentially being stood up.

He noticed Shannon stand up and then sit back down again, quickly. She wobbled on her stool and then seemed to find her balance. From the looks of it, she'd had one whiskey too many.

"So, is there anything I can get ya, luv?" the server said with a wink and a smile. David told her he was all set and noticed her slight frown. She was in her mid-to-late forties and had "cougar" written all over her. She wore the standard server outfit, black on black, but she made sure it was form-fitting and showed enough cleavage to pique interest but not enough to look trashy. She was attractive, and there was a time when David might have gone out with someone like her. He'd gone out with a few older women, back in the day, and he found them to be very interesting. But he'd grown tired of his college playboy persona after his first trip to Africa. Since then, he'd kept his relationships simple. And simple was one thing older women were not.

And apparently, neither was Megan. He didn't think she would intentionally blow him off. So, he would just go to her house to check on her. He stood to leave and noticed Shannon was doing the same—or attempting to. She had dropped her keys beneath a stool at the end of the bar and was looking down at them with a puzzled pout. He sighed. If she had her keys out, that meant she was driving, and from the looks of her, that was a very bad idea.

Walking up to her from the side, so as not to startle her, he placed a hand on her elbow. "Hey, Shannon. Are you on yer own tonight?" Eyes wide and startled, she put her hand on the stool for balance and David put an arm around her, ushering her to a stool. He grabbed her keys from the floor and sat next to her. "Why don't ya sit for another minute or two?"

"Thanks." She said, quietly. "I'm embarrassed you're seeing me like this."

"'Tis nothin', we've all had those days." He motioned for the bartender and asked for two waters.

She laughed bitterly. "I don't know why I came home. I forgot how bad it was. Ya know, you go away ... get away from the crap and you forget what it was really like. Or you tell yourself that things must have gotten better after all this time. But nope. Still the same old crap."

"I'm sorry. Family trouble? That's tough."

"Ha. Tough. That's one way to put it." She looked at him with pain in her eyes. "I'm tough, ya know. I was always the tough one. My sister would hide in her room and cry when we were little and Mam and Da would fight. I would just read a book and ignore them. I mean, I wasn't *really* ignoring. I was listening, trying to figure out how bad it was and if I'd have to jump in. But I *acted* like I was ignoring them." She placed her head in her open palm. "And things weren't always bad. But when Mam died, he went downhill fast."

"Yer mam?"

"Cancer."

Geez. Poor girl had been through a lot. "Sorry."

She shrugged, her eyes looking heavy, like she was having trouble keeping them open.

"Is yer dad an alcoholic?" he asked.

"Aye, drunk, alcoholic. Call it what ya want. He's only sober when he's at work."

"Are y'okay? Are ya safe?" he asked.

"I'm fine." She looked at him with a small smile. "Thanks for askin'."

"He doesn't get violent with you?"

"He was violent sometimes with my mam. But he's never touched me, and if he did, he wouldn't do it twice."

Amazing how you can think you have someone all figured out and then realize you don't know anything. He had written Shannon off as a silly girl without much substance. But she was right; she was tough. Still, at the moment, she was also drunk.

"Let's get ya home." He stood and offered her his arm for support. She took it and looked around for her keys, wobbling once again. "I've got yer keys. I'll drive you home and maybe you can get a ride back here tomorrow to get yer car, okay?"

She nodded. "Thanks."

Two nights this week, he'd driven her home, and the contrast couldn't be more stark. Wednesday, she'd talked the whole ride, with bright eyes and animated gestures. Tonight, she was quiet, looking out the window and at one point, he thought she may have drifted off to sleep. It was convenient she lived so close to Megan. He would drop her off and check on Megan, on the way back.

As they passed Megan's house, he almost veered off the road. Had he just seen Megan in a lip lock with some guy?

"Aw, Jamie's back." Shannon mumbled. David felt like his stomach dropped through the seat. Jamie? That was Jamie, and she was kissing him? *What the hell?* He tightened his grip on the steering wheel as thoughts whirred. First Katie and now Megan. What was it about him and girls with exes?

Anger coursed through him, and he struggled to keep his car at a safe speed. Shannon was oblivious as she dozed the two miles between Megan's house and hers.

"Shannon?" He gently shook her shoulder as he put his car in park at the top of her long driveway. He shook her again, a little harder. "Shannon." She was out cold. Great. Now what? He took a deep breath to calm his racing heart. Somewhere this night had gone very wrong. He sat there for several minutes with the music turned up, hoping it would wake her. No such luck. He tried shaking her again. "Shannon, ya need to wake up."

"Hmm?" Her bleary eyes were unfocused. Confused. "Oh, hi."

"Yer home." David pointed toward her house and decided he should probably make sure she got inside as he watched her fumble with her seat belt. "Hold on."

He walked around and opened her door, helping her out of the car. She leaned on him, heavily. At her front door, he asked her which key to use and opened the door.

"David, you don't know how much I needed a friend, tonight. Thank you." She kissed his cheek and then stumbled into her house. It was unusually dark inside, like they had blackout curtains. He heard a crack and then a sharp cry of pain.

"Shannon?" he called from the doorway. "Are ya okay?"

She whimpered something unintelligible, and he sighed. *Crap.* Pushing the door open, he let the outside light in. Then he flipped all the light switches by the door and saw Shannon sitting on her living room floor, squinting and rubbing her leg. She'd obviously tripped on the coffee table.

He helped her up, laughing softly. "Yer quite a mess, aren't you?"

He took her by the hand and walked down a long hallway, which he assumed led to the bedrooms, turning on lights as he went. "Why is it so dark in here?"

"Ummm, cuz Da likes it dark. Uses blackout curtains."

"Where is he?"

"Workin'. He's on second shift. Maintenance at the mill." She stumbled again, and he took her by the waist to keep her upright. She leaned in toward his neck. "You smmelll good."

"Which room's yours?"

"End of the hall."

He helped her take off her boots and tucked her into her bed, fully clothed. "Sleep tight."

"You wanna join me?" she asked with a lopsided grin.

"Yer drunk, Shannon." He laughed at her expression. "You need sleep."

She frowned and furrowed her brow. "I'm nnnnot gonna get in trouble at work, am I?"

He laughed again. "Are ya plannin' to show up to work in this state?"

Her droopy eyes widened. "No. Course not."

"Well, I think you're gonna have one heck of a headache in the morning, but by Monday, you should be fine. You've nothin' to worry about at work. We'll keep this between us, okay?" He noticed she had asprin on her bedside table so he took two out and handed them to her along with the conveniently placed water bottle she also kept at bedside. "Take these, it might help a little."

"I knew you were a great guy. Too bad we work together."

He ruffled her hair. "Get some sleep, kiddo."

"Maybe I should quit," she said softly as she turned over and snuggled under her covers.

⚓

Megan scanned the Blackwater for David while sliding between tables to the bar area. She didn't think he'd still be there, but it was worth a try. She saw a few people she knew, including the bartender, Jimmy. Maybe he'd seen David and would know how long ago he left.

"Hey, Jimmy."

"Hey, Megan, what are ya having?" he asked as he started to build a Guinness.

"Actually, I'm looking for a friend. He's the new doctor. Tall, blond. Have ya seen him tonight?"

"Aye, I know who he is. Don't think I don't hear my wife and her friends goin' on about him." Jimmy rolled his eyes. "He and Shannon left a little while ago."

"Shannon?" She worked to keep the surprise and jealousy out of her tone.

"They were sitting together down at that end of the bar. Left about ten minutes ago. Heard him say he was takin' her home." He made his last pour on the Guinness and passed it to a waiting server. "Prob'ly a good idea. She was puttin' 'em back as good as her da."

Megan nodded and made for the exit. The restaurant sounds faded, and all she heard was a rushing in her ears. He'd gone home with Shannon? She practiced deep breathing while she walked to her car. *Zen. What would Grania say?* Maybe there was an explanation. Maybe ... *no!* He had kept their previous relationship a secret, whatever it had been, and now he was taking Shannon home for the second time this week?

Sliding into her car, she thought about going to Brenna's, but Ryan was coming home tonight, and he'd been gone for a week. She certainly didn't want to walk in on anything. Then, she thought about going to Shannon's, just confronting the whole thing, head-on. But the thought of walking in on something there had her clenching her fists so hard she left nail marks on her palms.

She sat in her car long enough for the heater to warm up and take the chill out of the cooling night air. The only thing she could think to do was go home. At least no one was there tonight.

She drove out of town and had just started down her road when her car slowed and sputtered. She tried to accelerate, but it continued to slow and jerk awkwardly. *Crap!* She'd forgotten to get petrol on the way to the restaurant. She pulled as far to the side as she could, ten foot hedges on either side of the road making it tricky to actually get out of the way of any moving vehicles that might happen by. Of course, she lived on a dead-end country road, so it wasn't like she'd see much traffic. Frustrated, she pounded her steering wheel. She'd been forgetting to fill up all day long, but the stupid car couldn't have given her just one more mile?

Grabbing her purse and her thin sweater, she locked her car, slammed the door, and started walking—practically marching—toward home. The sun was low in the sky, with just an hour left of daylight, and she was walking directly toward it, making it difficult to see where she was going. *What's the upside of this one, huh, Meg?* She always tried to find an upside—a silver lining. But she was coming up blank. As she sidestepped a large pile of horse droppings, she found her upside. At least she didn't have to walk in the dark.

There were no cars in Megan's driveway when David sped by. He might have pulled in to talk to her if she'd been there. Then again, he was so angry, it might be best if he didn't see her—wait. Was that her? He zipped past a woman walking down the side of the road and, looking in his rearview mirror, he thought it might be Megan. He kept driving. It was probably his imagination.

Now he was hallucinating about her? Damn, she had him messed up. This was exactly why he didn't get involved with women anymore. Simple flirtations, weekend dates, lunches—those were all fine. But getting too close was just stupid. He knew better, and yet he'd let himself get burned again.

As he neared the turn, he saw a car pulled to the opposite side of the road. Megan's. Crap, it really was her. He turned around and sped back toward her house. She wasn't too far from her driveway when he pulled up next to her and opened the window.

"Get in."

She looked at him with furious eyes. "Nice of ya to come back. I'll walk, thank you." Chin up, she marched on. What was her problem? She was the one kissing another guy tonight. He, on the other hand, could have done anything he wanted with Shannon, but he didn't. Because he knew it wouldn't have been right when his heart was elsewhere; in the hands of the angry woman who marched alongside his car, which he'd slowed to five miles per hour.

"Megan, get in the car." If he weren't pissed, he would have laughed. She was being ridiculous. "I'm just going to keep pace with you, so ya might as well get in and tell me what's goin' on. I can see you're shivering. Just get in."

She stopped and turned toward him, arms crossed. "Fine." She pulled the door open and slammed it shut once she was seated.

Silently, he drove the remaining quarter-mile to her house. What the heck was her problem? She had stood him up to spend time with her ex-fiancé. She was in the wrong here. So, why was she acting like he was the one who should be apologizing?

He parked the car, and she opened her door, but he grabbed her arm before she could get out. "Megan, what is going on?"

She closed the door and took a deep breath. "I can't trust you." Her voice was flat and cold.

*What?* "You can't trust *me*? Just how is it that you've decided that?"

"I know there's something going on with you and Shannon. Save the indignation."

"That's ridiculous. There's nothing—"

"Why didn't ya tell me you'd gone out with her in Dublin? Hmm?"

Crap. Shannon had told her. "It didn't come up. If ya want a list of every woman I've gone out with, it will take a while."

She looked at him through narrowed eyes. "That's not what I'm saying, and I think you know it. We talked about Shannon on the way to the meeting Wednesday. It would have been a good time to mention ya knew her and had gone out before. The only reason I could think of that you would hide that would be if ya still had feelings for her—"

"That's absurd. We went out on one date. *And* I never called her back. But obviously, I've been pining for her all this time and fate has brought us back together."

"Obviously."

"Megan, I'm being sarcastic."

"Well, imagine my surprise when I see Shannon at the meeting, and she is all gaga over ya and won't stop talking about you. And I have to hear from her that you guys went out before, and she's hoping for more. I spent the whole night trying to figure out if you liked her."

"Did ya think I was lying when I said you had no competition?" He tried to keep from raising his voice, but he wasn't successful.

"I believed you when you said it, but then, when I realized ya didn't tell me the truth about Shannon, I started to wonder. I thought maybe you were hoping to keep something brewing there in case things went south with me."

"You mean, in case you decided to go back to Jamie?" He knew he was sounding cold. She looked at him, shocked.

"Excuse me? I told you it was over with him. I was honest about my past. You were not. And then ya took her home, Wednesday. You were sitting at the bar with her when we were supposed to have a date, and then ya took her home again. What am I supposed to think?"

"Maybe that I was just being nice. You're the one who didn't show up tonight. And you obviously don't know me very well."

"You're right. I don't. I knew we were going too fast, but I just ignored the red flags and plunged in. It was stupid."

A fury snaked through his gut. Red flags? *He* had red flags? "So that's why you decided to make out with Jamie in your driveway tonight?"

Her jaw dropped and eyes popped wide with surprise. "I ... how did you know Jamie was here?"

Not even a denial. Great. "I need to go, Megan. I assume you have someone who can help ya with your car?"

Tears glistened in her eyes, and she said quietly, "My da will, tomorrow." She got out and slammed the door.

David spun in reverse and sped from the driveway with exaggerated speed. He thought his head might explode. He hadn't allowed anyone to get him this angry since he'd walked in on Katie. He'd been completely in control for five years. And now he was undone, again, because of a woman. He was a damn fool.

# Chapter Thirty

Brenna had to admit, absence did make the heart grow fonder, and it made the reunion sizzle. Head on his pillow, behind her, Ryan's breathing had slowed, and she wasn't sure if he was still awake. He still had an arm firmly around her waist, though, like he wasn't planning to let her go for a long time.

She was glad she'd been able to get Ben down for an early bedtime tonight. After the crappy way she'd sent Ryan off to Limerick, the weekend before, she had planned to welcome him home in a way that would have him looking forward to coming home any time he was gone.

She had texted him when he was on the way home, telling him she was cooking up something special for him. She'd turned off all the lights and lit candles in a pathway to their bedroom. Then, wearing nothing but an apron, she read a romance novel and waited for her man to get home.

She heard him enter the kitchen. "Bren?" and then there was silence. Her excitement had been growing over the previous hour, so when he appeared at their bedroom door with a look of wonder on his face, it was all she could do to stay calm and just smile.

"Good Lord," he'd said. And then they'd gotten reacquainted.

Now, after snuggling for the last several minutes, she was pretty sure he was out. And she was drifting herself when she heard her phone ring in the kitchen. She ignored it. Until it rang again. And again. She sighed and eased herself from Ryan's grip and the bed. Grabbing her robe, she ran to the kitchen. She had five missed calls from Megan's house phone.

Her stomach lurched with fear that something was wrong. Megan wasn't the type to call over and over. And even more than that, Megan knew Ryan was coming home and normally wouldn't call at all. She dialed quickly.

"Hello?" Megan was clearly crying.

"Meg, what's wrong? Are you okay?"

Sniffle. "No. I mean, yes. I'm not hurt, physically. I'm sorry I'm calling tonight, but I really need to talk. Can ya come over?"

Brenna hesitated. Of course she would go, but she wasn't sure if she should wake Ryan and tell him or slip away.

Megan sniffled again. "I'm really sorry. You know I wouldn't ask if it wasn't important."

"I know, friend. Of course I'll come. I just have to take care of a few things first. Something happened with David?"

"David, Jamie, Shannon ... you name it. Just one big drama party tonight. Door's unlocked. My family decided to stay over at my uncle's, so just come on upstairs."

"Okay. Be there in twenty."

Brenna blew out all the candles and got dressed quickly. She wrote a note for Ryan, placing it on her pillow, just in case, and she made it to Megan's in fifteen minutes.

~~~

Megan was thankful Brenna didn't even ask her any questions at first. She just climbed onto her bed and pulled her into a hug. After David left, Megan had collapsed on her bed and cried for a long time. He never even denied something was going on with Shannon. And how did he know about Jamie? He must have been driving by ... to Shannon's? Of course— he saw them in the driveway when he was taking Shannon home.

She didn't even get a chance to explain what really happened. She was so angry, she didn't know if she cared to explain. He'd just assumed, and if he thought that little of her, well, then there wasn't much point in a relationship, anyway.

A small voice in her head said that it was perfectly understandable that he misunderstood. Anyone watching would have thought the hug and kiss were between lovers. Only she and Jamie would have known that they were a goodbye. It wasn't really fair for her to blame David for misunderstanding. And, she had stood him up, as far as he knew.

But then, the whole Shannon thing just didn't add up. He was hiding things from her, and she couldn't trust him. Even if he misunderstood what happened with Jamie, he was hiding stuff before that, so no matter how she spun it, bottom line, she didn't trust him. And that sucked. Cuz she *really* liked him.

She had tried to go to sleep. But she'd played the scenes back in her mind over and over to the point where she couldn't stop crying. That's why she'd called Brenna. She needed someone to come help her figure it all out or at least help her figure out how to sleep. If she had to lie there awake all night long with a loop of the night playing in her head, she'd go insane.

"Sorry I dragged ya out tonight. I know Ryan's home," she said through sniffles as Brenna grabbed a tissue box from the dresser. "I'm a wreck, aren't I?"

Every bit of eye makeup she'd donned earlier was probably spread around her face in a swirly mess. Her nose was definitely red and puffy.

Brenna nodded and crawled back up next to her. "Yeah. You look like you've had quite the night. Was that your car I saw at the corner?"

"Yep."

"What happened?"

"I'll get to the car. But I should start at the beginning." Megan wiped her eyes with a tissue. "So, right when I thought David was here to pick me up, I look out, and it's Jamie."

"Here?"

"Here. In the flesh."

"Oh my gosh. Okay, what happened?"

Taking a deep breath, Megan told her about Jamie's visit. From the poorly timed arrival to the goodbye kiss in the driveway.

"That's incredible!" Brenna said.

"I know. He was so sad, Bren. It was heartbreaking, really."

"He actually said he acted like a jerk on purpose?"

Megan nodded. "Can you imagine how scary it must have been for him? To constantly be making crazy choices and not know why you're feeling so different? He said he felt ashamed of the things he'd done and he knew he didn't deserve me, so he wanted me to hate him."

"Wow."

"I know. It's like, in some twisted way, he was trying to protect me."

"This whole thing just gets more and more crazy, doesn't it?"

"Just wait. There's more."

"David?"

Megan nodded and told what had happened with finding out David had taken Shannon home and then him picking her up on the road and their argument in the driveway.

"Aw, friend, what a night. No wonder you needed me. I'm glad you called."

"I didn't ... interrupt you, did I?"

"No, he's asleep now."

"Did ya do the apron thing?"

Brenna blushed. "Yes. He was speechless."

"You guys have the perfect marriage, ya know that?"

"Thanks. But no one has a perfect marriage. All marriages take work to make them strong."

Megan nodded and sighed. "I don't know what to do now. When I left for the Blackwater tonight, I was ready to tell David I was all in. Let's make a go of it and see where it leads. Let people talk; I don't care. But he acted like a total jerk. You should have seen him. He was sarcastic and ... I don't know, icy. Like he hated me, or something."

Brenna scootched back against the wall and leaned her head back. "Okay, well, you've told me what happened from your perspective. Now let's try and go through the night from his perspective."

Megan blew out a breath. "Fine." Brenna was always fair. Sometimes it irritated her. Sometimes she just wanted her to take her side, even if it wasn't rational or logical.

"So, he was running late, and he asked you to meet him there. He was probably stressed because he was making you meet him there instead of picking you up, like a proper date. And then you're not there. So, he probably sat down, maybe had a drink or something and waited. Think about how it feels to be waiting on someone and they aren't showing up. You don't know if you should be mad at them for being so late, or if you should be calling 9-1-1. It's a horrible feeling."

"You're good at this." *Too good.*

"Premarital counseling with Ben. Our pastor told us any time we were feeling like the other was acting completely irrational we should try to imagine things from their perspective. Works pretty well."

"Yeah, I can see that. So he waits around for me, and it's irritating that I'm not there. I get that. But where does Shannon come in?"

"Well, he's meeting you there for a date, right? Even if he did have something going with Shannon, it's not like he'd invite her along, right? He obviously ran into her there."

Megan suddenly remembered something Jimmy, the bartender, had said. "I think you're right. She must have already been there for a while cuz Jimmy said she was drinking like her dad. That means she was probably drunk." A sinking feeling settled on Megan's chest. He was probably just making sure she got home safely.

"And she wouldn't get drunk in thirty minutes. So, she was probably at the bar when he got there. Maybe she knew she shouldn't drive, and she asked him for a ride?"

"I'm sure she would have jumped at the chance. And he was doing the responsible thing, helping her out. And, if he were messing around with her, he wouldn't have been driving back down my road so soon, either. He would have still been at her house." Megan grabbed a fistful of hair. "Geez, I'm an eejit."

"No, friend. You were emotionally spent from dealing with Jamie, and you've been hurt before, so you're cautious."

"And stupid. Let's keep going with this. It's a trip." Megan rolled her eyes but pressed on. "So the poor guy takes a drunk girl home, and on the way, he sees what he thinks is his date, making out with her ex."

"Kind of makes his reaction understandable, huh?"

"Yeah, but it's not like we were actually making out. There were no tongues involved."

"Come on, be honest. From what you told me, it may not have been that kind of kiss, but it sounds like it was still quite intimate. Put it this way, would you have let anyone else kiss you the way Jamie did tonight?"

No, she would have slapped anyone who tried without her permission. Except—"Only David. Dang, you're right. It would have looked totally wrong to him." Megan sighed. "May as well finish. So he's angry cuz it looks like I'm going back to my ex, and he drives past me walking. Probably doesn't want to see me but he comes back for me, anyway. And I won't even get in the car." Megan put her head in her hands. "Brenna, I really screwed this up."

"Well, you both probably overreacted. Maybe you should call him. It's not too late."

Megan glanced at her alarm clock. It was 11:15 p.m. No, not too late to call. "I don't have his number. It's in my dead stupid phone."

Brenna pulled out her phone and read off his number.

Megan took a deep breath and dialed from her home phone. Placing her hand over the receiver, she whispered, "He won't know this number, I doubt he'll answer—"

"Hello?" He sounded gruff, and she hesitated, afraid to say who was calling. "Hello?"

Brenna hit her in the arm. "Hi, it's me, Megan." Now he was silent. "I'm sorry I overreacted earlier. I wondered if we could talk?"

"Whose phone are you using?"

"This is our home phone. My cell phone is completely dead now."

"Oh. Well, I'm sorry, Megan. I just don't feel like talking right now. Maybe another day." Dial tone.

She handed the phone to Brenna and stifled a sob. "He hung up."

"I'm sorry." Brenna rubbed her back as she put her head on her pillow.

"Listen, you are not going to fall asleep without help tonight. Do you have any sleep aids or chamomile tea or anything?"

Megan shook her head. "Oh, wait. Benadryl has the same active ingredient as a sleep aid. There's some in the bathroom cabinet."

"Okay, stay here. I'll get you some." Brenna was back in two minutes with Benadryl and a glass of water. "Here. Take this."

Megan swallowed the medicine. "Thanks. For this, and for coming over." She felt numb inside.

"No problem. I had to. It's part of the code. You obviously haven't read the handbook yet."

Megan smiled slightly. "I'm okay now. I'm gonna sleep. Thanks for coming over. Get back to that hunky husband of yours."

Brenna gave her a kiss on the cheek and left. Megan was not okay. But she knew there was nothing else Brenna could do to help. At this point, there was nothing else she could do, either. Except wait for the meds to kick in and take her off to la-la land.

# Chapter Thirty-One

David was awake before his alarm went off. Not that he was feeling rested. He wasn't sure he'd actually even fallen asleep. But he couldn't stand to lie there any longer, so he got up and went to take a shower. He winced when he saw the hole in his bathroom wall, and he outright swore when the hot water hit his swollen hand.

It took a lot to make him angry, but he had a bad habit of hitting inanimate objects when he reached a boiling point. He'd put the hole in the wall last night as soon as he'd gotten home and then had to ice his hand for an hour. He knew he had hit a stud, but this morning, it felt like he'd hit a brick wall.

He showered but didn't bother shaving. He didn't feel like eating anything. Instead, he downed a glass of juice and went out for a run. He had a five-mile circuit that he'd been running a few times a week. But even after that, he was restless. His mind wouldn't stop going over the night before. He couldn't get certain images from his head. What he really needed was a hard workout.

The town gym was small, but it had the latest equipment, if not a whole lot of it. He took ten minutes to fill out the necessary paperwork and became a card-carrying member of Millway Health & Fitness. He politely declined the tour offered by the perky blonde attendant and spent the next hour lifting weights and working his abs. It was exactly what he needed.

By the time he hit the shower, for the second time that morning, his head was clear and his muscles were fatigued, in a good way.

Next, he straightened up his flat and threw a load of laundry into the washer. It was days like these he wished he owned a house. There was always something to be fixed when you owned a home, and he liked fixing things. As a kid, he'd spent hours taking things apart so he could put them back together. His mother didn't always love it, but she let him do it, anyway.

She eventually found it quite useful and would bring him broken lamps or appliances to tinker with. He wondered if the church had a helping hands type ministry he could join. Surely there were elderly folks in the church who could use help around the house. He made a mental note to check into that after Mass tomorrow.

With his flat clean and his laundry done, David found there was nothing left to do but face what had happened with Megan and figure out what was next. Taking this apart and putting it back together wasn't as easy as fixing a toaster. He'd been too angry to even talk to her the night before. Now, he just felt numbed by the whole thing.

He considered why he'd gotten so angry at the sight of Megan and Jamie. He wasn't out of line. He and Megan might not have been officially dating yet, but they were about to be, and he had been ready to make a commitment to a serious relationship. So, the fact that she was kissing anyone, much less her ex-fiancé, was truly a problem. And she hadn't even tried to explain it.

Of course, he hadn't given her much chance to, either.

But regardless of what was actually going on with her and Jamie, David realized one thing: he wasn't ready for a serious relationship. Not yet. When he'd been hurt by Katie, he hadn't healed up properly. He'd gone on a dating binge. Went out with any lass who batted her eyelashes at him, which meant he had a date pretty much any night he chose. He'd filled the emptiness with more empty relationships. But it didn't work. On the outside, he was the envy of every guy he knew. He was studying to become a doctor, he had women throwing themselves at him, and no one was thinking, "Poor guy." But inside, he was a mess. He was angry all the time, he couldn't shake the bitterness he carried toward Katie, and even though he looked like he had it all together, he was miserable.

It wasn't until he went to Africa that he found something that made a difference. He was with the student team in a small, remote village. Houses made of mud, with roofs of woven straw and grass, dotted the landscape. Children ran through the dusty village with little to no clothing on. Anything they did wear was three sizes too big and filthy. They stared up at him with large, chocolate eyes when he first got out of the SUV. But as soon as he smiled at them, they came up to him and grabbed for his hands. Within minutes, they were fighting over who got to hold his hands.

He had followed his team through the village on red dirt pathways to the site where another organization had installed a deep water well, just a year before. You could tell the villagers took pride in their well. They had constructed a bamboo fence around it, woven together with grasses. And as they showed the team the clean water flowing from the hand-pumped well, David's eyes had landed on a young woman with a baby slung on her back. All he could actually see of the baby were two pink little feet on either side of the woman's hips. But the smile that radiated from this girl-mother took his breath away. And then, as the pastor of the village started a song and the villagers joined in, the glow on the young girl's face grew even brighter.

"Tell um tanky, tell um, tell Papa God tanky. Tell um tanky, tell um. Tell Papa God tanky."

That was about all that David could make out, but the meaning was clear. This group of literally dirt-poor, mostly uneducated, malnourished villagers was thanking God for all he'd done for them. *It blew his mind.* Suddenly he felt small. He thought of all that he had taken for granted. He thought of all the things he could have thanked God for and realized he'd never done so.

As the young pastor started a second song, David had made his way behind the crowd until he was just a few feet from the girl, and when the song ended, he introduced himself. Her name was Aminata, and her baby girl's name was Hawatu. Her English was surprisingly clear, although heavily accented. This meant she'd attended school and maybe wasn't as uneducated as he'd assumed. There wasn't time to be shy, so he asked her why she looked so happy.

"Because, God is good," she replied, as if it was the most obvious thing in the world. *God. Is. Good.* The woman was likely a single mother, not over twenty years old. She had no shoes and from the look of her, not much food. She must have lived in one of the dirt huts with dirt floors. And yet, she believed with every fiber of her being, that God was good.

Obviously, God's character, in her mind, was not tied to her circumstances. And that revelation had David searching for answers for the rest of the trip.

He began asking anyone he met who had the same kind of smile as Aminata what it was that made them so happy. And without fail, every person said something about how God had changed their lives. He'd healed some of them from physical ailments, but the overwhelming majority told stories of God healing their hearts. From bitterness, anger, hatred toward those who had done horrible things to their families, jealousy, pride, lust. You name it, they mentioned it, and they all gave credit to God for turning their lives around. The God that he'd grown up hearing about seemed small and tame compared to the God that he found in Africa. By the end of the trip, he had prayed and asked the God of Africa to be his God, even back in Ireland.

And He had. David's life was changed from the inside out. He stopped dating to fill a need. He still went out with women occasionally. But he kept it to a movie and dinner. Nothing serious. And he spent time reading the Bible, C.S. Lewis, N.T. Wright, and any other deep thinkers he came across.

But now, when faced with the anger he'd felt toward Megan, he realized he had never really dealt with what Katie had done. He had tucked it away, deep inside, so that he didn't think it really affected him. But he hadn't dealt with it. Hadn't asked God to heal him or take away his anger and bitterness. He just let it stay dark and hidden. And in reality, it had probably been affecting him all along.

So, sitting alone, on his couch on a Saturday afternoon, he prayed another heartfelt prayer. He asked God to heal him from all the junk that

Katie's betrayal had created in him. And then, he did something he'd never done. He asked God to help him forgive Katie. To truly, honestly forgive her. Surprising tears escaped his eyes as he prayed that last prayer. And he felt lighter than he had in a very long time.

～

"Megan!" Aidan yelled from the kitchen. "Phone's fer you!"

Megan rolled over on her bed and grabbed the phone. She had taken a nap and wasn't even sure what day it was.

"Hello?"

"Megan." David's voice was soft. Her stomach did a flip.

"Hi. Are you okay?" she asked, propping herself up on her elbow.

"Aye. You?"

"I've been better."

"Would ya still want to talk?"

Maybe she hadn't screwed it all up beyond repair. "I would."

"I'll pick ya up in twenty minutes, okay?"

"I'll be ready."

"And Megan?"

"Yes?"

"Bring yer stupid cell phone."

She smiled. He didn't hate her. "We're going to Killarney?"

"Aye. See ya in a few."

She jumped out of bed and nearly fell over from the head rush. No time for a shower, she ran to the bathroom to clean up a bit. One look in the mirror told her she would not be looking her best by the time David arrived. A ponytail was the best she could do to tame her hair, which had been sticking up in four directions. She had already cleaned the makeup off her face earlier in the day. Now she added a fresh coat of mascara and some lip gloss and decided that was as good as it was going to get.

She was dressed and waiting outside when David drove up in his sporty car. She didn't hesitate to get in this time, but she was hesitant once she was in and buckled and they were on their way. "Thanks for calling back." She thought it was extremely unfair that he could look amazing with his hair at odd angles and stubble all over his face.

"Sorry I hung up on you last night. That was rude."

"It was. But I think I understand."

He looked at her sideways. "We've a lot to talk about."

She nodded. "Do you want to start or should I?" He didn't answer right away. She fidgeted with her hands and then noticed his right hand on the wheel. It was swollen and red, with angry little cuts over his knuckles. "Oh my goodness, what happened to your hand?"

He took it from the wheel and winced when he dropped it to his side too quickly. "I might have punched a wall last night."

Was he serious? She stared at him, unsure.

"I'll start," he finally said. "First, I'm sorry I acted like a jerk last night. I told ya earlier this week that I had some baggage. And it's not fair to you that I let that come into our relationship."

"Okay."

"But before I get to that, from what ya said last night, you've been giving way too much weight to one date I had with Shannon, over a year ago."

She looked over at him. "I know. I was being silly. I wasn't thinking straight."

"Seems to be a lot of that going around." He smiled, and she realized she'd been waiting for that smile since they'd started driving. "But let me say it clearly, there is *nothing* going on between me and Shannon, okay?"

She felt about a foot tall. All this emotional upheaval, and this was the first time he'd even had a chance to tell her that. And when he said it, she knew without a doubt, he was telling the truth. If she'd just talked to him on Thursday, like he'd wanted, how much of the mess on Friday could have been avoided?

"I'm sorry. Really. I should have made time to talk to you about it on Thursday."

He shrugged. "So we're clear on that, right?"

"We are."

"Okay, so last night, I did take her home, but it was only cuz she was barely able to walk away from the bar, much less drive. I would have given anyone a ride in that situation."

"I know. I figured it out later. That's why I called you. I wanted to apologize."

"Well, I'm glad ya figured it out. I just wasn't ready to talk last night. I needed to work through some things. But I'm doing better now." He gave a small smile. "Is there anything else you want to know about me and Shannon?"

She would love to know why he didn't call Shannon back when they'd first gone out. Should she push it? No, she didn't want to go there. The important thing was that he obviously wasn't interested in her. It was painfully obvious now. "No. Thanks."

They sat in awkward silence until she grew too uncomfortable to maintain it. "Aren't ya going to ask me about Jamie?"

His brow furrowed, and he glanced her way. "I'm not sure I want to know."

"Hmm, well, I'm sure I want ya to know, so you're going to hear it, like it or not."

He chuckled and raised an eyebrow. "Okay."

"He showed up at my house last night, and I thought it was you in the driveway. I had no idea he was even in town. When I realized it was Jamie, I sent you a quick text to let ya know I'd be late—"

"I didn't get that."

"My phone died right after. I didn't know if it went through. But I had no way to call you. I had the house phone, but I didn't know your number. Actually, the only number I know by heart, other than my cell, is my house phone. So that was no help. But I *wanted* to let you know what was going on. It was totally stressing me out. I hated picturing you sitting there wondering where the heck I was and why I wasn't calling." She put her hand over his on the shifter. He didn't shake her off, but he didn't respond either. He didn't take her hand, like he would have before.

"I get it. Ya might want to write down some phone numbers for the future, though. I keep a small list in my wallet."

"Aye, trust me, I'm planning on it." She took her hand away and sighed.

"So what was he doing there?" David asked.

"He came to apologize. He told me about what's been going on with his diagnosis and what his symptoms have been. He was ... very upset. He was literally crying on my kitchen floor. I couldn't tell him I had to go. I kept watching the clock, but I didn't know what to do." Megan stopped because she could feel her voice getting shaky. Talking about it was like reliving it, and it wasn't pleasant.

David pulled over suddenly and put the car in park. He turned toward her. "I'm sorry. That had to be hard for you."

Megan just nodded, not trusting her voice.

"But I have to ask about what I saw in the driveway. It didn't look like a nice, friendly peck on the cheek, ya know?"

She nodded again and took a deep breath. "I know what it looked like. And I don't blame you if ya don't believe me when I tell you it was not what it looked like. The only one who can corroborate that is Jamie, and I doubt you two will be talking any time soon. So, my word is all ya have."

"Well, it looked like a real kiss."

"It was." He looked completely puzzled, and Megan knew she wasn't making much sense. "I don't know how to explain it. But I'll try. First, I didn't kiss him, he kissed me. I know that may not seem to matter, but it does to me. He had tears streaming down his face. I had just told him that I would always be his friend, and he knew that meant that I would be nothing else to him. And he was basically saying goodbye. He said something about not getting to say goodbye in January. So, I let him kiss me. I could have stopped him, but it didn't feel right. I thought it was okay to let him say goodbye in that way, because we both knew what it meant. And I'm sorry you saw it and were hurt by it. I never meant for that to happen."

"I'm sorry I didn't give you a chance to explain."

"It was all a mess, with both of us misunderstanding the other. Any way we can just forget it happened? Because what I didn't tell you yet was what Jamie's visit showed me. When he left, I knew for sure that I was over him and that you were the only one I wanted to be with." Her heart was pounding as he looked at her with a strange expression.

"Well, that certainly doesn't make this easier," he said, almost to himself.

She had been hoping when she told him how she felt, that he'd be glad to hear it. Maybe even tell her he felt the same. Instead, he was looking uncomfortable, which had her stomach slipping into knots.

"Geez, this was easier when I was saying it in my head. Without you sitting there, all pretty and wide-eyed. You weaken my resolve, woman. But I have to do this—"

"What are you talking about? Yer killin' me here."

He blew out a breath. "First, you need to know that how I feel about you now is exactly the same as how I felt about you two days ago. And to hear you say that you only want to be with me, it makes me want to take you in my arms and not let ya go. But the truth is, I'm going to let ya go, at least for a little while." He looked out the window.

What? Her heart raced. "I don't understand."

"Of course you don't. I'm not explaining it right." He hit the steering wheel with his good hand. "Let me start with the baggage. Maybe that will help. The reason I got so crazy about you and Jamie is because I've only had one serious relationship before. It was five years ago. Katie and I met through mutual friends at university. She was a year ahead of me, and I fell for her, pretty hard. Things seemed like they were going well. Everyone said we were the perfect couple, I thought we were happy. But one day, I came home early and caught her in bed with her ex-fiancé."

Megan took a sharp breath. "Oh, David. I'm sorry. That must have been awful."

He nodded. "Aye. 'Twas awful. She had never really been over him. I was kind of a rebound guy, I guess. And if I look back at it now, I can see the signs. But I didn't see them at the time. He was her first love. They were high school sweethearts, and they did end up getting married, not too long after we broke up."

Megan could see it cost him to tell the story. No wonder he was so freaked out by Jamie! "I wish I'd known. Not that I think you should have told me right away, 'Hi, I'm David. Nice to meet you. My girlfriend cheated on me with her ex.' I don't mean that. I know there's no way I really could have known. But I would have understood everything so much better. And I would have been more sensitive."

"I thought about telling ya last week. But I don't like to talk about it, so I put it off. There's a reason I'm telling you now, though." He ran his hands through his hair, and she had the strongest urge to do the same. Run her fingers through his hair. Yet she suspected that wasn't going to happen any time soon.

She sighed. "Go on."

"Well, last night, when I saw you with Jamie, I went ... a little crazy. As ya can see," he held up his hand, "I punched a hole in my bathroom wall. I haven't been that angry in a very long time. So, I did a lot of thinking today. And I realized something; I had never even tried to forgive Katie for what she did. Just the thought of her has always made me feel sick. If our mutual friends ever mentioned her by accident, I would stew about it for days. And eventually, I just buried it. I no longer thought about her much, but when I did, it was not pleasant." He rubbed the stubble on his jaw, and she again found herself wanting to do exactly what he was doing. She bit her lip as a distraction.

He continued, "Megan, I should never have been that angry at you last night. It was way out of proportion. And it was a huge red flag that I need to deal with my crap before I can even consider having a serious relationship." He had a determined look in his amber eyes.

She wasn't sure how to respond. "What does that mean?"

"I'm not exactly sure. I asked God to help me forgive Katie. That's probably a good first step toward me getting my head straight. I think forgiveness is sometimes a process, rather than a one-time thing. Meaning, I forgave her this afternoon, but it doesn't mean that when I think about what she did, I feel fine about it. I think it's going to take a while for me to get to a healthier place. And while I'm doing that, I don't think it's fair to bring you into it."

Megan swallowed a panicked feeling. "But what if I want to be in it? I want to help you get through it." She paused. "David, I'm really putting myself out there, and it feels scary to me, but ... I really like you."

"God, this is hard." He opened his door and got out.

She watched him for a minute as he paced. He appeared to be talking to himself, and he looked confused. She couldn't just sit in the car, so she got out and walked toward him.

When he saw her, he stopped and put his hand up. "Wait." She paused mid-stride. He took a deep breath and motioned for her to come forward. "If Jamie gets a goodbye hug and kiss, I get one, too."

He pulled her close and held her tight. She shook her head. "I don't understand why it's goodbye."

He took a step back but held her by the shoulders. "It's because I care about ya so much, that I'm telling you I need a little time. I don't want to screw us up. I don't know how long I need, and that sucks, and it's totally unfair to you. But I feel really strongly that I'm supposed to be on my own for a little while so I can concentrate on getting rid of all the crap in my head and my heart. Megan, if we're going to be together, do ya really want me punching walls when I don't like something I see?"

She shook her head, unable to speak.

"I don't either. I want to get my head on straight. I'm not saying I have to make myself perfect before we can be together. I know that's stupid. But I just need a little time to work through some stuff." He ran his fingers through his hair, hesitating. "And at the risk of making ya angry with me, I need to tell you that I don't think things are over with Jamie."

"What? I told you how I feel!"

"I know, and I don't doubt you. I believe it's over *for you*, but I guarantee it's not over for him."

"How can ya know that?"

"Megan, the man was weeping on your kitchen floor over how he treated you. And no man in his right mind would let you go without a fight. I think you and I both have some stuff to deal with before a relationship makes sense."

Megan didn't want to believe him. But as soon as he said it, she knew he was right. Jamie may have said the kiss was a goodbye, and for her it was. But she knew, deep down, it wasn't for him. She just hadn't wanted to admit it to herself.

She sighed and kicked at a loose stone, sending it skittering over dry earth. "Okay, you're probably right about Jamie. But isn't that all the more reason to be together? He'll certainly get the message if he knows we're a couple."

"True, that might make things easier for you, and it makes sense, what you're saying. But I guess it just comes back around to me needing a little bit of time. I can't explain why I know this is the right thing to do. And it's incredibly hard, but I guess what I'm asking is, if you'll wait a little while for me?"

Megan felt a huge pressure in her chest. All the stress of the last twenty-four hours made her feel like she would burst. She stepped back into his arms and held tight as tears blurred her vision. "I'll wait," she whispered into his chest. No matter how much he said it was on him, she couldn't help feeling like she'd caused this. Like she'd pushed him away without meaning to, and she was afraid she was going to lose him before she ever really had him.

He stroked her hair and ran his hands over her back. Then he whispered into her hair, "As sure as I am about needin' some time, I'm also sure that what I'm about to do is stupid of me, but I'm not ending this talk without getting *my* goodbye kiss—"

He barely had the words out when she hooked her arms around his neck and crushed her mouth to his, knocking him back to a sitting position on the hood of his car. She could taste her tears and smell his woodsy scent, and she lost herself for a moment. He was not slowing her down. In fact, his hands were roaming over her back and her sides, and she did something she'd only seen in movies. She sat on his lap and wrapped her legs around his waist. She figured if it was their last kiss for a while or maybe ever, she wouldn't let him be able to forget it any time soon. Her hands were in his hair and on his face.

He groaned as he stood up, strong arms supporting her legs. She knew she was playing with fire and warning bells were going off in her head. She was pushing this too far, too fast. She had to back off, but she didn't want to. She wanted him so much that it scared her.

But she'd made a commitment long ago to save herself for marriage. And she wasn't going to break that vow in a field by the side of the road. And yet, she had never felt anything like what she was feeling.

*Lord help me*, she thought in the faintest of prayers. Faint, but it was enough. Though it cost her, she put her feet on the ground and pushed off of him, hand on his chest. He looked a little drunk, and she noticed his mouth was red and slightly swollen, and if things hadn't been so intense, she might have laughed. Then she felt the burning on her own face and realized she probably looked just like he did, if not worse, from stubble burn.

"Damn," he said, raking fingers through his hair, a fierce look on his face. She wasn't sure they were out of the danger zone yet. Then a crooked smile passed over his lips and broke the tension.

"What's funny?"

"Well," he grinned, "I guess, if I compare that goodbye kiss to what I saw yesterday, I'm feelin' pretty good about my chances against Jamie."

She laughed, a little embarrassed at how bold and forceful she'd been. "Yeah, well, now ya know the difference between my goodbye-kiss and my see-you-soon-kiss."

"Do you have any idea how amazing you are? There's a huge part of me that thinks I'm an absolute eejit to put us on hold. But I have to listen to the part of me that had this all figured out before I had you in my arms." He tucked a stray hair behind her ear. "You mess with my brain, ya know that?"

"I'm not trying to. But I have to say, it's mutual. At least we know there's no problem with us being attracted to each other." She laughed.

"Ha! Aye, that's definitely not a problem," he said, scanning the fields behind her.

"What are ya looking for?"

He grinned again. "A cold shower."

# Chapter Thirty-Two

Brenna opened her eyes and tried to focus on the digital clock beside her bed. It said 3:00. Disoriented, she wondered why it was light out at 3:00 a.m.

A nap.

She'd taken a nap. And as her mind caught up with her reality, she felt a little sick to her stomach. She had planned to talk to Ryan this morning about the fact that Luke had called and might be moving back.

But the morning had been busy with getting stuff done around the house, and after staying out so late at Megan's the night before, she was zombie-like enough that Ryan had taken Ben to visit Anna and Bettie so Brenna could take a long nap. Which meant she still needed to talk to him about Luke, and she was dreading it.

Ryan was one of the kindest, most gentle men she'd ever known. But if he had an Achilles heel, it would be Luke. It was like he couldn't think rationally where Luke was involved. And she understood it. Luke had hurt her, and Ryan took that personally. She appreciated his protective stance. But at the same time, she wished they could just have a normal conversation about him, like they would anyone else. Because, like it or not, he might just be a continual presence in their lives, and she didn't want to develop an ulcer every time she had to bring his name up.

She sighed and slipped out of bed, freshening up a bit in front of the bathroom mirror. She didn't think the boys were home yet. The house was too quiet. So she was startled when Ryan came up from behind and wrapped his arms around her.

"Hey, sleeping beauty. Feel better now?" he whispered in her ear, sending a tingling down her spine.

She turned and faced him. "I feel much better. Thank you. Ben sleeping?"

"Aye," he said as he nibbled at her neck.

She knew where this would lead, and she couldn't do it. She had to get the conversation over with now. She kissed him and then pulled away. "Babe, I would love to keep this going, but Father Tim will be here for dinner in two hours, and we haven't had any time to talk since you got home. Can we go have some tea?"

He took a step backward. "Is everything okay?"

"Everything's fine. We just haven't had a face-to-face conversation in over a week. I'm a girl. I need that." She smiled sweetly.

"Okay. Tea and talk it is then."

They took a few minutes to get tea and some snacks together and seeing as the weather was pleasant, they settled on the porch swing.

"So you said on the phone that the buyer is really interested?" Brenna said.

"Aye, he sent a couple of his people to shadow me this week, and we talked yesterday. I think he's gonna make an offer. I was gonna try and wait to tell ya until it was definite. I don't want to get yer hopes up. But I'm pretty sure it's a go."

Brenna grabbed his hands. "Oh babe, that's awesome! Is he good with you staying on and managing local projects and everything?"

Ryan nodded. "He is. As a matter of fact, he wanted me to stay with the company for at least a year to create a smooth transition. Things like that don't always work unless the old and new owner get along well. And I think we will, so it's looking really good. I'll still have to figure out something else to do. I don't think I'll make much, since I probably won't be salaried. More of a per diem. And since there's not a whole lot of local work right now, I'll just need to be creative about what I can do. But the most important thing is that I won't be commuting to Limerick."

"This is the best thing I've heard in a long time." Brenna couldn't help but grin. The thought of having Ryan home every night made her giddy. "Can you even imagine not having to drive to Limerick all the time?"

"I can't. Been doing it so long I'm thinkin' I won't know what to do with all that free time. Any ideas?" He wiggled his eyebrows at her, and she laughed.

"I'm sure we'll figure something out." If Ryan needed help to keep them afloat, all the more reason for her to talk to Bettie.

"Maybe we'll give Ben a baby sister." Ryan said with a playful grin and a tug on her shirt. "Or at least we can practice."

Brenna laughed. "I'll be very happy to practice." She hated to break the mood ... but she had to. She exhaled a deep breath. "So, I need to tell you about something, and I don't want to because you're in such a good mood, I don't want to spoil it. But I'm just gonna trust that we can talk rationally about it and continue having a good day."

Ryan cocked an eyebrow. "Rationally? Well, the only time you accuse me of not being rational is when it's about Luke, so I'm assuming it's about him?"

Brenna's jaw dropped. "Well ... yes. You're good!"

The humor was gone from Ryan's face, but he looked more calm than she'd expected. "Go ahead. What's going on?"

"Well, you know his parents moved back."

"Aye, and I told ya I was sorry for being a jerk about it." He had.

"Yeah, well, he might be moving back, too."

Ryan's jaw twitched, but she could tell he was restraining himself. He took a deep breath. "Okay. How do ya know that?"

Now her stomach was somersaulting. His new tack for handling a Luke discussion was about to be tested. "He called."

"He called *you?* I don't want him calling you."

"I don't control what he does. And you know he's persistent. I guess he'd already called before that, and Megan took the call. I figured if I ignored him he would just keep calling, so better to get the conversation over with."

Ryan was staring out at the distant mountain, jaw set. "Has he called ya before?"

"No, I haven't talked to him since the day we went to the jail."

Ryan let out a breath. "Okay, so what did he say?"

"He said it was a courtesy call to let me know he might be moving back. I told him it would be better for all of us if he didn't. He said he had apologized for what he'd done, and that it's not fair that he should have to stay away from his hometown and his parents just because he made a mistake."

Ryan took a sip of tea and eyed her over the rim of the cup. "And what do you think?"

"I just said. I think it would be better for everyone if he didn't come back."

"But do ya think it's unfair?"

Brenna rubbed her forehead, trying to formulate her thoughts. Defending Luke was probably a stupid idea, but if she could help Ryan let go of his anger toward him it might be worth the risk. "I don't know. He was a jerk. He took advantage of me. But when he broke my ribs, he was drunk. I don't think he would have done that if he'd been sober. I don't think he's evil. I just think he was a jerk." She watched a bee land on a mini rosebush that Megan had planted in a terracotta pot. "I guess I think we've all done stupid things. You're the one that convinced me to forgive Luke in the first place. You said you forgave him, but it feels like you completely forgot that at some point. I don't really get it."

Ryan gave her such a vulnerable look she almost let him off the hook. But this discussion needed to happen, so she sat still and waited.

"Yer right. I did tell you to forgive him, cuz I know that's the right thing to do. And I think I forgave him, too. But when Ben was born, it was like all the anger came back, and twice as strong. Seeing Ben, loving him immediately like I did, I couldn't stand the thought of anyone coming between us. I think I've been afraid, all this time, that he'd try to take Ben. And I won't let that happen. So I've probably been getting more and more angry with him for something he hasn't even done." He looked at her with pain in his blue eyes. She grabbed his hands again as he grit his teeth and sighed. "And sometimes ... I see a look on Ben's face and I see Luke. And that just about kills me."

Brenna crawled into his lap, putting her hands on either side of his face. "Listen. You are Ben's father. There is no question about it, and you always will be. No one is going to change that."

He nodded and closed his eyes. Leaning back he set the swing into slight motion. "But remember, if things ... if I'd done things right with my girlfriend ten years ago, then I would have a ten-year-old son right now. And if she had kept him and gotten married to someone else, I can't help but think I would at least want to know him. So, a part of me won't be surprised if Luke wants to have some part in Ben's life." He pinched the bridge of his nose and breathed out heavily. "And that freaks me out, Bren."

Brenna ran her fingers through his hair and nodded. "I wonder about that, too. I worry about when Ben gets older. Do we tell him you're not his biological father? Will he want to meet Luke?"

"Sometimes I think we should have just kept it to ourselves and put my name on the birth certificate. Then we wouldn't have to worry about any of this. Most people would have just done that." He absently played with her hair.

"But we talked about it, and we both know we would always have felt like it was wrong."

He nodded. "I know. Nothing about this is easy." He pulled her to himself and squeezed and she wrapped her arms around his neck.

"We'll figure it out. All we can do is what we think is right and trust God to work out the details." She pulled back to look at his face. "We never do what most people do. If we had done what most people do, we probably wouldn't have Ben in our lives at all. We do what we think God wants us to do, and we agreed that lying about it was wrong. So that means, we have to trust God to help us with whatever comes next. But I want to be very clear about one thing. You, me, and Ben. We will always be a family. No matter what. Nothing will pull us apart. Okay?"

He buried his face in her neck and she held him close. "I love you," he whispered.

"I love you, too, babe.

# Chapter Thirty-Three

Megan had been up early. She was always up early on Sundays. Usually it was nervous energy that she got whenever she had to sing. But today was different. Her nerves were all about David.

After a crazy goodbye/snogging session by the side of the road, they had gone to Killarney, gotten her new phone, and had dinner. Conversation was easy and relaxed, and they spent a lot of time talking about each other's families and reminiscing about the summer that he had tutored her. It surprised her how easy it was just to be together, as friends. She had thought, when he told her he wanted to slow things way down, that it would mean awkward moments and stilted conversation. Yet the opposite had happened. As if removing the pressure of romance made it easier to just be themselves.

But she had dreamed about him all night long, and she could feel the heat in her face just thinking about it. She was not dreaming about friendship, and she wondered if the day before had just been an anomaly, if today things would get awkward. Or, if the reason it had been so easy to keep their hands to themselves the night before was because they had already released the tension on the way to Killarney. They certainly couldn't do that every time they saw each other. So, she didn't know what to expect when she saw him.

TidyTowns had painted the church fence the day before, and it made a surprising difference in the curb appeal. Megan noticed new flowers that had been planted along the front of the church and smiled at the obvious touch of her mother. Blue flax and violets filled the beds. As one of the first to arrive on Sundays, she went in the side door, knowing the front doors would still be locked from the inside.

Anna, who was in the office working, looked up and smiled when Megan walked in. "Hello, luv. How are we this morning?"

Megan noticed Anna's left wrist was wrapped in a flesh-colored bandage. "I'm well, thank you. What happened to your wrist?"

Anna glanced down and rolled her eyes. "I wasn't watching where I was going. Missed a step and fell on my wrist the other day. It's fine. Just a little sore."

"Aw, I'm sorry. Yer doing okay, today?"

Anna smiled. "I am having a wonderful morning. I love coming in when no one is here. I get so much done!"

Father Tim's office door was closed. She was wondering if she should ask him for some advice in dealing with all the weird stuff going on in her life. "Is Father Tim in a meeting?"

Anna glanced over her shoulder. "No, he's actually running behind this morning. Did ya need to see him?"

Megan shook her head. "No, it can wait. I'm going to go get the soundboard set up. We have a special song from little Lizzy Hogan. Something she wrote with her brother Tommy, who's playing guitar. Do you have the key for the annex? I need to get the guitar mic and stand from the Veritas stage."

By the time parishioners started filing into the sanctuary, Megan had everything in place, and her nervous energy was back. She tried not to look for David, but she couldn't stop herself from looking up every time the door opened. Which is why she saw Jamie as soon as he entered. He looked right at her, probably knowing her routine well enough to know where she would be. A thought of what David had said about it not being over for Jamie flitted through her mind. She watched him walk toward her and found herself, once again, completely unsure of how she should feel in his presence.

"Hey," he said with a small smile.

"Hey, yerself. How are ya?"

"I'm well." His eyes held hers, and she knew David was absolutely right.

"So, are ya headin' back this week?"

"No, actually I decided to stay."

Her stomach did a hard flip. "Oh." She could tell he was trying to gauge her reaction, so she kept her face neutral. "I thought you were seeing some doctors in London?"

"Aye, but I think being home with family and friends is more important than keeping the same doctors. Mam set up an appointment at Doctor Rob's for tomorrow, and we'll see if they think they can help me or if I need to find someone in Cork."

"Are ya seeing Doc Senior or Rob?" Please let it be one of the two.

"Neither. I guess there's a new doc. He was the one with the first available appointment. Have ya met him? Doctor O'Brien?"

Megan almost laughed and cried at the same time. "I have; he's a friend. He'll take good care of you." She felt her cheeks heating. "I have to check something in the office. I'll see y'around?"

He nodded. "Aye. Good to see you, Meg."

She spun on her heels and headed straight for the ladies room. Jamie and David were going to meet, and she had no idea what that would look like. Would David say anything? Should she warn him, or did he already know Jamie was coming in?

She ran her wrists under cold water, hoping it would cool her off. If she didn't have to sing in front of the congregation, she would have splashed cold water all over her face. After a few deep breaths, she checked her new phone for the time. It was past time that she got back out there. Father Tim would be wondering where she was.

Mass went smoothly, as usual. Lizzy Hogan sang at the very end and quickly found herself surrounded by friends and family giving her hugs and telling her what a lovely voice she had. She was only ten, but her voice would have carried through the sanctuary without the aid of a microphone.

Megan busied herself with tasks off to the side of the sanctuary, hoping not to run into Jamie again. It just made her feel awkward. She had seen David come in late but lost sight of him, and now she wondered if he would seek her out to say hi or just head home. She was coiling up the guitar cord when she felt a shadow over her and looked up to see his gorgeous smile.

"Need any help?"

"I do, actually. I have to put this stuff back in the annex. Can ya carry the mic stand?"

She led him through the back hallways and unlocked the Veritas room, turning on lights as she went.

"This is cool," he said, looking around at the coffeehouse-styled college meeting room. Wall sconces warmed the space with soft light. Café tables filled the center of the room, and a small coffee bar took up one corner. At the end of the room was a slightly raised platform with sound equipment and an Oriental rug covering the floor. This was where Megan spent her Thursday nights leading worship for the college group.

She returned the equipment to its place on the stage. "It has a great vibe in here, doesn't it?"

"It does." He was standing several feet from her and whichever way she moved, he kept the distance between them. She knew it was wise, but it didn't lessen the electric current in the room. Being alone with him, especially in a cozy atmosphere like this—well, it was just good that he was keeping his distance.

Her dreams from the night before flashed through her mind once more, and she silently scolded herself, turning back toward the stage to fiddle with something. In truth, she needed a moment to compose herself. She squatted down to pick up a stray cord and looked up at him. She could tell he was not finding it easy, either.

"Do ya think it will always be this hard?" she asked.

His lip quirked up at one corner, and he looked at her for a moment before responding. "I think it will get easier. I don't want to *not* be around you so the only option is to learn to keep myself under control. I can do it, can you?"

She laughed, the tension broken. "That sounds like a challenge. Yes, I can do it. As a matter of fact, I'm thinking we should make some kind of wager."

"A wager? You mean like, if I can't keep my hands off you, I lose the wager and vice versa?" His eyes danced with humor.

"Exactly. And the stakes have to be big enough that we don't want to lose."

"Hmm, okay. But rather than having it be you against me, I think it needs to be a team effort. We keep it platonic, or we lose the wager. Because I'm gonna need your help, and you'll probably need mine." He raised his eyebrows. "Right?"

He was absolutely right. The romance freeze wasn't her idea, but she wanted to respect his need for some time. And if she lost her resolve at some point, she'd want him to try to keep her on track. "Agreed. So what are the terms?"

"Well, the worst thing I can think of right now would be not being able to see you at all. So, how about ... if we kiss each other we aren't allowed to see each other for ... four weeks."

"Wow, that's brutal."

He took a step toward her. "Aye, but it will work, won't it?"

She stood and took a step toward him. "Only if we are both committed to it."

One more step. "I'm committed. Are you?"

Her next step took her within inches of him. She said with a shallow breath, "I guess I have to be if you are. She closed her eyes and took a few deep breaths, calming her racing pulse. When she opened her eyes, he was looking at her intently.

"This is important to me. I can do it because I don't want to mess up our future, just so I can feel good in the moment. You understand, right?"

She nodded. "I do. I don't like it. But I respect your decision, and I don't want to screw up our future either. So, I'll take the wager. Shake on it?" She stepped back and held out her hand.

He looked at her hand and then back at her face. "Mmm, better not." He grinned.

She laughed. "Okay, so we know what happens if we lose the wager. What if we win? What then?"

"If we make it a whole month, you can bet that you'll get more than a handshake to celebrate." With an intense parting look, he left her standing there, hating that her legs suddenly felt made of Jell-O.

Brenna had tried to find Megan after Mass, but she was nowhere to be found and not answering her texts. She had a new phone, so it couldn't be blamed on that. She just had to accept the fact that her friend was not a good texter. Which she knew all about, because Ryan was the same. He'd much rather call than text, which meant half of the time he didn't even see her texts until he dug out his phone to make a phone call.

At least Megan had called Saturday night to let her know that she'd worked things out with David. But she couldn't give her any details because they were at dinner, and he had just gone to the restroom. She had hoped to find out what happened, this morning. But no such luck.

By the time Brenna got to the B&B, Megan must have finally looked at her phone. Her reply pinged as Brenna plunged a masher into hot potatoes: *Sorry I missed ur messages! Was kind of talking to David. I'll tell u about it later.*

Brenna replied: *Talking?*

Megan: *Haha. Yes. Talking. Sooo much to tell you. Not working till noon tomorrow. What time does Ryan leave?*

Brenna: *First thing. I'm gonna paint my bedroom, wanna help and talk?*

Megan: *Sure. B there by 8. See u then. :)*

So, she wouldn't get the scoop from Megan till the morning, but maybe, if she was subtle, she could wiggle something from David. Ryan had invited him to join them at the B&B for Sunday dinner. They were in the living room watching a game on TV.

Anna and Auntie Pat had taken Ben for a short walk, just to get some fresh air. Probably as much for Auntie Pat as for Ben. She spent way too much time in her bedroom these days. Anna, who had hurt her wrist earlier in the week, convinced her she needed help to push the stroller. If she thought she was needed, she was much more likely to go than if she thought they were trying to con her into some exercise.

Brenna was helping Bettie in the kitchen, hoping to bring up the idea of working at the B&B part-time. She was trying to think of a way to bring it up that didn't make Bettie feel obligated but also let her know she really wanted the job if it was available.

"Are ya gonna play on that phone or mash the taters for me?" Bettie pretended to be irritated by all technology.

"I'm on it. Don't you worry."

"Good." Bettie pulled piping-hot bread from the oven. "So, Anna told me ya might be interested in a part-time job?"

*So much for worrying about how to bring it up.* "I am. If it's really something you were already looking to hire someone for. I feel a little weird taking a paycheck from you. Like I should be helping you for free, because we're family, ya know?"

"Oh, nonsense. I need help, and you need a job. It's a win-win. And yes, I was already considering hiring someone, so I'm thrilled it might be you instead of someone I hardly know."

"Okay, well I definitely want to talk more about it. I need to mention it to Ryan, though. We haven't had much chance to talk in the last week."

"That's fine. Why don't ya talk to him tonight, and then you can come over one day this week and we can hammer out the details?"

"Sounds good, boss-lady."

Bettie pointed at her with a wooden spoon. "Now don't you start with that! Let's say we're more like partners. I'm not comfortable with being a boss. It's one of the reasons I'm glad it will be you and not someone else who I would actually have to boss."

Brenna laughed as she poured a little milk into the potatoes and finished mashing. "We'll just take it day by day."

David could smell the roast chicken from two rooms away as it finished its time in the oven. His stomach grumbled, and he reached for some of the crisps Bettie had put out for them. The living room was comfortable yet still classy. Two large couches were arranged in an L shape and an antique armoire stood between the two front windows. While it had likely housed clothing for most of its years, it now held a fair sized flat-screen TV that sat hidden behind the large wooden doors when not in use.

But since Munster was playing Ulster it was definitely in use this afternoon. David was grateful for the dinner invite. It was a good distraction on a day when nothing else would be happening to occupy his mind and keep it away from thoughts of Megan. He smiled at the thought of their wager. It was a rather clever way to keep them both vested in doing something neither of them really wanted to do. He knew it was the right thing to do, but that didn't make it easier. Still, with the way they felt around each other, even if they were dating, they would probably need to be very careful if they wanted to keep from going too far, too soon.

David's thoughts on saving sex for marriage had changed over the years. In college, he just saw it as one more rule the Church tried to force on people, as another way the Church exercised its control. And he didn't like being controlled, so he did whatever felt good. And sex definitely felt good.

But something had changed in him the more he grew in his relationship with God. After his first trip to Africa, he decided to take a break from sex. He still dated but always kept it from going that far because he'd come to see it as something more sacred than casual. As something you saved for the right person and the right time. He had never talked with anyone about his thoughts on the subject. And he knew people probably assumed, with all the dating he'd done over the years, that he held a much more liberal view of things.

But getting as close to Megan as he had over the past couple weeks just confirmed that he was doing the right thing. Because some of the things she'd said in conversation made him think that she was still innocent, and he didn't want to take that lightly. He respected her for making that choice and hoped she'd respect him for the changes he'd made a few years back. Better late than never.

Ryan, at the other end of the couch, screamed something at the telly, bringing David out of his contemplations. Munster was losing, and it wasn't pretty.

"Dinner!" Brenna called from the dining room, rescuing the men from the unfortunate game.

David, being a closet carpenter, noticed the architectural details in the dining room. A sizable white crown molding topped the room, with precise dovetails at each corner. The fireplace, its Victorian-era mantle painted to match the trim, gave the room a focal point. And the cool, medium-grey walls made the white trim pop. It was a room that could be comfortable or formal, depending on the occasion.

But the large mahogany dining table was the star of the room and laden with potatoes, roast chicken and several varieties of veggies, it made David's stomach growl once again. And once he tasted Bettie's cooking he immediately began thinking of a way to secure another invite.

"Bettie, this is delicious," he said with a smile. "We may have to work out a barter. Medical services for occasional dinners?"

A blush crept up her cheeks. "Ah, this? This is just chicken and potatoes. Nothing special. Now, I've cherry pie for dessert, and you'll not find a better one in Millway. That might be worth a trade for ya."

David laughed.

"I hear I have you to thank," Brenna joined the conversation, while buttering a steaming piece of bread, "for Megan finally getting a better phone?"

And here he'd not thought about Megan for two whole minutes. "Aye, I guess ya just need to lead some people by the hand."

"Well, if you hadn't taken her yesterday, I was making plans to do it tomorrow. That phone of hers was driving me crazy."

David chuckled. "I wasn't a fan of it either. I couldn't sit by and let a friend use a slider phone. I talked her into the newest model iPhone. She has no clue what to do with most of the features, though. Maybe you can give her a lesson."

"I'll do that." Brenna popped a bit of her bread into her mouth.

"So, David," Auntie Pat chimed in, "I was just telling Bettie that maybe it was time I got a cell phone. What do you recommend?"

David watched Bettie's eyebrows lift and Brenna stifle a grin. "Well, ma'am, I guess it depends on what ya want to use it for."

"Ah, I don't like 'ma'am' so let's stick with Auntie Pat, shall we?" She waited for his nod and continued, "And what do ya mean, what I want to use it for? It's a phone. I want to use it for a phone." Auntie Pat shook her head as if he was daft, and he struggled not to laugh while glancing at Brenna and Ryan, hoping for some help.

"Patsy," Brenna said, "A lot of people use their phones for other things nowadays. They have phones with cameras, Internet, alarm clocks ... really, they can do so much."

Auntie Pat cocked her head to the side, raised her eyebrows, and gave a small shake of the head. "Well, I don't see why I would need all those things. I just want a phone."

Bettie set her fork down and looked at her mam. "I don't see why ya need a cell phone, Mam. We have a house phone and ya have an extension in yer room."

"Well, either I should get one, or you should. What if I need to call you from my room? I can't call the house from the house phone, now, can I? Besides, it's a safety thing. Mary Thornton told me that she carries hers in her pocket at all times. That way, if she falls or something, she can always get help."

Brenna absently tapped the table. "That's a good point. I'll take ya this week to get one, Patsy. How about Wednesday morning? Are you free?"

"I'll have to consult my busy calendar." Auntie Pat rolled her eyes. "Of course I'm free."

"Okay, well, I'm coming over to talk with Bettie about some things, and then I'll take you into town to the Phone Centre. They'll have the kind of phone that you need."

"That would be nice. I hardly hear from you anymore. Maybe if I have a cell phone, you'll call me more often."

David smiled at the universal language of the eldest generation—guilt.

Brenna laughed. "Even better, I'll teach you how to text!"

"Goodness," Bettie chimed in, "that might not be the best idea."

"Do ya think I'm not capable of doing what the youngsters do?" Another raised eyebrow from Auntie Pat.

"Ha! No, I know you're quite capable. Just don't expect me to get a phone so you can text me every time you think yer tea has cooled too much or ya can't find the remote to watch yer stories. I have no desire to get a cell phone." Bettie said. "But you do what ya want."

With the cell issue settled, conversation moved to sports, TidyTowns business, and upcoming church events.

David enjoyed the banter. At first, he couldn't figure out why he liked the conversation so much, when in reality, it was quite mundane. But then he realized that was exactly what made him feel comfortable. They weren't trying to entertain him. They were comfortable enough with him to be themselves, and that was a compliment. Between the comforting conversation and the first rate food, he would definitely be finagling another invite to Sunday dinner at the Maloney B&B.

# Chapter Thirty-Four

David looked over his schedule and tried not to zero in on his 10:30 appointment. Jamie O'Connor. *Shoot me, now*. He didn't think Jamie had a clue about him and Megan, so it wouldn't be awkward in that way. But certainly David would have to work to see Jamie as a patient, not a competitor. When Megan told him Jamie had scheduled an appointment, he considered having Doctor Rob switch patients with him for that time slot. He could easily make up some excuse.

But, in all honesty, he was curious. What was Jamie like? How serious was his TBI? It wouldn't hurt for him to know a little more about the guy. To listen to people talk, Jamie was the town saint. Elizabeth's confession at Mass had ignited a firestorm of gossip, and David heard the phrase "poor Jamie" everywhere he went.

Patricia had been conspicuously silent on the subject; likely unwilling to recant the lies she'd spread about Megan. He looked forward to going public with his and Megan's relationship for many reasons, not the least of which was to see Patricia's reaction.

He'd have to wait a little longer, now that he'd pressed the pause button. But he looked forward to personally sharing the news with her when it was time. He was a fairly objective guy, but since finding out the truth about Megan, he'd found it difficult to be around Patricia without getting irritated. On a positive note, she'd taken the day off, so he wouldn't have to deal with her today.

He closed his schedule and pushed his fingers through his hair. He needed coffee. Thankfully, he could smell a fresh-brewed pot. One of Peggy's administrative assistant duties was to be on top of the early morning caffeine supply. And the break room was conveniently located right next to his office.

Shannon had her back to him, wiping up a spill on the counter, when he entered the room. He considered quietly retreating back to his office. He didn't know how much she would remember from Friday but figured it would be awkward, regardless. Yet the pull of coffee was too strong.

"Morning, Shannon." He poured a tall cup of coffee and grabbed one sugar packet.

"Oh, Doctor David, hi." The color in her cheeks told him she remembered at least part of her night at the Blackwater. But he wouldn't mention it if she didn't. "Um, thank you for your help on Friday."

*So much for that.* He nodded. "No problem."

Her face was now a deep scarlet. "I, uh, I don't remember much of what happened?"

"Well, you needed a little help getting home, so I just made sure ya got there safely."

"I'm so sorry."

She looked mortified, and David wanted to assure her that all was fine, but at that moment, Ailish Keane, their other nurse, walked in. She had silver hair piled into a loose bun on top of her head. Her green eyes crinkled with good humor, whether she was praising you or scolding you. And she wore scrubs with puppies on them. Every day.

"Good morning to you both. I'm glad to see that coffee. I've already had two cups at home, but I'm after thinkin' it's a three-cup morning."

"I'm with you, there, Ailish." David said. "Something about a Monday."

Ailish nodded. "Shannon, are ya going to stand there all morning, lass? Doctor Rob is already in, and his first patient is in the waiting room."

Shannon glanced at David and hurried from the room. Doc Senior, himself, was the only person who'd worked at Rowan Family Practice longer than Ailish. She was both a nurse and a midwife and had no problem reminding Shannon that she had watched her come into the world and never had she heard such loud newborn wailing, before or since. David had heard her mention it a few times and could only assume it was meant to put Shannon in her place, lest she think she and Ailish were equals. David had actually been quite impressed with how well Shannon held up under Ailish's scrutiny.

"Ya gonna ease up on her a little bit, now?" he asked, turning on his charmer smile. "She had a great first week."

Ailish gave him a sideways grin. "Well, Doctor, I've been breaking in new nurses here for longer than you've been on God's green earth. So, don't you worry about her. I know she's a good lass, and she's got the makings of a good nurse, too. But she still has a lot to learn." She stirred three sugars and a good bit of milk into her tall travel mug. "I swear they only teach them a tenth of what they really need to know, in those nursing schools, these days."

He bowed slightly, "My apologies; you are certainly more qualified to evaluate such things."

"That I am. But it's kind of you to be concerned for her." She cocked an eyebrow. "Or, is it more than concern?"

"Now, Ailish, you know very well that if workplace romance was acceptable, you'd be the first one I'd call."

Her hearty laugh bounced off the walls, and she patted his cheek. "You are a smooth one. No wonder all the ladies are falling over themselves, trying to get ya to notice them. Now, I'm no hypocrite, so I need to get out there and see if your first patient is here. You all set?"

"I am. Open the floodgates." He sipped his coffee and headed back to his office to grab his notebook.

By the time Ailish came and told him that Jamie O'Connor was in Exam Room Two, David had seen three head colds, two viruses, two ear infections, and a broken finger. TBI was a change of pace, and he had read some newer journal publications on the subject after Elizabeth had announced Jamie's condition, so he was well-prepared on the medical side. But a feeling of dread settled on him the minute Ailish said Jamie's name, so he took his time getting to the exam room.

Jamie's mother was seated in the extra chair, and Jamie had taken a seat on the exam table. Even seated, David could see that he was tall. His dark hair was unruly, and he appeared somewhat disheveled. Shirt wrinkled. Jeans stained. It was obvious he wasn't trying to impress the doctor.

"Hello, ma'am. I'm Doctor David." He shook Elizabeth's hand and then Jamie's. "Nice to meet you, Jamie. How are we today?"

Elizabeth answered for him, "Yesterday was a tough day. He's not feeling great today."

"Well, I see in the notes from your phone call that you've been diagnosed with Traumatic Brian Injury. What can you tell me about how it happened?"

Jamie shook his head. "Not much. I was living near London. I was at my uncle's farm, in the barn. I had just been doing some maintenance on the ... the ... it's the thing that we use to ... it's for the feed ..." He swirled his hand around and around. "It does this to the feed? God, I don't remember the damn word!" He looked at his mam, who was wringing her scarf in her hands.

"Feed mixer," she said quietly.

"Aye, feed mixer." Jamie closed his eyes and took a deep breath while clenching and unclenching his fists. Forgetting words was a very common symptom of TBI.

Elizabeth turned toward David. "The therapist told me to let him try to remember the word."

David nodded. "I imagine this is difficult for you both." He took a couple notes to give them both a moment. "So, you were working on the feed mixer, and then what happened?"

Jamie was staring out the window. "The next thing I remember, I was in the hospital, and my Aunt Denni was crying, holding my hand. She says I had already been awake, but I don't remember getting to the hospital. They kept me there for several days, I guess. I don't remember any of that very clearly."

"Okay. I don't see any records from the hospital or any of your other doctors. I'm assuming you've had a CT or MRI already, but we may want to do that again. Are ya planning to stay in the area, or are you going back to London?" *Say London.*

"I'm going to stay here." Jamie said with a challenging glance toward Elizabeth.

"We were planning on him moving home in a couple months, continuing his care up there for a while, until I could do some more research on local treatment options. But—"

"But I need to be here. So, that's why we called Saturday to make the appointment with you. I need to know what kind of medical care is available locally."

"Jamie," his mam began, "you already have appointments scheduled in—"

"I'm not going back to London, dammit!" Jamie shouted and glared at his mam, and she gave David a pleading look that said "sorry" and "can you help us," all at the same time.

David cleared his throat. "Right. Well, we can help you in the short term and get you pointed in the right direction, as far as therapy goes. I know there's an excellent physiotherapy clinic in Cobh. It's about an hour and fifteen minutes from here, but people drive from all over the county. I'll get that information for you before ya leave. In the meantime, I'll ask you some more questions, and we'll do a physical exam and go from there, sound good?"

Jaime nodded but avoided eye contact with both David and Elizabeth. David could already see some classic TBI symptoms. The loss of words, the sudden outburst, the embarrassment afterward, the completely overwhelmed look on the caretaker's face. He would need to do a mental status exam, but asking the wide range of questions would be easier without Elizabeth in the room.

At this stage, most caretakers found it very difficult not to prompt the patient for the answers. He was impressed with the restraint she'd already shown when Jamie forgot how to say feed mixer. But he could also see, from the deep purple circles below her eyes, that exhaustion was setting in.

"Mrs. O'Connor, would you mind if I had ya speak with Ailish to make sure we have Jamie's full medical history? I imagine we have plenty of records from over the years, but she'll want to make sure we have everything in order."

"Sure, that's fine."

David called for Ailish, who led Elizabeth out of the exam room. After a full mental status exam and physical exam, David said goodbye to Jamie and told him Ailish would be back in a moment. Ailish had taken Elizabeth into the break room, and when David walked in, she was giving her a warm hug. Elizabeth wiped tears from her eyes and turned to David.

"Doctor, is there a way I can ask you a few questions without Jamie present?"

David nodded. "Sure, let's go to my office. Ailish, would you please check Jamie's vision and hearing? And they also need info on the Step by Step physio clinic in Cobh."

She nodded and headed toward the exam room as he directed Elizabeth to his office.

"How can I help?" They both sat.

She twisted her scarf again and took a slow breath. "Thank you for everything you're doing. In some ways, I think it's really helpful that you've never met Jamie. It might help you to be more objective. But it's also a disadvantage, in that ya don't know what he was like before, so the contrast might not be obvious to you."

"True. But I don't think that will influence his care here. However, if you'd prefer, I can have Doctor Rob take over." *That might be a wise idea, regardless.*

"No, I don't think that's necessary. It's just hard to watch someone get a first impression of your son and know that it's not a fair representation of who he is."

*Unfortunately, it may actually be who he is, now.* But it wouldn't do to tell her that. "All the behavior that you're referencing is influenced by TBI. I recognize it for what it is. But I can understand how this may be difficult for you."

"'Tis. But that's not actually what I wanted to talk with you about. As you can imagine, I've read every piece of information on TBI that I can get my hands on, and so much of it is conflicting. It's hard to sort out what might help him and what won't. But my question is in regards to relationships. Jamie was engaged ... well, I'm sure you heard what I said last week at Mass, so ya know some of that situation."

David nodded, hiding his discomfort with where the conversation might be going.

She continued, oblivious, "So, he spent some time with Megan on Friday and although he didn't tell me what happened, he woke up the next day the happiest I've seen him in over a year. He had such a good day. It was remarkable. And the only thing I can attribute it to is his visit with Megan." She looked down at her hands, now clasped and resting in her lap. "What I'm wondering is if it's possible that just being in her presence could help his recovery? I think that's why he suddenly decided to stay home. He recognizes the effect she has on him. Is that crazy?"

Everything in David wanted to tell her it was. Wanted to say that something like that wouldn't have any effect on his progress.

He took a deep breath as his stomach swirled. "Actually, positive relationship experiences have been known to trigger a spurt in functional gain. It's very hard to say, from a clinical standpoint, that those relationships are the cause of the improvement. All the evidence is anecdotal. But certainly, it's a possibility that a person would try harder to overcome obstacles if they felt that doing so would result in a favorable response from a loved one." *Damn.*

Elizabeth nodded and smiled. "Thank you. I read about some cases where that appeared to be true. I guess I just needed to hear it from a doctor."

David's head ached. "You understand, nothing is guaranteed."

"I know. Yesterday was a terrible day. But sometimes ya just need a little hope to cling to." She smoothed her scarf across her knees. "I know it could be so much worse. He's very high functioning compared to most TBI patients. We are fortunate, but it's still hard."

"I can imagine. Is there anything else ya wanted to ask me?"

She shook her head. "No, thank you fer yer time. I really appreciate it."

"Any time. I imagine Ailish is done with Jamie." He rose and shook her hand. "Would you mind closing the door when you go?"

Sitting back down with his head in his hands, David closed his eyes and tried to settle his racing mind, which was caught in an endless loop of thought. Just because Jamie was hopeful about his relationship with Megan, didn't mean that anything had changed for him and Megan. He believed her that she didn't see Jamie in that way anymore. But if she found out what Jamie was thinking, would she encourage him for a while just to help him? Would that be too hard for him once she let him down? Or even worse, what if she didn't let him down? What if, in the process of trying to help him, she fell back in love with him? It would be textbook Florence Nightingale Effect. *Double Damn.*

Suddenly, all the reasons he had for asking Megan to wait seemed idiotic; and he wondered if he hadn't just paved the way for her and Jamie to get back together. This was so messed up. Somehow, in the span of three days, the odds had shifted completely out of his favor. He was screwed, and he could do absolutely nothing about it.

⤙

Megan stepped back to admire her work. Brenna had chosen a soft tan paint, a huge departure from the barn red that had previously graced the walls of her cozy bedroom. It had taken Megan the entire first coat to fill Brenna in on her crazy weekend with David. She hadn't yet gotten to the part about Jamie staying. But Brenna had gone out to feed Ben, so Megan had just finished up the cutting-in around the top of the room.

Her arms ached. Since she was the taller one, she got the upper-half duty, which meant a lot of stretching and reaching. But as long as she didn't get the dreaded job of painting the ceiling, she didn't care.

"Bren, first coat's dry. Ready to do the second coat?" she yelled down the hallway.

"Yep, be there in a sec!"

Megan heard another voice in the kitchen, so she looked out the window. Anna's zippy little car was parked behind hers. Must have come to get Ben, as promised. Which was good, because Megan only had another hour to give Brenna before she had to go get cleaned up for work.

Moments later, Brenna appeared carrying a plate of deliciousness. "Try the square ones, they're amazing."

"Bettie's?" Megan asked around a mouthful and Brenna nodded. "Are these new recipes?"

"Mm-hm." Brenna took a moment to swallow. "Not new to her, but she hasn't done them for her pastry business before. Did I tell you I'm definitely gonna go work with her?"

"No! That's fabulous! Ryan's fine with it?" Megan sucked dark chocolate off her fingertips.

"Yep. He thinks it's a great idea. Gonna talk details with Bettie later this week. So I still don't know exactly what it will look like. But I'm excited!"

"Me too, cuz this means you can deliver chocolate pastries to me at Burke's." Megan grinned.

"Yeah, I should make the chocolate ones part of my benefits package." Brenna had filled the two paint trays again, and she handed Megan her roller. "Back to work!"

"'Tis looking great. I have to admit, I was sad to see the red go. It was so cozy in here. But I like the way ya just flipped the main and accent colors. It looks a little more, I don't know, classy or elegant?"

"Thanks. I wanted to freshen it up but Ryan was not into buying a new bedding set or curtains. The comforter is reversible, so I'll just put the red side up now. *Design On a Dime*, baby."

"Let me guess, *HGTV*?"

"Yup. Don't think it's on the air anymore. But it was a great show. And this is more like, design on a penny. I told Ryan I wouldn't spend over a hundred euro. So far, I'm at €68, so I'm doing good."

"Well done, my dear." Megan loaded her roller with paint. "So, I only have about 45 minutes left. I need to tell ya about Jamie."

"I saw him at Mass. Did he go back to London today?" Brenna had finished the bottom half of the outside wall so Megan started on the upper half.

"Nope. He said he's moving back to Millway. But that's not even the big thing. Guess where he's going today?"

Brenna bent to rearrange the tarp protecting the hardwood floors. "Um ... your house?"

"No. He has a doctor's appointment today at Rowan's."

"Get out. David?"

Megan sighed. "Of course."

"Well, that's awkward."

"Mm-hm. Made even more so by the fact that David won't even be able to tell me about it because of doctor-patient confidentiality."

"Right. That sucks. What a weird position that puts him in. Jamie has no idea, right?"

"I don't see how he could. You and Ryan are the only ones who know anything's happened between us. Oh, and my parents. But I'm sure Jamie doesn't have a clue. The only good thing is that I don't imagine he'll continue to see David for his medical care. You would think he'd need to go to a specialist in Cork or something, right?"

"Yeah, that would make sense." Brenna stood back from the completed wall as Megan reloaded her roller. "One wall down, three to go. If you can't stay till it's done, don't worry. Ryan can finish the high stuff later."

"No, we can get it done. More work, less talk."

"Aye, aye, Cap'n." Brenna saluted and Megan laughed.

"Ah, ya might want to go wipe off your forehead. Tan's not your color."

Brenna's eyes widened. "Did I get it in my hair?"

"Nope, just your forehead. Oh, and your elbow ... and your hand."

Brenna rolled her eyes as she headed toward the bathroom. "What else is new?" She was infamous for spilling or dropping food and drinks on herself. It was a wonder she wasn't covered in paint, head to toe.

Megan's phone rang, but she couldn't answer it. Too much paint on her hands. She could see that it was from Elizabeth, though. Things were definitely better between them, but her name still set off an automatic queasy response in Megan. She'd have to call her back after work.

# Chapter Thirty-Five ~ July

Megan noticed Brenna's car parked at the Maloney B&B as she drove past. Must be talking over the job details. Good for her. It would be smart for Brenna to get out of the house more. Focusing on the driveway ahead of her, Megan wondered how many times had she pulled into the O'Connor farm over the past few years? It had felt like a second home. And now, this was only the second time she'd pulled in since she'd called off the wedding. Elizabeth had asked her to come round for a *céilí*, but Megan wondered if she had more in mind than a simple visit over tea.

Windows down, she caught the familiar farm scent: fragrant trees mixed with sheep smells. It took her back. She'd spent many days here cooking with Elizabeth and helping Jamie with chores in the barns. She'd even helped deliver a little lamb, once. The memory threatened to bring tears to her eyes ...

She had stopped by one night to drop off Jamie's guitar, and he'd been in the barn with a struggling ewe, trying to help her with a difficult birth. When he saw Megan in the doorway of the barn, his eyes lit up with relief.

"Megan, thank God, I need your help. She's lambing, but she's really small, and I think the little guy is either too big or turned wrong. Ever done this before?"

"No. How can I help?"

He motioned toward the small sink in the corner. "Wash up quick and come over here. You might be able to save both their lives."

Sweat plastered his hair to his forehead as his blood-covered hands struggled to free the unborn lamb. The sight of it made her feel queasy at first, but as soon as she realized she was needed, she sprang to action and did exactly what Jamie told her to do.

"They normally lamb standing up, so when I saw her lying down I knew something was wrong. But she's so small, and I think my hands might be too big. I can't seem to reach the legs. Maybe you can?"

"I'll try."

Jamie nodded toward a tub of Vaseline, and she smeared it on her hands and arms up to the elbow, as he instructed. She tried not to think about where she was sticking her hand and instead focused on the fact that she could save the lives of both mam and baby.

"Okay, you should feel his head. I got that far already."

"Oh! I think I found the mouth."

"Great, feel beneath the chin. His legs should be tucked up in there."

She had to reach further in. "I can't find … wait. I think I feel one hoof."

"Okay, grab it and gently pull it down and toward you." Once she had the first leg out, Jamie tied a string to it so it wouldn't slip back in while she went looking for the other. Once both were out, they waited for a contraction and then pulled. The lamb came out in a mess of fluid but he wasn't breathing.

"Is he alive?" Tears sprang to Megan's eyes.

Jamie took some grass and tickled the lamb's nose. "Sometimes they'll sneeze and start breathing," he said.

"He's still not breathing. What should we do?"

Jamie was already on his feet. He picked the lamb up by his hind legs and swung him back and forth a few times, and to Megan's amazement, the lamb sputtered and started breathing. He put the lamb down by the mother's head, and she started to clean him.

"You did great, Meg." Jamie looked down at her with a look of wonder and kissed the top of her head. "You're amazing."

A loud bark shook Megan from her reverie. She had parked in front of the O'Connor farmhouse and their Bernese Mountain Dog, Jester, was obviously waiting for her to get out and pet him. She sighed. There were too many memories here. Why hadn't she suggested meeting Elizabeth at The Tea Shoppe? She got out of the car and bent to give Jester a warm hug. He was the sweetest dog ever. So warm and easygoing, with huge paws and smiling eyes.

"Hey buddy, long time no see, huh? Where were you last time I was here?"

"Looks like he's missed you." Jamie leaned against a porch column, his wet hair curling at the edges. Tired eyes with dark circles gazed at her as a smile tugged at his lips.

"I missed him, too." She walked up the porch steps and hoped Jamie wouldn't go for a hug.

He stuck his hands in his jean pockets and stayed where he was. "Mam's inside. She made scones."

"I can smell them from here. How are ya?"

"M'okay. Glad to be home."

She nodded. "I'm sure it's good for ya to be around family."

He moved toward the steps. "'Tis. I'm going to check on the sheep. I'll be back in soon for a scone."

She watched him walk toward the sheep fence, once again unsure how she should feel around him, but thankful he hadn't made things awkward.

"Megan, thanks for coming." Elizabeth opened the screen door. "Come on in. I've hot scones and tea."

Jax hissed at her and scurried from the kitchen as Megan took a seat. "What's up with him?"

"Ah, probably smells Jester on you. The two of them are having a spat. Just ignore him."

Setting the tea and scones on the table, Elizabeth took a seat opposite Megan. She couldn't be sure, but she thought the grey at Elizabeth's temples had multiplied a bit and new lines creased her forehead. She didn't look like she'd been getting much sleep either.

"I'm glad ya could come. I thought it might be nice just to catch up with each other."

"Sure, thanks for inviting me. How are you doing ... since he came home?"

Elizabeth glanced toward the screen door. "It's an adjustment. But I'm glad he's here."

"He told me he's staying?" Megan stirred sugar into her tea.

"He is. Originally, he was just visiting for the weekend, but he doesn't want to go back. So, Denni's getting his apartment packed up for him, and we'll go back at some point and bring all his stuff home."

Megan's mind flashed to Jamie's bare-bones apartment and zeroed in on the memory of the shoes by the door. "What about Annie?"

Elizabeth looked up over her teacup. "Oh, he and Annie broke up."

"Hmph. Is he sad?"

"Don't think so. Seems to me that was more a relationship of convenience. Are you sure ya want to be talking about stuff like that?"

Megan shrugged. "I want him to be happy. If she made him happy, then that's fine with me." In reality, she didn't like the thought of Jamie with the chick that broke up their relationship. But she knew that wasn't wholly rational. She distracted herself with a bite of cranberry scone.

"Well, that's very generous of you. But I think a clean break is a good thing. He needs to focus on therapy and recovery, in whatever form that takes. He's promised me he'll follow doctor's orders."

Megan's heart started to pound a little faster. "Yes, Jamie said he had a doctor's appointment on Monday. How'd that go?" She had known David wouldn't discuss it with her, but she was dying to know how the meeting of her past and her future had gone.

"It went very well. I like that new doctor. You've met him, right? Doctor David?"

Praying that her cheeks didn't give her away, she answered, "Aye." The less she said, the better.

"Well, everyone raved about what a sharp young man he is. I was a little leery to see someone new, but he's given me some very good suggestions, and he gave us the name of a clinic in Cobh that sounds very promising. I've made an appointment with them for the end of next week. In the meantime, we'll go back to Doctor David on Monday, once he's gotten all Jamie's records from the London docs. He said he may order another MRI or CT scan. I'm hopeful that between Doctor David and the clinic, we will be able to handle whatever Jamie needs and keep him here, at home."

"That's great news. I'm sure you're relieved."

"I am. I'm hopeful, too. The doctor said that having Jamie around loved ones can be very beneficial to his recovery."

"Really? That's good."

"Aye." Elizabeth eyed Megan over her teacup. "He said that if Jamie were motivated to please his loved ones, it could make a significant contribution to his progress."

"Makes sense. Have ya noticed a difference since he's been home?"

Elizabeth nodded and looked distractedly out the screen door once again. Megan noticed that she was twisting her napkin and wondered what was making her nervous.

"Are y'okay?"

"Hmm? Aye, I was just thinking about the last weekend. He saw you on Friday, right?"

"Yes, he came over and apologized for everything. He was so sad. It was hard to see him like that."

"It can be very hard some days. But Saturday was one of the best days he's had. He was very calm and relaxed. It was such a good day."

"Well, that must have been encouraging." Megan cleared crumbs from the table in front of her, dusting them on her small plate.

"It was. And it got me thinking ..." Elizabeth worried her lip as she hesitated. "We have no right to ask anything of you, and I'm not asking for things to go back to the way they were. But I'm wondering if you'd be willing to spend some time here, with Jamie. Just to see if it helps him." Elizabeth's napkin had been twisted so much that it came apart in her hands.

"Um, I don't know what to say." Dread rocked her stomach. She didn't want to hurt Elizabeth, or Jamie, but she didn't want to give them false hope, either. "I don't think Jamie and I will—"

"I'm not asking you to consider rekindling anything, luv. I just wonder if you'd consider being a good friend to him. He could use a friend and the bottom line, he responds well to you. For him to try to make a new friend at this point—well, that would be very difficult. But the two of you already had a friendship. There are so many positive memories associated with you that I think it just helps him to reconnect with who he was. He was more like himself on Saturday than I've seen him yet." Tears shimmered in her eyes. "I know it's a lot to ask, considering what he did, but I was hoping that ya would be willing, anyway. It may not have any effect, but I'm willing to try whatever I can, at this point, to make up for lost recovery time."

Megan realized she was biting her thumbnail and dropped her hand to her lap with a sigh. "I still love Jamie, as a friend. But I don't want to lead him on, or give him false hope for a future together, ya know? I'm worried that he'd take it the wrong way if I started coming around a lot."

Elizabeth nodded, looking down at the table. "Well, I can understand that. I wouldn't want you to give him false hope. I'm thinking that friendship will be enough for him. He told me he could tell you'd moved on. So, he's aware. Couldn't you just be very clear with him, that you want to be friends, only?"

She sipped her tea and shrugged. "I can try. What do you want me to do?"

"Well, I was thinking he needs something to do, to occupy his time. I mean, he's doing some work in the barns and helping his dad on the farm. But I thought maybe you could help him plant a small garden, out behind the shed. I have a good little plot there that I haven't used in a couple years. You could do some carrots and cabbage, beans, and probably some nice herbs. I think having a project would be a healthy thing for him. What do ya think?"

It sounded harmless. "Sure, I think that would be fun. Are you going to bring it up to him?"

"Aye, I'll talk with him later today. I'll have him get ahold of you to figure out when to meet and get things going. Probably want to have stuff planted this week. That will give it a good ten to twelve weeks before the first frost."

"Sounds like a plan. I'll look up what the best things are to plant in July and then we—"

The screen door banged as Jamie walked through.

"So, can I have one of those scones now, Mam?" He turned to Megan and said, behind his hand, "She refused to let me have even one, before ya got here."

"Yes, you can have one now." Elizabeth handed him a plate. "Want me to wet some more tea?"

"Sure. I'm gonna go wash up."

As he walked away, Elizabeth got up to put water on for more tea. "So, did ya hear about the TidyTowns project at Mountdonovan?"

"Aye, Marlene's very excited about it."

Jamie came back in and grabbed a towel from the drawer, next to the stove. "No towel in the bathroom again," he said.

Elizabeth rolled her eyes. "I swear, yer brothers take every towel I put in there. You should check their bedroom floor, ya should."

"I think they do it on purpose, just to drive ya crazy." He grinned, and Megan wondered if she truly could help him. He seemed so normal. Like nothing bad had happened. If she spent more time with him, what would she see? Would he be more like this guy or the one who called her when he was drunk and angry? Or maybe he'd be both. Maybe he simply was both now.

He sat at the table and grabbed a scone. "How was school this term?"

"I ... ah ... it was fine. But I'm taking some time off now. Just trying to figure out what I really want to do."

"Well, I'm sure you could do whatever ya set yer mind to."

"Thanks." Megan felt herself enjoying his attention and immediately scolded herself. Maybe she should tell Elizabeth she wasn't ready to do the garden thing. It wasn't a good idea. She had to leave—to gather her thoughts. Glancing at her phone for the time, she stood. "I'm gonna head on. But it was really nice to chat, Elizabeth. Thanks for the invite."

"Thanks for coming, luv. Sure we'll see ya soon." Elizabeth winked, and Megan had to get out. She took her plate and cup to the sink, and Elizabeth gave her a hug. She whispered a thank you in Megan's ear and Megan smiled back, feebly, giving a slight nod of her head.

Jamie stood and walked her to the door. "'Twas was nice to see you, again. Thanks for coming. I know it meant a lot to Mam."

She nodded and avoided a hug by opening the door before he could reach out for one. Sitting in her car, taking a deep breath, she wondered what she might be getting herself into.

Brenna sat at the old, wooden table beneath the lead-paned window in Bettie's country kitchen. The cheery yellow walls always lifted her mood. She'd had a great talk with Bettie about her new job. The plan was for her to come in on Monday, Wednesday, and Friday, from ten until two. She would start with organizing Bettie's pastry business. At the moment, Bettie had Post-it notes on her calendar and a stack of papers with scribbled names and numbers. That was the extent of her business plan. At the very least, she needed a spreadsheet, or two, to track clients and inventory. Brenna was confident she could make a significant impact in that area. She also pondered what systems she might be able to implement for the B&B that might make Bettie's life a little easier.

Bettie had gone upstairs to see if Auntie Pat was ready to go, and Brenna was making notes of some of the projects she wanted to tackle when she started working next week. Movement out the window caught Brenna's eye. She had a clear view of the O'Connor farmhouse. Megan was just getting into her car. She hadn't stayed very long.

Brenna sent a text: *Hey, just saw you leave Elizabeth's. How'd it go?*

Megan's car hadn't moved yet, and a text came back immediately: *Ummm ... too much to text. Went ok. But weird. Call me when you're home.*

Brenna and Auntie Pat were heading to the Phone Centre in Millway to get Auntie Pat a cell phone. The family all agreed that it wouldn't hurt for her to have the ability to call the house phone, if she needed help. There was some concern about her making random calls when she wasn't as lucid. But they figured they'd just worry about that if it happened. Bottom line, Auntie Pat asked for so little. If she wanted a cell phone, Brenna thought she should have one. If she'd needed an iPhone, they would have had to go into Killarney. But all she really needed was a phone with larger keys and the ability to make a phone call once in a while.

"Hello, luv," Auntie Pat said from the stairway. Her short, silvery-white hair framed her face in soft waves. Small wired glasses, perched on her thin nose, were attached to a delicate golden chain that kept them always at hand, hanging from her neck if she should decide to take them off. She had put considerable effort into her outfit today, pairing white pants with a peach shirt and a matching scarf. She had even donned some lipstick.

A twinge of sadness pricked Brenna when she thought about the fact that a trip to the store was a dress-up occasion and the highlight of Auntie Pat's week. Maybe, once she started working there, she would schedule in some time each day to take Auntie Pat out somewhere. She had to get lonely just hanging here in the B&B most days.

"Hi, Patsy!" Brenna rose and met her at the bottom of the stairs, giving her a hug and a kiss hello. "Ready to go?"

"Aye, just let me grab my jumper." She pulled her favorite sweater from a hook on the wall.

Bettie came down moments later, holding out twenty euro. "Brenna, while you're in town, would ya mind stopping at SuperValu and grabbing me some sugar and gelatin? I just ran out, and I need to make some tarts this afternoon."

"Sure. We'll be back in bit."

The drive into town took only a few minutes. They parked at the town square and set off down Main Street. Auntie Pat was very chatty today. Some days, she hardly spoke at all. More days than not, lately. So it always pleasantly surprised Brenna when she was full of conversation.

"I hear you're going to be working at the B&B now." Auntie Pat steadied herself with Brenna's outstretched arm. "I think that's a good idea. Bettie works too hard and I'm afraid I'm not much help anymore."

"Well, you built a lovely business there. You're entitled to a nice retirement." Brenna rubbed Auntie Pat's arm as they walked.

"Bah, I didn't want to retire. I could still help some, if they'd let me. But it was getting to be a bit much for me. Thank God for Anna. You two came at just the right time. Without her there, I think Bettie might have lost it."

"She's thrilled to be a help. And I'm excited to see what I can do to make things easier on you all."

Auntie Pat squeezed Brenna's hand. "You're a sweet lass. I'm glad you're going to be helping. I just don't know if it will be enough. They don't think I know what's going on, but I've looked at the books. I know that occupancy is down, and Bettie has no time to do anything about it. They all smile around me like everything is just fine, and they think I can't read their faces. Maybe, sometimes, they're right. But I know more than they think I do. And I think Bettie's considering selling the place."

Brenna glanced at Auntie Pat in surprise. Sometimes, it was hard to decipher if she was right on or completely off. "What makes you think that?"

"I heard her on the phone with an auctioneer. She's got some fancy person coming in to evaluate the property and give her a value on it."

"I didn't know that." Suddenly, her job security took a dive. But what would be the point of Bettie hiring her if she were just going to turn around and sell? Unless it was to help her get the records in order to make it easier to sell?

"Well, she doesn't think I know it, either. But I do, and I don't like it."

"Don't worry, Patsy, it will work out. Here we are." Brenna held the shop door open for Auntie Pat. "I've already looked at the phones they have available, and I found one that I really think you'll like."

It was a No Sim phone that had a standard number of talk minutes and was very popular with seniors. Large buttons, large display, and nothing fancy. And it didn't have a fancy price tag, either. So Auntie Pat was quite satisfied.

They went from there to the SuperValu and grabbed the items Bettie needed. As soon as they got back in the car, Auntie Pat called home to test it out. "Hello?" She paused. "Hello?" She put her hand over the receiver end and said to Brenna, "Bettie can't hear me. It's not working right."

Brenna heard a telltale beep. "It's okay, it's just the voicemail. You can leave a message." Auntie Pat looked utterly confused and passed the phone to Brenna. "Hi Bettie, just us. Patsy was testing her new phone. See you soon."

She noticed a glassy look in Auntie Pat's eyes. She was slipping into another place, and Brenna had seen it happen before. One minute she was completely lucid. The next she was far, far away. The fact that she didn't know what voicemail was should have clued Brenna in immediately.

They had planned to go for tea but Brenna headed for the B&B instead. "You're looking a little tired, Patsy. Let's get you home."

～

David had barely changed into jeans and a T-shirt when he heard a knock at his door. He wasn't expecting anyone and had to leave in twenty minutes to get Megan and Shannon for the ride to their C.A.M.P. meeting in Killarney. He and Megan had decided it wouldn't be very nice to leave Shannon out of the carpool loop, so to speak. And she would also be a good way to keep them from being alone in the car, which had led to some heated distractions in the past.

The soft knock came again just as David reached the door. He opened it and was surprised to see Megan there. "Hey."

"Hi," she said, and then stepped in and put her arms around his waist and laid her head on his chest.

He wrapped his arms around her. "Hey, are ya okay?"

She nodded, sighed, and spoke into his chest. "Yes, just had a weird day and really wanted a hug."

What was she thinking? Coming to his apartment all alone and vulnerable. She obviously had more faith in his self-control than he did. "Well, I'm always up for a hug. Better?"

She let go. "Yes, thanks. Sorry to drop in unannounced. I just figured I wouldn't have more than a minute alone with you if I waited for ya to pick me up." She had her hair back in a ponytail but several strawberry strands had escaped and now framed her face.

"Did you need to talk about something?"

She shrugged. "No, not really. Just came for the hug."

He laughed. "Okay, well, come on in for a few. If we leave now, we'll get to Shannon's too early."

She looked around at his little flat. It was supposed to be a temporary place to stay, an upper level apartment with an eighty-year-old landlord named, Breda Buckley living downstairs.

Mrs. Buckley had traveled a lot in her sixties and had decorated the upstairs apartment with souvenirs from Africa. David felt at home with the hand-carved wooden animals and paintings of small African villages. He thought she'd gone a little overboard with the animal print on pillows, chairs, and curtains. But he'd just gotten used to it. It wasn't until he looked at the place through someone else's eyes that he felt a little self-conscious about the decor.

He could get a bigger, more modern place, and originally that had been the plan, and the reason he hadn't bothered changing all the animal prints for something more ... manly. But he'd probably have to take on another part-time job if he wanted to afford a better place. By the time he paid his school loans and other bills each month, there wasn't much left from his first-year doctor's salary to spend on housing.

And despite the animal prints, the place suited his needs. He had a kitchen/dining room/living room combo, a bedroom, and a bathroom. A nice little deck off the living room even gave him a bit of outdoor space for those rare non-rainy days.

"So, you're a fan of animal prints, eh?" Megan's eyes twinkled with laughter as she moved a zebra print pillow to the end of the couch and took a seat.

"What if I am? Does that change things between us?" David raised an eyebrow in challenge and grinned when she just laughed at him. "The flat comes furnished."

"I figured. I know Mrs. Buckley's fondness for animal prints. She has a different print bag every time she comes into the pharmacy."

"Well, it's either grown on me, or I've become immune to it. Would ya like something to drink?"

"No, I'm fine. We have to leave in a little bit, anyway." She picked up a copy of *Woodworker* magazine from the coffee table. "Did you ever consider a career as a carpenter?"

He sat at the other end of the couch. "Maybe, at some point, in the back of my mind. But my grades in school, and all the aptitude tests, kind of put me on a trajectory towards either medicine or engineering. And I love medicine. So I figure, I'll do that full time, and carpentry can be a hobby someday, when I have time. And space. And equipment."

"Sounds like a good plan." She smiled, slightly. Despite her insistence that she didn't want to talk about anything, he could tell something was weighing on her mind.

"You sure you're okay? You wanna talk about yer day?"

She looked out the window for a moment. "It's nothing, really. Just had coffee with Elizabeth O'Connor. It was a weird conversation. I don't know. She told me they came to see you. I'm guessing you can't say much about it?"

He shook his head. "I wish I could talk with you about it. I really do. I can't talk about the specific case. But if ya have questions about TBI in general, I can answer those."

She nodded. "That's what I figured. It's okay. I did a lot of research online when Elizabeth first told me. I think I have a pretty good understanding of the general topic."

"Okay. Sorry."

"No, I'm sorry. I didn't want to bring it up. I know it puts you in a really awkward position. Geez, the whole thing is awkward, isn't it?" She pulled her knees up and circled them with her arms, resting her chin on top.

"I have to admit, I'd never thought I might need to excuse myself from a case due to a conflict of interest before. But I've considered it for this one."

Her eyes grew wide. "Oh, I'm so sorry. I won't bring it up anymore. I promise."

"No, it's not you. It's just that I want to make sure I have my patient's best interest in mind whenever I make decisions, and in this case, it requires a lot more thought and introspection on my part. But it's okay. If at any point I think I can't be objective, I'll ask Doctor Rob to take over his care."

Megan nodded. "I think the fact that you're so aware of it will ensure you do the right thing by him. But the whole thing gives me a headache. So, next subject. How are you doing ... ya know ... on dealing with the Katie stuff and getting to a better place?"

The hair on the back of his neck rose. The question shouldn't annoy him; it was a fair question. He'd asked her to wait for him until he had his head on straight. She had a right to know if he was making progress. "I set up a meeting with Father Tim on Saturday morning. Ryan suggested it. Said he's a great listener and really wise. So, I'm gonna see what he has to say. But if ya want the truth, I feel like an idiot. Like I don't know if I'm doing the right thing."

She knitted her brows and cocked her head to the side. "Right thing as in ... ?"

"Us. Putting on the brakes. Making us wait. A huge part of me wants to say, screw that, and just pretend the last week didn't even happen."

She gave a thoughtful nod. "Well, why don't you see what Father Tim says, and if he thinks you're being too hard on yourself or that you shouldn't worry about it, we can call off the wager and the pause on the relationship and pretend—like ya said—that last week didn't even happen. We just move forward.

"But if he thinks you should take some time without being focused on a relationship, to get yourself to ... wherever it is that you're wanting to get to, then we'll just take it a week at a time. Because I don't want to jump right back into things and then have you regret that, down the road."

"I don't see that happening."

"No, not right now, because we're just at the start of things. But we will hit bumps. And if we rush things now, I don't want one of those bumps to make you unsure. I'm not sure I could take it at that point."

He nodded and reached for her hand, rubbing the back of it with his thumb. "I feel so torn. I don't want to screw us up, by rushing things, but I don't want to lose you."

She took his hand in both of hers and pulled it to her lips, placed a soft kiss on his palm, then rested her cheek in his hand. "You're not going to lose me. And that doesn't count as a kiss, by the way." She smiled, returning his hand to his lap.

"Well, maybe not." He cleared his throat. "But if we stay here any longer, I don't know if—"

"I hear ya. Let's get outta here."

⌒◆⌐

As the C.A.M.P. meeting wound to a close, Megan took a breath to gather her courage. Shannon had crossed the room to catch up with some former trip-mates, and David stayed behind, apparently sensing her need for a pep talk. It was foolish for her to be anxious, but Moira made her feel like a silly schoolgirl who had no business talking with the adults.

"It's a great idea." David ran a hand back and forth over her arm. "Don't be nervous. Donal is harmless. And Moira? She's all bark, no bite."

Megan glanced over toward the queue of people waiting to talk with Donal. "What if they think I'm crazy? An outdoor event? It's awfully risky."

"Aye, but you've covered that with the tents. And with some hard work, the ballroom will be done in time and you can use that as a backup. I'm telling you, they will be thrilled just to have a place to hold the benefit. Want me to come with you to talk with them?"

"If ya don't mind? Just for moral support." Megan resisted the urge to grab his hand as she headed toward the dwindling queue.

Donal made eye contact and gave her a quick nod as he finished up with the team members who had waited to talk with him. Megan had sent him an email saying she wanted to talk with him and Moira after the meeting. So, as soon as he was free, he motioned toward Moira to join them, and they each grabbed a seat.

"Well, Miss Megan, you certainly have my curiosity piqued. What is it you wanted to talk about?"

"I have a proposal." She handed them both a packet of papers with her ideas outlined in detail. "I know you've been looking for a venue for the benefit, and I have an idea that's a little unconventional, but I think it could be a great opportunity."

Moira looked up sharply from the papers in her hands. "You want to hold the benefit out of doors? Absolutely not. We can't ask people to pay 100 euros per plate and then sit on the lawn."

A scene of ladies dressed in ball gowns, awkwardly sitting cross-legged on a picnic blanket, passed through Megan's head.

"I understand your concern. But I've been to several upscale weddings that were held outdoors with large tents to protect from the elements. They were all lovely. Besides, we won't be outside the whole time. As you can see, there will be tours of the Mountdonovan facility and dancing in the ballroom. If we do have an unfortunate weather situation, we can move the whole event indoors."

Moira huffed. "Well, then, why not plan it indoors to begin with?"

"Because this property is absolutely beautiful. You'll have to see it to understand. I just think it will be very elegant to dine on the grounds. And more than that, it sets the benefit apart. Everyone holds their charity events in a big hall or banquet room. This is something new and different. And because it would be a grand opening of sorts for the Mountdonovan Estate, I think it will increase attendance. Everyone will want to be a part of the event. It will create a buzz."

Donal turned to David. "What is your take, David?"

"I agree with Megan. It's a unique, beautiful property, and I think it will be a boon to both the Müller Haven House benefit and Mountdonovan. It's a win-win."

Moira flipped pages back and forth. "But I've already planned the entire event with the assumption that we'd be using a banquet hall. I don't have time to make all new arrangements. Not to mention the cost involved in catering and rentals. It's just not feasible, Donal."

Donal raised an eyebrow. "I know you've put a lot of time into the planning already, but the bottom line is we don't have a banquet hall to use. Everything from here to Dublin is booked for weddings. Unless you want to hold the benefit in a fire hall, I think this may be our best bet."

Moira shrugged. "Maybe. But there's still the cost to contend with. And I'm not sure I can get everything done in time, now."

"I am more than willing to help you, Moira." Megan said. "As a matter of fact, I can handle all the rentals and catering. And if I understand correctly, you were set to pay a good-sized fee just for the use of the room at McGovern's. My proposal to the TidyTowns committee is that they will allow us to use the estate for free, as it will be good publicity for them. So, provided they agree, the money you were going to use for the facility could be used for the rentals."

"I guess that could work." Moira said with a doubtful shrug.

"Excellent." Donal patted Megan on the back. "I love it. When will you present your idea to the TidyTowns Committee?"

"Tomorrow."

"Wonderful. Let us know if you need anything for your presentation."

"Will do. Thanks." Megan said.

As they crossed the room to collect Shannon, David leaned in and whispered, "I don't know what you were worried about. You nailed that."

Megan smiled. "Aye, that wasn't too bad. But tomorrow night is the TidyTowns Committee. And Patricia makes Moira look like a cuddly puppy."

# Chapter Thirty-Six

Megan wiped her palms on her jeans, thankful no one could see her do so beneath the table. She needed to appear strong and confident. That was hard to do with Patricia staring her down from the other end of the long conference table.

The seven TidyTowns Committee members had taken care of their usual Thursday night business, and it was just about time for Megan to propose her plan to have them host the Müller Haven House benefit on the Mountdonovan property. She had also filled out the Program Director job application online and hadn't heard back, so she wondered if that would come up as well. No pressure.

Her mother, presiding over the meeting, turned to her and gave a quick wink as she began. "Ladies and gentlemen, as I mentioned, Megan has a very interesting proposal regarding the Mountdonovan project. Megan?"

Megan blew out a breath, cleared her throat, and passed a printed version of her proposal to the committee members. "Thank you for taking time to hear my proposal. You may or may not be acquainted with the C.A.M.P. program. I've given you some details in your materials. In short, it's a volunteer medical organization that raises money for a number of projects in Sierra Leone, Africa, one of which is an annual benefit to support a children's home in Freetown. Doctor O'Brien is a member of the organization, as are Shannon Maguire and myself. It's come to my attention that the upcoming benefit is in need of a venue. I would like to propose that TidyTowns and Mountdonovan host the benefit as a sort of grand opening. I've outlined the details in your packet."

She sized them up as they all glanced at the papers in front of them. If Patricia weren't sitting there, she thought her proposal would probably be a slam-dunk. She could count on her mam, Bettie, and Anna, as well as Nessa Rose. Her boss, Tom, would back her, but she needed a unanimous vote. And she didn't know where Mike, of Mike's Hardware, would land. Ryan was at the table as well, but he wasn't a committee member and therefore had no vote. She assumed he was simply there because he was the contractor on the job. So, by her count, she had two wild cards. If Mike agreed, Patricia would have to have a really good reason to vote no.

Patricia leaned forward. "This says the benefit is scheduled for September fifth. Why in the world are they still without a venue? That seems like extremely poor planning."

"They had booked it at McGovern's in Killarney, where they've held the benefit for the last four years. Unfortunately, it has just been sold and is under renovations for the next three months, so that leaves C.A.M.P. scrambling for a place. However, as it's a Saturday just at the end of summer, most places are already booked with weddings. That's why I think we can provide the perfect solution. This event draws supporters from all over the country. If we offer to host this event, not only will we be helping a great cause, we will gain wonderful exposure for Mountdonovan." Megan paused and noticed heads nodding around the table.

Patricia drummed her nails on the table. "Yes, that would be a good thing. However, only if we can actually pull it off. This event is only eight weeks away. If the construction gets delayed at all, we won't be ready. And then, instead of impressing possible patrons, we will look like fools. Where would we put three hundred people if the ballroom isn't finished? I think the risk is too great." She folded her arms and sat back in her chair. "Not to mention, we don't have a Program Director yet. We aren't prepared. It's just too soon."

Megan nodded. "I agree the construction timetable is troubling. But I don't intend to use the ballroom for dinner. If it's ready, I would love to use it for dancing after dinner. But the plan is to make it an outdoor event with large tents to protect from the elements. I think focusing on the beauty of the grounds will make for a wonderful impression. Granted, if we had a storm, it wouldn't be as pleasant. But we all know a little rain won't hurt us."

Patricia's eyes narrowed. "And just how would we pay for all these tents and tables, and I'm assuming a caterer?"

"We wouldn't. That's the beauty of the plan. The budget for the event already included paying a rather large facility and food charge. I've priced out caterers and tent rentals, and we can easily keep it within the budget, as long as we don't charge a fee for the use of the property. And considering it's excellent publicity for us, I don't think it would make sense to charge anyway. I see it as a positive for both organizations."

Tom spoke up. "You've discussed this with C.A.M.P., and they are agreeable?"

"Yes. They are thrilled at the thought. Millway is more central than Killarney, and they are excited about doing something a little different."

Tom nodded. "I think it sounds like a great idea. Although, I am concerned that we don't have a Program Director to help organize the event."

Megan glanced toward committee secretary Nessa Rose, who was pulling a folder out of a large daisy-covered bag. "Well, this is as good a time as any," Nessa Rose said as she passed papers out to the committee. "We currently have three applicants for the position of Program Director. All three are interesting for different reasons. As you can see, two are from Cork and then the third is our very own—"

"Megan?" Patricia sputtered. It was no secret that Patricia was Megan's number one anti-fan. But the others didn't seem taken aback. Thoughtful smiles and nods went around the table. Patricia looked around at her fellow committee members. "This is certainly unorthodox. Marlene, you realize you will have to excuse yourself from the voting process on this, and your vote will have to be given to someone else to avoid a deadlock."

Marlene leveled a stare at Patricia. "I'm aware. That is why I asked Ryan Kelly to take my place for this decision. Since he is running the renovation project, it makes sense that he should have a say in who he will be working closely with to finish the project. Does anyone object to Ryan taking my vote regarding filling the position?"

All eyes were on Patricia. Her mouth was pressed into a thin line as she shook her head. Ryan was a town darling. It would not do for her to speak against him. Megan tried to hide a smile at the smooth way her mother had taken control of the situation.

Nessa Rose spoke up again. "Well, I'm glad that's settled. As I was saying, we have three applicants. I've provided you all with their résumés and a brief description of each candidate. If you'll all please take the time to review those, we will table this until our next meeting. At that time, all three candidates will be present to answer any questions the committee may have. Please come prepared to ask your questions and make a decision after that meeting. We don't have a lot of time to play with, as ya know."

Marlene nodded. "Thank you, Nessa Rose. Now back to the matter at hand. I understand that C.A.M.P. is asking for a decision as soon as possible. It sounds to me like this is a great opportunity for us. It's free publicity and an opportunity to help a reputable charity. Does anyone else have questions for Megan before we take a vote? It's not necessary for us to have made a decision on the Program Director position in order to decide on the benefit, as Megan has already offered to organize the benefit, if needed, regardless of whether or not she's chosen for the director position. Is that correct, Megan?"

Megan nodded. "Yes. Most of the planning has already been done by the C.A.M.P. organizers, so I would gladly do whatever I need to in order to make it a success on our end."

"Excellent. Any questions, then?" Marlene scanned the room as people shook their heads and Patricia crossed her arms and shrugged. "Right, then, shall we vote? All in favor?"

Hands went up around the table, and Megan held her breath as they waited for Patricia to raise her hand. It felt like this event would be an audition for the job, and the more she thought about it, the more she really wanted the position.

Patricia quickly flipped her hand up and down. "Fine, I'll agree to the event because it does sound like a good opportunity, but I won't be as easily persuaded when it comes to filling the Program Director position. Just so we're clear." She pinned Megan with a withering stare. But Megan was so excited about getting approval for the benefit she didn't even care.

# Chapter Thirty-Seven

Walking into the church office on a Saturday morning brought David back to childhood. He distinctly remembered sitting in the outer office for long stretches while his parents met with Father Dennis. Looking back, he imagined they were probably doing some sort of marital counseling. At about seven years old, he didn't grasp that. He just knew that Ms. Saorsie, the church secretary, always had a crystal bowl of butterscotch candies on her desk and a stack of coloring pages with crayons.

He instinctively glanced at the desk—now Anna's—to see if the candy dish was still there. Indeed, it was. Filled with chocolates instead of butterscotch, but it was still there. Anna, however, was not. Father Tim had told him to just come in and the door would be open.

He knocked on the slightly open door. "Hello, Father?"

"Ah, David. Please come in. Have a seat." He shook David's hand and moved a book off of the chair facing a large oak desk. The room was small and cozy and smelled of coffee. Well-built bookcases ran floor to ceiling behind the desk. A couple of wingback chairs stood in front of an unlit fireplace. It had the look of a study. Opened books lay in stacks on the desk, and notebooks full of loose sheets of paper were piled haphazardly on most surfaces.

"Thank you for seeing me. I don't really know how to do this."

Father Tim smiled graciously. "Let's just start with having a seat, shall we?"

David nodded and took a seat as Father Tim walked behind the desk and sat down. "I probably wouldn't normally meet with a priest to discuss my personal life, but Ryan said you've helped him work through some big issues in the past."

Father Tim nodded. "You're not the only one to ever feel uncomfortable coming here to talk. Don't worry, though. Nothing you say here will leave this room, and there's probably nothing I haven't heard before. Why don't ya tell me what you're struggling with."

"Hmm, okay. To make a long story really short ... about five years ago, I walked in on my girlfriend with her ex-fiancé. She was the only serious relationship I'd ever had. And I didn't take it very well."

"I shouldn't think anyone would."

"Right. So I was really angry for a while. Dated a lot ... and stuff." David raised an eyebrow, hoping Father Tim would get his meaning without details. He'd basically been a very bad Catholic for a time.

"I understand."

"Okay, so after a while, I kind of figured out I wasn't enjoying my life as much as everyone assumed I was, and I made some changes. I went on a couple mission trips to Africa, and my life changed a lot. But I didn't realize until last week that I never really forgave Katie for what she did. I just kinda stuffed it, ya know?"

Father Tim nodded. "I do. You're not alone; that's very common. So are you trying to figure out how to forgive her?"

"I don't know. I prayed about it last weekend, and I really think God's helping me with that part of it. I don't feel that sick feeling anymore when I mention her name. So that's a good sign."

"Very."

"But the reason I wanted to talk to you is because I've met someone, and I think I'm in love with her." David paused. He was surprised at how easy it was to tell such personal things to Father Tim. "So, I don't want to mess up what could be an amazing thing by bringing my baggage into the relationship. I saw her with her ex last week and I lost it. Punched a hole in my bathroom wall." He held up his bruised hand as Exhibit A. "That was kind of a wake-up call that I had some things to take care of before I had any business being in a relationship again. That's how I realized I hadn't forgiven Katie."

"That's good, David. It sounds like you're on the right track, to me."

"Well, here's the thing. I told this girl that I thought we should put our relationship on hold while I got my anger and all that stuff figured out. Neither of us really wants to do that, but it sounded like the right thing to do, at the time."

"I can see the wisdom in that. How did she take it?" Father Tim absently cracked his knuckles.

"She's supportive. I wouldn't say she likes the idea. But she respects that it's what I feel I need to do. And she said she would wait for me."

"Sounds like you've got an amazing woman there."

"I do, and that's why I'm worried I made a mistake. Her ex is back in town, so you've probably figured out who I'm talking about, by now."

He smiled. "I'm guessing we're talking about Megan."

David nodded. "So you know the situation is extremely complicated."

"Aye, extremely. Are ya concerned that Megan still has feelings for Jamie?"

David shrugged. "She says she doesn't see him in that way anymore. And I believe she believes that. But I'm not an idiot. She was engaged to the man. She obviously loved him, and that love broke because of something he did to hurt her, not because she decided she just didn't love him anymore. So, I don't think it's a big leap to think that she might fall in love with him, again. I don't think she's at that point right now. But I feel like I'm basically pushing her right into his arms by going through with this stupid break."

"Ah, I see." Father Tim's lips rested on steepled fingers. "That is a dilemma. Let me see if I understand what you're telling me. You're trying to do the right thing, get your emotions and anger figured out so that you don't damage your relationship with Megan. But just as you tell her that's what you want to do, her ex comes back into the picture, and now you're a little panicked that ya might lose her unless you toss the idea of putting the hold on your relationship. So what seemed like a mature, healthy decision now seems like a huge mistake."

"Um, exactly. I've never felt like this about anyone. I think we have a future together. But then I feel guilty. What if God wants her to help Jamie and get back together with him? What if I'm standing in the way of something that's supposed to be?" He blew out a breath. "Geez, I hate to even say that out loud. But it's true. That's what has me worried."

"Hmm. Okay, well, let me ask ya this. Do you think God has one specific person picked out for each of us?"

David had never really thought about it. Certainly, that's what movies and romance novels would have people believe. "I know that's the popular view, but it doesn't make a lot of sense from a logical standpoint. What if a few people get it wrong—then the whole system is shot, right?"

"Right. It would seem to be an easily broken design. Personally, I think it's more like God wants us to serve Him by loving Him and loving others. And He gives us the ability to choose someone to walk beside us in that journey. Someone we can serve with. I think we choose from all the potential relationships and once we make our vows, then that is the one God means for us to be with. That person then becomes our soul mate, so to speak. Until that point, though, I think there are probably hundreds of 'someones' we could have very successful, loving relationships with. I don't think it's an all or nothing proposition."

"So, are you saying that ya don't think God has a preference between me or Jamie, for Megan?"

"I can't speak to God's preferences. That would be a little presumptuous on my part. But I do think that she has the right to choose, and I believe God will work in each of your lives, regardless of whom she chooses. I don't think He's up there with a buzzer, waiting for us to choose the wrong person and then pressing the button. Ehhhh. Wrong choice. You lose."

"No, I don't suppose He is. But I'm still left with my dilemma. Do I stick with the plan and keep Megan at arm's length while I work through my issues, or do I say forget that, because I don't want to lose her and I'm afraid that if she's around him and not me, I will?"

"Well, that depends on you, really. I have a question, and I want you to take your time to answer it. Be honest with yourself. If you were to start actually dating Megan, do you think you would be so distracted by her that you wouldn't continue to seek God's help in healing your past hurts, or do ya think you can focus on both things at once?"

David rubbed his face. He knew the answer. "Sitting here in your office, having a rational conversation about it, I think to myself, of course I could do both. But the honest answer is that I find it really hard to keep my wits about me when we're together. We are, um ... very compatible. We don't have a very good track record for rational thought when we are together."

"What you're dancing around is that you have a strong physical attraction?"

"Yes. So, if you're asking if she's distracting to me, then I'd have to say yes."

"So, what are the issues that you feel ya need to address before you think you're ready to move forward with Megan?"

David wasn't sure how much to tell him. But at this point, it would probably be good to get everything in the open. "Last Friday, I drove by Megan's house and saw her and Jamie in the driveway, and he was kissing her. Now, we weren't officially a couple yet, but we were definitely talking as if that was what we both wanted. As a matter of fact, we were supposed to be on our first date at that moment. So, when I saw her with her ex, I went home and lost it. I felt like I was right back with Katie when she cheated on me. I punched the hole in the wall, and it took me hours to calm down. I was so angry. I haven't felt that way in five years and honestly, it scared me. I didn't even give her a chance to explain. Any trust I'd had with her vanished."

"And then what happened?"

"Well, Saturday I took some time to sort through what was going on in my head and why I overreacted. That's when I realized I hadn't forgiven Katie, so I asked God to help me forgive her."

"And do you feel any different about that situation?"

"Aye, like I said, the thought of her doesn't make me feel sick. I still don't love what she did. But what worries me is what if I'm just doing better because I now know that Megan was telling Jamie it was over. What if something else happens and I lose it again, only this time, she's around and I do something that scares her?"

"Have ya had issues with your temper before?"

Did he really have to admit it? He studied his scratched-up knuckles for a moment. "Aye, got into a few minor fights at university. But the big thing was after I caught Katie. I crashed her car into a pole."

Father Tim's eyebrows rose, and he appeared to be holding back a smile. "Okay, so I think you're probably wise in trying to get a handle on how you're doing with that, before you move things forward with Megan. But I think you're on the right track, just by admitting that it's an issue and working on it before it becomes something worse."

"I care too much about Megan to let her see me lose it like that."

"Well, from what you've told me, unless there's more that you're not remembering, I don't think you have a huge problem. You've gone five years without an issue, and you were under extreme duress at the time of the car incident. So, I think it would be valuable for you to talk with an anger-management counselor. I know of a couple good ones in Cork City. But I don't think you'll have to go for an extended period of time. You just need some ideas of how to deal with the anger in these difficult situations."

"Thanks. That sounds like a good plan. I'll call anyone you recommend."

Father Tim flipped through an old fashioned Rolodex until he found the contact information he was looking for. He handed David a notecard with a couple names and numbers and suggested he try them in the order listed. He walked David to the door and shook his hand.

"If ya need to talk again, my door is open."

"Thanks, Father. I really appreciate your time."

By the time David got home, he'd already made an appointment with the first counselor on the list. He felt like he was in a race against time. The sooner he could get to a counselor and get some tools to handle his anger, the sooner he could feel comfortable taking things to the next level with

Megan. And if he took too long, he might lose her. Then he'd really need a counselor.

━━✒━━

A warm breeze ruffled Ben's dark hair as they walked at a brisk pace through the Town Park. He did pretty well at staying in the stroller, as long as they moved quickly. The moment Brenna or Ryan slowed the pace too much, he began to strain against the belt that kept him captive.

The sun was out and surprisingly warm. So Brenna was thankful for the large trees that lined the pathway through the park. And even with the shade, she could feel her shirt sticking to her back. Teenage boys were practicing hurling in the large field on the other side of the trees. She kept vigilant watch for any stray balls flying their way from the pitch.

"So, how's the crew coming along at Mountdonovan?" she asked Ryan.

"They're doing well. I haven't been able to get over there to supervise as much as I'd like. But I've had Fergus there to keep an eye on things. He says they're actually ahead of schedule. Which is good, because at some point we are bound to hit a snag. And now that Megan has the benefit coming up, we can't afford any delays."

"True. Glad it's moving along."

"Aye, me too. And are you all set to start helpin' Bettie this week, then?"

"Yep, I start on Monday. Oh, did I tell you what Patsy said about selling the B&B?"

Ryan stopped abruptly, causing Ben to protest. "They want to sell it?"

"I don't know what they are planning. I just know that Patsy overheard Bettie talking to an auctioneer." Brenna pushed the pram forward. "We have to keep walking, or he'll start squealing."

"Well, they can't sell it without talkin' to me. I own a third of it."

"Oh, right. I'd forgotten that. Well, I'm sure it's nothing. Patsy gets very confused, ya know?"

"Aye, I know. But I think maybe I'll talk with Bettie just the same. If she's having financial troubles, maybe we can work something out."

"How? It's not like we are swimming in cash, right?" Brenna wished she knew more about their financial situation. She was looking forward to working with Bettie, if for nothing else but to feel like she was contributing.

Ryan shrugged and wore a smile that he'd seemed to be suppressing all morning. "Let's take a left up here." He indicated the pathway that led toward Main Street.

"What are you up to?" Brenna reached over and tickled his side. He jumped out of reach, full grin now on his face.

"You'll see. I have a surprise. Here, let me take the pram." In the switchover, their pace slowed, and Ben squealed and squirmed again.

Brenna tousled his hair as they walked. "You're going for a ride, baby boy! Isn't it fun?" She smiled and he mirrored her. He was becoming more strong-willed by the day, but he was still easily distracted, thank God.

Cars whizzed by on Main Street, and a few doors down from Rosie's, Ryan slowed to a stop and took Ben from his seat, pretending to munch on his neck as he snuggled him close. "Daddy's gonna get you."

Ben's laugh was probably the best noise Brenna had ever heard. She wondered if other people thought so, or if it was just a mom and dad thing. She knew Ryan felt the same because he took every opportunity to make the boy laugh.

"Well, here we are." Ryan said and pointed to a narrow storefront with cloudy windows and an auctioneer's phone number plastered on three identical signs in the window.

Brenna raised her eyebrows. "Where?"

Ryan pulled a key from his pocket with his free hand while Ben squirmed a bit in his other one. "You'll have to use a little imagination, right now, but would you do the honors, luv?" He handed her the key and nodded toward the faded red doorway.

She wiggled the key in the lock and held the door open. "And what am I supposed to be imagining?"

Ryan grabbed her hand and pulled her inside. "We are now standing in the regional office of Kelly Construction."

Brenna's stomach did a flip. "Really? The deal is done?"

"Really. Kelly Construction is officially a subsidiary of Byrne-Kavanagh, and this is my new office."

Brenna squealed, jumped up and down, and then wrapped her arms around Ryan and Ben. "I'm gonna cry."

"Ah, darlin', no crying. Give me a kiss, instead." Ryan leaned down and kissed her, and seconds later Ben leaned his forehead in toward theirs, laying an open-mouthed kiss on Brenna's nose. "He wants a part of the action." Ryan laughed, and munched at Ben's neck again.

Brenna looked around the room. He was right about the imagination part. The office space had obviously been vacant for some time. But it looked structurally sound, and all the needed improvements were cosmetic. "So, you're really going to be working here, in Millway?"

"I am."

"I can hardly imagine having you home every night." Brenna willed back tears.

"I've been imagining it for some time." Ryan grinned. "I've told ya, we'll find something to do with all that extra time."

Brenna laughed. "I don't doubt that. How long till you can work from here?"

"Starting Monday."

"Monday? Well, we have a lot of work to do this weekend, then. This place is a wreck."

"No, this weekend is for celebrating. I'll get the place cleaned up on Monday. Tonight, I'm taking ya to Cork City to a fancy restaurant, and we'll wear fancy clothes, and then we're gonna stay overnight in a fancy hotel. I've already spoken with Anna. She's gonna come stay with the munchkin."

Brenna's heart swelled. "That sounds amazing. This is happening." She shook her head. "I have to call Megan."

"Aye, you go ahead. We'll go get us a table at Rosie's for lunch. Lock the office when ya leave, darlin'." He kissed her again and pushed the empty stroller through the doorway while balancing Ben in his other arm.

Brenna watched them through the foggy window and as soon as they were out of sight, she did a dance to a soundtrack in her head. Fists pumping, butt shaking, twirling, she didn't think anything could ruin the high that she was on. Until she froze in place at the sound of a familiar voice.

"Well, that's quite a welcome-home sight."

Brenna whirled around. Luke stood in the doorway, framed by the sun. He looked much the same as he had when he'd lived in Millway. His hair was darker than it had been (she'd always suspected those blond highlights of his had been from a salon), but he was still quite handsome. His brown eyes still danced with mischief, and his crooked grin still made a pleasing picture. But Brenna was thrilled to realize that he didn't stir her in the least. At one time, his smile had had a potent effect on her. But no longer. Still, she could feel her face redden. She would have been embarrassed at being caught dancing, no matter who had caught her.

"Luke, wow. Hi, I ... didn't know you were back."

"I'm just visiting my parents fer the weekend."

Brenna felt her shoulders relax. "Oh, good."

He cocked an eyebrow.

"I mean ... you know, just cuz you said you'd let me know if you were moving back."

"Right. Well, don't be too relieved. I'm just visiting today, but I'm here to look for a flat. I've been offered a manager position at the Blackwater Grill. I start in two weeks."

Brenna's shoulders tensed again, and she could feel a violent swirl start in her stomach. She took a deep breath and bit her lip. "There's nothing I can say to change your mind, is there?"

He shook his head. "Listen, I understand it's awkward. But I'm sure Ryan and I can behave like adults about it, right?"

"Yeah, that would be good." Brenna stepped toward the door, and Luke backed out to give her room to come out. She pulled the door shut and locked it. "I need to get to Rosie's."

"I know. I saw them go in. I'll see you around."

As Brenna walked toward Rosie's, shock gave way to anger. She would not allow Luke to ruin their celebration night. Which meant she would just tell Ryan right away. Rip the Band-Aid off. If she waited, she'd have no fun all weekend. She blew out a big breath as she pulled on Rosie's brass-handled door. The hum of the lunch crowd greeted her, along with the aroma of onion gravy.

Ryan was seated at a table on the back wall, Ben's highchair was pulled up close, and he was playing with a multicolored, stuffed caterpillar.

"What did Megan say?" Ryan asked.

"I didn't call her yet. I got distracted. Luke came to the door." She held her breath as she took a seat across from him.

Ryan's blue eyes darkened a bit. "So, he's moved back?"

Ben was opening and closing his mouth; making spit bubbles and feeling them pop.

"Not yet. In two weeks. I'm sorry. Are you okay?"

He nodded and took a deep breath. "Sure, look, I'm fine. We've been waiting fer today a long time. Not gonna let anything ruin it." He grabbed her hand and squeezed. "I need to head to the jacks, though. Order me a coffee?"

She watched him head to the bathroom. Maybe they actually *would* all be adults about the situation. Time would tell.

# Chapter Thirty-Eight

*D*avid's office door was open, so he could see Patricia greeting her daughter, Char, with one of her awkward, I'm-not-really-sure-how-to-hug-people kind of hugs. As she turned and caught David's eye, she smiled and grabbed Char's hand, pulling her toward his office. He finished chewing a bite of his chicken-salad sandwich and wiped his mouth on a napkin.

"Doctor David, you remember my daughter, Char." He could see the strong resemblance between them. But Char's smile actually made her prettier, whereas Patricia's smile made her look scary.

"Yes, hi Char, how are you?"

"I'm well, and yerself?"

"Grand. Thanks. Are you two headed out to lunch, then?"

Patricia answered, "We are, and we wondered if you'd like to join us. You haven't had a chance to get to know Char much, yet."

Char's cheeks flushed at her mother's lack of subtlety.

"Ah, well, I thank you for the invite, but I usually work through lunch on Tuesdays." He held up the last bites of his sandwich. "Have a patient in five minutes, actually."

"Oh, okay. We'll take a rain check, then." Patricia said with a smile as she gave Char a slight nudge.

"It was nice to see you again, Doctor." Char said with a not-so-slight nudge back at her mother.

Five minutes later, he took his notebook and went to find Shannon. She had calmed down a bit over the last week. Before that, she'd apologized profusely, for two days straight, over her drinking episode at the Blackwater. Now they'd settled into an easy workplace relationship, and he hoped things would stay that way. When she acted weird, it made working with her very annoying.

She was typing on the computer at the nurse's counter, and she jumped when he said her name.

"Oh my, you put the heart crossways in me—I didn't know you were there." She laid her hand over her heart as if to calm it.

"Sorry, just wondering if we're on schedule? Next appointment is Jamie O'Connor?"

"Of course. I was just doing some research for Mrs. Thompson. After her appointment this morning, she asked if I'd send her more information on her thyroid condition. She doesn't have a computer." She pressed the print key on the computer keyboard. "I'm going to send her some info in the post."

"That's nice of you." He could see Mrs. O'Connor chatting with Patricia, through the waiting room door. "I'm ready for Mr. O'Connor."

"Right. I'll bring him right back." She scooted from her chair and out into the waiting room.

Jamie's physical exam was unremarkable. But the change in appearance, mood, and rapport was remarkable. One week ago, he had been disheveled, sleep-deprived, and generally unmotivated. He was still having some articulation issues, but overall, the man in front of him now looked completely different. He was clean-shaven, he'd had a haircut, and he looked like he'd been sleeping well. Not to mention, his clothing was clean and wrinkle-free.

The contrast was undeniable. Something had caused a profound change in Jamie's demeanor—in just over a week. And with a feeling of dread, David guessed that change had come from the attentions of a beautiful strawberry-blonde. She had told him that Mrs. O'Connor had asked her to help Jamie with a small garden, and she'd been over there working with him every day since Thursday, trying to get everything planted so it would have time to grow before the first frost.

"Well, everything looks good, Jamie. One question: I've reviewed your medical records from London. It seems like there was a lapse in care, shortly after your accident that only recently resumed. Were there any other doctors that you haven't included in your history?"

"No, I didn't stick with it back in November. They didn't tell me about TBI or anything. I thought I was okay. So, what you have there is all of my records."

"I see. Well, since you've had a CT quite recently, I don't see a need to repeat that test. Your therapist at the Step by Step clinic may order some baseline tests, though. You've made an appointment?"

"Aye, end of the week."

"Good. Well, unless you have questions for me, I think we can set up an appointment for four weeks. You'll be seeing the physio at Step by Step in the meantime. However, if you should have any trouble, or if you—or you, Mrs. O'Connor—"

"Please call me Elizabeth?"

David nodded. "Elizabeth, then. If either of you feel like he needs to be seen sooner, please call the office."

They stood and shook hands, and as David watched the O'Connors leave the office, he had a sudden urge to go park himself at one end of the bar in Rosie's and not leave until he was good and drunk.

⤝⤞

Megan sneezed as she swept up the last bits of dirt and debris in Ryan's new office. She hadn't seen the "before," but it was obvious Ryan had done a lot of work yesterday. Walls had been patched and smoothed. A half-wall now separated the front portion of the room from the back. The only things left to do, before getting the furniture put in, were to paint the walls and trim and polish the hardwood floors. Ryan had rented a machine to do the floors, so that left the painting to her and Brenna.

Brenna dragged a large container of paint from a supply room at the back of the office.

"That's as big as you." Megan said, as she wiped her watering eyes with the back of her hand. "So, last week your bedroom, this week the office. Are we going to start a painting business, you and I?"

Brenna had tied a bandana on her head to keep the dust and paint from her long brown hair. She took the bandana off and wiped her brow with it. "Right. No, this is it. If I don't see another paintbrush for a year, I'll be good. I wouldn't have done my bedroom last week, if I'd known!"

"Well, I think it's really sweet the way he surprised you, though." She poured the light grey paint into a tray on the tarp at her feet, only grunting slightly with the weight of the paint bucket. "Now, even I'm not tall enough to reach the top of these walls, so ya wanna take turns on the ladder, cutting in?"

"Sure. I'll take the first shift." Brenna grabbed a paintbrush and a small container of paint with a rubber handle that allowed her to slide her hand in and hold it steady with just her left hand. Climbing the ladder with the paintbrush between her teeth, she balanced near the top and began to paint a cautious line at the top of the wall.

"It's hard to tell if the walls were tan, or if they're just that dirty."

"They were white. Look over there, where Ryan removed that panel. That's the original wall color."

"Wow. I can almost hear the walls thanking us—ahhh, ouch." Megan massaged her thigh as she squatted down to load her roller with paint.

"What? Are you getting old on me?"

"Ha. No, I'm just sore. I did some gardening at Mountdonovan over the weekend and lots of digging, bending, and squatting last week, planting with Jamie."

"Oh, I saw him at Mass. He looks so much better!"

Megan nodded. It hadn't escaped her notice that since she'd been working with Jamie in the garden, he'd gotten his hair cut, started shaving again, and was looking healthier than he had in over a year.

"Do you think he thinks there's a shot of getting you back?" Brenna asked.

Megan sighed. "I dunno. I told him the first day we started on the garden that I only want to be his friend. He said he knows that. But I can't help but think that he's hoping for more."

"And how do you feel about that? David on one side, Jamie on the other." Brenna climbed down to reposition the ladder.

Megan massaged her temple with her free hand. "I'll admit it's weird. I want to be with David, but he's not ready. I don't want to be with Jamie, but he's practically waiting for me each day like an excited puppy. It's all gone arseways."

"Well, what does David think of the whole thing?"

Megan rolled a large W on the wall and filled it in before starting another W and another. "I think he's confused. His plan seemed all well and good on the day he proposed it. But then Jamie decided to stay, and I think it has David freaked out a bit. But he's told me some more things about his anger issues, and I think he's right. It makes sense that he should get some help dealing with it. He's definitely got a history of losing his temper. I don't want to be on the wrong end of that, ya know?"

"So you think the break is a good idea?"

Megan gave half a laugh. "No, not really. I think he can work on it while we're together. I don't see why we have to be apart."

"Can you fill this up for me?" Brenna handed down her small paint container. "So did you tell him that?"

"I did. He said he thinks I'm too much of a distraction." She felt her cheeks pink up at the idea of just how distracting she could be.

"Hm. He's probably using it as motivation. Like he can't have his reward—you—until he completes his task—getting the anger under control."

Megan hadn't looked at it that way before. She shrugged. "I guess. It just makes things harder. Harder to handle Jamie and stuff."

"Does Jamie know about David?"

"No!" Megan said, louder than she intended. "No, I don't think he'd handle it well." She pictured telling Jamie and the sudden realization that she was, indeed, leading him on hit her hard. It was painfully obvious, even if it wasn't intentional. Because if the thought of telling him made her worried that he'd regress, that must mean that on some level, she was allowing him to hold out hope that they'd get back together. She was practically dangling herself like a carrot.

"Are you afraid it will mess up his recovery?"

Megan nodded. "I guess. I think he might feel a little hopeless."

"So, what's the plan, then?"

"I don't know," Megan snapped. *Like there's a plan.*

"Whoa, what's wrong?" Brenna came down the ladder.

"Let's just stop talking about it, okay? Sorry I snapped."

"Sorry I upset you." Brenna mumbled something under her breath.

"No, not yer fault. It's just a mess, and I'd rather not think about it anymore today."

"Okay." Brenna refilled her paint bucket again. "Well, how are plans looking for the benefit?"

"Excellent." Megan grabbed a wet cloth to wipe up paint spatters on the floor. "I've rented all the tents and tables and chairs from Peter's Parties and Playhouses. They gave me a great discount, since it's for charity. Moira is a challenge to work with. She's very opinionated and a little rough around the edges. But Donal is thrilled with the new venue, and I think we're going to be able to pull it off in grand fashion."

"I'm sure you will. Can I help with anything?"

"Actually, I was thinking maybe you could contribute to the auction?"

"Like a donation?"

"No, of course not. I know money is tight. I want ya to paint something for me. I'll buy your supplies and everything. I'll even frame it."

Brenna's face lost its color. "I'm rusty, Meg. I wouldn't know what to paint. And I don't think anyone would bid on what I managed to put down on canvas."

"Nonsense. I've seen your college portfolio. You're very talented, and ya have a great eye. So don't even try that with me. You're just scared, and I'm not gonna accept that. Come on, this is for African orphans, for Pete's sake." Megan placed a hand on her hip and stared at Brenna, daring her to give another excuse.

"Way to make me feel like a loser." Brenna's fake pout didn't fool her. Deep down, she knew her friend was dying to start painting again. "Okay,

okay. I'll try. But if it turns out like crap, I'm not putting it in the auction, deal?"

"Deal." Megan held out a paint-speckled hand and Brenna shook it. "Now, tell me about the restaurant Ryan took ya to on Saturday."

She only half listened to the recap of Brenna's weekend, because hearing about their romantic getaway brought her right back to the reality of her own tangled-up "love life." A faint buzzing filled her head as she tried to make sense of the mess. If she pushed David to call off the break, and they started dating, for real, her life would be easier in so many ways. But Jamie would find out, and she was pretty sure he wouldn't be able to handle a blow like that yet. But if she didn't push for things to move along with David, she didn't know if she could handle being with Jamie so much without falling into a rhythm much like they had before the injury. She could already feel herself slipping into a weird place with him. All the work she needed to do for the benefit would be a good distraction from the madness.

⌖

Brenna appreciated the sunny days when they came. Growing up in Western New York, grey, drizzly weather was nothing new to her. But the summers there had always been full of sunshine. Here, three days of warm weather and sunshine in a row was usually considered a hot streak. But since the weekend, they'd had nothing but sun and heat. Five days and no sign of stopping.

It was like a true New York summer. Brenna was thrilled; most people were not. She'd heard the Marys in the Tea Shoppe complaining about the humidity and what it was doing to their (blue) hair. Bettie was sure she'd lost ten pounds with the heat of her kitchen and no breeze to cool it off.

Even Ryan seemed a little put out by it. Probably because he'd been working outside at Mountdonovan, never even considering that he would get a sunburn. Thankfully, Anna had an aloe plant, and Brenna had been able to treat his shoulders and nose the night before. He was fairly lobster-like. She understood why he was a little irritated.

But she was soaking it in. Donning a tank top, shorts, and sunscreen, she had fastened Ben into the jogging stroller and run all the way into town. He loved the rocking motion and rarely ever fussed when they were moving along at a good clip. Now, she was walking through the park, cooling down, and thinking that a rest on one of Megan's favorite little benches might be warranted.

It was a shady little spot, just past the playground, where two benches faced each other. She set the brake on the stroller and took a peek at her boy. He was knocked out. Good. That would give her a little recovery time. She wasn't used to running in the heat anymore.

She drank some water and then pulled the diaper bag out of the basket below the stroller. After pulling her book out, she used the bag as a pillow and lay down on the cool bench. A tiny stream meandered through this part of the park. The soft trickling soothed her as she removed her bookmark and entered the regency world of Jane Austen.

She woke with a start as the sun, filtering through the trees, temporarily blinded her. Had she heard talking? As her vision cleared, her heart jumped. There was a man standing over the stroller! Dropping her forgotten book to the ground, she jumped up and only then realized the backlit man was Luke, who immediately straightened and backed up a few steps.

"Hey, Brenna."

"What are you doing? You almost gave me a heart attack!" She covered her heart with her hand, willing it to slow it's pounding beat.

"I was walking by, saw ya sleeping. Wasn't gonna bother ya, but then I heard him making noise, so ..." He shrugged, "I just wanted to make sure he was okay."

Brenna's disobedient heartbeat sped up yet again, and she swallowed a hard lump. Luke was meeting Ben for the first time. As much as she wanted to kick him and chase him off, the vulnerable look on his face had her speechless. She gave a slight nod and watched him in silence.

He took a step back toward the stroller and knelt down in front of Ben. "Hey, little guy," he said softly. "How ya doin'?"

Ben held out his rainbow caterpillar. Luke glanced toward Brenna again and then accepted the offered toy. "Thanks, buddy." Ben immediately waved his hands in distress. He wanted the caterpillar back. Luke got the message. "Here ya go." But as he handed the toy back, Ben's finger closed around Luke's, and Brenna thought she might cry.

She had never seen Luke look so unsure. He stood up and rubbed the stubble along his jawline. He motioned to the bench. "Can I sit?"

Brenna took a deep breath and a quick glance around. "Okay." Ben started to fuss, so she sat him up in the stroller and placed some cereal on the tray before taking a seat on the bench. "You alright?" she asked.

He nodded. "Wasn't expecting this."

"What? Running into us?"

He shrugged. "Aye. But more than that. It's really weird to meet him. I didn't expect it to feel like this." He looked away, staring off.

She'd only seen Luke once since she'd had Ben. Now, talking to him and watching him with Ben, she was shocked to realize how much Ben looked like him. Her hands shook and a chill crept down her back. If she noticed it, would others? Was that was Ryan was talking about?

"How does it feel?" she asked, not sure she wanted the answer.

"Like I know him." He glanced toward her and then down at his hands. "I didn't know. I didn't realize ..." he trailed off and looked away again, lashes fluttering.

Holy crap, was he was crying? She couldn't do this. "I don't know what to say—"

"No need. I'm fine." He patted her knee and got to his feet. Without looking back at her or Ben, he said goodbye over his shoulder and took off down the hill.

Brenna sat there breathing deeply for a full minute before she was able to move.

"Well, little guy ..." She stowed the diaper bag and began their walk back home. "I think this is one conversation we might want to keep to ourselves, for now."

# Chapter Thirty-Nine

Megan wiped her sweaty forehead with a bandana and squinted at Jamie in the sunlight. "This is crazy. Eleven straight days of heat. It's unheard of!"

"Aye, I think my mam is ready to chop off all her hair." He patted down another mound of dirt around a leek stem, methodically moving from plant to plant. "But the sunlight is good for the plants as long as we keep them watered. I think they're already growing faster than normal." He waved a hand toward the neat rows with new green shoots sticking up from the ground.

Jester started barking and ran from the porch toward a truck moving slowly up the O'Connors' driveway.

"Jester!" Jamie walked toward the dog who swiftly changed direction and ran toward his master. "Good boy. That's just Nessa Rose come to bring us some plants. Be a good boy and don't knock her over, will ya?"

Nessa Rose parked and moved around to the truck bed to lift out a box of what Megan assumed were the last of their plants. Jamie had taken care of ordering everything and Nessa Rose had seemed particularly excited to help him research what would be best to plant in July.

Today, Nessa took on the appearance of a rose. She wore forest green slacks and a blouse that was a swirled mix of reds and pinks with a red slouch cap to top off the look. Megan watched her face light up when Jamie insisted on carrying the box for her. *Hmmm. Interesting.*

"Hey Megan." Nessa Rose sat on a crate at the edge of the garden. "It's looking great! You guys are almost done with the planting, it seems."

"Aye, I think that's the last of the plants and we planted all the seeds a couple weeks ago. So we should be done with stage one today. Thanks for all your help."

Nessa Rose waved her hand. "Aw, no trouble at all. Glad to help." She glanced at Jamie as he unpacked the box she had brought. The scent of basil wafted past Megan as he set each plant in a row where he intended to put them in the ground, finishing off the herb section of their garden.

Megan followed Nessa's gaze. Jamie was looking healthier every time she saw him. Where Megan's fair skin had simply freckled more with the repeated sun exposure, Jamie's had taken on a bronze tone giving him a strong, rugged appearance. He looked really good. But if he noticed Nessa Rose's appraisal of him, he didn't let it show. Megan wondered if the interest was a new thing or if Nessa Rose had always had a thing for Jamie and it was just now becoming obvious.

Nessa Rose stood with a sigh and dusted her hands together. "Well, I ought to get back to the shop. Megan, did yer mam mention the situation with the Program Director position?"

Megan nodded. "Aye, the committee has decided to wait to make a decision until after the benefit, right?"

"That's right. It seems a couple of the committee members aren't ready to make a decision and since you're already helping with the benefit, it wouldn't make much sense to bring someone else into the mix if the job goes to one of the other candidates. It just seems cleaner to wait to decide. I hope you're not upset by that?"

"Of course not." Megan shrugged. "I trust you all to do what's best."

"Seems a no-brainer to me." Jamie added, taking a spade to the ground at the base of the first basil plant.

"Yes, well, I can't really say anything about where everyone stands, but I have a feeling most of the committee would love to see one of our own take the helm at Mountdonovan." She smiled at Megan and shot a fleeting look back at Jamie before she walked back toward her truck.

"Thanks Nessa!" Megan called after her retreating form. Nessa raised a hand in acknowledgment and climbed into her truck.

"Nice of her to take the time to deliver those plants, huh?" Megan said.

Jamie shrugged. "I told her I would send John or David to pick them up but she insisted. Said something about customer service. Seems a waste of her time if ya ask me."

Megan blew out a breath. He was clueless. It would have been very convenient if he'd taken an interest in Nessa Rose but it was obvious the thought hadn't even crossed his mind.

***

As they zipped down the highway, Brenna's mind swam with possibilities. And fears. She tried to silence those, but somehow they were much louder than the possibilities. Ryan had discovered that Auntie Pat wasn't wrong; Bettie *had* been talking to an auctioneer about getting a value on the B&B. She was overwhelmed between taking care of Auntie Pat and running the B&B and her pastry business. She had planned to talk to Ryan about it but wanted to have her ducks in a row first. She wanted to come up with a plan before telling Ryan she wanted to sell.

But it seemed that Ryan had come up with a plan of his own, and Brenna was still trying to wrap her mind around it. He proposed that they would buy Bettie and Auntie Pat out of the B&B. That part seemed sane. It was the rest that had her losing sleep. He seemed to think it would be a grand adventure for him and Brenna to take over the running of the B&B. As in, move in and actually run the thing.

At first, she told him he was crazy. Young people don't run bed and breakfasts. Retired people do that. And for good reason. It would be very difficult to raise a family while inviting strangers into your home for constant sleepovers! But Ryan was so excited about the idea that over the past week he had infected Bettie and Anna. And even Auntie Pat was now on board. Only Brenna was left holding the "What if" bag.

What if it didn't work out? What if she hated running a B&B, but they couldn't find anyone to buy it? What if they wanted a vacation? What if they had another baby? What if, what if, what if?

Ryan took his hand off the shifter and squeezed her knee. "Whatcha thinkin' about?"

She looked at him sideways and offered a slight smile. "What do you think I'm thinking about, babe? I'm trying to look at the upside of the idea. But I'm scared by the downside. I don't want it to mess with our family. I only just got you back after all the commuting to Limerick. This is a big thing to take on. It just worries me."

"I understand. I just think it's a great solution. Bettie and Patsy can live in the cottage, and we can build our own family wing on the back of the B&B. We won't have to worry about keeping Ben quiet that way, and it will open up a couple more rooms to rent out. Anna said she'd stay and keep helping out. Bettie said she'd keep doing the cooking, and that way she can still use the kitchen for her pastry business. We can increase occupancy and begin to make a profit, which is a great solution as I phase out of the construction business over the next year. It's a perfect fit, don't ya think?" His fifty-watt smile made her feel like a jerk for even voicing any concerns.

"It does seem like a good idea ... I guess. No risk, no reward, right?"

He patted her leg. "Now you're talkin'. Just wait till ya meet Jim and Kathleen. You'll see it can work."

Ben was staying with Anna, and they were on their way to the little coastal town of Bantry to spend the night at the Moran-Magee Manor, a bed and breakfast owned by a couple in their thirties. Apparently, they had two children, two dogs, a kitten, and of course, a pony. Cuz who doesn't want a pony?

"I'm looking forward to seeing how they manage it."

⌐━✗

The stately Georgian style house was located on a forty acre working farm. Jim Magee's family had been farming for as long as they'd been breathing. And though Jim loved to work the farm, he had wanted to try something new. So when he decided to build a bed and breakfast, his father had given him his inheritance early. Ten acres of land. A perfect spot to build his dream home.

That was where Ryan entered the picture. Jim wanted to build a brand-new home that had the feel of something that had been there for hundreds of years. Ryan was well-known for his innovative building style, marrying modern convenience with historical architecture. Together, Ryan and Jim had designed and built the ten bedroom home—six years ago—finishing just in time for Jim and his new bride, Kathleen Moran, to move in.

Since then, they'd built a successful business, garnering recognition and awards from travel websites and national publications alike, all while adding children and pets to the mix. Ryan seemed confident that if Jim and Kathleen could do it, so could he and Brenna.

As they ambled along the quarter-mile driveway toward the main house, they passed two small barns and a duck pond. Two dogs chased each other through the tall grasses beside the house until they halted at the crunch of tires on gravel. Then they bounded toward Ryan's truck with enthusiasm.

"That's Finn and Fiona." Ryan pointed as the dogs grew closer. "They're harmless, unless you let them lick ya to death."

Brenna laughed. "You and the dog share a name?"

"Haha. Yes, and now you see why I prefer not to use my family's nickname for me." Brenna had heard both his parents and his cousins call him Finn on occasion. It always struck her as funny.

Ryan got out and greeted the dogs. Brenna waited inside the cab of the truck, not sure if she outweighed either dog. She didn't know what breed they were, but they were huge and likely would take her for a play toy. Ryan opened her door and shielded her from the dogs as the front door opened and the oddest couple walked out.

Jim looked to be about five foot six—maybe. He wore vintage glasses and a classic comb over struggled to hide his shiny head. He had a quiet smile, which he adoringly directed at the goddess beside him. Kathleen Moran-Magee had to be over six feet tall. She had ginger hair that fell in soft waves over her shoulders. Brenna was positive the woman had been a model, or an actress accustomed to the red carpet, at some point. She crossed the gravel driveway in four-inch heels as if she were strutting down a runway. How in the world did she end up with the little guy next to her?

"Ryan! It's been so long. Shame on you for keeping your bride from us for all this time." Kathleen made a beeline for Brenna, pulling her into a quick embrace, ending with a stooped-over kiss on each cheek. She then repeated the process with Ryan, without all the stooping. Jim held out a hand to shake Ryan's and then gave Brenna a kiss on the cheek.

"Nice to meet you, Brenna. Ryan's told us so much about you." Jim's voice was quiet but strong. Up close, Brenna noticed his bright blue eyes held a twinkle. And if she ignored the comb over, he was actually quite a handsome guy.

"Ryan has talked of nothing but the two of you for the last week. I'm glad to meet you. And thank you for inviting us."

Kathleen linked arms with Brenna—an impressive feat considering the height difference—and led them toward the house. "Come now, you must be ready for some tea and scones after a couple hours on the road."

After a late dinner, Kathleen put their two- and four-year-old girls to bed while Jim baked up some fresh scones. Brenna hadn't thought anyone could top Bettie's cooking. But Jim Magee had managed it. He'd been cooking with his grandma since he was a "wee lad." At eighteen, he'd done something rare in his farming family: he'd gone off to university. There he studied hotel management and culinary arts, interning with top hotels in Dublin. It was while working at an exclusive high-end hotel that he'd first met Kathleen, who had indeed been a model. Brenna congratulated herself for pegging that.

"I fell hard." Jim recalled. "But she didn't even notice me."

"Nonsense. You tell the story wrong, every time," Kathleen laughed and said from behind her hand, as if he hadn't heard her say the exact same thing before, "I think he tells it like that each time so he can hear me tell everyone how I was the one who fell hard."

Jim blushed. "Do tell, luv."

"So, I was there for a friend's rehearsal dinner. I was miserable ... ya know, 'always a bridesmaid, never a bride' kind of thing. Toward the end of the night, I went to get some coffee and I turned the knob the wrong way on the urn, and somehow I broke it. Steaming hot coffee poured over my hand, and I just yanked my hand back and froze. I didn't even cry out. I was in so much pain, but I was totally embarrassed.

"Thankfully, Jim was right there, and he calmly pulled me into the kitchen without a word. Then he filled a bowl with cold water and told me to keep my hand submerged. He kept refreshing the water so it would stay cold. It was actually a pretty nasty burn, but it would have been worse if he hadn't been so quick and thoughtful. He took such good care of me." She leveled him with a look of such sweet adoration that Brenna had to re-evaluate her first impression of Kathleen.

Kathleen continued. "So, he kept asking me questions to distract me from the pain. And the whole time I'm answering his questions I'm noticing that he's different from any guy I'd met before. And do you know what the difference was?"

She took Jim's hand across the table and with her other hand, she pointed toward her own eyes. "He only looked here. Right in my eyes. Most guys I'd met generally kept their eyes somewhere in the vicinity of my chest and only pulled their eyes up toward mine when they were caught. Not Jim. He was a prince."

Jim smiled. "Well, I didn't think I had any chance with her. What was the point of teasing myself?"

She smacked his arm. "Oh, stop."

He laughed and took over the telling of the story. "So imagine my surprise when I received a flower bouquet the next day with her number on the card! And the rest, as they say, is history."

"What a sweet story!" Brenna said before popping the last of an after-dinner scone in her mouth.

Kathleen leaned forward. "Now it's your turn. Tell us how you met."

Brenna and Ryan both laughed. Brenna said, "That's a long one."

Ryan added, "We might be here for a couple days if we start that story. How about we talk some about the B&B lifestyle, and then we'll give you an abridged version of how we ended up together?"

"Right." Jim said. "Well, where to start ..."

The next hour was a question and answer session with Jim answering quietly and thoughtfully and Kathleen breaking into spontaneous laughter and telling story after story about living in a B&B. Jim did the cooking and cleaning. Kathleen entertained guests and marketed the business. And they both took care of the kids. Brenna's fears eased a bit. They had figured out how to make it work. Maybe she and Ryan could too. Her thoughts were interrupted by her phone, vibrating on the table.

Anna's number came up on the caller ID. "Hi Anna, what's up?"

"Brenna, I don't want you to panic, but you need to come home. We have a—situation." Anna's voice was strained, and Brenna could hear shouting in the background.

"What's happening? Is Ben okay?"

There was a pause that made Brenna's stomach drop. She put the phone on speaker as Ryan leaned in to hear what was happening.

Anna replied, "I'm sure he's okay. It's just, well, we think Auntie Pat took him out for a walk and got lost. We can't find her."

Instant panic welled up inside her. "How long?"

More silence.

"Anna, how long have they been missing?" Ryan stood to his feet, and Brenna saw her fear mirrored in the three faces around her.

"We think about an hour or so. We have the Gardai here now. They are going to start the search, and neighbors are getting word now. I'm sure we'll have them by the time you get home, but I knew you'd want to know what was happening."

Brenna turned off the speaker. "We are leaving now. I'll call you on the drive to get more details."

# Chapter Forty

Brenna had never prayed so hard. The two-hour drive back to Millway was painfully slow. She hadn't been able to get much more information, as Anna was out searching, and her phone charge was almost dead. All they knew was that Bettie had gone upstairs for bed and when she checked on her mam, who she thought had been sleeping, she discovered she was missing. It took them a while to realize Ben was missing, too. As soon as they did, they called the Gardai and Brenna.

Brenna tore through the back door with Ryan right behind. All the lights in the house appeared to be on, even though it was well after midnight. Bettie was sitting at the table, red eyes swollen.

Bettie stood. "I'm so sorry! I don't even know what happened. I—"

Ryan gave her a hug. "Okay, take a deep breath and tell us what ya know. What's happening with the search?"

They sat down, and for the tenth time that night, Brenna's dinner threatened to come back up. Bettie wiped her eyes and began. "Well, I was out searching but they told me to come back here, so we'll know if they come home. There are lots of people looking. I'm sure they're gonna find them soon."

"Start at the beginning. Anna told us a little but I don't understand what happened. So start there," Brenna said.

Bettie nodded and blew out a breath. "Well, Mam went up to her room right after dinner, as she usually does. She took a bath. I know because I can hear the pipes here in the kitchen when she runs the water. That was around half six. Then I cleaned up from dinner and gave Ben a quick bath before I put him down. That was just after seven. And then, since Anna was out to dinner with a couple girls from church, and we had no guests, I thought I'd relax in front of the telly for a bit. I don't know how she could have left without me knowing. I think I must have dozed off. I'm so sorry." Bettie grabbed Brenna's arm across the table and dissolved into tears.

"Okay, I need you to focus, Bettie. What happened next?" Brenna asked, swallowing the fear that threatened to choke her.

Sniff. "Right. I'm sorry. So I was just heading up to bed around nine when I heard Anna come in. I thought I'd just check on Mam real quick and then go back down to say goodnight to Anna. But then Mam's bed was empty, and she wasn't in her bathroom. I called for Anna to come up, and we searched all the rooms. Then we looked downstairs and outside. I didn't look in Ben's little room because I didn't want to wake him, and there'd be no room for her in there, anyway. So we called a few people, and no one had seen her. Just before I called the gards, Anna opened the door to check on him and discovered that he was gone, too. I'm so sorry!"

"Bettie," Brenna leaned across the table and looked Bettie in the eyes. "Stop apologizing. We'll find them. But we need to focus. There must be clues as to what happened. Wait!" Brenna stood so fast that Ryan had to catch her chair. "The Life-Save bracelet. We can track her!" Why hadn't she thought of that sooner? Because of the Alzheimer's, Auntie Pat wore a tracking device on her ankle.

Bettie shook her head and reached into her pocket, revealing the tracking bracelet that was supposed to help them avoid situations like this. "She took it off for her bath. And her new cell phone is sitting on her bed."

"Damn it." Brenna slammed the table, and tears raced down her cheeks. Ryan pulled her close.

"Shhh, we're gonna find him, luv. You'll see. We'll find them both, and they'll be okay." He turned back toward Bettie. "Is the pram gone?"

Bettie nodded. "Aye, it was on the back porch. Anna took him for a walk before she left for dinner. It's gone now."

"Okay, so that's good." Ryan ducked his head to look Brenna in the eyes. "It means she most likely stuck to the roads and footpaths, as she wouldn't have been able to push the pram through the tall grasses behind the house. That will make them easier to find, right?"

Brenna wiped her eyes with the back of her hand. "They've been looking for a couple hours already. They must have covered all the streets in town by now. Where could she have taken him? Bettie, was she herself today, or was she stuck in the past?"

"Past. She kept calling me Pammy all through dinner. And she thought Luke was my cousin Denny—"

"Luke?" Both Brenna and Ryan said.

"Aye, Luke was by earlier, and she thought he was Denny and that Ben was his wee one, Thomas. "

"But why was Luke here?" Brenna glanced at Ryan, whose jaw was now twitching. Bettie didn't know that Luke actually was Ben's father. They had managed to keep that secret to just a few people. Still, Luke couldn't be involved, could he?

She knew that was where Ryan's mind was going. But it didn't make sense. Even if Luke wanted to get ahold of Ben, she couldn't imagine him actually taking him in the night. And then why would Auntie Pat be part of it? It made no sense at all.

"He stopped over before dinner to talk with me about doing some desserts for the Blackwater. He's managing it now." Bettie waved her hand as if the information was insignificant. But Brenna had a feeling it wasn't. There was a link, even if she couldn't see it.

"Did you tell the gards that Luke was here?" Brenna asked.

Bettie raised her brows. "No, I didn't think it was relevant. Do you think it is?" Puzzlement danced across her face as she glanced at Ryan. His nostrils were flared, and he was obviously working to control his breathing.

"I don't know. But my gut is telling me it is."

Brenna felt Ryan grasp her elbow. "We'll be right back," he said, pulling her toward the front room.

"Is there something you're not telling me?" Ryan's fierce gaze sent a chill through her.

"What do you mean?"

"I *mean*, why would your gut be telling you that Luke is involved?" His harsh whisper had her cringing.

"I don't think he's *involved*. That's not what I said. I said I thought the fact that he was here is relevant. I don't know why. I just have a feeling, okay?" She wrenched her elbow from his grasp and went back into the kitchen, ignoring his sputtering protest. Anna was just coming through the door with three or four neighbors in tow.

"Oh, luv," Anna held her arms open, and Brenna crumpled in her embrace. "We're gonna find them. It'll be okay. You'll see. We just need to figure out what Auntie Pat was thinking."

Brenna mumbled through her tears but knew Anna couldn't understand a word. *Pull yourself together, woman.*

Two of the gards came in next, and as they spread out their maps on the table, Brenna flashed back to when Auntie Pat had been lost the first time, a couple of years ago. It was scary. But this? This was a whole new level of terrifying. Her baby was lost somewhere out there with a delusional woman who didn't even recognize her own family members half the time. She knew Auntie Pat would never intentionally hurt Ben. But there was no telling what decade the woman was even in, so how were they supposed to guess what she was thinking!?

At the exact same moment, Ryan came in from the dining room door and Luke came through the back door. Brenna tensed as Ryan covered the distance to Luke in three steps.

"What are you doing here?" His eyes flashed a wild look.

"Not the time." Brenna said quietly, as she pulled on Ryan's bulging arm.

Luke's hands were in the air in a surrender pose. "I'm just trying to help."

Anna patted Ryan's other arm and casually turned Ryan away from Luke. "We stopped in the Blackwater to see if Auntie Pat took him there, and Luke joined the search, as many of the people in town have done."

Ryan shook his head slightly, as if coming out of a daydream. "Sorry. Anna, did you get any leads?"

Anna filled them in on the progress of the search. But as more and more people filled the kitchen, Brenna's panic rose. Were they calling off the search? Had they given up? She looked back at the map. *Where are you, Patsy? What are you thinking?*

"I'm sorry." Luke said from just behind her. She turned as his eyes darted to Ryan, who was leaning over the maps and discussing the search with the gards. His pale face told her he wasn't just along for the ride. He was scared, too. "I couldn't just stay at work. I just want to help."

"Thanks. I know. Ryan's not thinking clearly."

"I get it. How are you holdin' up?"

"I don't have time to think about that. I have to get inside Patsy's head. Bettie said she thought you were her nephew, Denny. Did she say anything to you?"

"Aye, she was calling me Denny. She kept asking me if I was leaving for America. I just played along."

"Anything else?"

"Yeah, she kept asking me about someone named Tommy. Bettie said that was Denny's son. And then, when Anna came in with Ben, she kept calling him Tommy. We all just played along, ya know? Do you think it has something to do with her taking off?"

"I don't know. But I feel like it's important. Like there's something just beyond where I can see. Can you think of anything else? Even something that seems insignificant. Anything?" Brenna forced the panic down.

Luke ran his fingers through his hair, and suddenly he looked up, grabbing Brenna's arm. "The train! When I left, she asked me if I was taking the train to Cork to go to America. What if she thought I left without Tommy and she had to bring him to me?"

Puzzle pieces clicked together. "Yes, that's exactly what she would think! Ryan!" She yelled, grabbing everyone's attention. She explained their theory, and the gards immediately made some calls. The last train out left around 8:00 p.m. every night. She could have made that train, but she would have had to change trains at Mallow in order to get to Cork. Maybe she got off the train in Mallow and was still there at the station? Brenna could hear one of the gards talking to someone in Mallow, asking them to check the train station and surrounding areas. Calls were made to each of the stops with the same request.

⟋⟍

It was almost two-thirty in the morning, and Brenna was nursing a strong coffee, staring out the window at the darkness. Bettie was pacing the kitchen behind her as she tried not to think about Auntie Pat and Ben being out in the cold somewhere. She felt helpless sitting there while the search continued, but Anna had convinced her that the quickest way for her to see her son was to stay at the B&B. Because anyone who found him would take him straight there and he would most certainly be wanting his mam.

Several people, including Ryan, had left to drive to the stations along the rail. The entire O'Connor family had spread out in different cars. David had gone with Ryan. And Anna and Father Tim were searching as well. She envied those who were actively doing something. Waiting was killing her.

The door burst open, stopping Bettie in her tracks and causing Brenna to spill her coffee. Megan, clad in Hello Kitty PJ pants and a wrinkled AC/DC T-shirt, ran to Brenna and pulled her into a hug. Brenna had known she was coming, because she'd called while Brenna was talking to Ryan ten minutes earlier. But she didn't realize how much she'd wanted her there until that moment.

"I'm so sorry I didn't get the messages sooner. I went to bed early, and I just woke up to go to the bathroom. I saw all the missed calls and texts. My family's all at my uncle's house in Limerick. I would have slept clean through if I hadn't had too much water tonight. Any news?"

"We have a theory that she might have taken him on the train to Cork. Ryan's driving to the stops on the way. A bunch of people went out looking. I'm stuck here doing absolutely nothing but losing my mind. I'm so glad you're here."

Brenna's phone rang. "Luke?"

"I've got them!" His shout rang in her ears, and tears immediately ran down her cheeks.

"Where are you? Are they okay? Are you on your way here? Is anyone with—"

"Slow down. It's okay, they're fine. A little cold, but they're fine. I convinced Patsy to walk with me, and we're heading for my car."

"How'd you find them?"

"I went straight to the end of the line in Cork, cuz I knew the others were searching in between. She was hiding, but she came out when she heard me calling for her and "Tommy." Says she got scared when the gards came by earlier, so she hid. I think she must have dozed off."

"Ben?"

"He's asleep in the pram. He'll probably wake up when we get in the car, but I don't have a car seat. I guess I should have her hold him?"

Brenna could hear the ding of an open car door and then the sweet music of her baby's voice. "Mamamama."

"Can ya hear that?" Luke asked.

Brenna laughed and cried all at once. She nodded although she knew Luke couldn't see her. And then she laughed again at the thought of Luke being the hero who saved the day. Who'd have thought?

# Chapter Forty-One

Megan hoisted the bag full of groceries onto her hip, so she could close her car door. She knew Brenna was taking a much-needed late nap after the horror of the previous night's drama, so she figured she would slip inside and make them some dinner. Setting the bag on the table, she crept toward Brenna's room and peeked inside. Ben was cuddled up, spoon fashion, with his thumb lazily hanging from his mouth. Brenna's arm held him close. Her eyes fluttered open, and she gave a quick nod when she saw Megan.

"Stay asleep," Megan whispered and backed away from the door.

Thirty minutes later, Megan had just finished peeling the potatoes when Brenna padded into the room in slippers and PJs. "You are an angel."

Megan covered a smile at the sight of Brenna's hair wildly sticking up in all directions.

"I'll put the potatoes on and by the time they're done, the chicken should be done baking. Why don't ya take a minute to freshen up? I'm all set in here."

Brenna raised a brow. "I know I look like a banshee. I'll take care of it. But first, coffee." She helped herself to the pot that Megan had brewed, pouring a large cup full and sweetening it with vanilla creamer. Inhaling deeply, she turned back toward her room. "Truly an angel."

A few minutes later Brenna was back, looking slightly more awake and much more presentable.

"There's my friend. I knew you were under that hair, somewhere," Megan said, holding up the coffee to offer Brenna a top off.

"Your angel status keeps getting more solid." Brenna dropped into a chair. "I feel like I could sleep for a week."

"How's Benny boy?"

"He's fine. It was probably a grand adventure, in his eyes."

Megan opened the oven a crack to check on the chicken. "How about Auntie Pat? Does she remember?"

Brenna shook her head. "I talked with Anna earlier. Patsy doesn't even realize anything happened. Bettie's beside herself. Nobody knows exactly how she managed to get all the way to the train station without anyone seeing her. I mean, it's walkable, but it's quite a ways. So this obviously takes the concern for her condition to a whole new level. It looks like Ryan's plan to take over the B&B couldn't be more timely."

"So you're gonna move ahead with that?"

"I think so. Before the craziness last night, we had a really good visit with the couple in Bantry. They seem to be making a go of it. I'm sure we can, too." Brenna stood and looked out the window. "Ryan should be home soon. I imagine you're wanting to ask how he handled the Luke thing?"

"Well, yes, since you bring it up."

"Really well. He shook his hand and thanked him for finding them. Such a strange sight."

"I can imagine. I understand why you guys had everyone go home, but I wouldn't have minded sticking around to see that."

"I know. We just didn't want it to be a circus when they got back. I think we're in for some uncomfortable conversations about what happens now with Luke. He's going to be around, and we won't be able to avoid him. So we have to come up with something that works for everyone. He's not Ben's dad, but he is the biological father, and I have a feeling he's not going to settle for completely fading back into the cracks." Brenna paced and ran her fingers through her long hair.

"Well, if you need a mediator, I'm happy to try to help."

"Thanks. I should wake the boy, or he'll never sleep tonight."

"I'll have the potatoes mashed before you have him dressed. Ready, set, go."

# Chapter Forty-Two

Megan's hands were confused. She had put the power sander down five minutes ago and still they were vibrating, refusing to settle. She really didn't have time to be refinishing furniture, but she needed a break from all the planning and decision-making. She just wanted to work with her hands for a while. And since the efficient Nessa Rose had taken over the committee tending to the Mountdonovan grounds, there was nowhere for her to get her hands into the dirt.

So getting them into some stain was the next best thing. The smell of the stain took her back to her dad's workshop, when she was a kid. He did side jobs for people, building small pieces of furniture, and his workshop always had the smell of wood shavings and stain. She breathed deeply and took a seat on the folding chair behind her. She couldn't start staining when her hands were still shaking, so maybe a little breather was in order.

She surveyed the grounds. They were shaping up nicely. The new roof glistened in the late July sun after the midday rain. Her eyes landed on a tall blond doctor walking the path. He came toward her with purpose, and she suddenly worried about the state of her hair, her clothes, her nails—basically all of her. She was a wreck. She'd been so busy getting everything rolling for Mountdonovan that she'd barely seen him in a couple weeks. She wondered again how it was fair that he could look gorgeous without even trying. He didn't appear to have shaved in a few days; his jeans and T-shirt both were riddled with holes. And he looked amazing. Unfair.

"Hi there," she said, standing and wiping her still shaky hands on her jeans.

"Hi yerself." He held out a hand. "Come with me, will ya?"

The intense look in his eyes threw her for a moment. He looked focused and almost dangerous. "Is everything okay?" She placed her hand in his.

"It will be in a minute."

He quickly pulled her behind the old kitchen building. In a swift move, he came toward her until she was backed up against the cobblestone wall. Hands braced on the wall on either side of her head, he leaned in and whispered, "Do ya know what today is?"

She shook her head as the benefit deadline dates swam through her mind. She'd made lists so she wouldn't drop the ball. Had she forgotten something? Her mental calendar flew from her head as David's lips turned up into a smile just before they landed on hers.

After a rocking kiss, he braced himself on the wall again. "Congratulations, darlin'. We made it the full month, and I've been trying not to think about this moment the entire time."

Megan wasn't sure she trusted her legs to hold her up after that, so she slid down into a squat, and he mirrored her. "Hmm. That was definitely better than a handshake." She laughed briefly, but her attention was caught by Jamie's truck ambling along the winding driveway.

"Meg, I've had a lot of time to think over the last month. I've met with a great anger-management counselor several times, and I'm feeling really good about that whole thing. I'm ready to make a go of this if you are."

She tried to focus on what he was saying, but all she could think about was Jamie seeing them and making some huge scene out of shock and anger. He was doing so much better, but he was still unstable. She might have been ready to move forward with David, but she wasn't ready to tell Jamie that. She watched him park his truck and turned back in time to see David following her line of sight.

His jaw tightened, and he stood up and backed away. "I see you're not ready."

"No, I am. I just ..." She glanced back toward Jamie. Had he seen them together?

David gave a caustic laugh. "I've got to go."

She leaped up. "No, David, wait."

He held up a hand as he walked away in the opposite direction of the parking lot. "I'll see ya around."

She took a peek around the corner of the building to see where Jamie was before she chased David down. But Jamie was walking right toward her. "Hey! It's looking great around here," he beamed.

She sighed, and with one last glance toward David, she rounded the corner toward Jamie.

David used every single bit of technique he'd learned over the past month to keep himself from losing it. He sat in his car and watched as Megan laughed at something Jamie had said. The irony was unbelievable. He'd finally learned to control his temper so he wouldn't hurt the woman he loved, and because he took the time to learn those skills, he now watched her slip from his grasp. *Un-freaking-believable.*

He knew this would happen. He had to be the biggest eejit on the planet. He'd practically pushed her into Jamie's arms. But geez, she couldn't even keep herself from looking for Jamie while they were kissing! *What the—*

*Breathe, man. Breathe.* He had to interrupt his thoughts, or he was going to spiral into a bad place. He felt his heart rate slow and his face cool. She obviously wanted to be with Jamie, so he would just back off. Or he'd figure out a way to prescribe poison to his patient.

# Chapter Forty-Three ~ August

The transformation of Mountdonovan was almost complete. Megan wasn't sure she'd slept a full night the entire month of August, but with only one week to go before the Haven House benefit, she knew she wouldn't be catching up on her sleep any time soon. She barely heard the hammers and power tools anymore, until it was time to go to sleep. Then construction noises in her head kept her awake. But during the day, they faded into background music.

The facade was completely finished, and now the crew was inside the stately house, working feverishly to finish the ballroom. All the public areas had priority. Offices and staff rooms would take a back seat until after next week, which was fine, because those areas of the house would not be on the tour that she hoped to be able to give the guests at the banquet. From what she'd seen on her morning walkthrough with Ryan, she would guess they wouldn't be fully tour-ready for another month. But Ryan assured her they would finish what was needed for the benefit on time.

The TidyTowns volunteers, led by Nessa Rose, had come through with great results on the grounds. The weeds were history, and colorful flowers dotted the pathways, with freshly mulched beds perfectly placed across the estate. Although Marlene had instructed the group to get rid of the meadow buttercups, Nessa had overruled her, saying they would make great centerpieces. Which is what the volunteers would be working on today: Mason jars, wrapped with a jute bow and filled with buttercups. They weren't actually picking the flowers today, as they would die before the banquet. But they were cutting the jute and wrapping the Mason jars, so all that would be left to do next week was put the flowers in the jars.

Megan surveyed the field of wild buttercups and thought of David. He'd been avoiding her for a month—ever since that day he pulled her behind the kitchen building. She had tried to call and talk it over with him, but he politely put her off every time. She needed to deal with it, but in all honesty, she'd had no extra time or energy while planning the banquet, so she kept shoving it to the back of her mind.

Brenna came toward her carrying two full boxes of Mason jars. "Hey, where do you want these babies?"

Megan grabbed a box from her and nodded toward one corner of the tent where several more boxes were stacked on a table. "We'll just start a new stack."

"So, I have news. We signed the papers, and everything's official."

Megan rearranged the stacks of boxes. "So that's it? You're now the owners of the Maloney B&B?"

Brenna nodded. "Yep. It's a done deal. We'll transition everything over the next couple months. Ryan's gonna start the addition as soon as he's done here at Mountdonovan. But even if it doesn't get done right away, I think we're going to move in by November. Once Bettie and Patsy are moved into our cottage, we can use their rooms until the addition is done."

"Are you excited?"

"I am, actually. I've been talking with Kathleen on the phone a lot, and she's given me tons of great ideas. Ryan is so excited about it, I can't help but be a little excited. How 'bout you? Are you glad all this is almost over?"

Megan blew out a breath. "I can't wait for the benefit to be over. I mean, I'm looking forward to it, of course. But the stress of it all has been a bit much."

"Do you think the committee will make a decision before that?"

"Can ya grab the scissors?" Megan pointed toward a can full of scissors and grabbed two rolls of jute. "I think they are going to wait to see how the event goes off. They've eliminated one candidate from the list, so it's down to me and one other guy. And you know, he doesn't have a mental illness, so ..."

Brenna raised a brow.

"Oh, I didn't tell you Patricia's latest technique to discredit me?"

"No. What's she making up now?" Brenna pulled an arm's length of jute onto the table and cut it free from the roll.

"Well, this one's not made up, and if anyone really knew what she was doing, I bet she would lose her job. She must have looked in my records and found out I'm on antidepressants because she made a motion that the committee should investigate the mental health of all candidates, as that is sometimes overlooked in the interview process." Megan made air quotes to emphasize Patricia's words.

Brenna set down the scissors, looking at them like she thought she might stab someone with them. "Are you freaking kidding me?"

Megan nodded. "Nope."

"I can't believe Ryan didn't tell me that! What did the committee say?"

"I know. I'm actually surprised my mam told me. But she was pissed, I could tell. They told Patricia that was overreaching and as long as the background checks come back fine on the candidates, that will be sufficient."

"You should tell David!" Brenna still looked dangerous.

Megan shrugged. "Maybe. We're not talking much."

"Still?"

"I don't know what to do, Bren. I have to tell Jamie before I talk to David. I have to clean up my mess, but I'm so worried about how Jamie's gonna react."

"Meg, you can't keep stringing both of them along."

Anger coursed through Megan. "I'm not!"

"I know you don't see it that way. But that's the way it looks. You want David, but you've left him twisting in the wind, and you don't want to be with Jamie, but you're so afraid to tell him, that every day you dig yourself in deeper. You're leading him on. Sorry, friend. I gotta be honest."

Megan choked back tears. "Geez. I don't have time for this. You can show everyone how to do the centerpieces. I have work to do inside."

Megan barely made it into her unfinished, makeshift office before the tears came fast and furious. She hated it, but Brenna was right. She had to do something—something other than be a coward.

# Chapter Forty-Four

Megan stood at the edge of Jamie's garden, shading her eyes with her right hand. It had bloomed beautifully. And except for an incident with white butterflies eating the cabbage, all had gone smoothly. Today, they were harvesting the leeks and onions. Elizabeth would use them to make her famous potato-leek soup this weekend, signaling to the whole family that autumn had begun.

Jamie had already peeled down the leaves and left the bulbs to cure for a couple days. He was now on his knees, carefully digging out the first of the bulbs. Megan grabbed a large basket and knelt beside him. "How're they lookin'?" she asked.

"Excellent." He beamed.

As the garden thrived, so did Jamie. He had made remarkable progress, and his therapy at Step by Step had been invaluable. When he'd first come back to Millway, Megan had noticed a lot of small things that were different about him. The most prevalent was the lost words. Common things that shouldn't have been hard to remember would just be completely gone from his brain. He couldn't think of what some things were called, and he got pretty frustrated by it. She didn't blame him. He also got lost a few times and seemed to be very sensitive to light and sounds.

Now, two months later, he had improved in every one of those areas. He still got frequent headaches, and lights and sound played a role in those. But he wasn't sensitive in general; only when his head was already bothering him. The words ... so many had come back. She rarely heard him struggling anymore, and she gave him so much credit on that one. He read thick novels and did crossword puzzles every day, to improve his vocabulary and retention, even though it didn't come easily. She was really proud of him. She shook her head, trying not to think about the fact that she had to break his heart. As much as she tried to convince herself that he just saw her as a friend, she knew she was full of it.

"We did good, Meg." He handed her the first onion, and she set it in the basket. She took the second spade and began working alongside him. There was something just so satisfying about harvesting plants that you grew from seeds. It never ceased to amaze her—that such a small, insignificant-looking seed could grow into an onion, a tomato plant, or even a towering tree. By the time the basket was almost full, she noticed Jamie had stopped digging and was looking her way.

"What is it?" she said.

"You look really happy. You should see your face."

She shrugged. "It's probably weird, but I feel closer to God when I'm gardening. I just see little miracles all around me, and it reminds me that there's something so much bigger than we can see."

"I don't think that's weird at all. I feel the same way around you. Being with you reminds me of Him." Jamie stood and reached down with his dirt-caked hand. She placed her own dirt-caked hand in his so he could help her to her feet.

Warning bells. This was the conversation she'd been avoiding for two months. By the look in his eyes, she had no doubt where this was going.

"Jamie, I just—"

"Wait. Let me say what I need to say. You've been changing the subject for weeks now. I just need to say my piece. Okay?"

Megan bit her lip and nodded. Jamie continued, "So, I know ya told me right from the start that you just want to be my friend. And I've tried to look at you that way. I really have. But I'm sure ya know I still love you. It's getting hard to be around you without telling—"

"I'm sorry. I didn—"

"No, let me finish. I know I'm not the best with words, but I have to tell ya what's in my head." He motioned toward the work shed where they could wash their hands, and they started walking. "What we had was the best thing that had ever happened to me. And I screwed it up. I know that. I know I hurt you, and you didn't have to forgive me, but ya did. More than that, you've been by my side through all the therapy, you've helped me with my exercises, and you've been there for me, whatever I needed. So, first I have to say thank you. I owe you—"

"You don't owe me anything. You're my friend, and you would have done the same for me." They washed their hands in the work sink. Megan made use of the nailbrush that dangled from the faucet by a piece of twine.

"Tis true, but I still owe you a huge debt of gratitude. There's no way I can thank you properly. But this is about more than that. If I thought you hadn't been able to forgive me, I would understand that, and I would leave it alone. But I can tell ya have. I know you don't blame me for what happened. So, I can't understand why you keep pushing me away when I try to talk to you about us. I know I don't deserve a second chance, but if you're willing to—"

"Stop. Jamie, I can't." She faced him and looked into his eyes, willing him to take her seriously. "I do care for you, but not in the way you care for me, I'm so sorry."

Undeterred, he took her hand. "But ya loved me once; we're so good together. Maybe you can love me again. You could try. Unless ..."

She could see the light of understanding dawn in his eyes, and she looked down at their hands just as he dropped hers. "Are ya seeing someone else?"

Continuing to stare down at her hands, she said quietly, "It's complicated."

Jamie took a step backward, shock radiating off of him. He was clearly blindsided. And with a glance at his face, the pain she saw in his eyes made it hard for her to breathe. She just wanted to take it all back. To tell him there was no one else, and that she would make things work with him.

But she couldn't.

"Who? When?" He ran his hands through his hair and then shook his head. "I never see you with anyone. You're always working or you're here. How ..."

"As I said, it's complicated. You were gone, Jame. You hurt me, and I had no idea why. I didn't know about your injury. If I had, maybe things would have turned out differently. If everything that's happened in the last two months had happened six months ago, well, it would have made this conversation very different. But six months is a long time." She sat down on a hay bale that rested along the outer wall of the work shed. Jamie sat beside her, elbows on his knees and head in his hands.

"Who is it? Do I know him?" He looked at her sideways.

She leaned back against the wall, closed her eyes and answered, "Yes." How was she supposed to tell him?

"Well, are ya gonna tell me who it is or not?"

"Okay, but like I said, it's really complicated. Officially, we've never even dated. We—"

"Well if ya haven't dated, you're not really seeing anyone, then."

"No, I'm not. But if you weren't here, I would be."

"What the hell does that mean?"

"It means that we've been waiting. It means that I've been trying to do the right thing—"

"What, like I'm some charity case?" Jamie stood and paced. "You're saying all of this was just a duty to you?"

"No!" She stood and grabbed his arm, making him face her. "Do you think this has been easy for me, either? I do love you, Jamie. A part of me always will. But what we had broke. And before I had any idea it could have been healed, I met someone else. And both of us have tried to do what was best for you, all this time."

"Both of you? Megan, who the hell are we talking about here?"

"David," she said with an exhale.

"David? God, my brother?" The color drained from his face.

"No! Not yer brother. Good Lord. No, David O'Brien."

"Doctor David? My doctor is your boyfriend?" He shook her hand from his arm and walked toward the wall, pounding it a couple times with his fist. "What the hell. How is that even—isn't that some kind of conflict of interest? That's fecked up, Meg."

"He and I have never talked about his professional relationship with you. Anything I know about your visits with him is from you or yer mam. And I know him well enough to know that he wouldn't have let his feelings for me interfere with his professional opinion or recommendations for your situation."

Jamie sat on the hay bale again. His head back in his hands. After a silent minute or two, Megan sat beside him and laid a hand on his arm. "We didn't plan any of this."

"No, but I'm sure ya had a good laugh at my expense. I'm an effin' eejit."

"Jamie, what are you even talking about? Why would we be laughing at you? Everything I've done has been to help you. Trust me, none of this has been funny to me or David."

"So then what was the point of keeping it from me?"

Megan blew out a breath. "Okay, let me start at the beginning. David and I knew each other when we were kids. He tutored me one summer. So, when he came back to town, we already knew each other. We got reacquainted, and we were supposed to have our first official date the night you came back. When you showed up at my door, I was just leaving to meet him."

"Why didn't ya tell me that when I showed up?"

Megan raised an eyebrow. "Seriously? It's the first time I've seen you since I threw my ring at your head, you're apologizing and crying, and I'm going to say, sorry—got a date! I don't think so."

Jamie nodded. "Okay, valid."

"So, you coming back just made things very complicated, and there were other factors as well, that just made us decide to wait to start dating."

"Wait till what? Did ya think I was going to leave town again?"

"No, I just didn't think that telling you would help your recovery. And besides, there were other factors that made us hold off."

"And now?"

"Now, I don't know. We've hardly talked. But we're supposed to attend the banquet together this weekend, so I imagine it will come up."

Jamie leaned back against the wall and stared straight ahead. His jaw was clenched, and Megan could see he was trying to control his temper. A temper he'd never had before and had controlled quite well over the last month or so. But this was a very harsh test of his self-control.

"So, what did the doctor think of you spending all your time with me this summer?" he asked without looking her way.

She shrugged. "I imagine it wasn't easy for him. But I think he understood why it was important to me to be able to help you. Honestly, Jame, we've barely talked about it, because it was too sticky. He couldn't talk at all about your visits and what he knew, so it was easier just to avoid the subject altogether. And like I said, we've hardly seen each other. I don't even know how he feels anymore. He's kept his distance. So, I don't know."

He looked at her with narrowed eyes. "Let me get this straight. You won't even consider making things work with me, because there's a guy that you almost went out with who's barely talking to you, and ya don't know how he feels about you. Does that sum it up?"

Megan rolled her eyes. "There's more to it than that. But if that's how you see it, that's fine. I have to do what I have to do. For the last two months, that was to help you. But now I have to see if I can—if he's still waiting for me, or if I've blown it and he's moved on."

David didn't call her anymore, and he didn't text unless it was one-word replies to her texts. It was very likely she'd lost him by spending all her time with Jamie. And she wouldn't blame him if he'd decided to walk away. But she wouldn't let him go without a fight. The fact that she could sit here and tell Jamie "no" was even more proof of how she felt about David.

"Do you love him?" Jamie asked, his voice laced with anger and defeat.

She nodded. "Pretty sure I do. I'm sorry. I really am."

Jamie shrugged and reached down for the basket of onions. He stood and looked down at her, eyes more cold than hurt. "Well, thanks. Good luck with your party."

He walked toward the house, and Megan let out a shaky breath. Closing her eyes, she whispered a prayer. "Lord, I need your help right now. I'm a mess. Now Jamie's a mess. And I'm guessing David is a mess, too. But if anyone can make something from this mess, it's you."

⌒⌒

Brenna carried a box filled with pastries with one arm while her other arm was stretched down toward her toddling son. She had a firm grip on his soft little hand while he set a pace so slow she had to resist the urge to haul him up onto her hip. But he loved walking. He'd been at it for a month now, and he'd gone from not taking a step without holding her hand to not wanting anyone to hold him back as he toddled off to explore his world.

But right now, they were on the sidewalk, much too close to the traffic to let him wander free. Though he struggled a bit to free himself from her grasp, he was easily distracted by the colorful flowers and frequent passersby. They were actually to blame for the slow pace, more than Ben's little legs. Almost every person stopped and bent down to his level to have a pretend chat with him. He still didn't use very many words. But she was pretty sure he understood most of what was said to him.

'Wohzee!" He pointed toward the deep red walls as they approached Rosie's Pub.

"That's right, buddy. It's Rosie's." Usually, she made deliveries during his morning nap time, so she could leave him with Bettie and get them done quickly. But Rosie's had two deliveries a day: one in the morning for the lunch crowd, and a fresh one for the upcoming dinner crowd. And one day, she'd had to bring Ben with her when Bettie was in Cork, shopping. Since then, she couldn't get away with not bringing him. She had tried a couple times, but all the regulars at Rosie's were so disappointed that she decided the afternoon run would be a mother/son job. It took longer, but it also gave them something fun to do together, and it warmed her heart to see how people's eyes lit up when he walked into the pub.

They were hardly through the door before he was scooped up into Paddy Joe's arms. Paddy Joe had been eating lunch at the end of the bar for

as long as it had been open. Somewhere along the line, the previous owners had made a little brass sign with his name on it and had it fastened to
the back of the last chair at the bar. He'd spent a year with his grandson in
Dublin, when he'd been sick a while back. But as soon as he was healthy
enough to come home, he was back on his chair at the end of the bar.

"How's my little guy doin' today? Look at you, happy out workin' with
yer Mammy." Ben smiled and reached for Paddy Joe's long ears.

"Hi there, PadJoe, how are you doing today?" Brenna asked as he followed her, with Ben, to the pastry case.

"Fair to middlin,' lass. This wee one is bigger every time I see him.
What're ya feedin' him, steak and potatoes?"

Brenna laughed. He said the same thing every time. "Of course, what
else would I feed a young Irish lad?"

"Good form, there. Good form. Will ya take a mineral and a bag o'
crisps while you stock the case?" he asked. It was funny how some people
were so regular at an establishment that the lines blurred between customer and employee.

"Sure, thanks. I'll take a Coke." She could see Tara watching their conversation and already pouring her a Coke and grabbing a bag of chips from
behind the bar.

She always had her hands free when she delivered at Rosie's because
Ben was passed from person to person at the bar. Most were retired folk
who came in several days a week. Rosie's was something of a family for
them, and Ben was just the youngest, newest member.

She took a look around the restaurant as she straightened and stretched
from her bent position behind the pastry case. That's when she noticed
Megan sitting alone, in a corner booth. She had a far away look on her face
and obviously hadn't even noticed Brenna coming in. Glancing over her
shoulder to make sure Ben was well attended, she crossed to where Megan
sat.

"Hey, stranger."

Megan looked up, surprised. "Oh, hi there. Yer afternoon delivery?"

"Yup." Brenna slid into the booth seat opposite her. "You look like
someone killed your dog. What's up?"

"Jamie. I told him about David," she said, looking at Brenna through red-rimmed eyes.

"Ahh, probably worse than someone killing your dog, huh?"

Megan nodded. "It wasn't pretty. He's angry I kept it from him. But I still think it was the right thing. I mean, in reality, there was nothing to keep from him. We're not dating. So ..."

"Has he called you at all?"

Megan shook her head. "David? No. He's still responding to my texts, but very quick little answers. No conversation."

"Well, now that Jamie knows, just go talk to him. Find out what he's thinking."

"I will. I'm just thinking through it all."

"Good. I'm sure he's fine. He's probably just keeping his distance to give you space to deal with Jamie, you know? I've seen the way he looks at you, friend. He's still waiting for you, even if he doesn't know it. As soon as you tell him that Jamie is out of the picture, you'll see. He'll be all over you."

Megan gave a mirthless laugh. "I hope yer right." She stood and dropped some euros on the table. "I've gotta go. I'll call ya later."

Brenna went back to the bar to claim her son. She wasn't as confident as she pretended, regarding David's feelings for Megan. In reality, she'd hardly been able to get him to say two words about her in the last month. But she hadn't heard him talking about anyone else, either. So she was placing her bets on Megan and letting it ride.

# Chapter Forty-Five ~ September

*D*avid changed his workout routine as the mornings began to get cooler. Instead of running first, he'd spend an hour at the gym with free weights, and then he'd do a five-mile run in the hills. Since Rob had offered him a permanent position, he'd been given Wednesdays off, which was a nice mid-week break. This morning he was glad for the five miles to clear his head.

Megan had called the night before. She wanted to talk, so they were going to meet at Mountdonovan at eleven. He was obviously distracted by the thought because he'd dropped three weights on his foot this morning, and now it was throbbing. But the run was still welcome. Usually, by the third mile, his mind felt free of all the extra stuff it held, and he was able to concentrate on whatever was bothering him. Today, by mile two, he was fast at work on the problem.

He'd managed to avoid her for weeks, but it wasn't that hard. She was distracted and distant anyway. He'd obviously done what she wanted when he backed off. So now that she insisted they talk, he figured she was finally going to officially tell him she was going back to Jamie. Of course he'd been expecting it. They seemed to spend every spare minute together. Jamie's progress, in just two months, was nothing short of miraculous. It was obvious that Megan was the reason, so she must have been giving him some sort of encouragement.

David wanted to hate her for it, for breaking his heart. But the truth was, everyone was right; Jamie was a really nice guy who deserved a second chance at a happy life. And David almost found himself rooting for Jamie, despite the fact that it meant he was losing Megan. As much as he wanted to, he found it impossible to hate the guy.

Not at first. When Megan blew him off at the end of their wager, he might have hated Jamie for a day or two. But then, as soon as he saw him in the office and watched the excitement on his and Elizabeth's faces as they described how well he was doing, the hate deflated like a punctured balloon. Apparently his anger-management counseling had worked.

So now, even though he dreaded "the talk," there was a part of him that was glad. Better to just have it out in the open and move on than keep things unsaid. He was determined to respond in a calm, understanding way. That was one of the anger management techniques he'd learned.

*Respond, don't react.*

He was already thinking about how he would respond. "Megan, you know how I feel about you. That hasn't changed for me. But I understand you were with Jamie before I came into the picture, and I respect your decision." It sounded stupid in his head. But it was the right thing to say. Let her go graciously. It's what his therapist had encouraged him to do, and he had his last session coming up with her on Friday. He didn't want to go in there and have to admit that he lost his cool. No, he'd keep it all under control. Deep breathing. *Think of sun and sandy beaches or anything else that makes you calm.* He could do it.

After a quick shower and change, he decided he'd walk to Mountdonovan. But he forgot to grab his umbrella, and halfway there, it started to pour. So by the time he climbed over the stile, rain had soaked him through. *Calm. Beaches.*

Her car was parked at the stile, but he didn't see her when he first came over the hill. Then he remembered her alcove. Construction was almost done on the main house, but the outbuildings weren't set to begin for a while, so her alcove was still intact for now. To his surprise, she wasn't there.

"Megan?" he called as he circled the building. He thought he heard a response from the front of the property. "Megan? Where are you?"

"Up here!" Her voice floated from the direction of the great tree. Had she really climbed the tree?

From under the branches, he could see her, about halfway up. "Are ya mad? What are you doin' up there?"

She smiled, "Just felt like it. Wanted to get out of the rain. Look at you, you're soaked. Think you can make it up here?"

Looking at her smiling, teasing him, how was he supposed to let her go? His heart pounded, and it had nothing to do with climbing the tree. *Beaches.*

She had made a seat for herself on a double branch that grew out from the tree at an odd angle. David had used it as a seat before, himself. He stood on a lower branch and leaned back against another, facing her.

"How are ya?" he asked. She looked a little nervous. Maybe he should just tell her he knew what she was going to say and get it over with.

"I'm fine. How've you been? I haven't seen ya much."

"Right, well, I knew you were busy, so I didn't want to interfere." *You should fight for her. What are you thinking, letting her go? Beaches. Sun.*

She looked down at a blue and green canvas tote she'd slung over a small side branch. "I'm sorry about that. I know this has probably been really hard for you. It was just such a weird situation."

"I know. Look, I understand. I'm not sure why ya brought me all the way up here. But I understand why you're doing what you are. And honestly, although I want to fight for you, I don't feel right about it. You and Jamie deserve a second chance, and if I got in the way of that, I'd never feel right about it." There. He'd said it.

But the look on her face was not one of relief or gladness; she looked puzzled. And then shy. "You want to fight for me?"

"Megan, please don't make this harder than it already is. Yes, I want to fight for you, but I'm not going to. It wouldn't be right. It'd be like boxing a man who had a hand tied behind his back. So, thanks for telling me, face to face. That takes guts and I ... I appreciate it. I guess we should talk about how we're going to handle the benefit this weeken—"

"Stop." She placed two fingers over his lips. "Take a breath. I haven't told you anything face to face, yet. Have I?" She had a glimmer in her eye now, and he was completely confused.

"You said you—well, no. I guess you didn't say it, I did. Maybe it's easier for me to hear it from myself." He gave a wry laugh.

She reached into her bag and pulled out a beautiful wooden box with her initials carved into the top. She set it on her lap and ran her fingers along its edge. "David, I think you're assuming the wrong thing. And I probably was, too. I was assuming I had lost you because I'd spent so much time with Jamie, but you said ya wanted to fight for me, so ..."

David's heart began to pound again. She wasn't going back to Jamie? "I thought you decided to make things work with him. He's had such an amazing recovery; I just backed off cuz I thought—"

"I know. Thank you for giving me time to do what I needed to do. But David, I can't make things work with Jamie, because it wouldn't be fair to him, or you or me. We have something here. You and I. And it has roots. It goes back a long time. This is my keepsake box." She opened it and pulled out a faded red, flat pencil. "Do ya know what this is?"

"A ... carpenter's pencil?"

She laughed. "Of course it's a carpenter's pencil. But look at it closely."

He took it from her and inspected it. At the top, the letters *DTO* had been carved. *With a needle.* He remembered carving them when he was young. "Mine? Where did you get it?"

She giggled. "I guess I stole it from you. I found it in my box the other day, wrapped in this." She held up a small piece of yellow paper. "I didn't remember writing this until I read it. I don't think I'd looked in here for years. I'll read it to you."

*Dear Diary,*

*Today was the last day of math lessons. David brought me a notebook with all the formulas written out for me to study from. He's really sweet. I was so embarrassed Da asked him to come help me. But I'm really glad he did. I like him. He's kind of shy, but he's really smart, and he has beautiful eyes. I don't think he likes me cuz he's*

*way older than me. Besides, I don't know if I like him, like him. But*
*maybe when I'm older.*

*P.S. I took his pencil when he wasn't looking. Shhhh. Don't tell!*
*~Meggie*

He smiled and told himself to stay calm. She really wasn't going back to Jamie. "Meggie?"

She looked up at him with a grin. "My da calls me that. I guess I used it as my sign off in my diary for a while."

"So, you didn't *like me, like me*?"

She scrunched her nose and shrugged. "I was what, twelve? Thirteen?"

"But you're older now."

She nodded and looked up at him through her lashes. "I am. And there's something else from a couple years later." She reached back into the box and pulled out a small notebook. Flipping to the middle, she pulled out a dried yellow flower and handed it to him.

"What is this?"

"It goes with this." She held up a yellowed envelope with her name written in neat script on the front. He knew that writing. It was his own.

"But ... you threw it away." He had seen her toss both the yellow flowers and the letter into the trash bin.

Now her face pinked up, and she smiled. "Aye, but I went back after everyone left, and took them both out of the bin."

He was stunned. "You are just full of surprises, aren't you? I suppose it's too much to hope that ya never actually read it?"

She laughed. "Oh, I read it."

He tried to grab it, but she was too quick. "Megan, I was a lad of sixteen. I can only imagine what it says."

"Well, lucky for you, I saved it, so ya don't have to imagine."

He groaned and put his hand over his face, peeking out at her through his fingers. "You're not seriously gonna read it to me."

"Sure and I am. You were quite eloquent for a sixteen-year-old lad. Ahem ..."

*Beautiful Megan,*

*I know you probably don't know this, but I've liked you for a really long time. I never told you, because I didn't know how. But I may be moving later this year, and if I don't tell you, I'll regret it. I mean, what's the worst thing that could happen?*

Megan cringed a bit at those words and mouthed, "Sorry," before continuing.

*I guess I should tell you why I like you. It's not just because you're beautiful. It's not just because your hair looks like fiery gold in the sunlight, or because you sing like an angel. It's because you look past people's bad stuff, and you see right into who they are. I've seen you do it, time after time. Someone at school will be sitting alone at lunch, and you'll go sit with them. Or the girls will be picking on someone, and you'll tell them to stop. And with me, you always smile and say hi.*

*No one else does. Did you know that? I think you're the only girl at school who even speaks to me. But even if every girl spoke to me, I'd still choose you. And if every lad in school wanted you, I'd fight them for you. Because I think you are a rare gem, Megan McKenna. And I know I said I like you, but that's not the truth. Truth is, I'm fierce in love with you. I don't expect you to return the feelings, but maybe someday you will? I hope you understand that I just had to tell you how I feel.*

*Yours Forever,*

*David Trevor O'Brien*


David let out a breath. It wasn't actually as bad as he'd thought it would be. "I still can't believe you pulled it from the trash."

"I'm so glad I did." She stood on a lower branch, put the box back in its bag, and leaned into him, wrapping her arms around his waist. "So, I'm older now, and someday is definitely here. And while I appreciate the fact that you said then and now that you'd fight for me, you don't have to. I'm all yours, and no one is standing in your way. So, if you'll still have—"

"Enough talk." He secured them to the tree with one hand and pulled her close with the other. "Cuz I'm still fierce in love with you, Megan McKenna."

Their lips met for a long overdue kiss that stretched into several minutes. He was just thinking it was a blessing and a curse that they were in a tree, which meant he had to hold on to the branch above and her waist—leaving him no extra hands to do the things he wanted to do but knew he shouldn't—when he heard the loud crack.

The branch beneath him split, and his feet slipped. He held to both the upper branch and Megan with every bit of strength he had, but he could feel her slipping.

"David, let go of me. I can get to the branch but you have to let go," she said in a rush.

He was losing his hold on the upper branch, but he couldn't let her go. She battered his chest. "David, please let go. It's okay, just let go."

There was a large branch just six inches below her feet. She was right. She'd be okay, so why was it so hard to let her go?

"Okay, I'm gonna let go. Ready?"

She nodded, and he dropped her. She landed on the lower branch and grabbed behind her for a handhold. With his other arm free now, David pulled himself over to the double branch she had been sitting on and reached down for her hand. "You okay?"

She nodded and laughed. "I'm fine, but my heart is beating out of my chest."

"Me too. Whose idea was it to be snogging up in a tree, anyway? Let's get our feet on the ground. I call a do-over." He grabbed her bag, and they made their way to safety. Where they had a proper do-over snogging session.

# Chapter Forty-Six

"It's a disaster!" Megan whispered to Brenna.

"It is not. It's fine. No one knows you were going to have a string quartet playing through dinner, so no one will miss it. I'll hook up my iPhone, and we will play some nice, soothing classical music over the speakers. It will be fine. Really."

"Well, no one knows that the catering staff dropped Bettie's gorgeous cake or that the programs are printed on the wrong paper, either. But if the committee finds out, I'll be cut from the list for sure. I thought everything was going so well. I was so prepared. And now all these things keep happening. It's a disaster."

"Meg, everything is going well. Take a deep breath and look around you." From their vantage point by the hobbit tree, Megan sighed and did as Brenna told her. "Now, don't look at it through the eyes of the organizer. Just pretend for a minute that you're here for the very first time."

To her right, Megan took in the massive white tents where hors d'oeuvres were being hand-passed at the moment, and dinner would soon be served. Vintage string lights twinkled in the twilight, and the tables glistened with stemware and silver. The long tent beside the dining tent was practically bursting with auction items, Brenna's beautiful painting of Alahaji anchored the whole display. It was stunning and Megan was so proud of her.

People were buzzing with excitement over the auction, which would take place after dinner. Most of the three hundred and sixty guests had arrived and were scattered around the grounds. Some mingled with appetizers in hand. Others, led by TidyTowns volunteers, toured the estate.

And directly in front of Megan, center stage, stood the fully restored Mountdonovan House. Ryan had installed lighting that would reflect off the facade at all the right spots. A warm glow escaped each window, and the house that had looked like an angry old giant for so long was now the belle of the ball.

Brenna leaned in and nudged her. "Look at their faces. Do you see anyone who isn't smiling?"

Megan smiled. "They all look happy, don't they?" Even Jamie had a slight smile on his face as Nessa Rose flitted around him, showing him the various garden projects she'd implemented. "Well, I can guarantee there's one person who isn't smiling."

"Patricia." They said in unison and then laughed.

"She probably arranged to have the cellist's fingers broken," Megan said in a mock serious tone.

"Yeah, and I bet she tripped the girl carrying the cake, too."

"I bet!" They giggled, and Megan rubbed her neck, trying to alleviate some of the built-up tension.

"I've gotta go check on something," Brenna said suddenly with a grin as she took off toward the tents.

"I can help you with that," David whispered into Megan's ear as his strong hands began kneading her knotted shoulders.

"Hi there." Megan rolled her head forward, fully relaxing for a moment. "That feels so good. You may have missed your calling, doc."

"Glad to be of service." He pulled her close, hugging her from behind. "You nailed this, Meg. I'm so proud of you."

She turned to face him. "Well, save that until we know if I got the job."

"I'm proud of you either way. I've been to these banquets for the last five years. I've never seen one sold out before, and this is, by far, the classiest event C.A.M.P. has ever held. Even Moira is impressed!"

Megan felt her cheeks heat. "Really? Well, if you hear Patricia say anything nice, I'll know I've entered the Twilight Zone."

"Right. I wouldn't hold my breath on that one. But everyone else? Totally impressed."

Megan glanced back toward the house and tensed. All seven committee members, plus Ryan, were walking toward them. She turned back toward David. "Oh my gosh, the committee is coming this way. Ahh! Why are they coming over here? We haven't even had dinner yet. Are they still coming?"

David laughed. "Aye, and ya might want to lose the deer-in-the-headlights look. But Ryan is smiling, and so is yer mother. So just take a breath and turn around. You've got this."

Megan blew out a breath and turned to face the committee. David was right. The only one not smiling was Patricia. If they were coming to give her bad news, Patricia would most certainly have been grinning.

"Hello, everyone." Megan forced a smile, though her heart threatened to pound out of her chest.

Marlene took Megan's hands and gave her a quick kiss on the cheek. "You look lovely, dear. Stunning. That yellow dress is perfect on you."

"Thanks, Mam."

Marlene nodded. "Well, as you may have guessed, we are here on official business. The committee just voted you in as the Program Director of Mountdonovan Estates. Congratulations."

Megan held back joyful tears. She wanted to keep her professional face on. But it was hard. "Thank you so much. I thought you'd wait until after the benefit to vote."

Nessa Rose jumped in. "No need. You practically performed a miracle here, Megan. We were all rooting for you, but it was hard to see how you were gonna pull it off. Yet ya did. Not to mention, we took bronze this year for TidyTowns, and this amazing project wasn't even part of it. Just imagine the points we'll rack up for next year's competition!" Nessa Rose's hands clapped together in excitement, and nods of agreement came from the entire group.

"Well, obviously next year we'll take the gold," David said with a wink.

Megan shook each committee member's hand, including icy Patricia's, and thanked them again for the opportunity.

"I should probably start moving people toward the dinner tables," she said to David as the others left.

"In a minute. I have something for you." He took her hand and pulled her under the canopy of leaves. From behind the massive trunk, he picked up something and held it behind his back.

"What are you up to?" Megan giggled.

"Nothing major." He pulled out a beautiful bouquet of yellow butter-cups and handed them to her, along with a card. "I just picked you some flowers and wrote ya a little note. I hope ya like them."

Megan laughed. "Oh my. Very smooth, Doctor. Very smooth. I don't just like them, I love them. Can I read the note later? I like to read things like that in private."

"Somehow I already knew that." He smiled and moved a stray hair from her face, golden eyes going from playful to serious in an instant. "You already know what it says anyway—that I'm fierce in love with ya, Megan McKenna. Always have been."

He leaned in for a kiss and for a few moments the sounds and lights faded away, and no one else was around.

The sound of Ryan on the speaker, inviting the guests to take their seats, broke the moment. "Hmmm," Megan hummed, "if you had tried that the first time around, I wonder what would have happened?"

"I probably would never have moved away and gotten braces, and you'd be stuck with Beaver Boy."

"That's okay, I liked Beaver Boy. I mean, I think I liked him, liked him." She grinned.

"And now that you're older and wiser?" David ran his hand over her cheek.

"And now," Megan lifted the flowers and inhaled their scent, "Now I know I love him, love him."

# Author's Note

I hope you enjoyed getting to know David and Megan as much as I enjoyed creating them. There's just something about an ugly duckling turned swan that captivates the imagination.

Some have asked how I came up with the topic of Traumatic Brain Injury. Years ago, I heard a speaker talk about her father who suffered a head injury when she was a child and how he radically changed into a violent, angry man. She may or may not have mentioned TBI but I was deeply struck by the story. Can you imagine someone you love having such a radical personality transformation? What must that have been like? I often thought about that story, so when I was working through the plot lines for this book, I knew I wanted to research TBI and make it part of my story.

The research was sobering. According to the Brain Injury Association of America, 1.7 million Americans sustain a TBI each year. Over 52,000 of those head injuries are fatal and 125,000 of the patients are permanently disabled as a result. And all of that is just in America. Imagine the numbers worldwide!

One of the scarier elements of TBI is the number of people who *aren't* diagnosed, so they go home without knowing what is actually happening to them or how they can get help. I chose to focus on that scenario and the effect it can have on relationships.

I encourage you to be aware of TBI and how it can affect those you love. I have noticed in my children's schools that there is an excellent effort being made to educate and protect children from concussions. So word is getting out that brain injury is nothing to shrug off. But I'm sure caretakers of TBI patients would agree that more education is in order. If you would like more information on TBI, check out the fabulous resources at Brainline.org.

Thank you for reading my second novel, *Where the Yellow Flowers Grow*. Even with the tough subject matter, I thoroughly enjoyed immersing myself in the little Irish town of Millway. I hope you enjoyed your "visit" as well and that you'll tell all your friends about it. And if you haven't read the first book in the series, *Where the Pink Houses Are*, what are you waiting for? It's on Amazon.com ... check it out!!

If you enjoyed this book, it would be awesome if you would leave a review on Amazon.com and/or Goodreads.com. You will have my undying gratitude ☺

Also, I love getting feedback from readers so feel free to contact me at:
    reb@rebekahruthbooks.com
You can also find more information, on my website (including book club questions):
    www.rebekahruthbooks.com
Or on Facebook:
    www.facebook.com/rebekahruthbooks
(Like my Facebook page or subscribe to my blog at rebekahruthbooks.com and you will get updates when book three in the Millway Novel series comes out in 2016! The story continues ... )

    Thank you and God Bless!
    Rebekah Ruth